D0810423

ALSO BY TESS GERRITSEN

THE SILENT GIRL

THE SILENT GIRL

A RIZZOLI & ISLES NOVEL

TESS GERRITSEN

DOUBLEDAY LARGE PRINT HOME LIBRARY EDITION

BALLANTINE BOOKS NEW YORK

Copyright © 2011 by Tess Gerritsen

All rights reserved.

Published in the United States by Ballantine Books, an imprint of The Random House Publishing Group, a division of Random House, Inc., New York.

BALLANTINE and colophon are registered trademarks of Random House, Inc.

ISBN 978-1-61129-696-9

Printed in the United States of America

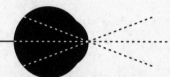

This Large Print Book carries the
Seal of Approval of N.A.V.H.

To Bill Haber and Janet Tamaro,

for believing in my girls

"What you must do," said Monkey, "is lure the monster from its hiding place, but be certain it is a fight you can survive."

—Wu Cheng'en,
The Monkey King: Journey to the West, c. 1500–1582

THE SILENT GIRL

ONE

SAN FRANCISCO

All day, I have been watching the girl.

She gives no indication that she's aware of me, although my rental car is within view of the street corner where she and the other teenagers have gathered this afternoon, doing whatever bored kids do to pass the time. She looks younger than the others, but perhaps it's because she's Asian and petite at seventeen, just a wisp of a girl. Her black hair is cropped as short as a boy's, and her blue jeans are ragged and torn. Not a fashion statement, I think, but a result of hard use and life on the streets. She puffs on a cigarette and exhales a cloud of smoke with the nonchalance of a street thug, an attitude that doesn't match her pale face and delicate Chinese features. She is pretty enough to attract the hungry stares of two men who pass by. The girl notices their looks and glares straight back at them, unafraid, but it's easy to be fearless when danger is merely an abstract concept. Faced with a real threat, how would this girl react, I wonder. Would she put up a fight or would she crumble? I want to know what she's made of, but I have not seen her put to the test.

As evening falls, the teenagers on the corner begin to disband. First one and then another wanders away. In San Francisco, even summer nights are chilly, and those who remain huddle together in their sweaters and jackets, lighting one another's cigarettes, savoring the ephemeral heat of the flame. But cold and hunger eventually disperse the last of them, leaving only the girl, who has nowhere to go. She waves to her departing friends and for a while lingers alone, as though waiting for someone. At last, with a shrug, she leaves the corner and walks in my direction, her hands thrust in her pockets. As she passes my car, she doesn't even glance at me, but looks straight ahead, her gaze focused and fierce, as if she's mentally churning over some dilemma. Perhaps she's thinking about where she's going to scavenge dinner tonight. Or perhaps it's something more consequential. Her future. Her survival.

She's probably unaware that two men are following her.

Seconds after she walks past my car, I spot the men emerging from an alley. I recognize them; it's the same pair who had stared at her earlier. As they move past my car, trailing her, one of the men looks at me through the windshield. It's just a quick glance to assess whether I am a threat. What he sees does not concern him in the least, and he and his companion keep walking. They move like the confident predators they are, stalking weaker prey who cannot possibly fight them off.

I step out of my car and follow them. Just as they are following the girl.

She heads into a neighborhood where too many buildings stand abandoned, where the sidewalk seems paved with broken bottles. The girl betrays no fear, no hesitation, as if this is familiar territory. Not once does she glance back, which tells me she is either foolhardy or clueless about the world and what it can do to girls like her. The men following her don't glance back, either. Even if they were to spot me, which I do not allow to happen, they would see nothing to be afraid of. No one ever does.

A block ahead, the girl turns right, vanishing through a doorway.

I retreat into the shadows and watch what happens next. The two men pause outside the building that the girl has entered, conferring over strategy. Then they, too, step inside.

From the sidewalk, I look up at the boarded-over windows. It is a vacant warehouse posted with a NO TRESPASSING notice. The door hangs ajar. I slip inside, into gloom so thick that I pause to let my eyes adjust as I rely on my other senses to take in what I cannot yet see. I hear the floor creaking. I smell burning candle wax. I see the faint glow of the doorway to my left. Pausing outside it, I peer into the room beyond.

The girl kneels before a makeshift table, her face lit by one flickering candle. Around her are signs of temporary habitation: a sleeping bag, tins of food, and a small camp stove. She is struggling with a balky can opener and is unaware of the two men closing in from behind.

Just as I draw in a breath to shout a warning, the girl whirls around to face the trespassers. All she has in her hand is the can opener, a meager weapon against two larger men.

"This is my home," she says. "Get out."

I had been prepared to intervene. Instead I pause where I am to watch what happens next. To see what the girl is made of.

One of the men laughs. "We're just visiting, honey."

"Did I invite you?"

"You look like you could use the company."

"You look like you could use a brain."

Not a wise way to handle the situation, I think. Now their lust is mingled with anger, a dangerous combination. Yet the girl stands perfectly still, perfectly calm, brandishing that pitiful kitchen utensil. As the men lunge, I am already on the balls of my feet, ready to spring.

She springs first. One leap and her foot thuds straight into the first man's sternum. It's an inelegant but effective blow and he staggers, gripping his chest as if he cannot breathe. Before the second man can react, she is already spinning toward him, and she slams the can opener against the side of his head. He howls and backs away.

This has gotten interesting.

The first man has recovered and rushes at her, slamming her so hard that they both go sprawling onto the floor. She kicks and punches, and her fist cracks into his jaw. But fury has inured him to pain and with a roar he rolls on top of her, immobilizing her with his weight.

Now the second man jumps back

in. Grabbing her wrists, he pins them against the floor. Youth and inexperience have landed her in a calamity that she cannot possibly escape. As fierce as she is, the girl is green and untrained, and the inevitable is about to happen. The first man has unzipped her jeans and he yanks them down past her skinny hips. His arousal is evident, his trousers bulging. Never is a man more vulnerable to attack.

He doesn't hear me coming. One moment he's unzipping his fly. The next, he's on the floor, his jaw shattered, loose teeth spilling from his mouth.

The second man barely has time to release the girl's hands and jump up, but he's not quick enough. I am a tiger and he is nothing more than a lumbering buffalo, stupid and helpless against my strike. With a shriek he drops to the ground, and judging by the grotesque angle of his arm, his bone has been snapped in two.

I grab the girl and yank her to her feet. "Are you unhurt?"

She zips up her jeans and stares at me. "Who the hell are *you*?"

"That's for later. Now we go!" I bark.

"How did you do that? How did you bring them down so fast?"

"Do you want to learn?"

"Yes!"

I look at the two men groaning and writhing at our feet. "Then here is the first lesson: Know when to run." I shove her toward the door. "That time would be now."

I watch her eat. For a small girl, she has the appetite of a wolf, and she devours three chicken tacos, a lake of refried beans, and a large glass of Coca-Cola. Mexican food was what she wanted, so we sit in a café where mariachi music plays and the walls are adorned with gaudy paintings of dancing señoritas. Though the girl's features are Chinese, she is clearly American, from her cropped hair to her tattered jeans. A crude and feral creature who slurps up the last of her Coke before noisily gnawing on the ice cubes.

I begin to doubt the wisdom of this venture. She is already too old to be taught, too wild to learn discipline. I should release her back to the streets, if that's where she wants to go, and find another way. But then I notice the scars on her knuckles and remember how close she came to single-handedly taking down the two men. She has raw talent and is fearless—two things that cannot be taught.

"Do you remember me?" I ask.

The girl sets down her glass and frowns. For an instant I think I see a flash of recognition, but then it's gone. She shakes her head.

"It was a long time ago," I say. "Twelve years." An eternity for a girl so young. "You were small."

She shrugs. "No wonder I don't remember you." She reaches in her jacket, pulls out a cigarette, and starts to light it.

"You're polluting your body."

"It's my body," she retorts.

"Not if you wish to train." I reach across the table and snatch the cigarette from her lips. "If you want to learn, your attitude must change. You must show respect."

She snorts. "You sound like my mother."

"I knew your mother. In Boston."

"Well, she's dead."

"I know. She wrote me last month. She told me she was ill and had very little time left. That's why I'm here."

I'm surprised to see tears glisten in the girl's eyes and she quickly turns away, as though ashamed to reveal weakness. But in that vulnerable instant, before she hides her eyes, she brings to mind my own daughter, who was younger than this girl when I lost her. My eyes sting with tears, but I don't try to hide them. Sorrow has made me who I am. It has been the refining fire that has honed my resolve and sharpened my purpose.

I need this girl. Clearly, she also needs me.

"It's taken me weeks to find you," I tell her.

"Foster home sucked. I'm better off on my own."

"If your mother saw you now, her heart would break."

"She never had time for me."

"Maybe because she was working two jobs, trying to keep you fed? Because she couldn't count on anyone but herself to do it?"

"She let the world walk all over her. Not once did I see her stand up for anything. Not even me."

"She was afraid."

"She was spineless."

I lean forward, enraged by this ungrateful brat. "Your poor mother suffered in ways you can't possibly imagine. Everything she did was for you." In disgust, I toss her cigarette back at her. This is not the girl I'd hoped to find. She may be strong and fearless, but no sense of filial duty binds her to her dead mother and father, no sense of family honor. Without ties to our ancestors, we are lonely specks of dust, adrift and floating, attached to nothing and no one.

I pay the bill for her meal and stand. "Someday, I hope you find the wisdom to understand what your mother sacrificed for you."

"You're leaving?"

"There's nothing I can teach you."

"Why would you want to, anyway? Why did you even come looking for me?"

"I thought I would find someone different. Someone I could teach. Someone who would help me."

"To do what?"

I don't know how to answer her question. For a moment, the only sound is the tinny mariachi music spilling from the restaurant speakers.

"Do you remember your father?" I ask. "Do you remember what happened to him?"

She stares at me. "That's what this is about, isn't it? That's why you came looking for me. Because my mother wrote you about him."

"Your father was a good man. He loved you, and you dishonor him. You dishonor both your parents." I place a bundle of cash in front of her. "This is in their memory. Get off the street and go back to school. At least there, you won't have to fight off strange men." I turn and walk out of the restaurant.

In seconds she's out the door and

running after me. "Wait!" she calls. "Where are you going?"

"Back home to Boston."

"I do remember you. I think I know what you want."

I stop and face her. "It's what *you* should want, too."

"What do I have to do?"

I look her up and down, and see scrawny shoulders and hips so narrow they barely hold up her blue jeans. "It's not what you need to do," I reply. "It's what you need to *be.*" Slowly I move toward her. Up till this point, she's seen no reason to fear me and why should she? I am just a woman. But something she now sees in my eyes makes her take a step back.

"Are you afraid?" I ask her softly.

Her chin juts up, and she says with foolish bravado: "No. I'm not."

"You should be."

TWO

SEVEN YEARS LATER

My name is Dr. Maura Isles, last name spelled I-S-L-E-S. I'm a forensic pathologist, employed by the medical examiner's office in the Commonwealth of Massachusetts."

"Please describe for the court your education and background, Dr. Isles," said the Suffolk County assistant district attorney Carmela Aguilar.

Maura kept her gaze on the assistant DA as she answered the question. It was far easier to focus on Aguilar's neutral face than to see the glares coming from the defendant and his supporters, dozens of whom had gathered in the courtroom. Aguilar did not seem to notice or care that she was arguing her case before a hostile audience, but Maura was acutely aware of it; a large segment of that audience was law enforcement officers and their friends. They were not going to like what Maura had to say.

The defendant was Boston PD officer Wayne Brian Graff, square-jawed and broad-shouldered, the vision of an all-American hero. The room's sympathy was with Graff, not with the victim, a man who had ended up battered and broken on Maura's autopsy table six months ago. A man who'd been buried unmourned and unclaimed. A man who, two hours before his death, committed the fatal sin of shooting and killing a police officer.

Maura felt all those courtroom gazes burning into her face, hot as laser points, as she recited her curriculum vitae.

"I graduated from Stanford University with a BA in anthropology," she said. "I received my medical degree from the University of California in San Francisco, and went on to complete a five-year pathology residency at that same institution. I am certified in both anatomical and clinical pathology. After my residency, I then completed a two-year fellowship in the subspecialty of forensic pathology, at the University of California–Los Angeles."

"And are you board-certified in your field?"

"Yes, ma'am. In both general and forensic pathology."

"And where have you worked prior to joining the ME's office here in Boston?"

"For seven years, I was a pathologist with the ME's office in San Francisco, California. I also served as a clinical professor of pathology at the University of California. I hold medical licenses in both Massachusetts and California." It was more information than had been asked of her, and she could see Aguilar frown, because Maura had tripped up her planned sequence of questions. Maura had recited this information so many times before in court that she knew exactly what would be asked, and her responses were equally automatic.

Where she'd trained, what her job required, and whether she was qualified to testify on this particular case.

Formalities completed, Aguilar finally got down to specifics. "Did you perform an autopsy on an individual named Fabian Dixon last October?"

"I did," answered Maura. A matter-of-fact response, yet she felt the tension instantly ratchet up in the courtroom.

"Tell us how Mr. Dixon came to be a medical examiner's case." Aguilar stood with her gaze fixed on Maura, as though to say: *Ignore everyone else in the room. Just look at me and state the facts.*

Maura straightened and began to speak, loudly enough for the courtroom to hear. "The decedent was a twenty-four-year-old man who was discovered unresponsive in the backseat of a Boston Police Department cruiser. This was approximately twenty minutes after his arrest. He was transported by ambulance to Massachusetts General Hospital, where he was pronounced dead on arrival in the emergency room."

"And that made him a medical examiner's case?"

"Yes, it did. He was subsequently transferred to our morgue."

"Describe for the court Mr. Dixon's appearance when you first saw him."

It didn't escape Maura's attention that Aguilar referred to the dead man by name. Not as *the body* or *the deceased.* It was her way of reminding the court that the victim had an identity. A name and a face and a life.

Maura responded likewise. "Mr. Dixon was a well-nourished man, of average height and weight, who arrived at our facility clothed only in cotton briefs and socks. His other clothing had been earlier removed during resuscitation attempts in the emergency room. EKG pads were still affixed to his chest, and an intravenous catheter remained in his left arm . . ." She paused. Here was where things got uncomfortable. Although she avoided looking at the audience and the defendant, she knew their eyes were upon her.

"And the condition of his body? Would you describe it for us?" Aguilar prodded.

"There were multiple bruises over the

chest, the left flank, and the upper ab-
domen. Both eyes were swollen shut,
and there were lacerations of the lip and
scalp. Two of his teeth—the upper front
incisors—were missing."

"Objection." The defense attorney
stood. "There's no way of knowing when
he lost those teeth. They could have
been missing for years."

"One tooth showed up on X-ray. In
his stomach," said Maura.

"The witness should refrain from com-
menting until I've ruled," the judge cut
in severely. He looked at the defense
attorney. "Objection overruled. Ms.
Aguilar, proceed."

The assistant DA nodded, her lips
twitching into a smile, and she refocused on Maura. "So Mr. Dixon was
badly bruised, he had lacerations, and
at least *one* of his teeth had recently
been knocked out."

"Yes," said Maura. "As you'll see from
the morgue photographs."

"If it please the court, we would like
to show those morgue photos now,"
said Aguilar. "I should warn the audience, these are not pleasant to look at.

If any visitors in the courtroom would prefer not to see them, I suggest you leave at this point." She paused and looked around.

No one left the room.

As the first slide went up, revealing Fabian Dixon's battered body, there were audible intakes of breath. Maura had kept her description of Dixon's bruises understated, because she knew the photos would tell the story better than she could. Photos couldn't be accused of taking sides or lying. And the truth staring from that image was obvious to all: Fabian Dixon had been savagely battered before being placed in the backseat of the police cruiser.

Other slides appeared as Maura described what she had found on autopsy. Multiple broken ribs. A swallowed tooth in the stomach. Aspirated blood in the lungs. And the cause of death: a splenic rupture, which had led to massive intra-peritoneal hemorrhage.

"And what was the manner of Mr. Dixon's death, Dr. Isles?" Aguilar asked.

This was the key question, the one

that she dreaded answering, because of the consequences that would follow.

"Homicide," said Maura. It was not her job to point out the guilty party. She restricted her answer to that one word, but she couldn't help glancing at Wayne Graff. The accused police officer sat motionless, his face as unreadable as granite. For more than a decade, he had served the city of Boston with distinction. A dozen character witnesses had stepped forward to tell the court how Officer Graff had courageously come to their aid. He was a hero, they said, and Maura believed them.

But on the night of October 31, the night that Fabian Dixon murdered a police officer, Wayne Graff and his partner had transformed into angels of vengeance. They'd made the arrest, and Dixon was in their custody when he died. *Subject was agitated and violent, as if under the influence of PCP or crack,* they wrote in their statement. They described Dixon's crazed resistance, his superhuman strength. It had taken both officers to wrestle the prisoner into the cruiser. *Controlling him required force, but he did not seem to notice pain. During this struggle, he was making grunts and animal sounds and trying to take off his clothes, even though it was forty degrees that night.* They had described, almost too perfectly, the known medical condition of excited delirium, which had killed other cocaine-addled prisoners.

But months later, the toxicology report showed only alcohol in Dixon's system. It left no doubt in Maura's mind that the manner of death was homicide. And one of the killers now sat at the defense table, staring at Maura.

"I have no further questions," said Aguilar. She sat down, looking confident that she had successfully made her case.

Morris Whaley, the defense attorney, rose for the cross-examination, and Maura felt her muscles tense. Whaley appeared cordial enough as he approached the witness stand, as if he intended only to have a friendly chat. Had they met at a cocktail party, she might have found him pleasant company, an attractive enough man in his Brooks Brothers suit.

"I think we're all impressed by your credentials, Dr. Isles," he said. "So I won't take up any more of the court's time reviewing your academic achievements."

She said nothing, just stared at his smiling face, wondering from which direction the attack would come.

"I don't think anyone in this room doubts that you've worked hard to get where you are today," Whaley continued. "Especially taking into account some of the challenges you've faced in your personal life in the past few months."

"Objection." Aguilar heaved out an exasperated sigh and stood. "This is not relevant."

"It is, Your Honor. It goes to the witness's judgment," said Whaley.

"How so?" the judge countered.

"Past experiences can affect how a witness interprets the evidence."

"What experiences are you referring to?"

"If you'll allow me to explore that issue, it will become apparent."

The judge stared hard at Whaley. "For

the moment, I'll allow this line of questioning. But only for the moment."

Aguilar sat back down, scowling.

Whaley turned his attention back to Maura. "Dr. Isles, do you happen to recall the date that you examined the deceased?"

Maura paused, taken aback by the abrupt return to the topic of the autopsy. It did not slip past her that he'd avoided using the victim's name.

"You are referring to Mr. Dixon?" she said, and saw irritation flicker in his eyes.

"Yes."

"The date of the postmortem was November first of last year."

"And on that date, did you determine the cause of death?"

"Yes. As I said earlier, he died of massive internal hemorrhage secondary to a ruptured spleen."

"On that same date, did you also specify the manner of death?"

She hesitated. "No. At least, not a final—"

"Why not?"

She took a breath, aware of all the

eyes watching her. "I wanted to wait for the results of the toxicology screen. To see whether Mr. Dixon was, in fact, under the influence of cocaine or other pharmaceuticals. I wanted to be cautious."

"As well you should. When your decision could destroy the careers, even the lives, of two dedicated peace officers."

"I only concern myself with the facts, Mr. Whaley, wherever they may lead."

He did not like that answer; she saw it in the twitch of his jaw muscle. All semblance of cordiality had vanished; this was now a battle.

"So you performed the autopsy on November first," he said.

"Yes."

"What happened after that?"

"I'm not sure what you're referring to."

"Did you take the weekend off? Did you spend the following week performing other autopsies?"

She stared at him, anxiety coiling like a serpent in her stomach. She didn't know where he was taking this, but she didn't like the direction. "I attended a pathology conference," she said.

"In Wyoming, I believe."

"Yes."

"Where you had something of a traumatic experience. You were assaulted by a rogue police officer."

Aguilar shot to her feet. "Objection! Not relevant!"

"Overruled," the judge said.

Whaley smiled, his path now cleared to ask the questions that Maura dreaded. "Is that correct, Dr. Isles? Were you attacked by a police officer?"

"Yes," she whispered.

"I'm afraid I didn't hear that."

"Yes," she repeated, louder.

"And how did you survive that attack?"

The room was dead silent, waiting for her story. A story that she did not want to even think about, because it still gave her nightmares. She remembered the lonely hilltop in Wyoming. She remembered the thud of the deputy's vehicle door as it closed, trapping her in the backseat behind the prisoner grating. She remembered her panic as she'd futilely battered her hands against the window, trying to escape a man she knew was about to kill her.

"Dr. Isles, how did you survive? Who came to your aid?"

She swallowed. "A boy."

"Julian Perkins, age sixteen, I believe. A young man who shot and killed that police officer."

"He had no choice!"

Whaley cocked his head. "You're defending a boy who killed a cop?"

"A *bad* cop!"

"And then you came home to Boston. And declared Mr. Dixon's death a homicide."

"Because it was."

"Or was it merely a tragic accident? The unavoidable consequence after a violent prisoner fought back and had to be subdued?"

"You saw the morgue photos. The police used far more force than was necessary."

"So did that boy in Wyoming, Julian Perkins. He shot and killed a sheriff's deputy. Do you consider that justifiable force?"

"Objection," said Aguilar. "Dr. Isles isn't on trial here."

Whaley barreled ahead with the next question, his gaze fixed on Maura. "What happened in Wyoming, Dr. Isles? While you were fighting for your life, was there an epiphany? A sudden realization that cops are the enemy?"

"Objection!"

"Or have cops always been the enemy? Members of your own family seem to think so."

The gavel banged down. "Mr. Whaley, you will approach the bench *now.*"

Maura sat stunned as both attorneys huddled with the judge. So it had come to this, the dredging up of her family. Every cop in Boston probably knew about her mother, Amalthea, now serving a life sentence in a women's prison in Framingham. The monster who gave birth to me, she thought. Everyone who looks at me must wonder if the same evil has seeped into my blood as well. She saw that the defendant, Officer Graff, was staring at her. Their gazes locked, and a smile curled his lips. *Welcome to the consequences,* she read in his eyes. *This is what happens when you betray the thin blue line.*

"The court will take a recess," the judge announced. "We'll resume at two this afternoon."

As the jury filed out, Maura sagged back against the chair and didn't notice that Aguilar was standing beside her.

"That was dirty pool," said Aguilar. "It should never have been allowed."

"He made it all about me," said Maura.

"Yeah, well, that's all he has. Because the autopsy photos are pretty damn convincing." Aguilar looked hard at her. "Is there anything else I should know about you, Dr. Isles?"

"Other than the fact my mother's a convicted murderer and I torture kittens for fun?"

"I'm not laughing."

"You said it earlier. I'm not the one on trial."

"No, but they'll try to make it about you. Whether you hate cops. Whether you have a hidden agenda. We could lose this case if that jury thinks you're not on the level. So tell me if there's anything else they might bring up. Any secrets that you haven't mentioned to me."

Maura considered the private embarrassments that she guarded. The illicit affair that she'd just ended. Her family's history of violence. "Everyone has secrets," she said. "Mine aren't relevant."

"Let's hope not," said Aguilar.

THREE

Wherever you looked in Boston's Chinatown, there were ghosts. They haunted quiet Tai Tung Village as well as garish Beach Street, hovered along Ping On Alley and flitted down the dark lane behind Oxford Place. Ghosts were everywhere on these streets. That, at least, was tour guide Billy Foo's story, and he was sticking to it. Whether he himself believed in ghosts hardly mattered; his job was to convince the tourists that these streets were haunted by spirits. People *wanted* to believe in ghosts; that's why so many of them were willing to pony up fifteen bucks apiece to stand shivering on the corner of Beach and Oxford and listen to Billy's gory tales of murder. Tonight, an auspicious thirteen of them had signed up for the late-night Chinatown Ghost Tour, including a pair of bratty ten-year-old twins who should have been put to bed three hours ago. But when you need the money, you don't turn away paying guests, even bratty little boys. Billy was a theater major with no job prospects on the horizon, and tonight's haul was a cool $195, plus tips. Not a bad payday for two hours of telling tall tales, even if it came with the humiliation of wearing a satin mandarin robe and a fake pigtail.

Billy cleared his throat and held up his arms, drawing on skills he'd learned from six semesters of theater classes to get their attention. "The year is 1907! August second, a warm Friday evening." His voice, deep and ominous, rose above the distracting sound of traffic. Like Death singling out his next victim, Billy pointed across the street. "There, in the square known as Oxford Place, beats the heart of Boston's Chinese quarter. Walk with me now, as we step back into an era when these streets teemed with immigrants. When the steamy night smelled of sweating bodies and strange spices. Come back to a night when *murder* was in the air!" With a dramatic wave, he beckoned the group to follow him to Oxford Place, where they all moved in closer to listen. Gazing at their attentive faces, he thought: Now it's time to enchant them, time to weave a spell as only a fine actor can. He spread his arms, and the sleeves of his mandarin robe flapped like satin wings as he took in a breath to speak.

"Mahhhh-*mee*!" one of the brats whined. "He's *kicking* me!"

"Stop it, Michael," the mother snapped. "You stop it right this minute."

"I didn't *do* anything!"

"You're annoying your brother."

"Well, he's annoying *me*."

"Do you boys want to go back to the hotel? *Do* you?"

Oh Lord, *please* go back to your hotel, thought Billy. But the two brothers just stood glowering at each other, arms crossed, refusing to be entertained.

"As I was saying," continued Billy. But the interruption had ruined his concentration, and he could almost hear the *pffft!* of the dramatic tension leaking away like air from a balloon with a hole in it. Gritting his teeth, he continued.

"It was a steamy night in August. In this square, after a long day's work in their laundries and grocery stores, a crowd of Chinamen sat resting." He hated that word *Chinamen,* but forced himself to say it anyway, to evoke an era when newspapers regularly referred to *furtive and sinister Orientals.* When even *Time* magazine had seen fit to describe *malice palely half-smiling from faces as yellow as telegraph blanks.* An era when Billy Foo, a Chinese American, would have found no jobs open to him except as laundryman or cook or laborer.

"Here in this square, a battle is about to erupt," said Billy. "A battle between two rival Chinese clans, the On Leongs and the Hip Sings. A battle that will leave this square awash in blood . . .

"Someone lights a firecracker. Suddenly the night explodes with gunfire! Scores of Chinamen flee in terror! But some do not run fast enough, and when the bullets fall silent, five men lie dead or dying. They are just the latest casualties in the bloody and infamous tong wars . . ."

"Mommy, can we go *now*?"

"Shhhh. Listen to the man's story."

"But he's *borrrring*."

Billy paused, hands twitching to grab the little brat around the throat. He shot the boy a poison glance. The unimpressed kid just shrugged.

"On foggy nights like this one," Billy said through clenched teeth, "you can sometimes hear the distant sound of those firecrackers. You can see shadowy figures flit past in mortal terror, forever desperate to escape the bullets that flew that night!" Billy turned, waving an arm. "Now follow me across Beach Street. To another place where ghosts dwell."

"Mommy. *Mommy!*"

Billy ignored the little turd and led the group across the street. *Keep smiling, keep up the patter. It's all about the tips.* He had to maintain the energy for only another hour. First they'd head to Knapp Street for the next stop. Then it was on to Tyler Street and the gambling parlor where five men were massacred in '91. In Chinatown, there were murder sites galore.

He led the group down Knapp Street. It was scarcely more than an alley, poorly lit and little traveled. As they left behind the lights and traffic of Beach Street, the temperature suddenly seemed to plummet. Shivering, Billy wrapped his mandarin robe tighter. He had noticed this disturbing phenomenon before, whenever he ventured down this section of Knapp. Even on warm summer nights, he always felt cold here, as if a chill had long ago settled into the alley, never to dissipate. His tour group seemed to notice it as well and he heard jackets zip up, saw gloves emerge from pockets. They fell silent, their footsteps echoing off the buildings that loomed on either side. Even the two brats were quiet, as if they sensed that the air was different. That something lingered here, something that devoured all laughter and joy.

Billy came to a halt outside the abandoned building, where a locked gate covered the door and steel bars secured the ground-floor windows. A rusting fire escape clambered up to the third and fourth floors, where every window was boarded up tight, as if to hold prisoner something that lurked inside. His group huddled closer together, seeking escape from the chill. Or was it something else they sensed in this alley, something that made them draw into a tight circle as if for protection?

"Welcome to the setting of one of Chinatown's most grisly crimes," said Billy. "The sign on the building is now gone, but nineteen years ago, behind these barred windows, was a little Chinese seafood restaurant called the Red Phoenix. It was a modest establishment, just eight tables inside, but known for its fresh shellfish. It was late on March thirtieth, a damp and cold night. A night like this one, when the normally bustling streets of Chinatown were strangely quiet. Inside the Red Phoenix, only two employees were at work: the waiter, Jimmy Fang. And the cook, an illegal immigrant from China named Wu Weimin. Three customers came to eat that night—a night that would be their last. Because in the kitchen, something was very wrong. We'll never know what made the cook snap and go berserk. Maybe it was the long, hard hours he worked. Or the heartbreak of living as a stranger in a strange land."

Billy paused. His voice dropped to a chilling whisper. "Or maybe it was some alien force that took hold of him, some evil that possessed him. An evil that made him pull out a gun. Made him storm into the dining room. An evil that still lingers here, on this dark street. All we know is that he pointed his gun and he . . ." Billy stopped.

"And he what?" someone prompted anxiously.

But Billy's attention was fixed overhead, his gaze riveted to the roof, where he swore something had just moved. It was merely a flutter of black on black, like the wing of a giant bird flapping against the sky. He strained to catch another glimpse of it, but all he saw now was the skeletal outline of the fire escape hugging the wall.

"Then what happened?" one of the brats demanded.

Billy looked at the thirteen faces staring at him expectantly and tried to remember where he'd left off. But he was still rattled by whatever had flitted against the sky. All at once, he was desperate to get out of that dark alley and flee this building. So desperate that it took every ounce of willpower not to run back toward Beach Street. Toward the lights. He took a deep breath and blurted: "The cook shot them. He shot them all. And then he killed himself."

With that, Billy turned and quickly waved them on, leading them away from that blighted building with its ghosts and its echoes of horror. Harrison Avenue was a block ahead, its lights and traffic beckoning warmly. A place for the living, not the dead. He was walking so quickly that his group fell behind, but he could not shake off the sense of menace that seemed to coil ever tighter around them. A sense that something was watching them. Watching *him*.

A woman's loud shriek made him spin around, heart hammering. Then the group suddenly erupted in noisy laughter, and one of the men said, "Hey, nice prop! Do you use it on all your tours?"

"What?" said Billy.

"Scared the crap out of us! Looks pretty damn realistic."

"I don't know what you're talking about," said Billy.

The man pointed at what he assumed was part of the performance. "Hey, kid, show him what you found."

"I found it over there, by the trash bin," said one of the brats, holding up his discovery. "Ewww. It even *feels* real. Gross!"

Billy took a few steps closer and suddenly found he couldn't move, couldn't speak. He froze, staring at the object the boy was holding. He saw inky droplets trickle down and spatter the boy's jacket, but the boy didn't seem to notice it.

It was the boy's mother who started screaming first. Then the others joined in, shrieking, backing away. The baffled boy just stood there holding up his prize as blood dripped, dripped onto his sleeve.

FOUR

"I had dinner there just last Saturday," said Detective Barry Frost as they drove toward Chinatown. "I took Liz to see the ballet at the Wang Theater. She loves ballet, but man, I just don't get it. I fell asleep halfway through. Afterward, we walked over to the Ocean City restaurant for dinner."

It was two AM, way too early in the morning for anyone to be so damn chatty, but Detective Jane Rizzoli let her partner babble on about his latest date as she focused on driving. To her tired eyes, every streetlamp seemed too bright, every passing headlight an assault on her retinas. An hour ago, she'd been warmly cocooned in bed with her husband; now she was trying to shake herself awake as she navigated traffic that had inexplicably slowed to a stall and crawl at an hour when sane citizens should be home sleeping.

"You ever eat there?" Frost asked.

"What?"

"Ocean City restaurant. Liz ordered these great clams with garlic and black bean sauce. It's making me hungry just thinking about it. I can't wait to go back for more."

"Who's Liz?" said Jane.

"I told you about her last week. We met at the health club."

"I thought you were seeing someone named Muffy."

"Maggie." He shrugged. "That didn't work out."

"Neither did the one before her. Whatever her name was."

"Hey, I'm still trying to figure out what I want in a woman, you know? It's been, like, forever since I was on the market.

Man, I had no idea there were so many single girls around."

"Women."

He sighed. "Yeah, yeah. Alice used to pound that into my head. You're supposed to say *women* now."

Jane braked at a red light and glanced at him. "You and Alice talk very much these days?"

"What's there to talk about?"

"Ten years of marriage, maybe?"

He looked out the window at nothing in particular. "There's nothing else to say. She's moved on."

But Frost hasn't, thought Jane. Eight months ago, his wife, Alice, had moved out of their home. Ever since, Jane had been subjected to a chronicle of Frost's frantic but joyless adventures with women. There'd been the buxom blonde who told him she was wearing no underwear. The frighteningly athletic librarian with the well-thumbed copy of the Kama Sutra. The fresh-faced Quaker who drank him under the table. He related all these tales with a mingling of bewilderment and wonder, but it was sadness, more than anything else, that she saw in his eyes these days. By no means was he a bad catch. He was lean and fit and good-looking in a bland sort of way, so dating should be easier for him than it had been.

But he still misses Alice.

They turned onto Beach Street, driving into the heart of Chinatown, and were nearly blinded by the flashing rack lights of a Boston PD cruiser. She pulled up behind the cruiser and they stepped out, into the bone-chilling dampness of a spring night. Despite the ungodly hour, there were several onlookers gathered on the sidewalk, and Jane heard murmurs in both Chinese and English, everyone no doubt posing the universal question: *Does anyone know what's going on?*

She and Frost walked down Knapp Street and ducked under the strand of police tape, where a patrolman stood guard. "Detectives Rizzoli and Frost, homicide," she announced.

"It's over there" was the cop's terse response. He pointed down the alley at a dumpster, where another cop stood guard.

As Jane and Frost approached, she realized that it wasn't the dumpster the cop was guarding, but something lying on the pavement. She halted, staring down at a severed right hand.

"Whoa," said Frost.

The cop laughed. "That was my reaction exactly."

"Who found it?"

"Folks on the Chinatown Ghost Tour. Some kid in the group picked it up thinking it was fake. It was fresh enough to still be dripping blood. Soon as he realized it was real, he dropped it right where it is now. Guess they never expected *that* on the tour."

"Where are these tourists now?"

"They were pretty freaked out. They all insisted on going back to their hotels, but I got names and contact info. The tour guide's some local Chinese kid, says he's happy to talk to you whenever you want. No one saw anything except the hand. They called nine one one, and dispatch thought it was a practical joke. It took us a while to respond 'cause we got held up dealing with some rowdies over in Charlestown."

Jane crouched down and shone her flashlight on the hand. It was a startlingly clean amputation, the severed end crusted over with dried blood. The hand appeared to be a woman's, with pale and slender fingers and a disconcertingly elegant manicure. No ring, no watch. "It was just lying here on the ground?"

"Yeah. Fresh meat like that, rats'd be at it pretty quick."

"No nibbles that I can see. Hasn't been here long."

"Oh, I spotted something else." The cop aimed his flashlight and the beam landed on a dull gray object lying a few yards away.

Frost moved in for a closer inspection. "This is a Heckler and Koch. Expensive," he said. He glanced at Jane. "It's got a suppressor."

"Did any of the tourists touch the gun?" asked Jane.

"No one touched the gun," the cop said. "They never saw it."

"So we've got a silenced automatic and a freshly severed right hand," said

Jane. "Who wants to bet they go together?"

"This is a really nice piece," said Frost, still admiring the weapon. "Can't imagine anyone tossing something like this."

Jane rose to her feet and looked at the dumpster. "Have you checked in there for the rest of the body?"

"No, ma'am. I figured a severed hand was more than enough to call you folks straight in. Didn't want to contaminate anything before you got here."

She pulled a pair of gloves out of her pocket. As she snapped them on, she felt her heart starting to thump hard, in anticipation of what she'd find. Together she and Frost lifted the lid, and the stench of rotting seafood rose up and smacked them in the face. Battling nausea, she stared down at crushed cardboard boxes and a bulging black garbage bag. She and Frost looked at each other.

"You wanna do the honors?" he asked.

She reached in, tugged on the bag, and immediately knew that it didn't contain a corpse. It wasn't heavy enough.

Grimacing at the smell, she untied the bag and looked inside. Saw shrimp and crab shells.

They both backed away, and the dumpster lid swung shut with a thunderous clang.

"No one at home?" the cop asked.

"Not in there." Jane looked down at the severed hand. "So where's the rest of her?"

"Maybe someone's scattering parts all over town," said Frost.

The cop laughed. "Or maybe one of these Chinese restaurants cooked her up and served her in a nice stew."

Jane looked at Frost. "Good thing you ordered the clams."

"We did a walk-around already," the patrolman said. "Didn't find anything."

"Still, I think we'll take a stroll around the block ourselves," said Jane.

Together, she and Frost moved slowly along Knapp Street, their flashlights cutting through the shadows. They saw shards from broken bottles, scraps of paper, cigarette butts. No body parts. The buildings rising on either side had dark windows, but she wondered if eyes were watching from those unlit rooms above, tracking their progress down the silent passage. They would have to make this same inspection again by daylight, but she did not want to miss any time-sensitive clues. So she and Frost inched their way up the alley to another strand of police tape blocking off access from Harrison Avenue. Here were sidewalks and streetlights and traffic. Yet Jane and Frost continued their painstaking circle around the block, from Harrison to Beach Street, gazes sweeping the ground. By the time they'd finished their circuit and were back at the dumpster, the crime scene unit had arrived.

"Guess you didn't find the rest of her, either," the cop said to Jane and Frost.

Jane watched as the weapon and severed hand were bagged, wondering why a killer would dump a body part in such an exposed place where someone was sure to spot it. Was it a rush job? Was it meant to be found, a message of some kind? Then her gaze lifted to a fire escape that snaked up the four-story building facing the alley.

"We need to check the roof," she said.

The bottom rung of the ladder was rusted, and they couldn't pull it down; they'd have to reach the roof the conventional way, up a stairwell. They left the alley and returned to Beach Street, where they could access the front entrances to that block of buildings. Businesses occupied the first levels: a Chinese restaurant, a bakery, and an Asian grocery store—all closed at that hour. Above the businesses were apartments. Peering up, Jane saw that the windows on the upper floors were all dark.

"We're going to have to wake someone to let us in," said Frost.

Jane approached a group of ancient Chinese men, who'd gathered on the sidewalk to watch the excitement. "Do any of you know the tenants in this building?" she asked. "We need to get inside."

They stared at her blankly.

"This building," she said again, pointing. "We need to go upstairs."

"You know, talking louder doesn't

help," said Frost. "I don't think they understand English."

Jane sighed. *That's Chinatown for you.* "We need an interpreter."

"District A-1's got a new detective. I think he's Chinese."

"It'll take too long to wait for him." She climbed to the front entrance, scanned the tenant names, and pressed a button at random. Despite repeated buzzes, no one answered. She tried another button, and this time, a voice finally crackled over the intercom.

"*Wei?*" a woman said.

"It's the police," said Jane. "Can you let us into the building, please?"

"*Wei?*"

"Please open the door!"

A few minutes passed, then a child's voice answered: "My grandma wants to know who you are."

"Detective Jane Rizzoli, Boston PD," said Jane. "We need to go up on the roof. Can you let us in the building?"

At last the lock buzzed open.

The building was at least a hundred years old, and the wooden steps groaned as Jane and Frost climbed the stairs. When they reached the second floor, a door swung open and Jane caught a glimpse into a cramped apartment, from which two girls stared out with curious eyes. The younger was about the same age as Jane's daughter, Regina, and Jane paused to smile and murmur hello.

Instantly the smaller girl was snatched up into a woman's arms and the door slammed shut.

"Guess we're the big bad strangers," said Frost.

They kept climbing. Past the fourth-floor landing and up a narrow set of steps to the roof. The exit was unlocked, but the door gave off a piercing squeal as they swung it open.

They stepped out into the predawn gloom, lit only by the diffuse glow of city lights. Shining her flashlight, Jane saw a plastic table and chairs, flower-pots of herbs. On a sagging clothesline, a full load of laundry danced like ghosts in the wind. Through the flapping sheets, she spotted something else, something that lay near the roof's edge, beyond that curtain of linen.

Without saying a word, both she and Frost automatically took paper shoe covers from their pockets and bent down to pull them on. Only then did they duck under the hanging sheets and cross toward what they had glimpsed, their booties crackling over the tar-paper surface.

For a moment neither spoke. They stood together, flashlights trained on a congealed lake of blood. On what was lying in that lake.

"I guess we found the rest of her," said Frost.

FIVE

Chinatown sat in the very heart of Boston, tucked up against the financial district to the north and the green lawn of the Common to the west. But as Maura walked under the *paifang* gate, with its four carved lions, she felt as if she were entering a different city, a different world. She'd last visited Chinatown on a Saturday morning in October, when there had been groups of elderly men sitting beneath the gate, sipping tea and playing checkers as they gossiped in Chinese. On that cold day she'd met Daniel here for a dim sum breakfast. It was one of the last meals they would ever eat together, and the memory of that day now pierced like a dagger to the heart. Although this was a bright spring dawn, and the same checkers-playing men sat chattering in the morning chill, melancholy darkened everything she saw, turning sunshine to gloom.

She walked past restaurants where seafood tanks teemed with silvery fish, past dusty import shops crammed with rosewood furniture and jade bracelets and fake ivory carvings, into a thickening crowd of bystanders. She spotted a uniformed Boston PD cop towering over the mostly Asian crowd and worked her way toward him.

"Excuse me. I'm the ME," she announced.

The cold look he gave her left no doubt that the police officer knew exactly who she was. Dr. Maura Isles, who'd betrayed the brotherhood of those tasked to serve and protect. Whose testimony might send one of their own to prison. He didn't say a word, just stared at her, as if he had no idea what she expected of him.

She returned the stare, just as coldly. "Where is the deceased?" she asked.

"You'd have to ask Detective Rizzoli."

He was not going to make this easy for her. "And where is she?"

Before he could answer, she heard someone call out: "Dr. Isles?" A young Asian man in a suit and tie crossed the street toward her. "They're waiting for you up on the roof."

"Which way up?"

"Come with me. I'll walk you up the stairs."

"Are you new to homicide? I don't believe we've met."

"Sorry, I should have introduced myself. I'm Detective Johnny Tam, with District A-1. Rizzoli needed someone from the neighborhood to translate, and since I'm the generic Chinese guy, I got pulled onto her team."

"Your first time working with homicide?"

"Yes, ma'am. Always been a dream of mine. I only made detective two months ago, so I'm really psyched." Briskly ordering onlookers aside, he cleared a path for her through the crowd and opened a door to a building that smelled of garlic and incense.

"I notice you speak Mandarin. Do you speak Cantonese, too?" she said.

"You can hear the difference?"

"I used to live in San Francisco. A number of my colleagues were Chinese."

"I wish I could speak Cantonese, but it's like Greek to me," he said as they climbed up the stairwell. "I'm afraid my Mandarin's not very useful around here. Most of these old-timers speak Cantonese or the Toisan dialect. Half the time, I need an interpreter myself."

"So you aren't from Boston."

"Born and raised in New York City. My parents came over from Fujian province."

They reached the rooftop door and stepped outside, into the glare of the early-morning sun. Squinting against the brightness, Maura saw crime scene unit personnel combing the rooftop and heard someone call out: "Found another bullet casing over here."

"What is that, five?"

"Mark it and bag it."

Suddenly the voices went silent and Maura realized they'd noticed her arrival and were all looking at her. The traitor had arrived.

"Hey, Doc," called out Jane, crossing toward her, the wind scrambling her dark hair. "I see Tam finally found you."

"What's this about bullet casings?" asked Maura. "On the phone, you said it was an amputation."

"It is. But we found a Heckler and Koch automatic down in the alley below. Looks like someone fired off a few rounds up here. At least five."

"Were there reports of gunshots? Do we have an approximate time?"

"Gun had a suppressor, so no one heard a thing." Jane turned. "Victim's over here."

Maura pulled on shoe covers and gloves and followed Jane to the shrouded body lying near the roof's edge. Bending down, she lifted the plastic sheet and stared, unable to speak for a moment.

"Yeah. It kind of took our breath away, too," said Jane.

The woman was a Caucasian in her early thirties, slim and athletic, dressed all in black in a hoodie sweatshirt and leggings. The body was in full rigor mortis. She lay on her back, face staring up at the sky, as though she'd stretched out to admire the stars. Her hair, a rich auburn, was gathered at the nape of her neck in a simple ponytail. Her skin was pale and flawless and she had a model's jutting cheekbones, faintly Slavic. But it was the wound that Maura focused on, a slash so deep that it divided skin and muscle and cartilage, severing the lumen of the trachea and exposing the pearly surface of the cervical spine. The arterial gush that had resulted was powerful enough to spray blood in a shockingly wide radius that left splatters across the curtain of sheets hanging on a nearby clothesline.

"The amputated hand fell in the alley right below," said Jane. "So did the Heckler and Koch. My guess is, her fingerprints are on the grip. And we're gonna find gunshot residue on that hand."

Maura tore her gaze away from the neck and focused on the right wrist, which had been cleanly divided, and she tried to picture what sort of instrument could have so efficiently slashed through cartilage and bone. It had to be appallingly sharp, wielded without hesitation. She imagined the slash of the blade and the hand falling away, tumbling over the roof's edge. Imagined that same blade slicing across that slender neck.

Shuddering, she rose to her feet and stared down from the roof at the police officers standing at the far end of Knapp Street, holding back onlookers. The crowd looked twice as large as it had only moments before, and the day was still early. The curious, ever relentless, can always smell blood.

"Are you sure you really want to be here, Maura?" Jane asked quietly.

Maura turned to her. "Why wouldn't I be?"

"I'm just wondering if it's too soon for you to be back in rotation. I know it's been a tough week for you, with the trial and all." Jane paused. "It's not looking too good for Graff right now."

"It shouldn't look good. He killed a man."

"And that man killed a cop. A good cop, who had a wife and kids. I have to admit, I might've lost it, too."

"Please, Jane. Don't tell me you're defending Officer Graff."

"I worked with Graff, and you couldn't ask for a better man to watch your back. You do know what happens to cops who end up in prison, don't you?"

"I shouldn't have to defend myself on this. I've gotten enough hate mail about it. Don't you join in the chorus."

"I'm just saying, it's a sensitive time right now. We all respect Graff, and we can understand how he lost it that night. A cop killer's dead, and maybe that's a kind of justice all its own."

"It's not my job to deliver justice. I just deliver the facts."

Jane's laugh was biting. "Yeah, you're all about the facts, aren't you?"

Maura turned and looked across the rooftop at the criminalists scouring the scene. *Let it roll off and focus on your job. You're here to speak for this dead woman, and no one else.* "What was she doing on this roof?" she asked.

Jane looked down at the body. "No idea."

"Do we know how she gained access?"

"Could've been a fire escape or a stairwell. Once you're on one roof, you can access all the roofs on this block, from Harrison Avenue to Knapp Street. She could have entered any of these buildings. Or been dropped from a helicopter, for that matter. No one we've spoken to remembers seeing her last night. And we know it happened last night. When we found her, rigor mortis was just starting to set in."

Maura focused on the victim again, and frowned at her clothes. "It's strange, how she's dressed all in black."

"Goes with everything, as they say."

"ID?"

"No ID. All we found in her pockets was three hundred bucks and a Honda car key. We're searching the area for the vehicle." Jane shook her head. "Too bad she didn't drive a Yugo. This is like looking for a needle in a whole damn haystack of Hondas."

Maura replaced the sheet, and the gaping wound vanished once more beneath plastic. "Where is the hand?"

"It's already bagged."

"Are you sure it belongs to this body?"

Jane gave a startled laugh. "What are the odds it doesn't?"

"I never make assumptions. You know that." She turned.

"Maura?"

Once again, she looked at Jane. They stood face-to-face in that blinding sunshine, where it felt as if all of Boston PD could see them, hear them.

"About the trial. I do understand where you're coming from," said Jane. "You know that."

"And you don't approve."

"But I understand. Just as I hope you understand that it's guys like Graff who have to deal with the real world. They're the ones on the front lines. Justice isn't as clean as a science experiment.

Sometimes it's pretty damn messy and the facts just make things messier."

"So I should have lied instead?"

"Just don't forget who the real bad guys are."

"That's not in my job description," said Maura. She left the rooftop and retreated into the stairwell, relieved to escape the sharp glare of the sun and the eyes of Boston PD personnel. But when she emerged on the ground floor, she came face-to-face once again with Detective Tam.

"It's pretty bloody up there, isn't it?" he said.

"Bloodier than most."

"So when's the autopsy?"

"I'll do it tomorrow morning."

"May I observe?"

"You're welcome to be there, if you have the stomach for it."

"I watched a few while I was at the academy. Managed not to keel over."

She paused to regard him for a moment. Saw humorless dark eyes and sharply handsome features, but no hostility. On a morning when all of Boston PD seemed to regard her as the enemy,

Detective Johnny Tam was the only cop who didn't seem to stand in judgment of her.

"Eight AM," she said. "I'll see you there."

SIX

Maura did not sleep well that night. After a heavy meal of lasagna, washed down with three glasses of wine, she climbed into bed exhausted. She awakened a few hours later, painfully aware of the empty space beside her. Reaching out, she touched cold sheets and wondered, as she had on so many other nights over these past four months, if Daniel Brophy was also lying awake, also lonely. If he, too, was desperate to pick up the telephone and break this silence between them. Or did he sleep soundly, without regrets, relieved their affair had finally ended? While she might be her own woman again, freedom came with a price. An empty bed, sleepless nights, and the unanswerable question: *Am I better with him or without him?*

The next morning, she arrived at work groggy and nauseated from all the coffee she'd consumed to make herself alert. As she stood in the morgue anteroom donning mask and paper cap and shoe covers, she looked through the viewing window and saw that Jane was already standing by the table, waiting for her. Yesterday they had not parted on the most congenial of terms, and Maura still felt stung by Jane's sarcastic retort: *You're all about the facts, aren't you?* Yes, facts mattered to her. They were immutable things that could not be denied, even when they threatened a friendship. The trial of Officer Graff had driven a wedge between her and Jane, reminding Maura how unlikely their friendship had been from the start. As she tied on her gown, it was not the corpse she dreaded confronting, but Jane.

With a deep breath, she pushed through the door.

Her assistant, Yoshima, had already transferred the body bag onto the table. On a tray beside it was the severed hand, covered by a drape. Acutely aware that Yoshima was listening to their conversation, Maura gave Jane a businesslike nod and said, "Isn't Frost joining us?"

"He's going to miss this one, but Johnny Tam's on his way here. In fact, I think he can't wait to watch you start slicing."

"Detective Tam seems eager to prove himself."

"I think he's got his eye on joining homicide. From what I've seen so far, he may have what it takes." She glanced up. "Speak of the devil."

Through the viewing window, Maura saw that Tam had arrived and was tying on a surgical gown. A moment later he entered, jet-black hair hidden beneath a paper cap. He approached the table, his gaze calm and impassive as he focused on the draped body.

"Before we start, Tam," said Jane, "I

just want to point out to you that the barf sink is right over there."

He shrugged. "I won't need it."

"You say that now."

"We'll start with the easy part," said Maura, and she uncovered the tray with the severed hand. It looked plastic. No wonder the Chinatown tour group had mistaken it for a Halloween prop with fake blood. It had already been swabbed and found positive for gunshot residue. Fingerprints from this hand were found on the grip of the Heckler & Koch, leaving no doubt that the victim had fired the bullets, scattering five casings on the rooftop. Maura swung the magnifier over the hand and examined the severed wrist.

"The cut sliced right between the distal radius and the lunate bone," she said. "But I can see a good chunk of the triquetral here."

"And that would mean?" asked Jane.

"Whatever made this cut divided a carpal bone. And these bones are very dense."

"So it had to be a sharp blade."

"Sharp enough to amputate with a

single slice." Maura looked up. "I don't see any secondary cut marks."

"Just tell me this hand matches that body."

Maura turned to the table and un-zipped the body bag. The plastic parted, releasing the stomach-turning smell of refrigerated meat and stale blood. The cadaver inside was still fully clothed, the head tipped backward, exposing the gaping wound in her neck. As Yo-shima took photos, Maura's gaze was drawn to the woman's auburn hair, caked in blood. Beautiful hair, she thought, and a beautiful woman. A woman who was armed and shooting at someone on that rooftop.

"Dr. Isles, we've got some hair and fiber evidence staring at us," said Yo-shima. He was bending over the corpse's black sweatshirt, peering at a single pale strand that clung to the sleeve.

With a pair of tweezers, Maura plucked up the hair and examined it un-der the light. It was about two inches long, silvery gray and slightly curved. She glanced at the cadaver. "This obvi-ously is not her hair."

"Look, there's another one," said Jane, pointing to a second strand clinging to the victim's black leggings.

"Maybe animal hairs," said Yoshima. "Could be a golden retriever."

"Or maybe she got whacked by a gray-haired grandpa."

Maura slipped the strands into separate evidence envelopes and set them aside. "Okay, let's undress her."

First they removed the only item of jewelry she was wearing, a black Swiss Hanowa watch, from her left wrist. Next came the shoes, black Reeboks, followed by the hoodie sweatshirt and a long-sleeved T-shirt, leggings, cotton panties, and an athletic bra. What emerged was a well-toned body, slim but muscular. Maura had once heard a pathology professor assert that in his many years of performing autopsies, he'd never come across an attractive corpse. This woman proved there could be exceptions to that rule. Despite the gaping wound and dependent mottling of her back and buttocks, despite the glassy eyes, she was still a stunningly beautiful woman.

With the corpse now fully stripped of clothing, Maura and the two detectives stepped out of the room so that Yoshima could take X-rays. In the anteroom, they watched through the viewing window as he donned a lead apron and positioned the film cartridges.

"A woman like that," said Maura, "is going to be missed by someone."

"You saying that because she's good-looking?" Jane said.

"I'm saying it because she looks incredibly fit, she has perfect dentition, and those are Donna Karan leggings she was wearing."

"Question, please, from an ignorant man," said Tam. "Does that mean they're expensive?"

Jane said, "I'll bet Dr. Isles here can quote you the exact retail price."

"The point is," said Maura, "she's not some penniless stray off the street. She was carrying a lot of cash, and she was armed with a Heckler and Koch, which I understand is not your usual street gun."

"She also had no ID," said Tam.

"It could have been stolen."

"But the thief leaves behind three hundred bucks?" Tam shook his head. "That would be weird."

Through the viewing window, Maura saw Yoshima give a wave. "He's done," she said, and pushed through the door back into the lab.

Maura examined the incised neck first. Like the cut that had amputated the hand, this wound appeared to be a single slice, delivered without hesitation. Inserting a ruler into the wound, Maura said: "It's almost eight centimeters deep. Transects the trachea and penetrates all the way to the cervical spine." She reoriented the ruler. "Wider than it is deep, around twelve centimeters side to side. Not a stab but a slash." She paused, studying the exposed incision. "Odd how smooth it is. There's no bread-knifing, no secondary cuts. No bruising or crushing. It was done so quickly, the victim never had a chance to struggle." She cradled the head and tilted it forward. "Can someone hold the cranium in position for me? I want to approximate the wound edges."

Without any hesitation, Detective Tam

stepped forward and cradled the head in his gloved hands. While a human torso can be viewed as merely imper-sonal skin and bone and muscle, a corpse's face reveals more than most cops want to see. Johnny Tam, though, did not shy away from the view. He stared straight into the dead woman's eyes, as though hoping they might pro-vide answers to his many questions.

"That's it, right there," said Maura, sliding the magnifier over the skin. "I don't see any serration marks. Nothing that would tell me what kind of knife . . ." She paused.

"What?" asked Jane.

"This angle is strange. It's not your usual slashed throat."

"Yeah, those are so boring."

"Consider for a moment how you'd go about cutting a throat," said Maura. "To penetrate this deep, all the way to vertebrae, you'd approach it from be-hind. You'd grab the victim's hair, pull the head back, and slice across the front, from ear to ear."

"The commando method," said Tam.

"The rear approach gives you control

of the victim and maximizes exposure of the throat. And it usually results in a curved incision when the wound's later approximated. But this slash is angled slightly upward, right to left. It was delivered with the head in a neutral position, not tilted back."

"Maybe the killer was standing in front of her," said Jane.

"Then why didn't she resist? There's no bruising to indicate a struggle. Why would she just stand there while someone practically slices off her head?"

Yoshima said: "I've put up the X-rays."

They all turned to the viewing box where the radiographs were now displayed, bones glowing white on the backlit screen. She focused first on the films of the right wrist stump and the severed hand, mentally comparing the angles of the transected triquetral bone. They were a match.

"It's definitely her hand," Maura confirmed.

"Not that I ever doubted it," said Jane.

Maura next focused on the neck X-rays, on the gap in the soft tissues where the flesh had been so cleanly divided. Her gaze instantly fixed on a bright sliver in the cervical vertebra. "Did you do a lateral on this C-spine?" she asked.

Yoshima had clearly anticipated her request, because he immediately pulled down the hand and wrist films and clipped up a new radiograph, this one a side view of the neck. "I saw that thing earlier. Thought you'd want to see more detail on it."

Maura stared at the lateral view of the fifth cervical vertebra. The object, razor-thin, was visible on this X-ray as well.

"What is that?" asked Jane, moving close beside her.

"It's something metallic, and it's embedded in the anterior fifth vertebra." She turned to the autopsy table. "I think part of the blade sheared off when the killer made his cut, and a chip is lodged in her neck bone."

"Which means we might be able to analyze the metal," said Jane. "Identify who manufactured the knife."

"I don't think it was a knife," said Maura.

"An ax?"

"An ax would leave a cleft, and we'd see crush changes on the soft tissues. She has neither. This incision is fine and linear. It was made by a blade that's razor-sharp, and long enough to practically transect the neck with one sweep."

"Like a machete?" asked Jane.

"Or a sword."

Jane looked at Tam. "We're looking for Zorro." Her laugh was interrupted by the sound of her ringing cell phone. She stripped off her gloves and reached for the phone clipped to her belt. "Rizzoli."

"Have you seen any sword injuries before, Dr. Isles?" Tam asked, still studying the X-ray.

"One, in San Francisco. A man hacked his girlfriend to death with a samurai sword."

"Would metal analysis tell you if this was a samurai sword?"

"They're mass-produced these days, so it probably wouldn't help us unless we could find the weapon itself. Still, you never know when trace evidence like this ends up being just the puzzle piece needed to convict." She looked at Tam, whose face was bathed in the glow from the viewing box. Even though a bouffant paper cap covered his hair, she was once again struck by his intensity. And lack of humor. "You ask good questions," she said.

"Just trying to learn."

"Rizzoli's a smart cop. Keep up with her, and you'll do fine."

"Tam," said Jane, hanging up her phone. "You stay and finish up here. I have to go."

"What's happened?"

"That was Frost. We found the victim's car."

The fourth floor of the Tyler Street parking garage was nearly empty, but the blue Honda Civic sat all by itself in a remote corner space. It was a dim and isolated spot, the sort of place you would choose if you did not want anyone to see you walking to your car. As Jane and Frost inspected the vehicle, their only audience was a lone garage employee and the two Boston PD officers who'd spotted the car earlier that morning.

"The entry ticket on the dashboard

has a time stamp of eight fifteen PM Wednesday," said Frost. "I checked the security tape, and it shows the Honda driving in at that time. Five minutes later, a woman walks out of the garage. Her hoodie's up, so you can't see her face on the camera, but it looks like her. Car hasn't left the garage since."

As Frost spoke, Jane did a slow walk-around of the Honda. It was a three-year-old model with no major dings or scratches. The tires were in good condition. The trunk was open, the hatch lifted for her to inspect the interior.

"License plates were reported stolen five days ago in Springfield," said Frost. "Vehicle was stolen a week ago, also in Springfield."

Jane frowned into the trunk, which was empty except for the spare tire. "Geez, it's a lot cleaner than mine."

Frost laughed. "You could say that about a lot of cars."

"Says the guy with OCD."

"Looks like it's been recently detailed. Glove compartment's got the real owner's registration and insurance card. And you're gonna love what was left on the front seat." He pulled on gloves and opened the driver's door. "Handheld GPS."

"Why do you always get to find the fun stuff?"

"I'm guessing it's a brand-new unit, because she'd plugged in only two addresses. Both in Boston."

"Where?"

"The first is a private residence in Roxbury Crossing, owned by a Louis Ingersoll."

Jane glanced at him in surprise. "Would that be *Detective* Lou Ingersoll?"

"One and the same. It's the address Boston PD has listed for him."

"He retired from homicide, what? Sixteen, seventeen years ago?"

"Sixteen. Can't get hold of him right now. I called his daughter, and she says Lou took off up north to go fishing for the week. There may not be cell coverage wherever he is. Or he turned off his phone and doesn't want to be bothered."

"What about the second address on the GPS?"

"It's a business, right here in Chinatown. Someplace called the Dragon and Stars Martial Arts Academy. Their answering machine said they open at noon." Frost glanced at his watch. "Which would be ten minutes ago."

SEVEN

The Dragon and Stars Academy of Martial Arts was located on the second floor of a tired brick building on Harrison Avenue, and as Jane and Frost climbed the narrow stairway, they could hear chants and grunts and thumping feet, and could already smell the sweaty locker-room odor. Inside the studio, a dozen students garbed in black pajama-like costumes moved with such total focus that not a single one seemed to notice the two detectives' entrance. Except for a faded martial arts poster, it was a starkly empty room with bare walls and a scuffed wood floor. For a moment Jane and Frost stood ignored near the door, watching the class leap and kick.

Suddenly a young Asian woman stepped out of formation and ordered: "Complete the exercise!" Then she crossed the room to meet the two visitors. She was slender as a dancer, her skin aglow with sweat, but despite her exertions she did not seem at all out of breath. "May I help you?" she asked.

"We're from Boston PD. I'm Detective Jane Rizzoli, and this is Detective Frost. We'd like to speak to the owner of this studio."

"May I see identification?" The request was brusque and not at all what Jane expected from someone who looked like she was barely out of high school. As the girl studied Jane's ID, Jane studied the girl. Maybe not as young as she appeared, Jane decided. Early twenties and American Chinese, by the sound of her voice, with a tattoo of a tiger on her left forearm. With her short, spiky hair and her sullen gaze, she looked like an Asian version of a Goth girl, small but dangerous.

The girl handed back the ID. "I see you're with homicide. Why are you here?"

"First, may I ask your name?" said Jane, pulling out a notebook.

"Bella Li. I teach the beginning and intermediate classes."

"Your students are amazing," Frost marveled, still watching the class as they leaped and whirled.

"This is the intermediate class. They're rehearsing for a martial arts demonstration next month in New York. They're now practicing the leopard moves."

"Leopard?"

"It's one of the ancient animal techniques from northern China. The leopard relies on speed and aggression, which is what you see in this exercise. Each animal technique is a reflection of that animal's nature. The snake is sly and sleek. The stork excels in balance and evasion. The monkey is quick and clever. Students choose which animal best suits their own personality, and that's the form they master."

Frost laughed. "It's like what you see in kung fu movies."

His remark was met with an icy stare. "The proper name for this art is wushu, and it was invented thousands of years ago. What you see in those movies is fake Hollywood crap." She paused as her class ended its exercise and stood watching her, waiting for further instructions. "Get the swords. Sparring practice," she ordered, and the students headed for a weapons rack where they collected wooden practice swords.

"May we speak to the owner?" asked Jane.

"*Sifu* Fang is in the back room, teaching a private student."

"How do you spell that name? You said it was She—"

"*Sifu* isn't a name," Bella retorted. "It's the Chinese word for 'master' or 'teacher.' A term of respect."

"Then may we speak to the *master*?" Jane snapped, irritated by the girl's attitude. "This isn't a social call, Ms. Li. It's official business."

Bella weighed her request. The students began sparring practice, and the room echoed with the clacks of wooden swords. "A minute," she finally said.

She knocked at a door, waited a respectful moment before opening it, and announced: "*Sifu,* there are two policemen here to see you."

"Send them in," said a voice. A woman.

Unlike lithe young Bella Li, the Chinese woman who rose from her chair to greet them moved slowly, as if struggling with aching joints, although she appeared to be only in her fifties. Middle age was barely etched in her face, and her long black hair was streaked with only a few strands of silver. She faced them with the confidence of an empress. Although she was Jane's height, her regal posture made her seem far taller. Beside her stood a small blond boy of about six, dressed in a martial arts uniform and clutching a wooden staff almost as large as he was.

"I am Iris Fang," the woman said. "How can I help you?" Both her formality and her accent told Jane the woman was foreign-born.

"Detective Rizzoli and Detective Frost," said Jane. She glanced at the little boy, who looked back at her, pugnaciously unafraid. "Could your student step out? We need to speak in private, ma'am."

Iris nodded. "Bella, take Adam into the other room to wait for his mother."

"But *Sifu,*" the boy protested. "I want to show you how I practiced with the monkey pole!"

Iris smiled down at him. "You will show me next week, Adam," she said, affectionately brushing her fingers through his hair. "Monkeys must also learn patience. Now go." The smile remained on her lips as Bella led the boy out of the room.

"That little guy's a martial arts student?" said Frost.

"He has both talent and passion. I do not waste my effort on just anyone." The smile was gone from Iris's face as she regarded her visitors with cool appraisal. Her gaze fixed on Jane, as if she understood in which visitor the authority lay. "Why have the police come to my studio?"

"We're from the homicide unit, Boston PD," said Jane. "We need to ask you a few questions about something that happened in Chinatown last night."

"I assume this is about the dead woman on the roof?"

"Then you already know about it."

"Everyone is talking about it. This is a small neighborhood, and like any Chinese village, it has its gossips and its busybodies. They say her throat was cut, and her hand was thrown off the rooftop. And they say she had a gun."

Whoever *they* were, they knew too damn much, thought Jane.

"Are these stories true?" asked Iris.

"We can't really talk about it," said Jane.

"But that is why you're here, isn't it? To talk about it?" Iris said placidly.

They regarded each other for a moment, and Jane suddenly realized: I am not the only one seeking out information. "We have a photo we'd like to show you," she said.

"Is there a reason you're asking me?" Iris asked.

"We're talking to a number of people in the neighborhood."

"But this is the first I've heard about

any photo. And I think I *would* have heard about it."

"First, we need to show you a picture. Then we'll talk about why." Jane looked at Frost.

"I'm sorry you have to see this, ma'am," he said. "This might be a little upsetting for you. Maybe you'd like to sit down first?"

His quietly respectful tone seemed to melt some of the ice from the woman's eyes, and she nodded. "I am feeling weary today. Perhaps I will sit down, thank you."

Frost quickly scooted a chair closer, and Iris sank down with a sigh of relief that told them how much she welcomed his gesture. Only then did Frost reveal the digital image that Maura had emailed from the morgue. Although the victim's wound was discreetly covered by a drape, the facial pallor, the slack jaw and half-open eyes, left no doubt that this was a photo of a dead woman.

In silence, Iris stared at the image for a solid minute, her expression unchanging.

"Ma'am?" said Frost. "Do you recognize her?"

"She is beautiful, isn't she?" Iris said, and looked up. "But I don't know her."

"You're sure you've never seen her?"

"I have lived in Chinatown for thirty-five years, ever since my husband and I emigrated from Taiwan. If this woman came from my neighborhood, I would know." She looked at Jane. "Is this all you came to ask me?"

Jane didn't immediately answer, because she'd noticed the fire escape, which snaked right past the window. From this room, she thought, you could access the roof. Which meant you'd have access to all the rooftops on this block, including the building where the victim died. She turned to Iris. "How many employees work here?"

"I am the primary instructor."

"What about that young woman who just showed us in?" Jane glanced at the name in her notebook. "Bella Li."

"Bella has been with me for almost a year. She teaches some of the classes, and collects tuition from her own students."

"You mentioned your husband. Does Mr. Fang also work here?"

The woman blinked a few times and looked away. "My husband is dead," she said softly. "James has been gone for nineteen years."

"I'm sorry to hear that, Mrs. Fang," Frost said quietly, and it was apparent that he actually meant it.

A moment passed, silent except for the noisy clack of wooden practice swords in the next room, where the class was sparring.

"I am the sole owner of this school," said Iris. "So if you have questions, I am the one to ask." She straightened. Her composure had returned, and her gaze settled on Jane, as if she understood who was most likely to challenge her. "Why did you think I might know this dead woman?"

They could not avoid the question any longer. Jane said, "We found the victim's car this morning, parked in a Chinatown garage. It had a GPS unit in it, and one of the addresses in the memory was yours."

Iris frowned. "Here? My studio?"

"This was the victim's destination. Do you know why?"

"No." The answer was immediate.

"May I ask where you were Wednesday night, Mrs. Fang?"

Iris paused, eyes narrowing as she stared at Jane. "I taught an evening class. Then I walked home."

"What time did you leave here?"

"Around ten. I was home by ten fifteen. It is only a short walk, to Tai Tung Village. I live on Hudson Street, just at the edge of Chinatown."

"Did anyone walk with you?"

"I was alone."

"And do you live alone?"

"I have no family, Detective. My husband is gone, and my daughter . . ." She paused. "Yes, I live alone," she said, and her chin lifted, as though to ward off any pity her answer might inspire. But there was a flash of brightness in her eyes, tears that, with a few blinks, were quickly banished. Invincible though she tried to appear, this was a woman still wounded by loss.

In the next room, the class had ended,

and they could hear shoes thudding down the stairs. Iris looked up at the clock on the wall and said, "My next student will be arriving soon. Are we finished?"

"Not quite," said Jane. "I have one more question. There was another address in the victim's GPS. It was a private residence, here in Boston. Are you acquainted with a retired Boston PD detective named Louis Ingersoll?"

In an instant, all color drained from the woman's cheeks. She sat frozen, her face as rigid as stone.

"Mrs. Fang, are you all right?" said Frost. He touched her on the shoulder, and she flinched as though seared by the contact.

Jane said, quietly: "So you do know that name."

Iris swallowed. "I met Detective Ingersoll nineteen years ago. When my husband died. When he . . ." Her voice faded.

Jane and Frost glanced at each other. *Ingersoll worked homicide.*

"Mrs. Fang," said Frost. This time, when he touched her, she didn't flinch but let him rest his hand on her shoulder. "What happened to your husband?"

Iris lowered her head, and her answer was barely a whisper. "He was shot to death. In the Red Phoenix restaurant."

EIGHT

From my studio window, I can see the two detectives walk out of my building and pause on the street below. They glance up, and although every instinct tells me to back away, I stubbornly remain in full view, knowing that they're watching me watching them. I refuse to hide from either friends or enemies, so I face them through the glass, my gaze focused on the woman. DETECTIVE JANE RIZZOLI, it says on the business card that she left me. At first glance, she seemed an unlikely combatant, just another hardworking woman in a gray pantsuit and practical shoes, her hair a wiry tangle of dark curls. But her eyes reveal much more. They search and observe and assess. She has the eyes of a hunter, and she's trying to decide if I'm her prey.

I stand unafraid in open view, where she, and the rest of the world, can see me. They may study me as long as they wish, but all they'll see is a quiet and unassuming woman, my hair streaked with the first light snow of the passing years. Old age is still many years away, to be sure, but today I feel its relentless approach. I know that I am running out of time to finish what I've started. And with this visit by the two detectives, the journey has just taken a disturbing detour that I had not anticipated.

On the street below, the two detectives finally depart. Back to the hunt, wherever it takes them.

"*Sifu,* is there a problem?"

"I don't know." I turn to look at Bella, and once again marvel at how flawless and young her skin is, even in the harsh light through the window. The only imperfection is the scar on her chin, the consequence of an instant's inattention during sparring practice. It was a mistake that she has never repeated. She stands straight and unafraid and confident. Perhaps too confident; on the battlefield, arrogance can prove fatal.

"Why did they come here?" she asks.

"They're detectives. It's their job to ask questions."

"Did you learn anything else about the woman? Who she was, who sent her?"

"No." I look out the window again, at passersby walking down Harrison Avenue. "But whoever she was, she knew how to find me."

"She won't be the last," says Bella darkly.

She does not need to warn me; we both know the match has been struck and the fuse is lit.

In my office, I sink into my chair and stare at the framed photo that sits on my desk. It is a photo that I do not even need to look at, the image is so thoroughly burned into my memory. I pick it up and smile at the faces. I know the exact date the picture was taken, because it was my daughter's birthday. Mothers may forget many things, but we always remember the day our children were born. In the picture, Laura is fourteen. She and I stand together in front of the Boston Symphony Hall, where we went to hear Joshua Bell perform. For a month before that concert, all Laura talked about was Joshua Bell this, Joshua Bell that. *Isn't he handsome, Mommy? Doesn't his violin practically* sing? In the photo, Laura is still aglow from watching her idol's performance. My husband, James, was also with us that evening, but he is not in the photo; he does not appear in any of our photos because he was always the one holding the camera. How I wish I had thought, just once, to take that camera from his hands and snap a picture of his sweet, owlish face. But it never occurred to me that the opportunity, so precious, would suddenly vanish. That his smile would survive only in my memory, his image frozen at age thirty-seven. Forever, my young husband. A tear plops onto the frame, and I set the photo back on the desk.

They are both gone now. First my daughter, then my husband, ripped from my arms. How do you go on living when your heart has been cut out not just once, but twice? Yet here I am, still alive, still breathing.

For the moment.

NINE

"I remember the Red Phoenix massacre very well. It was a classic case of *amok.*" Criminal psychologist Dr. Lawrence Zucker leaned back in his chair, looking across his desk at Jane and Frost with the penetrating stare that had always made Jane feel uneasy. Although Frost sat right beside her, Zucker seemed to look only at her, his gaze crawling into her mind, probing for secrets, as if she were the sole object of his curiosity. Zucker already knew too many of her secrets. He had witnessed her rocky start with the homicide unit, when she had still been battling for acceptance as the lone woman among twelve detectives. He knew about the nightmares that haunted her after a series of particularly brutal murders by a killer named the Surgeon. And he knew about the scars she would always carry on her hands, where that same killer had plunged scalpels through her flesh. With just one look, Zucker saw through all her defenses to the raw wounds beneath, and Jane resented how vulnerable that made her feel.

She focused instead on the folder lying open on his desk. It contained his nineteen-year-old report on the Red Phoenix, including the psychological profile of Wu Weimin, the Chinese cook responsible for the shootings. She knew Zucker to be a painstakingly thorough clinician whose analyses sometimes ran dozens of pages long, so she was surprised by how thin the file appeared.

"This is your complete report?" she asked.

"It's everything I contributed to the investigation. It includes the psychological postmortem of Mr. Wu, as well as the four victim reports. There should be a copy of all this in the Boston PD file. Detective Ingersoll was the lead on that case. Have you spoken to him?"

"He's out of town this week and we haven't been able to reach him," said Frost. "His daughter says he's up north somewhere, at some fishing camp where he has no cell phone coverage."

Zucker sighed. "Retirement must be nice. Seems like he left the force ages ago. What is he now, in his seventies?"

"Which is like a hundred and ten in cop years," said Frost with a laugh.

Jane steered them back on topic. "The other detective on the case was Charlie Staines, but he's deceased. So we were hoping you could share your insight into the case."

Zucker nodded. "The basics of what happened were apparent just from the crime scene. We know that the cook, a Chinese immigrant named Wu Weimin, walked into the dining room and pro- ceeded to shoot four people. First to die was a man named Joey Gilmore, who'd dropped in to pick up a take-out order. Victim number two was the waiter,

James Fang, reportedly the cook's close friend. Victims three and four were a married couple, the Mallorys, who were seated at a dining table. Finally the cook walked into the kitchen, put the gun to his own temple, and killed himself. It was a case of *amok* followed by suicide."

"You make *amok* sound like a clinical term," said Frost.

"It is. It's a Malaysian word for something Captain Cook described back in the late 1700s, when he was living among the Malays. He described homicidal outbursts without apparent motive, in which an individual—almost always male—goes into a killing frenzy. The killer slaughters everyone within reach until he's brought down. Captain Cook thought it was a behavior peculiar to Southeast Asia, but it's now clear that it occurs worldwide, in every culture. The phenomenon's now got the unwieldy name of SMASI."

"And that stands for?"

"Sudden Mass Assault by a Single Individual."

Jane looked at Frost. "Otherwise known as going postal."

Zucker shot her a disapproving look. "Which is unfair to postal workers. SMASI happens in every profession. Blue-collar, white-collar. Young, old. Married, single. But they're almost always men."

"So what do these killers have in common?" asked Frost.

"You can probably guess. They're often isolated from the community. They have problems with relationships. Some sort of crisis precipitates the attack—loss of a job, collapse of a marriage. And finally, these individuals also have access to weapons."

Jane flipped through her copy of the Boston PD report. "It was a Glock 17 with a threaded barrel, reported stolen a year earlier in Georgia." She looked up. "Why would an immigrant on a cook's salary buy a Glock?"

"For protection, maybe? Because he felt threatened?"

"You're the psychologist, Dr. Zucker. Don't you have an answer?"

Zucker's mouth tightened. "No, I

don't. I'm not psychic. And I had no chance to interview the one person closest to him—his wife. By the time Boston PD requested my consult, she had left town and we had no idea how to find her. My psychological profile of Mr. Wu is based on interviews with other people who knew him. And that list wasn't long."

"One of those people was Iris Fang," said Jane.

Zucker nodded. "Ah, yes. The wife of the waiter. I remember her very well."

"Any reason in particular?"

"For one thing, she was a beautiful woman. Absolutely stunning."

"We've just met her," said Frost. "She's still stunning."

"Really?" Zucker flipped through the pages in his file. "Let's see, she was thirty-six when I interviewed her. Which makes her . . . fifty-five now." He glanced at Frost. "Must be those Asian genes."

Jane was beginning to feel like the ignored and ugly stepsister. "Getting beyond the fact you both think she's gorgeous, what else do you remember about Mrs. Fang?"

"Quite a lot, actually. I spoke with her several times, since she was my primary source of information about Wu Weimin. That was my first year working with Boston PD, and that particular incident was so horrific, it's hard not to remember it. You go out for a late-night dinner in Chinatown, and instead of enjoying kung pao chicken, you end up getting slaughtered by the cook. That's why the story attracted so much attention. It made the public feel vulnerable because anyone could have been a victim. Plus, there was the usual hysteria about dangerous illegal immigrants. How did Mr. Wu get into the country, how did he get a gun, et cetera, et cetera. I was only a few years out of my doctoral program, and there I was, consulting on one of the splashiest cases of the year." He paused. "That was a poor choice of words."

"What did you conclude about the shooter?" asked Frost.

"He was a rather sad character, really. He came over from Fujian province and slipped into the US when he was maybe twenty. It's impossible to be certain about the dates, because there's no documentation. All the information came from Mrs. Fang, who said Mr. Wu was close friends with her husband."

"Who died in the shooting," said Frost.

"Yes. Despite that, Mrs. Fang refused to say anything negative about Wu. She didn't believe he did it. She called him gentle and hardworking. Said he had too much to live for. He was supporting his wife and daughter, as well as sending money to a seven-year-old son from a previous relationship."

"So there was an ex-wife?"

"In another city. But Wu and his wife, Li Hua, had been settled in Boston for years. They lived in the apartment right above the restaurant where he worked, and pretty much kept to themselves. Probably afraid to attract attention, because they were illegal. Also, language may have made life difficult since they spoke Mandarin plus their very local dialect known as Min."

"While most of Chinatown speaks Cantonese," said Frost.

Zucker nodded. "Those dialects are

incomprehensible to each other, and that would have isolated the Wu family. So the man's got multiple sources of stress. He's hiding his illegal status. He's isolated. And he's got a family to support. Add to that the long hours he's working, and anyone would agree that's a lot of pressure for any man."

"But what made him snap?" asked Jane.

"Mrs. Fang didn't know. The week of the shooting, she was out of the country visiting relatives. I interviewed her after she returned home, when she was still in a state of shock. The one thing she kept insisting on, again and again, was that Wu would never kill anyone. He certainly wouldn't have killed her husband, James, because the two men were friends. She also claimed that Wu didn't even own a gun."

"How would she know that? She wasn't married to the man."

"Well, I couldn't ask Wu's wife. Within days of the shooting, she and her daughter packed up and disappeared. There was no Homeland Security tracking aliens back then, so it wasn't hard for

illegals to slip in and out of view, or vanish entirely. That's what Wu's wife did.
She vanished. And even Iris Fang had
no idea where they went."

"You're going entirely by Mrs. Fang's
word. How do you know she was telling
the truth?" said Jane.

"Maybe I'm naïve, but I never doubted
her sincerity, not once. There's just
something about her." Zucker shook his
head. "Such a tragic figure. I still feel
sorry for her. I don't know how anyone
survives as many losses as she's had."

"Losses?"

"There was also her daughter."

Jane suddenly remembered what Iris
had said, about living alone. About no
longer having a family. "Did her daughter die?"

"I guess I didn't put that in my report,
since it wasn't relevant to the Red Phoenix incident. Iris and James had a four-
teen-year-old daughter who'd vanished
two years earlier. No trace of the girl
was ever found."

"Jesus," said Frost. "We had no idea.
She didn't say anything about it."

"She's not the kind of woman who'd

welcome anyone's pity. But I remember looking in her eyes and seeing the pain. The kind of pain I couldn't even imagine. And yet, such incredible strength." Zucker fell silent for a moment, as though still moved by the memory of the woman's grief.

This was pain that Jane could not imagine, either. She thought of her own daughter, Regina, only two and a half years old. Thought of trying to go on, year after year, not knowing if her child was dead or alive. That torment alone could drive a woman to madness. *And then to lose a husband as well . . .*

"In the wake of any tragedy," said Zucker, "there are always aftershocks. But what happened after the Red Phoenix went beyond the devastation to the immediate families. It's as if the massacre had a curse attached to it. And it just kept claiming more and more victims."

The room suddenly felt colder. So cold that Jane's arms prickled from the chill. "What do you mean, a curse?" she asked.

"Within a month, a host of bad things

happened. Detective Staines keeled over and died of a heart attack. A technician working the crime scene unit was killed in a car accident. Detective Ingersoll's wife had a stroke and later died. Finally, there was the girl who disappeared."

"What girl?"

"Charlotte Dion. She was the seventeen-year-old daughter of Dina Mallory, one of the restaurant victims. A few weeks after Dina was killed in the Red Phoenix, Charlotte vanished during a school outing. She's never been found."

Jane could suddenly hear her own heartbeat, loud as a drum in her ears. "And you said Iris Fang's daughter vanished, too."

Zucker nodded. "They disappeared two years apart, but it's still an eerie coincidence, isn't it? Two victims of the Red Phoenix both had daughters go missing."

"*Was* it a coincidence?"

"What else would it be? The two families didn't know each other. The Fangs were struggling immigrants. Charlotte's parents were Boston Brahmins. There was no other connection between them. You might as well blame it on the Red Phoenix curse." He looked at the case file. "Or maybe it's that building. In Chinatown, they consider it haunted. They say that when you step inside, evil attaches itself to you." He looked at Jane. "And follows you home."

TEN

Jane did not like coincidences. In the complex fabric of life they happened, of course, but she always felt compelled to examine what made the threads cross, whether it was truly random or if there was some grander design at work, a pattern that could only be seen when you traced those threads back to their origins. And so she sat at her desk trying to do exactly that, tracing five disparate threads that had tragically intersected in a Chinatown restaurant nineteen years ago.

The Red Phoenix file was not a particularly thick one. For homicide detectives, a murder-suicide is a lucky catch, the kind of case that comes neatly wrapped up with a bow, justice conveniently dispensed by the perp himself in the form of a self-inflicted bullet. The police report by Staines and Ingersoll focused not on the *who* but the *why* of the shooting, and their analysis relied heavily on what Dr. Zucker had already told Jane and Frost about Wu Weimin.

So she looked instead at the four victims.

Victim number one was Joey Gilmore, age twenty-five, born and raised in South Boston. There was a great deal more information about Gilmore in the report, because he had a police record. Burglary, trespassing, assault and battery. That record, plus his employer's name—Donohue Wholesale Meats—instantly caught Jane's attention. Boston PD was all too familiar with the owner of the company, Kevin Donohue, because of his deep and enduring ties to local organized crime. Over the past four decades, Donohue had advanced through the ranks from a common street thug to one of the three most powerful names in the local Irish mafia. Law enforcement knew exactly who and what Donohue was; they just couldn't prove it in court. Not yet.

Jane pulled out the folder of crime scene photos and flipped to the image of Joey Gilmore's body, lying on the floor amid scattered take-out cartons. He'd been felled with a single bullet to the back of his head. Dr. Zucker might call this a case of *amok,* but to Jane, it looked a hell of a lot like a gangland execution.

Victim number two was James Fang, age thirty-seven, who worked as host, waiter, and cashier in the Red Phoenix restaurant. He and his wife, Iris, had immigrated from Taiwan sixteen years earlier, when he arrived in the United States as a graduate student in Asian literature. The restaurant was merely his evening job; during the day, he taught in the after-school enrichment program at the Boston Chinatown Neighborhood Center. He and Wu Weimin were described as good friends who had worked together in the Red Phoenix for five years. There were no known conflicts between them. Jane found no mention in the report of the Fangs' daughter, Laura, who had gone missing two years before. Perhaps Staines and Ingersoll were not even aware of the earlier tragedy that had struck the Fang family.

Victims three and four were a married couple, Arthur and Dina Mallory of Brookline, Massachusetts. Arthur was forty-eight, president and CEO of the Wellesley Group, an investment firm. No occupation was listed for Dina, age forty; judging by her husband's job title, she did not need to work. For both Arthur and Dina, this was a second marriage, and a blending of two families. Arthur's first wife was the former Barbara Hart, and they had a son, Mark, age twenty. Dina's ex-husband was Patrick Dion, and they had a daughter, seventeen. The police report specifically addressed the issue that every good homicide investigator automatically explores: any and all conflicts that resulted from the victims' divorces and remarriages.

According to Arthur Mallory's son, Mark Mallory, relations between the Mallory and Dion families were extremely cordial despite the fact Dina and Arthur left their first spouses for each other five years earlier. Even after the divorce and remarriage, Dina Mallory and her ex-husband, Patrick, remained on friendly terms, and the families often shared holiday dinners.

How bizarrely civilized that was, thought Jane. Patrick's wife leaves him for another man, and then they all spend Christmas together. It sounded too good to be true, but the information came straight from Arthur Mallory's own son, Mark, who would know. It was the ideal reconstituted family, all smiles and no conflict. She supposed it was possible, but she certainly could not see it happening in her own family. She tried to imagine a Rizzoli reunion that included her father, her mother, her father's bimbo, and her mother's new boyfriend, Vince Korsak. Now, *there* was a massacre waiting to happen, and all bets were off as to who'd be left standing.

But the Mallorys and Dions had somehow made it work. Perhaps it was for the sake of Charlotte, who would have been only twelve when her parents divorced. Like most children of divorce, she'd probably shuttled between two households, the poor little rich girl, bouncing between the homes of her mother, Dina, and her father, Patrick.

Jane turned to the last page in the file and found a brief addendum to the report:

Charlotte Dion, daughter of Dina Mallory, was reported missing April 24. Last seen in vicinity of Faneuil Hall while on school field trip. According to Detective Hank Buckholz, evidence points to likely abduction. Investigation continuing.

That addendum, dated April 28, was signed by Detective Ingersoll.

Two missing girls, Laura Fang and Charlotte Dion. Both of them were daughters of victims killed in the Red Phoenix, but nothing in this report indicated that this was anything more than a sad coincidence. It was just as Dr. Zucker had said. Sometimes there is no pattern, no plan, but merely the blind cruelty of fate, which keeps no running tally of who has suffered too much.

"You know, Rizzoli, all you had to do was ask me."

She looked up to see Johnny Tam standing beside her desk. "Ask you what?"

"About the Red Phoenix massacre. I just ran into Frost. He told me you two have been hunting down all the files. If you'd just talked to me, I could have told you all about the case."

"How would you know about it? You were like, what, eight years old when it happened?"

"I'm assigned to Chinatown so I have to know what goes on there. The Chinese still talk about the Red Phoenix, you know. It's like a wound that never healed. And never will, because it's all tied up in shame."

"Shame? Why?"

"The killer was one of our own. And by *our own,* I mean all Chinese." He pointed to the folders on her desk. "I reviewed that case file two months ago. I spoke to Lou Ingersoll. I read the ME's reports." He tapped his head. "The info's all right here."

"I didn't know you were familiar with it."

"Did it occur to you to ask me? I thought I was part of the team."

She didn't like the accusatory note in his voice. "Yes, you're part of the team," she acknowledged. "I'll try to remember it. But things'll go a lot easier for all of us if you got rid of that chip on your shoulder."

"I just want to be right in front of the hunt. Not treated like the geeky backup guy, which happens way too often around here."

"What do you mean?"

"Boston PD's supposed to be one big, happy melting pot, right?" He laughed. "Bullshit."

For a moment she studied him, trying to read his stony expression. Suddenly she recognized herself at his age, hungry to prove herself and resentful that, too often, she was ignored. "Sit down, Tam," she said.

Sighing, he pulled up the nearest chair and sat. "Yeah?"

"You think I have no idea what it's like to be a minority?"

"I don't know. Do you?"

"Look around this place. How many female homicide detectives do you see? There's one, and you're talking to her. I know what it's like having guys shut me out of the loop because I'm the girl and they think there's no way I'm good enough to do the job. You just need to learn to deal with all the jerks and the bullshit, because there's an endless supply of both."

"It doesn't mean we stop calling them on it."

"For all the difference it makes."

"You must have made a difference. Because now they accept *you.*"

She thought about whether that was true. Remembered what her life used to be like when she'd first joined the unit and had to put up with the snickers and the tampon jokes and the deliberate snubs. Yes, things were better now, but the war had been hard-fought and had taken years.

"It's not complaining that makes the difference," she said. "It's all about doing the job better than anyone else." She paused. "I hear you aced the exam for detective on your first try."

His nod was curt. "Top score, as a matter of fact."

"And you're what? Twenty-five?"

"Twenty-six."

"That's working against you, you know."

"What, the fact I'm seen as just another Asian geek?"

"No. The fact you're still a kid."

"Great. Yet another reason not to be taken seriously."

"The point is, there's a dozen different reasons to feel like you're at a disadvantage. Some are real, some are in your head. Just deal with it and do the job."

"If you'll try to remember that I'm part of the team. Let me do some of the legwork on the Red Phoenix, since I'm al-

ready up on it. I can make calls, talk to
the victims' families."

"Frost already plans to interview Mrs.
Fang again."

"So I'll talk to the other families."

She nodded. "Fine. Now tell me where
you've gone with the case already."

"I first checked it out back in Febru-
ary, when I got assigned to District A-1
and I heard some of the Chinatown lo-
cals talking about it. I remembered the
case from back when I was a kid in New
York City."

"You heard about it in New York?"

"If it's big news and it involves someone Chinese anywhere in the country,
trust me, the whole Chinese community
gossips about it. Even in New York, we
talked about the Red Phoenix. I remember my grandmother telling me how
shameful it was that the killer was one
of us. She said it reflected badly on everyone who was Chinese. It made us all
look like criminals."

"Geez. Talk about collective guilt."

"Yeah, we're really good at that.
Grandma, she'd pitch a fit if I tried to
leave the house wearing ripped jeans,

because she didn't want people to think all Chinese were slobs. I grew up with the burden of representing an entire race every time I stepped out the door. So, yeah. I already had an interest in the Red Phoenix. Then when that ad in *The Boston Globe* came out in March, I got even more interested. I read through the case file a second time."

"What ad?"

"It came out on the thirtieth, the anniversary of the shooting. Took up about a quarter page in the local section."

"I didn't see it. What did the ad say?"

"It ran a photo of the cook, Wu Weimin, with the word *innocent* in bold letters." He stared across the desks in the homicide unit. "When I saw that ad, I wanted it to be true. I wanted Wu Weimin to be innocent, just so we could erase that black mark against us."

"You don't really think he was innocent, do you?"

He looked at her. "I don't know."

"Staines and Ingersoll never doubted he was the shooter. Neither does Dr. Zucker."

"But that ad got me thinking. It made

me wonder if Boston PD got it wrong nineteen years ago."

"Just because Wu was Chinese?"

"Because people in Chinatown never believed he did it."

"Who paid for the ad? Did you ever find out?"

He nodded. "I called the *Globe.* It was paid for by Iris Fang."

Jane's cell phone rang. Even as she reached for it, she was processing that last piece of information. Wondering why, nineteen years after the event, Iris would buy an ad in defense of the man who had murdered her husband. Glancing at her phone, she saw that the incoming call was from the crime lab and she answered: "Rizzoli."

"I'm looking at those hairs right now," said criminalist Erin Volchko. "And I'll be damned if I can identify what they are."

It took a moment for Jane to shift her focus to what Erin was talking about. "You mean those hairs from the victim's clothing?"

"Yes. The ME's office sent over two strands yesterday. One was plucked off the dead woman's sleeve, the other from her leggings. They have similar morphology and color, so they're probably from the same source."

Jane felt Tam watching her as she asked: "Are these hairs real or synthetic?"

"These aren't manufactured. They're definitely organic."

"So are they human?"

"I'm not sure."

ELEVEN

Jane squinted into the microscope's eyepiece, trying to make out some distinguishing feature, but what she saw through the lens looked scarcely different from all the other hairs that she'd seen over the years. She moved aside to let Tam have a peek.

"What you're seeing on that slide is a guard hair," said Erin. "Guard hairs function as an animal's outer coat."

"And that's different from fur?" asked Tam.

"Yes, it is. Fur is from the inner coat,

and it provides insulation. Humans don't have fur."

"So if this is a hair, what does it come from?"

"It might be easier," said Erin, "to tell you what it doesn't come from. The pigmentation is consistent throughout the shaft length, so we know it's an animal whose hair has the same color from root to tip. There are no coronal scales, which eliminates rodents and bats."

Tam looked up from the microscope. "What are coronal scales?"

"Scales are structures that make up the cuticle—the outside of the hair, like the scales of a fish. The patterns in which the scales line up are characteristic of certain animal families."

"And you said that coronal scales are on rodents."

She nodded. "This hair lacks spinous scales as well, which tells us it didn't come from a cat, a mink, or a seal."

"Are we going down the whole list of animal species?" asked Jane.

"To some extent, this is a process of elimination."

"And so far you've eliminated rats, bats, and cats."

"Correct."

"Great," muttered Jane. "We can cross Batman and Catwoman off our list of suspects."

Sighing, Erin pulled off her glasses and massaged the bridge of her nose. "Detective Rizzoli, I'm just explaining how difficult it is to identify an animal hair using only light microscopy. These morphologic clues help me eliminate some animal groups, but this specimen isn't like anything I've encountered in this lab."

"What else can you eliminate?" asked Tam.

"If it were deer or caribou, the root would be wineglass-shaped, and the hair would be coarser. So it's not in the deer family. The color argues against raccoon or beaver, and it's too coarse for rabbit or chinchilla. If I were to go by the shape of the root, the diameter, and the scale pattern, I'd say it's most similar to human hair."

"Then why couldn't it be human?" asked Jane.

"Take another look in the microscope."

Jane bent down to peer into the eyepiece. "What am I supposed to focus on?"

"Notice how it's fairly straight, not kinked like a sexual hair from the pubic or underarm regions."

"Making this a head hair?"

"That's what I thought at first. That this was a human head hair. Now focus on the medulla, the central core of the strand. It's like a channel running down the length of the hair. There's something very strange about this specimen."

"Can you be more specific?"

"The medullary index. It's the ratio between the diameter of the medulla and the diameter of the hair. I've looked at countless human specimens and I've never seen a medulla this wide in a head hair. In humans, the normal index is less than a third. This is more than half the diameter of the strand. It's not just a channel, it's a huge, honking pipe."

Jane straightened and looked at Erin. "Could it be some kind of medical condition? A genetic abnormality?"

"None that I know of."

"Then what is this hair?" asked Tam.

Erin took a deep breath, as though trying to find the right words. "In almost every other way, this looks human. But it's not."

Jane's startled laugh cut through the silence. "What are we talking about here? Sasquatch?"

"I'm guessing it's some sort of non-human primate. A species I can't identify with microscopy. There are no epithelial cells attached, so the only DNA we can look at would be mitochondrial."

"It would take forever to get those results," said Tam.

"So there's one more test I'm thinking about," said Erin. "I found a scientific article out of India, about electrophoretic analysis of hair keratin. They have a huge problem with the illegal fur trade, and they use this test to identify the furs of exotic species."

"Which labs can run that test?"

"There are several wildlife labs in the US I can contact. It may turn out to be the quickest way to identify the species." Erin looked at the microscope.

"One way or another, I'm going to find out what this hairy creature is."

Retired Detective Hank Buckholz looked like a man who'd fought a long, hard war with devil alcohol and had finally surrendered to the inevitable. Jane found him in his usual spot, sitting at the bar in J. P. Doyle's, staring into a glass of scotch. It wasn't even five PM yet, but by the looks of him Buckholz had already gotten a good head start for the evening, and when he stood up to greet her, she noticed his unsteady handshake and watery eyes. But eight years of retirement could not break old habits, and he still dressed like a detective, in a blazer and oxford shirt, even if that shirt was frayed around the collar.

It was still early for the usual crowd at Doyle's, a favorite hangout for Boston PD cops. With one wave, Buckholz was able to catch the bartender's attention. "Her drink's on me," he announced, pointing to Jane. "What would you like, Detective?"

"I'm good, thanks," said Jane.

"Come on. Don't make an old cop drink alone."

She nodded to the bartender. "Sam Adams lager."

"And a refill for me," added Buckholz.

"You want to move to a table, Hank?" asked Jane.

"Naw, I like it right here. This is my stool. Always has been. Besides," he added, glancing around at the nearly empty room, "who's here to listen in? This is such an old case, no one's paying attention anymore. Except for maybe the family."

"And you."

"Yeah, well, it's hard to let go, you know? All these years later, the ones I never closed, they still keep me up at night. The Charlotte Dion case especially, because it ticked me off when her father hired a PI to follow up on it. Implication being I'm a lousy cop." He grunted and took a gulp of scotch. "All that money he wasted, just to prove that I didn't miss anything."

"So the PI never got anywhere, either?"

"Nope. That girl just plain vanished.

No witnesses, no evidence except her backpack, left in the alley. Nineteen years ago, we didn't have nearly as many surveillance cameras around to catch anything. Whoever snatched her did it quick and clean. Had to be a spur-of-the-moment thing."

"How do you figure that?"

"It was a school field trip. She went to this fancy boarding school, the Bolton Academy, out past Framingham. Thirty kids came into the city on a private bus to walk the Freedom Trail. Their stop at Faneuil Hall was a last-minute decision. Teacher told me the kids got hungry, so that's where they went for lunch. I'm thinking the perp spotted Charlotte and just moved in." He shook his head. "Talk about a high-profile snatch. Patrick Dion's a venture capitalist and he was in London when it happened. Flew home on his own private jet. Considering who he was, and his net worth, I expected there'd be a ransom demand. But it never came. Charlotte just dropped off the face of the earth. No clues, no body. Nothing."

"Her mother was killed in the Red

Phoenix restaurant just a month before that."

"Yeah, I know. Rotten luck in that family." He sipped his scotch. "Money can't stop the Grim Reaper."

"You think that's all it was? Rotten luck?"

"Lou Ingersoll and I talked and talked about it. We couldn't see a way to tie the two events together, and we looked at it every which way. Custody fight over Charlotte? Nasty divorce? Money?"

"Nothing?"

Buckholz shook his head. "I've gone through a divorce myself, and I still hate the bitch. But Patrick Dion, he and his ex-wife stayed friends. He even got along with her new husband."

"Even though Arthur ran off with Patrick's wife?"

He laughed. "Yeah, can you figure? They started off two happy families. Patrick, Dina, and Charlotte. Arthur, Barbara, and their son, Mark. Both kids attended that snooty Bolton Academy, which is how the families met. They started having dinners together. Then Arthur hooks up with Patrick's wife, and everyone gets divorced. Arthur marries Dina, Patrick gets custody of twelve-year-old Charlotte, and they all go on being friends. It's unnatural, I tell ya." He set down his glass. "The normal thing would've been to hate each other."

"Are you sure they didn't?"

"I guess it's possible they hid it. It's possible that five years after their divorce, Patrick Dion stalked his ex-wife and her husband to that restaurant and shot them in a fit of rage. But Mark Mallory swore to me that everyone was friendly. And he lost his own father in that shooting."

"What about Mark's mother? Was she hunky-dory about losing her husband to another woman?"

"I never got a chance to talk with Barbara Mallory. She had a stroke a year before the shooting. The day Charlotte vanished, Barbara was in a rehab hospital. She died a month later. Yet another bad-luck family." He waved at the bartender. "Hey, I need another one here."

"Um, did you drive, Hank?" asked Jane, frowning at his empty glass.

"It's okay. I promise, this'll be my last."

The bartender set another scotch on the counter and Buckholz just stared at it, as though its mere presence was enough to satisfy him for the moment. "So that's the story in a nutshell," he said. "Charlotte Dion was seventeen, blond, and gorgeous. When she wasn't attending that boarding school, she lived with her rich daddy. She had everything going for her, and then—poof. She's snatched off a street. We just haven't found her remains yet." He picked up the scotch, his hand now steady. "Hell of a thing, life."

"And death."

He laughed and took a sip. "So true."

"You have any thoughts about the other girl who vanished? Laura Fang?"

"That was Sedlak's case, rest his soul. But I did review it, because of the Red Phoenix connection. Didn't find anything to make me think the abductions were related. I think Charlotte was a spontaneous spot and snatch. Laura, she was a different case. It happened right after school got out and she was walking home. One of her schoolmates saw Laura voluntarily climb into some-one's car, like she knew the driver. But no one got a license plate and the girl was never seen again. So that's another body that's never been found." He stared at the bottles lined up on the other side of the counter. "Makes you wonder just how many skeletons are piled up in the woods, in the landfills. Millions of people missing in this coun-try. All those bones. I can accept the fact I'm gonna die someday, as long as there's a nice marker to tell the world it's me buried there. But to never be found? To end up hidden under some weeds? That's like you never even ex-isted." He shuddered. "Anyway, that's the Charlotte Dion case in a nutshell. Does that help any?"

"I don't know. Right now, it's just one piece of a very confusing puzzle." Jane waved to the bartender. "Let me have the tab."

"No way," said Buckholz.

"You just did me a favor, telling me about Charlotte."

"I'm here all the time anyway. This

seat, this bar. You know where to find me." He looked down at her ringing cell phone. "I see you're a girl in demand. Lucky you."

"Depends who's calling." She answered her phone. "Detective Rizzoli."

"I'm sorry to have to make this call." It was a man's voice, and he did indeed sound reluctant to be talking to her. "I believe you're Detective Tam's supervisor?"

"Yes, we work together."

"I'm calling on behalf of all the victims' families. We'd prefer not to deal with Detective Tam anymore. He's managed to upset everyone, especially poor Mary Gilmore. After all these years, why are we being subjected to these questions again?"

Jane massaged her head, dreading the talk she would need to have with her younger colleague. *You are a public servant. Which means you must not piss off the public.* "I'm sorry, sir," she said. "I didn't catch your name."

"Patrick Dion."

She straightened. Looked at Buckholz, who was following the conversation with keen interest. Once a cop, always a cop. "Dina Mallory was your ex-wife?" she said.

"Yes. And it's painful, being reminded of how she died."

"I understand it's difficult for you, Mr. Dion. But Detective Tam needs to ask these questions."

"Dina died nineteen years ago. There was never any doubt about who killed her. Why is this coming up again?"

"I can't really discuss it. It's—"

"Yes, I know. It's part of *a current investigation.* That's what Detective Tam said."

"Because it's true."

"Mark Mallory is livid about this, and it's got both Mary Gilmore and her daughter upset. First we get those notes in the mail, and then Detective Tam starts calling us. We'd all like to know why this is happening now."

"Excuse me," she cut in. "What's this about getting notes?"

"It's been going on for six, seven years. Every March thirtieth they show up in our mailboxes, like some grim anniversary reminder."

"What's in these notes?"

"I always get a copy of Dina's obituary. On the back, someone writes: *Don't you want to know the truth?*"

"Do you still have those notes?"

"Yes, and Mary has hers. But Mark was so angry, he tossed his out."

"Who's sending these things? Do you know?"

"I have to assume they come from the same person who took out the ad in the *Globe.* That Iris Fang."

"Why would Mrs. Fang be doing this?"

There was a long pause. "I hate to speak badly of Mrs. Fang. She lost her husband so I know she's suffered, too. I feel sorry for her. But I think the issue is quite obvious."

"What's obvious?"

"The woman," said Patrick, "is insane."

TWELVE

By the time her doorbell rang, Maura had the dinner table set and a leg of lamb roasting in the oven. Teenage boys were notorious for their appetites, so she had brought home both a blueberry and an apple pie, had baked four potatoes and shucked half a dozen ears of corn. Did the boy eat salad? She didn't know. During those desperately hungry days they'd spent together in the Wyoming wilderness, she and Rat had survived on whatever they could forage. She had watched him devour dog biscuits and tinned beans and tree bark.

Surely he wouldn't turn up his nose at lettuce, and he could probably use the vitamins. When she'd last seen him in January, he'd been pale and thin, and it was that undernourished boy she was cooking for tonight. No matter how the week goes, she thought, he will not leave my house hungry. It was the one detail she could prepare for, the one variable she could control.

Because everything else about his first visit to her house was fraught with unknowns.

She owed her life to Julian "Rat" Perkins, yet she scarcely knew him, and he scarcely knew her. Together they had fought to stay alive, and there was no more intimate bond two people could know than to stare death in the face together. Now they were about to find out if that bond could survive the acid test of a week in each other's company, under civilized conditions.

At the sound of the doorbell, she dried her hands on a dish towel and hurried down the hall, aware that her heart was suddenly thumping hard. Relax, he's only a boy, she thought as she opened the front door. And was almost knocked down when an enormous black dog reared up to greet her, its two front paws landing on her chest.

"Bear! *Down, boy!*" yelled Rat.

She laughed as the dog gave her a sloppily joyful lick on her face. Then it dropped to all fours, tail wagging, and barked. Maura smiled at the boy, who looked thoroughly appalled by his companion's bad manners. "Well?" she said. "Aren't you going to give me a hug, too?"

"Hello, ma'am," he said and awkwardly wrapped long arms around her. She was startled by how much bigger he seemed, how much muscle he'd put on since she'd last seen him. Was it possible for a boy to grow so much in only a few months?

"I missed you, Rat," she murmured. "I missed you both so much."

Footsteps creaked on the porch stairs and the boy suddenly pulled away from her, as though embarrassed to be seen hugging her. Maura looked at the man now standing behind Rat. Anthony Sansone had always seemed a forbidding figure, physically imposing, his face impossible to read, but on this gloomy afternoon, he was smiling as he set down Rat's backpack on the porch.

"There you go, Julian," he said.

"Thank you for driving him all the way to Boston," she said.

"It was a pleasure, Maura. It gave us a chance to talk." He paused, his gaze searching her face, and as always he seemed to see too much. "It's been a long time since we spoke. How are you?"

"I'm fine. Busy." She forced a smile. "I never have any shortage of clients. Would you like to come in for a bit?"

He looked at the boy, who'd been glancing back and forth between them, following their conversation with great interest. "No, I should let you and Julian catch up. Are you two going to be fine for the week?"

"I have to go in to work Monday and Tuesday, but starting Wednesday I have some time off. We'll take a tour of the city."

"Then I'll pick you up next Saturday,

Julian," said Sansone, extending his arm to him.

The man and boy shook hands. It was an oddly formal farewell, but between these two it seemed perfectly natural, and just what was expected. Rat waited until Sansone returned to his car and drove away. Only then did he look at Maura.

"We talked about you," he said. "On the drive down."

"All good things, I hope."

"I think he likes you. A lot." Rat picked up his backpack. "But he's kind of strange."

People could say the same about you, she thought, looking at the boy. About both of us. She draped an arm around him and felt him flinch at the unaccustomed affection. For too long, the boy had lived like a wild animal, foraging in the Wyoming mountains, and in his eyes she still saw traces of the abandoned child. The world had not been kind to Julian Perkins, and it would take time for him to trust another human being.

They walked into the house, and the

boy glanced around the living room. "Where did Bear go?"

"I think he's already made himself at home here. I bet he's discovered all the goodies in the kitchen."

That was indeed where they found him, gobbling up the lamb trimmings that she'd placed in the ceramic dog bowl. She had never owned a dog, and the bowl was brand-new, as was the extra-large dog bed and the leash and the flea powder and the cans of Alpo stacked in the closet. Where the boy went, so did Bear, which meant that this week she was sharing her house with two alien creatures, a dog and a teen-ager. In the oven, drippings from the roasting lamb sizzled and she saw the boy lift his nose, like a beast scenting his supper.

"Dinner should be ready in an hour. Let me show you your room," she said and frowned at his backpack. "Where's your suitcase?"

"This is all I brought."

"Then it looks like you and I need to go shopping for clothes."

"No, I don't really need anything," he

said as they walked up the hall. "We all wear uniforms at the school."

"This room's yours."

Bear trotted in first, but the boy hesitated in the doorway, as if wondering whether a mistake had been made. It suddenly struck Maura what an absurdly feminine room this was for a boy and a dog. Reluctantly Rat stepped into the room and surveyed the white duvet, the vase of freshly cut flowers on the dresser, and the pale green Turkish rug. He touched nothing, as if these were all museum pieces and he was afraid to break something. Carefully he set his backpack in a corner.

"How is school?" she asked.

"It's okay." He knelt down to unzip the backpack. Out came two shirts, a sweater, a pair of trousers, all neatly rolled up.

"So you like being at Evensong? You're happy there?"

"It's different from my old school. People are nice to me." It was a matter-of-fact statement, said without self-pity, and it revealed how painful his life must once have been. She had read his files from Wyoming, so she knew about his fistfights in the school yard, the taunts he'd endured about his ragged clothes and his fractured family. So many people, from his social worker to his psychologist, had warned her that the boy was too troubled, that taking him into her life could lead to consequences she'd regret. Now she watched that troubled boy calmly unpack his clothes and hang them neatly in the closet, and she thought: Thank God I never listened to them. To any of them.

"Have you made friends at school?" she asked. "Do you like the other students?"

"They're a lot like me," he said. He opened a dresser drawer and placed socks and underwear inside.

She smiled. "You mean they're special."

"They don't have parents, either."

This was news to her. When Sansone had told her he was offering the boy a scholarship to the Evensong School, he had emphasized the institution's academic strengths and rural campus, its international faculty and superb library.

He had said nothing about it being a school for orphans.

"Are you sure about that?" she asked. "There must be some parents who come to visit."

"Sometimes I see someone's aunt or an uncle. But I've never met anyone's mom or dad. He says we're each other's family now."

"He?"

"Mr. Sansone." Rat closed the dresser drawer and looked at her. "He asks about you all the time."

Maura felt her face redden and she focused on Bear, who was turning around and around in the dog bed, getting a feel for this new luxury. "What sort of things does he ask?"

"If you've written me any letters lately. If you're ever coming to visit the school. Whether you'd like to teach a class there."

"At Evensong?" She shook her head. "I'm not sure a class in forensic pathology is appropriate for high school students."

"But we're learning a lot of cool stuff. Last month, Ms. Saul showed us how to build a Roman catapult. And they let me teach a class on animal tracks, because I know so much about it. We even dissected a horse."

"Really?"

"He broke his leg, and they had to put him down. We cut him open and studied his organs."

"Didn't you find that upsetting?"

"I've dressed deer. I know what dead things look like."

Yes, you do, she thought. In Wyoming, he had watched a man bleed to death. She wondered whether he sometimes startled awake at night, as she did, haunted by the memories of what had happened to them both in the mountains. He seemed so calm and controlled as he set his schoolbooks on the dresser, as he took his toothbrush into the bathroom, all his emotions shuttered up tight. *He is more like me than I care to admit.*

In the kitchen, her cell phone was ringing.

"Can I go outside and see the yard?" he asked.

"Go ahead. Let me get this call."

She walked into the kitchen and pulled the cell phone out of her purse. "Dr. Isles," she answered.

"This is Detective Tam. I'm really sorry to be calling you on the weekend."

"Not a problem, Detective. How can I help you?"

"I wondered if I could ask your opinion on an old homicide. It happened nineteen years ago, a shooting in a Chinatown restaurant. There were five victims. At the time, they called it a murder-suicide."

"Why are you pursuing something that happened nineteen years ago?"

"It could be connected to our Jane Doe on the rooftop. It may be the reason she came to Chinatown. It seems she was seeking out people who knew about that restaurant shooting."

"What do you want me to do, exactly?"

"Review the autopsy reports on those five people, particularly the shooter's. Tell us if you agree with the conclusions. The pathologist who performed them is no longer with the ME's office, so I can't ask him."

From the kitchen window, she saw Rat and the dog were outside and circling the yard, as though hunting for a way out, an escape into the wider world. He was a boy meant for the wilderness.

"I'm busy this week," she said. "You might try asking Dr. Bristol instead."

"But I was really hoping . . ."

"Yes?"

"I'd rather have your opinion, Dr. Isles. I know you always tell it like it is, no matter what. I trust your judgment."

That startled her, because it was not an opinion shared among Boston PD's rank and file these days. She thought of the stares and cold silence she'd endured from police officers during the past week. Thought of all the different ways they had made her feel like the enemy.

"I'll be home this evening," she said. "You can drop off the files anytime."

It was after nine pm when Bear began barking at the front door. Maura opened it to find Detective Tam standing on her porch. He and the dog warily regarded each other for a moment, but after a few exploratory sniffs, Bear signaled his approval by trotting back into the house, allowing the visitor to enter. Tam moved with the same coiled energy that she'd noticed when they'd met in Chinatown, and he paused in her foyer, head alertly swiveling toward the sound of the running shower. He didn't ask the question, but she could read it in his eyes.

"I have a houseguest staying with me this week," she said.

"I'm sorry about intruding on your weekend." He handed her a bundle of photocopied pages. "That's all five autopsy reports, plus the Boston PD report filed by Detectives Ingersoll and Staines."

"Wow. It looks like you put a lot of effort into this."

"This is my first homicide case. Freshman effort, you know?" He pulled a flash drive out of his pocket. "They wouldn't let me take any originals out of the ME's office, so I scanned the photos and X-rays for you. I realize it's an overwhelming amount of work, and I'm sorry about dumping this on you." As he pressed the flash drive into her hand, he looked straight at her, as though to emphasize how important this was to him, and that he was placing all his confidence in her.

Flushing at his touch, she looked down at the flash drive. "Before you leave, let me make sure these files load up on my computer," she said. They went into her office and as she booted up her laptop, Tam eyed the dog, who had followed them and now sat at Tam's feet, watching this new visitor.

"What kind of dog is this?" Tam asked.

"I have no idea. Probably shepherd, plus some wolf or husky. He belongs to my houseguest."

"You're a very nice hostess, letting your guest bring a dog."

"I owe my life to that dog. As far as I'm concerned, he can stay anywhere he wants." She inserted the flash drive, and after a moment a series of thumbnail photos appeared on the monitor. She clicked on the first, revealing a grisly view of a woman's nude body on the autopsy table. "Looks like this loads up fine. I can't promise when I'll review them, but I can tell you it won't be until next week."

"I really appreciate this, Dr. Isles."

She straightened and looked at him. "Drs. Bristol and Costas are both very good pathologists. You can trust their judgment as well. Is there a reason you didn't go to them?"

He paused, turning toward the sound of the shower shutting off. Bear's ears pricked up, and he trotted out of the office.

"Detective?" she asked.

He said, reluctantly: "I'm guessing you know what's being said about you. Because of the Wayne Graff trial and all."

Her mouth tightened. "I'm sure that none of it is flattering."

"It may be a thin blue line, but that line holds firm. It doesn't take kindly to criticism."

"Even when it's the truth," she said bitterly.

"That's why I came to you. Because I know you do tell the truth." His eyes met hers, direct and unflinching. The day they'd met in Chinatown, she had thought him unreadable, a man who might or might not like her. That same detached expression was now on his face, but it was merely a mask that she had not yet learned to penetrate. There was more to this man than she knew, and she wondered if he ever allowed anyone a glimpse behind that mask.

"What are you hoping I'll find in these reports?" she asked.

"Contradictions, maybe. Things that don't add up or don't make sense."

"Why do you think there'd be any?"

"Practically from the moment that Staines and Ingersoll walked onto the scene, it was called a murder-suicide. I read their report and they didn't explore alternative theories. It was too easy to sign it off as a crazy Chinese immigrant shooting up a restaurant. And then himself."

"Do you think it wasn't a murder-suicide?"

"I don't know. But nineteen years later, it's giving off some strange echoes. Our Jane Doe on the roof had two addresses in her handheld GPS. One was

Detective Ingersoll's residence. The other was for Iris Fang, the widow of one of the massacre victims. This dead woman was obviously interested in the Red Phoenix case. We don't know why."

They heard the dog whine, and Maura turned to see Rat standing in the doorway, his hair still damp from the shower. He was staring at the autopsy photo on her computer screen. Quickly she minimized the program, and the disturbing image shrank from sight.

"Julian, this is Detective Tam," she said. "And this is my houseguest, Julian Perkins. He's been going to school up in Maine, and he's down here for spring break."

"So you're the owner of the scary dog," Tam said.

The boy kept staring at the monitor, as if he could still see the image displayed there. "Who was she?" he asked softly.

"It's just a case we're talking about," said Maura. "We're almost through here. Why don't you go watch TV?"

Tam waited until they heard the television turn on in the living room, and he said: "I'm sorry he got a look at that. It's not something you want a kid to see."

"I'll review the files when I have the time. It may not be for a while. There's no hurry, I assume?"

"It would be nice to make some progress on Jane Doe."

"The Red Phoenix happened nineteen years ago," she said and turned off her laptop. "I'm sure this can wait a little longer."

THIRTEEN

Even before I see him, I know that he has entered my studio, his arrival heralded by the whoosh of damp night air as the door opens and closes. I do not interrupt my exercise to greet him, but continue to whirl and swing my blade. In the wide mirror I can see Detective Frost watching in fascination as I enact the chant of the saber. Today I feel strong, my arms and legs as limber as when I was young. Each of my moves, each turn, each slash, is dictated by a line from an ancient sonnet:

Up the seven stars to ride the
  tiger.
Soaring, turning, dodging as
  spirits soar,
To become the white crane,
Spreading its wings as it thrusts
  out a leg.
The wind blows
And the lotus flower trembles.

All the moves are second nature to
me, one blending into the next. I do not
have to think about them, because my
body remembers, as surely as it knows
how to walk and how to breathe. My
saber slices and whirls, but my thoughts
are on the policeman, and what I will
say to him.

I reach the final and thirteenth line of
the sonnet. *The phoenix returns to its
nest.* I stand at attention, my weapon
finally at rest, sweat cooling my face.
Only then do I turn to face him.

"That was beautiful, Mrs. Fang," says
Detective Frost, his eyes wide with ad-
miration. "Like a dance."

"A beginner's exercise. It brings a
calming end to my day."

His gaze drops to the saber I'm holding. "Is that a real sword?"

"Her name is Zheng Yi. She was passed down to me from my great-great-grandmother."

"So it must be really old."

"And battle-tested. It was meant for combat. If you never practice with a combat sword, you'll never learn to work with its weight, to know how it feels in your grip." I make two lightning slashes through the air and he flinches away, startled. With a smile, I extend the handle to him. "Take it. Feel its weight."

He hesitates, as if it might give him an electric shock. Cautiously he grasps the handle and gives the sword a clumsy swing through the air. "It doesn't feel natural to me," he said.

"No?"

"The balance seems strange."

"Because it's not merely a ceremonial sword but a genuine *dao*. A true Chinese saber. This design is called a willow leaf. You see how it's curved along the length of the blade? It was the standard sidearm for soldiers during the Ming dynasty."

"When was that?"

"About six hundred years ago. Zheng Yi was crafted in Gansu province during a time of war." I pause and add ruefully, "Unfortunately, war was too often a normal state in old China."

"So this sword saw actual combat?"

"I know it did. When I hold her, I can feel old battles still singing in the blade."

He laughs. "If I'm ever attacked in a dark alley, Mrs. Fang, I want you by my side."

"You're the one with the gun. Shouldn't you protect *me*?"

"I'm sure you do a good job of that all by yourself." He hands the sword back to me. I can see it makes him nervous, just being in proximity to that razor-sharp edge. With a bow, I take back the sword and look straight at him. He flushes at my directness, a reaction I don't expect from a policeman, and certainly not from a seasoned detective who investigates murders. But there is a surprising sweetness to this man, a vulnerability that suddenly reminds me of my husband. Detective Frost is about the same age as James was when he died, and in this man's face I see James's abashed smile, his innate eagerness to please.

"You had more questions to ask me, Detective?"

"Yes. Concerning a matter that we weren't aware of when we spoke to you before."

"What would that be?"

He seems reluctant to say what is on his mind. Already I can see the apology in his eyes. "It's about your daughter. Laura."

The mention of Laura's name is like a shocking blow to my chest. This I did not expect, and I sway from the impact.

"I'm so sorry, Mrs. Fang," he says, reaching out to steady me. "I know this has to be upsetting. Are you all right? Do you want to sit down?"

"It's just that . . ." I give a numb shake of my head. "I have not eaten since this morning."

"Maybe if you ate something now? Could I bring you somewhere?"

"Perhaps we should talk another day."

"It would only be a few questions."
He pauses. Adds, quietly: "I haven't had
dinner, either."

For a moment his words hang in the
air. It is a trial balloon. My hand tightens
around the grip of my sword, an instinc-
tive reaction to a situation fraught with
uncertainties. In danger, there is opportunity. He is a policeman, but I see nothing about him to be wary of, only an
attentive man with a kind face. And I
want desperately to know why he is
asking about Laura.

I slide Zheng Yi into its scabbard.
"There is a dumpling house on Beach
Street."

He smiles, and the change in his face
is startling. It makes him seem far
younger. "I know the place."

"Let me get my raincoat, and we'll
walk."

Outside, we stroll together through a
fine spring drizzle, but keep a discreet
distance between us. I have brought
along Zheng Yi because the sword is
too valuable to leave behind at the studio. And because she has always been
my protection, against all the threats I

cannot see. Even on this wet evening, Chinatown is bustling, the streets crowded with dinner-hour patrons hungry for roast duck or ginger-steamed fish. As we walk, I try to stay focused on my surroundings, on every unfamiliar face that passes by. But Detective Frost, talkative and exuberant, is a continual distraction.

"This is my favorite part of Boston," he says, throwing his arms wide, as though to embrace Chinatown and everyone in it. "It has the best food, the best markets, the most interesting little side streets. I always love coming here."

"Even when you're here to see a dead body?"

"Well, no," he says with a rueful laugh. "But there's just something about this neighborhood. Sometimes I feel like I belong here. Like it's an accident I wasn't born Chinese."

"Ah. You think you're reincarnated."

"Yeah. As the all-American kid from South Boston." He looks at me, his face gleaming in the dampness. "You said you're from Taiwan."

"Have you ever been there?"

He gives a regretful shake of the head. "I haven't traveled as much as I'd like. But I did go to France on my honeymoon."

"What does your wife do?"

The pause makes me look at him, and I see his head has drooped. "She's in law school," he says quietly. It takes him a moment before he adds: "We separated. Last summer."

"I'm sorry."

"It hasn't been a very good year, I'm afraid," he says, then suddenly seems to remember who he's talking to. The woman who has lost both her husband and her daughter. "I have nothing to complain about, really."

"Loneliness isn't easy for anyone to live with. But I'm certain you will find someone else."

He looks at me, and I see pain in his eyes. "Yet you never remarried, Mrs. Fang."

"No, I didn't."

"There must have been men who were interested."

"How can you replace the love of your

life?" I say simply. "James is my husband. He will always be my husband."

He takes a moment to absorb that. Then he says: "That's the way I always thought love should be."

"It is."

His eyes are unnaturally bright when he looks at me. "Only for some of us."

We reach the dumpling house, where the windows are fogged with steam. He steps forward quickly to open the door, a gentlemanly gesture that strikes me as ironic, since I am the one carrying a lethal sword. Inside, the cramped dining room is packed, and we are lucky to claim the last empty table, tucked into a corner near the window. I hang the scabbard over the back of my chair and pull off my raincoat. From the kitchen wafts the tempting scents of garlic and steamed buns, painfully savory reminders that I have not eaten since breakfast. Out those kitchen doors come platters of glistening dumplings stuffed with morsels of pork or shrimp or fish; at the next table chopsticks clack against bowls, and a family chatters in such noisy Cantonese that it sounds like an argument.

Frost looks bewildered as he scans the long menu. "Maybe I should let you order for both of us."

"Are there any foods you won't eat?"

"I'll eat everything."

"You may be sorry you said that. Because we Chinese really *do* eat everything."

He cheerfully accepts the challenge. "Surprise me."

When the waitress brings out an appetizer platter with cold jellyfish and chicken feet and pickled pig's feet, his chopsticks hesitate over the unfamiliar selection, but then he bites into a translucent chunk of pork cartilage. I watch his eyes widen with a look of delight and revelation.

"This is wonderful!"

"You haven't tried it before?"

"I guess I haven't been very adventurous," he confesses as he dabs chili oil from his lips. "But I'm trying to change all that."

"Why?"

He pauses to think about it, a strip of

jellyfish dangling from his chopsticks. "I guess . . . I guess it's about getting older, you know? Realizing how few things I've actually experienced. And how little time there is to do it all."

Older. At that I have to smile because I am almost two decades older than he is, so he must consider me ancient. Yet he does not look at me that way. I catch him studying my face, and when I return the gaze, his cheeks suddenly flush. Just as my husband's did the first night we courted, on a spring evening heavy with mist, like this one. *Oh James, I think you would like this young man. He reminds me so much of you.*

The dumplings come, soft little pillows plump with pork and shrimp. I watch in amusement as he struggles to pick up the slippery morsels and ends up chasing them around the plate with his chopsticks.

"These were my husband's favorites. He could eat a dozen of them." I smile at the memory. "He offered to work here without pay for a month, if they would just give him their recipe."

"Was he also in the restaurant business in Taiwan?"

His question makes me look straight at him. "My husband was a scholar of Chinese literature. He was descended from a long line of scholars. So no, he was not in the restaurant business. He worked as a waiter only to survive."

"I didn't know that."

"It's too easy to assume that the waiter you see here is just a waiter, and the grocery clerk is only a clerk. But in Chinatown, you can't assume anything about people. Those shabby old men you see playing checkers under the lion gate? Some of them are millionaires. And that woman over there, behind the cash register? She comes from a family of imperial generals. People are not what they seem here, so you should never underestimate them. Not in Chinatown."

He gives a chastened nod. "I won't. Not now. And I'm sorry, Mrs. Fang, if I in any way sounded disrespectful of your husband." His apology sounds utterly sincere; it is yet another reason I find this man so surprising.

I set down my chopsticks and regard him. Now that I have eaten, I finally feel able to address the subject that has been hanging over our meal. The noisy family at the next table rises to leave with a squeal of chair legs and a noisy chorus of Cantonese. When they walk out the door, the room suddenly seems silent in their absence.

"You came to ask about my daughter. Why?"

He takes a moment to answer, wiping his hands and neatly folding his napkin. "Have you ever heard the name Charlotte Dion?"

I nod. "She was the daughter of Dina Mallory."

"Are you aware of what happened to Charlotte?"

"Detective Frost," I say, sighing, "I was forced to live through those events, so they are embedded here, forever." I touch my head. "I know Mrs. Mallory was married before, to a man named Patrick Dion, and they had a daughter named Charlotte. A few weeks after the shooting, Charlotte disappeared. Yes, I know about all the victims and their families, because I'm one of them." I look down at my empty plate, glistening with grease. "I've never met Mr. Dion, but after his daughter vanished, I wrote him a condolence card. I don't know if he still cared about his ex-wife, or if he mourned her death. But I do know what it feels like to lose a child. I told him how sorry I was. I told him I understood his pain. He never wrote back." I look up at Frost again. "So yes. I know why you're asking about Charlotte. You're wondering the same thing everyone else did. The same thing I've wondered. How is it possible for two families to be so cursed? First my Laura disappears, and then two years later, his Charlotte. Our families linked by both the Red Phoenix and the loss of our daughters. You wouldn't be the first policeman to ask me about it."

"Detective Buckholz did, I assume."

I nod. "When Charlotte vanished, he came to see me. To ask if the two girls might have known each other. Charlotte's father is very wealthy, so of course she received a great deal of attention.

Far more attention than my Laura ever received."

"In his report, Buckholz wrote that both Laura and Charlotte studied classical music."

"My daughter played the violin."

"And Charlotte played the viola in her school orchestra. Is there any chance they met? At a music workshop, maybe?"

I shake my head. "I've already gone over this with the police, again and again. Except for music, the girls had nothing in common. Charlotte went to a private school. And we live here, in Chinatown." My voice trails off and I focus on the next table, where a Chinese couple sits with their young children. In the high chair is a little girl, her hair done up in tiny pigtails that stick up like spiky devil horns. The way I used to arrange Laura's hair when she was three years old.

The waitress brings the check to our table. I reach for it, but Frost snatches it up first.

"Please," he says. "Let me."

"The elder should always pay for dinner."

"That is the last word I'd use to describe you, Mrs. Fang. Besides, I ate ninety percent of this meal." He sets cash on the table. "Let me give you a ride home."

"I live only a few blocks from here, in Tai Tung Village. It's easier for me to walk."

"Then I'll walk with you. Just to be on the safe side."

"Is this for your protection, or for mine?" I ask as I reach for my sword, which has been hanging over the chair.

He looks at Zheng Yi and laughs. "I forgot that you're already armed and dangerous."

"So there's no need to walk me home."

"Please. I'd feel better if I did."

It is still drizzling when we step outside, and after the steamy heat of the restaurant it's a relief to breathe in the cool air. The mist sparkles in his hair and glazes his skin, and despite the chill I feel unexpected warmth in my cheeks. He has paid for dinner and now he insists on walking me home. It's been a long time since a man has been so solicitous toward me, and I don't know whether to feel flattered or irritated that he considers me so vulnerable.

We walk south on Tyler Street, toward the old enclave of Tai Tung Village, moving into a part of Chinatown that is quieter, emptier. Here there are no tourists, just tired buildings that house dusty shops on the ground floors, all barricaded at this hour behind locked gates. While in the brightly lit restaurant, I could let down my guard. Now I feel exposed, even though an armed detective is at my side. The lights fade behind us and the shadows thicken. I am aware of my own heartbeat and the sigh of air flowing in and out of my lungs. The chant of the saber flows through my mind, words that both calm me and prepare me for whatever may come.

Green dragon emerges from the water.
The wind blows the flowers.
White clouds move overhead.
Black tiger searches the mountain.

My hand moves to the pommel of my sword, where it rests in readiness. We pass through darkness and light and darkness again, and as my senses sharpen, the night itself seems to tremble.

Beat the grass to search for the snake on the left.
Beat the grass to search for the snake on the right.

The darkness comes alive. Everywhere there is movement. A rat skittering in the alley. The drip of water trickling from a rain gutter. I see it all, hear it all. The man beside me is oblivious, believing that it is his presence that keeps me safe. Never imagining that perhaps it is the other way around.

We turn onto Hudson Street and arrive at my modest row house, which has its own ground-floor entrance. As I pull out my keys, he lingers beneath the yellow glow of the porch light where insects buzz and tick against the bulb. He is a gentleman to the end, waiting until I am safely inside.

"Thank you for dinner and the armed escort," I say with a smile.

"We don't really know what's going on yet. So do be careful."

"Good night." I insert my key into the lock and suddenly go very still. It's my sharp intake of breath that alerts him.

"What is it?"

"It isn't locked," I whisper. The door hangs ajar. Already Zheng Yi is out of the scabbard and in my hand; I do not even remember pulling her free. My heart is thumping as I give the door a shove with my foot. It swings all the way open and I see only darkness beyond. I step forward, but Detective Frost pulls me back.

"Wait here," he orders. Weapon drawn, he steps inside and flips on the light switch.

From the doorway I watch as he moves through my modest home, past the brown sofa, the striped armchair that James and I bought so many years ago when we first arrived from Taiwan. Furniture that I could never bear to replace, because my husband and my daughter once sat in them. Even in furniture, beloved spirits still linger. As Frost heads to the kitchen, I walk into the middle of the living room and stand very still, inhaling the air, scanning the room. My gaze halts on the bookcase. On the empty picture frame. I feel a thrill of fear.

Someone has been here.

From the kitchen, Frost says: "Does it look okay to you?"

I don't answer but move toward the stairs.

"Iris, wait," he says.

Already I'm darting up the steps, moving silently. It's my heartbeat that thunders. It sends blood rushing to limbs, to muscles. I grip my sword with both hands as I step toward my bedroom door.

Scatter the clouds and see the sun.

I sniff and know at once that the intruder has been in this room, has left his scent of aggression. The air is foul with the smell, and for a few heartbeats I cannot bring myself to advance and meet the enemy. I hear Detective Frost come running up the stairs. He defends my back, but it's what waits ahead that terrifies me.

Use the seven stars to ride the tiger.

I step across the threshold just as Frost turns on the light. The room comes into sudden, shocking focus. The missing photograph is on my pillow, fixed there by a knife blade. Only when I hear Frost punching numbers into his cell phone do I turn to look at him.

"What are you doing?" I ask.

"Calling my partner. She needs to know about this."

"Don't call her. Please. You don't know anything about this."

He looks up at me, his gaze suddenly focused with an intensity that makes me realize I have underestimated him. "Do you?"

FOURTEEN

Jane stood in Iris Fang's bedroom, staring at the photograph that had been stabbed through by a butcher knife. It was a picture of a much younger Iris, her face aglow and smiling as she held an infant in her arms.

"She says the knife is from her own kitchen," said Frost. "And the baby is her daughter, Laura. That photo is supposed to be in a frame downstairs, on the bookcase. Whoever broke in deliberately took it out of the frame and brought it upstairs, where she certainly couldn't miss seeing it."

"Or the message. Stabbing a knife in her pillow sure as hell isn't wishing her sweet dreams. What is this all about?"

"She doesn't know." He dropped his voice so Iris couldn't hear him from downstairs. "At least, that's what she says."

"You think she's not being straight with us?"

"I don't know. The thing is . . ."

"What?"

His voice dropped even lower. "She didn't want me to call you. In fact, she asked me to forget the whole thing. That doesn't make sense to me."

Or me either, thought Jane, frowning at the knife, which had been plunged hilt-deep, crushing the picture against the linen. It was an act of sheer rage, meant to terrify. "Anyone else would be screaming for police protection."

"She insists she doesn't need it. Says she's not afraid."

"Are we sure someone else was actually in here?"

"What are you implying?"

"She could have done this herself. Taken a knife from her own kitchen."

"Why would she?"

"It would explain why she's not scared."

"That's not how it happened."

"How do you know?"

"Because I was right here when she found it."

Jane turned to him. "You came up to her bedroom?"

"Don't look at me like that. I walked her home, that's all. We noticed her front door was open, so I came in to check the place."

"Okay."

"That's all it was!"

Then why do you look so guilty? She stared down at the mutilated photo. "If I came home and found something like this, it would scare the hell out of me. So why doesn't she want us to look into it?"

"It could be just a cultural thing about the police. Tam says that folks in Chinatown are leery of us."

"I'd be a lot more leery of whoever did this." Jane turned to the door. "Let's have a talk with Mrs. Fang."

Downstairs she found Iris seated on

the faded brown sofa, looking far too calm for a woman whose home had just been violated. Detective Tam was pacing nearby, cell phone pressed to his ear. He glanced up at Jane with a look of *I don't know what's going on here, either.*

Jane sat down across from Iris and just studied her for a moment without saying a word. The woman stared straight back at her, as though understanding that this was a test, and she had already girded herself for the challenge. It was not the gaze of a victim.

"What do you think is going on, Mrs. Fang?" Jane said.

"I don't know."

"Has your home been broken into before?"

"No."

"How long have you lived in this building?"

"Almost thirty-five years. Since my husband and I immigrated to this country."

"Is there anyone you know who'd do this? Maybe some man you've been dating, someone who's angry that you rejected him?"

"No." She hadn't paused to even think about it. As if that answer was the only one she was prepared to give. "There is no man. And there's no need for the police to be involved."

"Someone breaks into your home. Someone stabs a butcher knife through your photo and leaves it on your pillow. The message couldn't be clearer. Who's threatening you?"

"I don't know."

"Yet you don't want us to look into it."

The woman stared back, displaying no fear. It was like looking into pools of black water, revealing nothing at all. Jane leaned back and let a moment pass. She saw Tam and Frost standing on the periphery, intently following their conversation. Three sets of eyes were focused on Iris, and the silence stretched on, yet the woman's composure did not crack.

Time for a new approach.

"I had an interesting conversation today," said Jane. "With Patrick Dion, the ex-husband of one of the Red Phoenix victims. He tells me that every year in March, you've mailed notes to him and the other families."

"I've sent no one any notes."

"For the past seven years, they've been getting them. Always on the anniversary of the Red Phoenix massacre. The families believe you're doing it. Sending them copies of their loved ones' obituaries. Trying to bring back the bad memories."

"Bring *back* the memories?" Iris stiffened. "What kind of families are these, needing to be *reminded*?" For the first time, agitation shook her voice, made her hands tremble. "I live with my memories. They never leave me, not even when I sleep."

"Have you received any notes?"

"No. But then, no one needs to remind *me.* Of all the families, it seems I'm the only one who's asked questions. Demanded answers."

"If you aren't sending them, do you know who might be?"

"Maybe it's someone who believes the truth has been suppressed."

"Like you."

"But I'm not afraid to say it."

"And in a very public way. We know you placed the ad in the *Globe* last month."

"If your husband were murdered, and you knew the killer was never punished, would you do any less? No matter how many years went by?"

A moment passed, the two women staring at each other. Jane imagined herself waking up every morning in this shabby home, imagined living with unspeakable grief, obsessing over happiness lost. Searching for reasons, for any explanation for her ruined life. Sitting in this room, on this threadbare armchair, she felt despair settle on her shoulders, dragging her down, smothering all joy. This is not even my world, she thought. I can go home and kiss my husband. I can hug my daughter and tuck her into bed. But Iris will still be trapped here.

"It's been nineteen years, Mrs. Fang," said Jane. "I understand it's not easy to move on. But the other families want to. Patrick Dion, Mark Mallory—they have no doubt that Wu Weimin was the killer.

Maybe it's time for you to accept what they accepted long ago."

Iris's chin lifted and her eyes were hard as flint. "I won't accept anything less than the truth."

"How do you know it's *not* true? According to the police report, the evidence against Wu Weimin was overwhelming."

"The police did not know him."

"Can you be sure you did?"

"Yes, completely. And this is my final chance to make things right."

Jane frowned at her. "What do you mean, your final chance?"

Iris drew a breath and lifted her head. The look she gave Jane was both dignified and calm. "I am sick."

The room went silent. That simple statement had stunned them all. Iris sat perfectly composed, staring back at Jane as if daring her to offer any pity.

"I have a chronic form of leukemia," said Iris. "The doctor tells me I could live another ten years. Or perhaps even twenty years. Some days I feel perfectly well. Other days, I'm so tired I can scarcely lift my head off the pillow. One day, this illness will probably kill me, but I'm not afraid. I merely refuse to die without knowing the truth. Without seeing justice done." She paused, and the first note of fear slipped into her voice. "I feel time running through my fingers."

Frost moved behind Iris and placed his hand on her shoulder. It was simply a gesture of sympathy, something anyone might do, but Jane was troubled by that touch, and by the stricken look she saw in his eyes.

"She can't stay here alone tonight," Frost said. "It's not safe."

Tam said, "I just got off the phone with Bella Li. Mrs. Fang can spend the night with her while CSU processes the scene."

Frost said, "I'll drive her there."

"No," Jane said. "Tam will take her. Mrs. Fang, why don't you pack a bag?" She rose from the chair. "Detective Frost, can you step outside with me? We need to check the perimeter."

"But—"

"Frost."

He glanced back and forth between Iris and Jane, and finally followed Jane out the front door, into a night that was filmy with mist.

The instant the door swung shut, she said: "Do you want to tell me what's going on?"

"I wish I could. Obviously someone's trying to scare her. Trying to stop her from asking questions."

"No, I'm talking about *you.* How you ended up taking her to dinner. Turning into her white knight."

"I came to ask about what happened to her daughter. You know that."

"How did an interview turn into dinner?"

"We were hungry. It just happened."

"Accidents just happen. But going out to dinner with a subject you're questioning? That's something else entirely."

"She's not a suspect."

"We don't know that."

"For God's sake, Rizzoli, she's a victim. She lost her husband in a shooting and now all she wants is justice."

"We don't know what she really wants. Frankly, I can't figure out what you want, either."

The glow of the yellow porch light,

diffused by mist, framed his head like a spectral halo. Saint Barry, the Boy Scout, she thought. The cop you could always count on to do the right thing. Now he stood before her, avoiding her gaze, looking as guilty as a man could look.

"I feel sorry for her," he said.

"Is that all you feel?"

"And I just wish . . ." He sighed. "It's been nineteen years since her husband died, and she still loves him. She still carries a torch for him. Alice couldn't even make it ten years before she walked out on me. I look at Iris and I think, Why the hell didn't I marry someone like her?"

"The woman's almost old enough to be your mother."

"That's *not* what I'm saying. I'm not talking about going out with her! And what does age have to do with anything? This is about loyalty. About loving someone your whole life, no matter what happens." He turned away and said softly: "I'm never going to know what that's like."

The front door opened and they both

turned as Tam escorted Iris out of the building. She gave a nod to Frost, a tired smile, then she climbed into Tam's car. Even as the taillights faded into the mist, Frost was still staring after her.

"I have to admit," said Jane thoughtfully, "she's got me wondering now."

He turned to her. "About what?"

"You're right about one thing. She's obviously rattled someone. Someone who's angry enough or feels threatened enough to break into her house. To stab a knife in her pillow."

"What if she's right about the massacre? And the cook didn't do it?"

Jane nodded. "I think it's time to take a closer look at the Red Phoenix."

FIFTEEN

Hidden behind tall hedges, Patrick Dion's Brookline property was a private Eden of woods and lawn where footpaths meandered from intimate shade to sunlit flower beds. The wrought-iron gate at the entrance hung open, and as Jane and Frost drove through, they glimpsed the residence through a stand of ghostly white birches. It was a massive Colonial set on a knoll, commanding a view of Dion's expansive estate.

"What the heck is a venture capitalist, anyway?" said Frost as they passed a tennis court tucked into a shady grove. "I hear that term used all the time."

"I think they use money to make money," Jane said.

"But how do you get the money to start with?"

"From friends who have it."

"I gotta get me some new friends."

She pulled to a stop in the driveway, where two cars were parked, and stared up at the mansion. "But think about it. You have all this money, this nice house. Then your wife leaves you for another man. And your daughter gets snatched off the street. Me, I'd rather be poor." She looked at him. "Okay, now we've got to do some damage control in there. From what Mr. Dion said, Tam didn't exactly charm them."

Frost shook his head. "We gotta get that boy to cool his jets. He goes at everything full-throttle. It's like he's stuck on overdrive."

"But you know who Tam reminds me of?"

"Who?"

"Me. He says he wants to make homicide before he's thirty." She pushed open her door. "He might just do it."

They climbed granite steps to the front door, but before Jane could ring the bell, the door swung open and a silver-haired man stood before them. Though in his late sixties, he was still fit and handsome, but there was a gauntness to his face, and the baggy trousers told Jane that he had recently lost weight.

"I saw your car coming up the driveway," he said. "I'm Patrick Dion."

"Detective Rizzoli," she said. "And this is my partner, Detective Frost." They shook hands and Patrick's grip was firm, his gaze steady.

"Come in, please. We're all in the parlor."

"Mr. Mallory's here?"

"Yes. And I invited Mary Gilmore to join us as well. A united front, because we're all upset about this, and we want to know how to put an end to it."

As they entered the house, Jane saw polished wood floors and a graceful banister that curved up toward a soaring second-floor gallery. It was far too brief a look; Patrick led them straight into the front parlor, where the other two visitors were already waiting.

Mark Mallory rose with athletic grace from the sofa. He was in his mid-thirties, fit and tan, with not even a hint of gray in his dark hair. Jane surveyed his alligator belt, his Sperry Top-Siders, and his Breitling watch, all the little clues that sneered: *I have more money than you ever will.* His handshake was perfunctory, a clue that he was impatient to get on with the business at hand.

The third person in the room would have been easy to overlook, had Jane not already been alerted she was there. Mary Gilmore was about Patrick's age, but so tiny and hunched over that she was almost invisible, swallowed up in a huge armchair by the window. As the woman struggled to stand, Frost quickly moved to her side.

"Please don't bother, Mrs. Gilmore. You just sit right back down, okay?" Frost urged and helped her settle back into the chair. Watching the woman beam up at him, Jane thought: What is it about Frost and older ladies? He loves them, and they all love him.

"My daughter wanted to be here, too," said Mrs. Gilmore. "But she couldn't get off work, so I brought the note she got." She pointed an arthritic hand at the coffee table. "It came in the mail the same day mine did. Every year they arrive on March thirtieth, the day my Joey died. It's just like she's stalking us. It's emotional harassment. Can't the police do something to stop her?"

On the coffee table were three envelopes. Before touching them, Jane reached into her pocket and took out a pair of gloves.

"There's no point with gloves," said Mark. "There are never any fingerprints on the letters or the envelopes."

Jane frowned at him. "How do you know there aren't any prints?"

"Detective Ingersoll had them analyzed in the crime lab."

"He knows about these?"

"He gets them, too. So does anyone connected with the victims, even my father's business associates. It's up to a dozen people that we know about. It's

been going on for years, and the crime
lab never finds anything on the envelopes or the mailings. She must wear
gloves when she sends them."

"Mrs. Fang denies sending any
notes."

Mark snorted. "Who else would do
it? She's the one who ran that ad in the
Globe. She's obsessed by this."

"But she denies sending any notes."
With gloved hands, Jane picked up the
first envelope, addressed to Mrs. Mary
Gilmore. It had a Boston postmark;
there was no return address. She slid
out the contents: a single folded sheet
of paper. It was a photocopied obituary
of Joseph S. Gilmore, age twenty-five,
killed in the Chinatown restaurant mass
murder–suicide. Survived by his mother,
Mary, and his sister, Phoebe Morrison.
Funeral mass celebrated at St. Moni-
ca's. Jane flipped over the mailing and
saw a single sentence written in block
letters.

I know what really happened.

"It's the same damn note I got," said
Mark. "The same thing we get every
year. Except I get my father's obituary."

"And I get Dina's," said Patrick quietly.

Jane picked up the envelope addressed to Patrick Dion. Inside was the photocopied obituary of Dina Mallory, age forty, killed with her husband, Arthur, in the Red Phoenix shooting. Survived by a daughter from a previous marriage, Charlotte Dion. On the reverse side was written the same sentence that was on Mary Gilmore's mailing:

I know what really happened.

"Detective Ingersoll told us the envelope's a standard brand sold by the millions in Staples," said Mark. "The ink's the same as what you'd find in any Bic pen. The crime lab found microscopic starch granules inside the envelopes, indicating the sender was wearing latex gloves, and the stamps and envelopes are self-adhesive, so there's no DNA. Every year it arrives in my mailbox on the same day. March thirtieth."

"The day of the massacre," said Jane.

Mark nodded. "As if we need to be reminded of the date."

"And the handwriting?" asked Jane. "Does it vary?"

"It's always the same block letters. The same black ink."

"But the note's different this year," said Mrs. Gilmore. She spoke so quietly her voice was almost lost in the conversation.

Frost, standing closest to her, gently touched her on the shoulder. "What do you mean, ma'am?"

"Before, all the other years, the notes said: *Don't you want to know the truth?* But this year it's different. This year it says, *I know what really happened.*"

"It's basically the same bullshit," said Mark. "Just said in a slightly different way."

"No, the meaning is completely different this year." Mrs. Gilmore looked at Jane. "If she knows something, why doesn't she just come out and tell us what the truth is?"

"We all know what the truth is, Mrs. Gilmore," Patrick said patiently. "It's the same answer we've known for nineteen years. I have complete faith that Boston PD knew what it was doing when they closed the case."

"But what if they were wrong?"

"Mrs. Gilmore," Mark said, "these notes have only one purpose: to make us pay attention to her. We all know that woman's not exactly balanced."

"What do you mean by that?" asked Frost.

"Patrick, tell them what you found out about Mrs. Fang."

The older man looked reluctant to speak. "I'm not sure it's necessary to go into that right now."

"We'd like to hear it, Mr. Dion," said Jane.

Patrick looked down at his hands, resting in his lap. "Some years ago, when Detective Ingersoll was first looking into these mailings, he told me that Mrs. Fang suffers from, well, delusions of grandeur. She believes she's descended from an ancient line of warriors. She believes it's her sacred mission in life, as a warrior, to track down her husband's killer and exact vengeance."

"Can you believe it?" Mark laughed. "It's like something out of a Chinese soap opera. The woman is completely nuts."

"She is a martial arts master," said Frost. "Her students certainly believe in her, and you'd think they'd recognize a fraud."

"Detective Frost," said Patrick, "we're not saying she's a fraud. But surely, her claims must strike you as being more than a little absurd. I know that ancient traditions run deep in martial arts, but a lot of it is fanciful. The stuff of legends and Jackie Chan movies. What I think, and what Detective Ingersoll thinks, is that Mrs. Fang was deeply traumatized by her husband's death. She's never accepted it. And her way of coping with grief is to search for a deeper meaning, something that gives his death significance and makes it more than just a random act by a madman. She needs to prove that something bigger killed her husband, and she'll never stop searching for this nameless enemy, because it's the one thing that gives her life purpose." Sadly, he looked around the room at Mark. At Mary Gilmore. "But we know the truth. That it was just a senseless crime committed by an unstable man. Arthur and Dina and Joey died for no reason whatsoever. It's not easy to accept, but we do accept it. Mrs. Fang can't."

"So we have to put up with that harassment," said Mark, pointing to the mailings on the coffee table. "And we can't get her to stop sending them."

"But there's no proof she's sending them," said Frost.

"Well, we do know she's the one behind *this*," said Mark, and he pulled from his pocket a folded clipping from *The Boston Globe.* It was the quarter-page ad that Detective Tam had earlier described to Jane, a stark box enclosed in black. Under the word INNOCENT was a smiling photo of the Red Phoenix cook, Wu Weimin. Beneath the photo was the date of the massacre, and a single sentence: THE TRUTH HAS NEVER BEEN TOLD.

"With this ad, it's now gotten much worse," said Mark. "Now she's got the whole city paying attention to her delusions. Where does this stop? When does it stop?"

"Have any of you actually spoken to Mrs. Fang about this?" Jane looked around the room, and her gaze settled on Mark Mallory.

He snorted. "I, for one, wouldn't waste my time talking to her."

"Then you haven't gone to her residence? Tried to confront her?"

"Why are you asking *me*?"

"You seem the angriest about this, Mr. Mallory," she observed. But was he angry enough to break into Iris's home? To stab a warning into her pillow? She didn't know Mark well enough to have a sense of what he was capable of.

"Look, we're all upset," said Patrick, although his voice sounded weary more than anything else. "But we also know that it would be unwise to establish any contact with the woman. I called Detective Ingersoll last week, thinking he might intervene on our behalf. But he hasn't returned my call yet."

"He's out of town this week," said Jane. She collected the mailings and slipped them into evidence bags. "We'll speak to him about this when he returns. In the meantime, please let me know if you receive anything else like this."

"And we'd appreciate it if you kept us informed," said Patrick.

Again, she shook hands with them all. Again, Mark's grasp was a brusque sign-off, as if he'd already decided the police were useless to him. But Patrick's hand lingered around hers, and he walked them to the door, clearly reluctant to see them go.

"Please call me anytime," he said. "About this matter, or . . ." He paused, and a shadow seemed to pass over his eyes. "Anything else."

"We're sorry this had to come up again, Mr. Dion," said Jane. "I can see it's hard for you."

"Especially since it's so closely connected to the . . . other event." He paused, his shoulders drooping. "I assume you know about my daughter."

Jane nodded. "I spoke to Detective Buckholz about Charlotte."

Just the mention of his daughter's name made his face contract in pain. "Dina's death was difficult. But nothing compares to losing a child. My only child. These mailings, and that ad in the newspaper, they bring it all back. That's what really hurts, Detective. That's why I want this stopped."

"I'll do what I can, Mr. Dion."

Although they had already shaken hands, he grasped hers once again, a farewell that left her depressed and silent as she and Frost walked back to her car. She unlocked the doors but did not immediately climb in. Instead she stared across the lawn, at the trees, at garden paths that led into the deepening shadows of afternoon. He owns all this, yet he has nothing, she thought, and you can see it in his face. In the drooping mouth, the hollows under his eyes. Nineteen years later, the ghost of his daughter still haunted him, as it would haunt any parent. Having a child meant your heart was always at the world's mercy.

"Detectives?"

Jane turned to see Mrs. Gilmore coming down the porch steps. She walked toward them with grim determination, her spine bent forward in a dowager's hump.

"I have to say this before you leave. I know Patrick and Mark are convinced that the matter's been settled. That there's no question about what happened in the restaurant. But what if they're wrong? What if we really *don't* know the truth?"

"So you do have doubts," said Jane.

The woman's mouth tightened into hard lines. "I'll admit this. My son, Joey, wasn't a saint. I raised him to be a good boy, I really tried. But there were so many temptations, and it's easy to fall in with the wrong people." She stared hard at Jane. "You probably know that Joey got into trouble."

"I know he was working for Kevin Donohue."

At the mention of that name, Mrs. Gilmore spat out: "Piece of crap! The whole Donohue clan is. But my Joey, he admired power and he liked easy money. He thought Donohue was the one who'd show him the ropes. By the time he realized what was involved, he couldn't get out of it. Donohue wouldn't let him."

"You think he had your son killed?"

"It's what I've wondered from the start."

"There was no evidence for it, Mrs. Gilmore."

The woman hacked out a cough, noisy and bronchial. "You think Donohue couldn't buy off a few cops? He could throw any investigation."

"That's a serious charge."

"I'm a Southie girl. I know what goes on in this town, and I know what money can buy." Her eyes narrowed, her stare fixed on Jane. "I'm sure you do, too, Detective."

The implied charge made Jane stiffen. "I'll give your concerns the attention they deserve, Mrs. Gilmore," she said evenly and slid into her car. As she and Frost drove away, she saw the woman in the rearview mirror, still standing in the driveway and glaring after them.

"That," muttered Jane, "is not a nice old lady."

Frost gave a disbelieving laugh. "Did she just accuse us of taking bribes?"

"That's exactly what she did."

"And she looked so sweet."

"To you, they're all sweet. You've never met one you didn't like." *Or one who didn't like you.*

Frost's cell phone rang. As he answered it, she thought about how easily Frost always managed to charm the older ladies. He certainly seemed to have made inroads with Iris Fang, a woman who was still young enough to be both handsome and formidable. She remembered what Patrick had said about her: *Deeply traumatized. Delusions of grandeur. Believes she's descended from warriors.* Iris might be delusional, but someone real had broken into her residence and stabbed a knife into her pillow. *Whose cage did you rattle, Iris?*

Frost sighed as he hung up the cell phone. "Guess our day's not over yet."

"Who was that?"

"The realtor for the Knapp Street building. I've been trying to get hold of him all day. He says he's on his way out of town tonight, but if we want to see the place, he'll meet us in an hour."

"I take it we're headed back to Chinatown?"

Frost nodded. "Back to Chinatown."

<u>SIXTEEN</u>

In the fading twilight, Knapp Street was a shadowy canyon, cast in gloom between four-story brick buildings. Jane and Frost stood outside what had once been the Red Phoenix restaurant and tried to peer inside, but beyond the barred windows, Jane saw only thin curtains that were tattered and almost translucent with age.

Frost looked at his watch. "Mr. Kwan's now fifteen minutes late."

"Don't you have a cell number for him?"

"I don't think he has a cell. I played

phone tag with him all day through his office."

"A realtor who doesn't have a cell phone?"

"I just hope we understood each other. He had a pretty strong Chinese accent."

"We could really use Tam here. Where is he?"

"He said he'd be here."

Jane backed into the street and peered up at the rusting fire escape and boarded-up windows. Only last week, she and the crime scene unit had walked this same block of rooftops searching for bullet casings. Just around the corner was the alley where Jane Doe's severed hand had been found. This street, this building, seemed to be ground zero for everything that had happened. "Looks like it's been abandoned a long time. Center of town, you'd think it'd be prime real estate."

"Except for the fact it's a crime scene. Tam says that in this neighborhood, they really believe in ghosts. And a haunted building's bad luck." He paused, staring up the alley. "I wonder if that's our man coming?"

The elderly Chinese man walked with a limp, as if he had a bad hip, but he moved with surprising alacrity in his bright white Reeboks, easily stepping over a trash bag as he negotiated his way along the uneven pavement. His jacket was several sizes too large, but he wore it with panache, like a nattily dressed professor out for a night stroll.

"Mr. Kwan?"

"Hello, hello. You Detective Frost?"

"Yes, sir. And this is my partner, Detective Rizzoli."

The man smiled, revealing two bright gold teeth. "I tell you now, I always follow the law, okay? Okay? Everything always legal."

"Sir, that's not why I called you."

"Very good location here, Knapp Street. Three apartment upstairs. Downstairs, very good space for business. Maybe restaurant or store."

"Mr. Kwan, we'd just like to look around inside."

"Behind, two places for tenant to park car . . ."

"Is he going to show it or sell it to us?" muttered Jane.

". . . development company in Hong Kong doesn't want to manage anymore. So they sell for very good price."

"Then why hasn't it sold?" asked Jane.

The question seemed to take him aback, abruptly cutting off his sales patter. Eyeing her in the gloom, his wrinkles deepened into a scowl. "Bad thing happen here," he finally admitted. "No one wants to rent or buy."

"Sir, we're here only to look at the place," said Frost.

"Why? Empty inside, nothing to see."

"This is police business. Please just open the door."

Reluctantly, Kwan pulled out an enormous set of keys that clanked like a jailer's ring. In the dim alley, it took an excruciatingly long time for him to find and insert the correct key in the padlock. The gate swung open with a deafening screech, and they all stepped into what had once been the Red Phoenix restaurant. Mr. Kwan flipped the light switch, and a single bare bulb came on overhead.

"Is that the only light in here?" Jane asked.

The realtor looked up at the ceiling and shrugged. "Time to buy lightbulbs."

Jane moved to the center of that gloomy space and looked around the room. As Kwan had said, the place was empty, and she saw a bare linoleum floor, cracked and yellow with age. Only the built-in cashier counter offered any hint that this had once been a restaurant dining room.

"We have it cleaned, painted," said Mr. Kwan. "Make it just like it was before, but still no one wants to buy." He shook his head in disgust. "Chinese people too superstitious. They don't even like to come inside."

I don't blame them, thought Jane as a cold breath seemed to whisper across her skin. Violence leaves a mark, a psychic stain that can never be scrubbed away with mere soap and bleach. In a neighborhood as insular as Chinatown, everyone would remember what had happened in this building. Everyone would shudder as they walked past on Knapp Street. Even if this building were torn down and another erected in its place, this bloodied ground would remain forever haunted in the minds of those who knew its ugly past. Jane looked down at the linoleum, the same floor where blood had flowed. Although the walls were repainted and the bullet holes plastered over, in the seams and nooks of this floor, chemical traces of that blood still lingered. A crime scene photo that she had earlier studied suddenly clicked into her head. It was an image of a crumpled body lying amid fallen take-out cartons.

Here is the spot where Joey Gilmore died.

She looked across the cashier counter, and the memory of another crime scene photo superimposed itself on that patch of floor: the body of James Fang, his glasses askew, dressed in his trim waiter's vest and black pants. He had crumpled into the nook behind the register, dollar bills scattered around him.

She turned. Stared at the corner

where a four-top table had once been. She imagined Dina and Arthur Mallory sitting at that table, sipping tea, warming themselves after the chill of a March night. That image suddenly vanished, replaced by the police photos taken hours later. Arthur Mallory, still in his chair, slumped forward over the spilled teacups. And a few feet away his wife, Dina, lying facedown on the floor, her chair tipped over in her panic to escape. Standing in this vacant room, Jane could hear the echo of gunshots, the clatter of breaking china.

She turned toward the kitchen, where the cook had died. Suddenly she did not want to step through that doorway. It was Frost who walked in first, who flipped the light switch. Again, only a single bulb came on. She followed him, and in the dim glow she saw the blackened cookstove, a refrigerator, and stainless-steel countertops. The concrete floor was pockmarked with wear.

She moved to the cellar door. Here, with his body blocking that door, was where Wu Weimin, the cook, had drawn his final breath. Staring down, she almost imagined that the floor was darker here, the concrete still stained with old blood. She remembered how eerily intact his face had been, except for the lone bullet hole punched into his temple. That bullet had ricocheted within his skull, shredding gray matter, but it had not immediately killed him. They knew this because of how copiously he had bled during his final moments while his heart continued to pump and his wound spilled a waterfall that poured down the cellar steps.

She opened the door and peered down a wooden stairway that descended into darkness. A light cord dangled overhead. She gave it a tug, but nothing happened; this bulb had burned out.

Frost crossed the kitchen to another door. "Does this lead outside?"

"Goes to back of building," said Mr. Kwan. "Parking."

Frost opened the door and saw another locked gate. "The alley's here. Report said this is how the cook's wife walked in. She heard a gunshot, came down to check on her husband, and found him dead in the kitchen."

"So theoretically, if that door was unlocked, any intruder could have come in that way," said Jane.

Kwan looked back and forth at the two detectives, and he seemed confused. "What intruder? Cook, he kill himself."

"We're reexamining the incident, Mr. Kwan," said Frost. "Just to be certain nothing was missed."

The realtor shook his head in dismay. "That was very bad thing for Chinatown," he muttered, no doubt surrendering all hope of unloading this cursed building. "Better to forget about it." He squinted at his watch. "If you finished now, we leave, okay? I lock up."

Jane glanced up toward the second floor. "Wu Weimin and his family lived on the second floor. Could you take us up to their apartment?"

"Nothing to see," said Kwan.

"Nevertheless, we need to look at it."

He sighed deeply, as though they were asking him for a favor beyond all human measure. Once again he took out his heavy key ring and went through the painstaking process of locating the right key. Judging by how many were jangling on that enormous ring, this man controlled half the properties in Chinatown. At last, he found the right one and led them out the kitchen exit, into the back alley.

Like the front entrance to the Red Phoenix restaurant, the door to the upstairs apartments was secured behind a steel gate. The shadows had deepened to night, and Frost had to shine his flashlight on the lock so Kwan could insert the key. Rusty hinges squealed as he swung open the gate, and yet another key had to be inserted into another lock before he could open the inner door.

Inside was blackness. The stairwell light had burned out, so Jane turned on her flashlight and saw steps leading upward, the railing rubbed smooth by the oils of countless hands sliding over wood. The darkness seemed to magnify the sound of their shoes creaking on the steps, and she heard Mr. Kwan's labored breathing behind them as he struggled to climb the stairs.

At the top of the flight, she paused outside the door to the second-floor apartment. It was unlocked, yet she did not want to open that door, did not want to see what lurked beyond. She stood with her hand frozen on the knob, the metal cold as ice against her skin. Only when she heard Mr. Kwan reach the top step, wheezing right behind her, did she finally push open the door.

She and Frost stepped into what had once been the home of Wu Weimin.

The windows were boarded shut, closing off any light from outside. Although the apartment had been vacant for years, she could still smell the scents left by those who had once lived here. The ghostly fragrance of incense and oranges still lingered, trapped in the tomb-like darkness. As her flashlight beam skittered across the wood floor, she saw the gouges and scratches of a century's worth of wear, scars left by scraping chair legs and dragged furniture.

She crossed to a doorway at the far

end of the room, and when she walked through it, the scent of incense, the presence of ghosts, seemed stronger. These windows, too, were covered by boards, and her flashlight seemed a feeble weapon to cut through the curtain of darkness. Her beam swept across the wall, across the scars of old nail holes and a Rorschach blot of mold.

A face stared back at her.

She gasped and jerked backward, colliding with Frost.

"What?" he said.

Shock had frozen her voice; all she could do was shine her light at the framed portrait hanging on the wall. As she approached it, the smell of incense grew overpowering. Beneath the portrait was a low table where she saw the remains of joss sticks, burned down to nubs among a mound of ashes. On a porcelain plate were five oranges.

"It's him," Frost murmured. "It's a photo of the cook."

It took Jane a moment to see it, but as she stared at the face she realized he was right. The man in the photo was indeed Wu Weimin, but this was no

homicidal maniac glaring back at them.
In this picture he was laughing as he
clutched a fishing pole, a Boston Red
Sox cap tilted rakishly on his head. *A
happy man on a happy day.*

"This looks like some kind of shrine
to his memory," said Frost.

Jane picked up an orange from the
plate and took a sniff. Saw that the stem
end was tinged with green. Real, she
thought. She turned to Mr. Kwan, whom
she could barely make out in the doorway. "Who else has a key to this building?"

"No one," he said, rattling his jailer's
ring. "I have the only key."

"But these oranges are fresh. Someone's been in here recently. Someone
left this offering and burned this incense."

"These keys *always* with me," he insisted, noisily jangling the ring for em-
phasis.

"The gate downstairs has a dead
bolt," said Frost. "There's no way you
could pick the lock."

"Then how could anyone . . ." She

went dead silent. Turned toward the doorway.

Footsteps were thumping up the stairs.

In an instant her weapon was drawn and clutched in both hands. Pushing aside Mr. Kwan, she quickly slipped out of the bedroom. As she eased her way across the living room, she felt her heart banging, heard Frost's footsteps creaking on her right. Smelled incense and mold and sweat, a dozen details assaulting her at once. But it was the stairwell door she focused on, a black portal to something that was now climbing toward them. Something that suddenly took on the shape of a man.

"Freeze!" Frost commanded. "Boston PD!"

"Whoa, Frost." Johnny Tam gave a startled laugh. "It's just me."

Behind her, Jane heard Mr. Kwan give a squawk of fear. "Who is he? Who is he?"

"What the hell, Tam," said Frost, huffing out a breath as he holstered his weapon. "I could have blown your head off."

"You did tell me to meet you here, didn't you? I would've gotten here sooner, but I got stuck in traffic coming back from Springfield."

"You talk to the owner of that Honda?"

"Yeah. Said it was stolen right out of his driveway. And that wasn't his GPS in the car." He swept his flashlight around the room. "So what's going on in here?"

"Mr. Kwan's giving us a tour of the building."

"It's been boarded up for years. What's there to see?"

"More than we expected. This is Wu Weimin's apartment."

Tam's flashlight revealed patches of mold and crumbling plaster from the ceiling. "This place looks like it's from the lead-paint era."

"No lead paint here," snapped Kwan. "No asbestos, either."

"But look what we did find," said Jane, turning back toward the bedroom. "Someone's been visiting this apartment. And they left behind . . ." She halted, her beam frozen on blank wall.

"Left behind what?"

I must be looking at the wrong spot, she thought, and shifted her light. Again, she saw blank wall. She swept the beam all around the room until she flashed on the little table with the joss sticks and oranges. Above it, the wall was empty.

"What the hell?" Frost whispered.

Through the pounding of her own heart, she heard three gun holsters simultaneously snick open. As she slid out her weapon, she whispered: "Tam, take Mr. Kwan into the stairwell and stay with him. Frost, you're with me."

"Why?" protested Mr. Kwan as Tam pulled him out of the room. "What's going on?"

"Doorway there," she murmured, her light shining on a black rectangle.

Together she and Frost inched toward it, their beams wildly crisscrossing, scanning every dark corner. Her breath was a roar in her ears, every sense sharpened to diamond points. She registered the smell of the darkness, the strobe-like glimpses as her beam flicked here, there. The weight of the gun, heavy and reassuring. *On the rooftop, Jane*

Doe had a gun, too, and it didn't save her.

She thought of blades slicing through wrist bones, through neck and wind-pipe, and she dreaded stepping through that doorway and confronting what waited on the other side.

One, two, three. Do it.

She was first through, dropping to a crouch as she swung the light around. Heard Frost's harsh breathing behind her as she glimpsed a porcelain toilet, a sink, a rust-stained bathtub. No bogey-man with a blade.

Another doorway.

Frost took the lead this time, slipping through into a bedroom where wallpaper hung peeling, like a room shedding its skin. No furniture, nowhere to hide.

Through one more doorway, and they were back in the living room. Back in familiar territory. Jane walked out into the stairwell, where Tam and Mr. Kwan stood waiting.

"Nothing?" said Tam.

"That photo didn't walk off on its own."

"We were right here in the stairwell the whole time. No one came by us."

Jane reholstered her gun. "Then how the hell . . ."

"Rizzoli!" called out Frost. "Look at this!"

They found him standing by the window in the bedroom where the portrait had hung. Like all the other windows, this one had been boarded over, but when Frost nudged the board, it easily swiveled aside, suspended in place by only a single nail above the frame. Jane peered through the opening and saw that the window faced Knapp Street.

"Fire escape's here," said Frost. He poked out his head and craned to look up toward the roof. "Hey, something's moving up there!"

"Go, go!" said Jane.

Frost scrambled over the sill, all clumsy long arms and legs, and clanged onto the landing. Tam exited right after him, moving with an acrobat's grace. Last out the window was Jane, and as she dropped onto the metal grate of the landing, she caught a glimpse of the street below. Saw splintered crates, broken bottles. A bad drop, any way you looked at it. She forced herself to focus on the ladder above, where Frost was clanging up the rungs, noisily announcing to the whole world that they were in pursuit.

She scrambled up right behind Tam, her hands gripping slippery metal, the breeze chilling the sweat on her face. She heard Frost grunt, saw the silhouette of his legs flailing against the night sky as he pulled himself over the edge and onto the rooftop. Jane felt his movements transmitted through the rungs as the fire escape shuddered, and for a panic-stricken moment she thought the brackets might give way, that the weight of three bodies would make the whole rickety structure twist off in a screech of metal and fling them to the pavement below. She froze, gripping the ladder, afraid that even a puff of wind would tip them into disaster.

A shriek above her made every hair stand up on the back of her neck. *Frost.*

She looked up, expecting to see his

body hurtling toward her, but all she glimpsed was Tam as he scaled the last rungs and vanished onto the rooftop. She clambered after him, sick with dread. As she reached the roof edge, a piece of asphalt tile crumbled at her touch and dropped away, plummeting into darkness below. With shaking hands, she pulled herself up over the edge and crawled onto the roof. Spotted Tam crouched a few feet away.

Frost. Where is Frost?

She jumped to her feet and scanned the roof. Glimpsed a shadow flitting away, moving so swiftly that it might only have been a cat darting with feline grace into the darkness. Under the night sky, Jane saw empty rooftops, one blending into the next, an aerial landscape of slopes and valleys, jutting chimneys and ventilation shafts. But no Frost.

Dear God, he's fallen. He's on the ground somewhere, dead or dying.

"Frost?" Tam yelled as he circled the roof. *"Frost?"*

Jane pulled out her cell phone. "This

is Detective Rizzoli. Beach and Knapp Street. Officer down—"

"He's here!" Tam yelled. "Help me pull him up!"

She spun around and saw Tam kneeling at the roof's edge, as if he were about to take a swan dive to the street below. She thrust the phone back into her pocket and ran to his side. Saw Frost clinging with both hands to the rain gutter, his feet dangling above a four-story plummet. Tam dropped to his belly and reached down to grab Frost's left wrist. The roof sloped here, and a misstep could send them both sliding off the edge. Jane flopped onto her belly beside Tam and grabbed Frost's right wrist. Together they pulled, straining to drag him up across gritty tiles that snagged Jane's jacket and scraped her skin. With a loud grunt, Frost flopped onto the roof beside them, where he sprawled, gasping.

"Jesus," he whispered. "Thought I was dead!"

"What the hell, did you trip and fall?" said Jane.

"I was chasing it, but I swear, it was *flying* over this roof, like a bat out of hell."

"What are you talking about?"

"Didn't you see it?" Frost sat up; even in the darkness Jane could see he was pale and shaking.

"I didn't see anything," said Tam.

"It was right there, standing where you are now. Turned and looked straight at me. I jumped back and lost my footing."

"It?" said Jane. "Are we talking about a man or what?"

Frost let out a trembling breath. Turning, he gazed across the sweep of Chinatown rooftops. "I don't know."

"How can you not know?"

Slowly Frost rose to his feet and stood facing the direction that the thing—whatever it was—had fled. "It moved too fast to be a man. That's all I can tell you."

"It's dark up here, Frost," said Tam. "When you're hyped up on adrenaline, it's hard to be sure of what you're seeing."

"I know it sounds crazy, but there was

something here, something I've never seen before. You've got to believe me!"

"Okay," Jane said, clapping him on the shoulder. "I believe you."

Frost looked at Tam. "But you don't, do you?"

In the darkness, they saw Tam's shoulder lift in a shrug. "It's Chinatown. Weird stuff happens here." He laughed. "Maybe there's more to that ghost tour than we thought."

"It was no ghost," said Frost. "I'm telling you, it was flesh and blood, standing right there. It was *real.*"

"No one saw it but you," said Tam.

Frost stalked away across the roof and stood staring down at the street below. "That may not be entirely true."

Jane followed him to the edge and saw the fire escape that they'd clambered up only moments earlier. Below them was Knapp Street, dimly lit by the glow of a streetlamp.

"Do you see it?" said Frost, and he pointed toward the corner, at what was mounted on the building.

A surveillance camera.

SEVENTEEN

Even at nine thirty pm, the employees of Dedham Security were on the job, monitoring properties all over the Greater Boston area.

"Bad guys usually get to work after dark," said Gus Gilliam as he walked the trio of detectives past a bank of surveillance monitors. "So we have to stay awake, too. If any of our alarms gets tripped, we're talking to Boston PD like *that.*" He snapped his fingers. "You ever need a security system, call us."

Tam surveyed the video feeds on the

monitors. "Wow. You really do have eyes all over the city."

"All over Suffolk County. And *our* cameras are actually operational. Half the security cameras you see mounted around town are just dummies that don't record a damn thing. So if you're a bad guy, it's a shell game. You don't know which cameras are really watching and which aren't. But when they spot any camera, they tend to shy away and go for easier pickings, so just having a camera in view is a deterrent."

"We're lucky that camera on Knapp Street is real," said Jane.

"Yeah. We have about forty-eight hours' worth of video stored on that one." He led them into a back room, where four chairs were already set up around the monitor. "Usually gives us enough postincident time to be notified so we can save relevant footage. That particular camera was installed about five years ago. Last time we were asked to pull video off it, we caught a kid breaking a window." He sat down at the monitor. "You said you were interested in a second-floor fire escape landing?"

"I'm hoping it's in your camera's field of view," said Jane. "The building in question is about twenty, twenty-five yards away."

"I don't know. That could be too far to see much detail, and second floor might not be visible. Plus, we're talking low resolution. But let's take a look."

As the three detectives crowded in to watch the monitor, Gilliam clicked the Play icon, and a live view of Knapp Street appeared. Two pedestrians could be seen walking past, in the direction of Kneeland Street, their backs to the camera.

"Look," said Frost. "You can just see a corner of the fire escape."

"Unfortunately, not the window itself," said Jane.

"It might be enough." Frost leaned in closer to read the date and time on the recording. "Go back around two hours. Seven thirty. Let's see if we can catch a glimpse of our intruder."

Gilliam rewound to 7:30 PM.

At 7:35, an elderly woman walked slowly along Knapp Street, arms weighed down by grocery sacks.

At 7:50, Johnny Tam appeared outside the Red Phoenix restaurant. He peered into the window, looked at his watch, then vanished through the unlocked front door. A moment later he reemerged, glanced up toward the apartment windows above. Circling toward the back of the building, he disappeared around the corner.

At 8:06, something jerked into view on the fire escape. It was Frost, tumbling clumsily out of the window. He jumped to his feet and climbed out of view.

"What the hell?" Frost murmured. "Nothing came out ahead of me. I know I chased something up that ladder."

"It doesn't show up," said Jane.

"And there's you, Rizzoli. How come Tam doesn't show up, either? He came out right after me."

Tam snorted. "Maybe I'm a ghost."

"Your problem is the field of view," said Gilliam. "We're catching just a corner of the fire escape, so the camera misses anyone who makes a more, er, graceful entry and exit."

"In other words, Frost and I make lousy cat burglars," said Jane.

Gilliam smiled. "And Detective Tam here would make a good one."

Jane sighed. "So we caught nothing on this camera."

"Assuming this was the only time the intruder entered."

Jane remembered the scent of incense, the fresh oranges on the plate. Someone was regularly visiting that apartment, leaving offerings in memory of Wu Weimin. "Go back," she said. "Two nights ago and move forward."

Gilliam nodded. "Worth a look."

On the monitor, time wound back to 9:38 PM, forty-eight hours earlier. As the video once again advanced to 10:00 PM, then to midnight, pedestrians walked past, their movements accelerated and shaky. By 2:00 AM, Knapp Street was deserted, and they watched an unchanging view of pavement across which only a stray bit of paper fluttered.

At 3:02 AM, Jane saw it.

It was just the twitch of a shadow on the fire escape landing, but it was enough to make her rock forward in her chair. "Stop. Go back!" she snapped.

Gilliam reversed the video and froze the image on a shadow darkening the fire escape.

"It doesn't look like much," said Tam. "It could be nothing but a cat casting that shadow."

"If someone went into that building," said Frost, "they've gotta come out again, right?"

"Then let's see what happens next," said Gilliam, and he advanced the video. They watched as the minutes progressed. Saw two clearly drunken men stagger down Knapp Street and around the corner.

Seconds later Jane gave a gasp. *"There."*

Gilliam froze the image and stared at a crouching shadow on the fire escape. Softly he said: "What the hell is that?"

"I *told* you I saw something," said Frost. "That's *it.*"

"I don't even know what we're looking at," said Tam. "You can't see a face, you can't even be sure it's a man."

"But it's bipedal," said Frost. "Look

how it's down on its haunches. Like it's about to leap."

Jane's cell phone rang, the sound so startling that she had to take a breath and steady her voice before she answered. "Detective Rizzoli."

"You left a message on my voice mail," a man said. "I'm returning your call. This is Lou Ingersoll."

She sat up straight in her chair. "Detective Ingersoll, we've been trying to reach you all week. We need to talk to you."

"About what?"

"A homicide in Chinatown. Happened last Wednesday night. Victim is a Jane Doe, female in her thirties."

"You do know that I've been retired from Boston PD for sixteen years? Why are you asking me about this?"

"We think this death could be connected to one of your old cases. The Red Phoenix massacre."

There was a long silence. "I don't think I want to talk about this on the phone," he said.

"How about in person, sir?"

She heard his footsteps moving across

the floor. Heard his labored breaths. "Okay, I think that vehicle's gone now. Wish I'd gotten the goddamn license plate."

"What vehicle?"

"The van that's been parked across the street ever since I got home. Probably the same son of a bitch who broke in while I was up north."

"What, exactly, is going on?"

"Come over now, and I'll give you my theory."

"We're in Dedham. It'll take us half an hour, maybe more. You sure we can't talk about it now?"

She heard his footsteps moving again. "I don't want to say anything over the phone. I don't know who's listening, and I promised I'd keep her out of this. So I'll just wait till you get here."

"What is this all about?"

"Girls, Detective," he said. "It's all about what happened to those girls."

"At least now you believe me," Frost said, as he and Jane drove toward Boston. "Now that you've seen it for yourself."

"We don't know what we saw on that video," she said. "I'm sure there's a logical answer."

"I've never seen a man move that fast."

"So what do you think it was?"

Frost stared out the window. "You know, Rizzoli, there's a lot of things in this world we don't understand. Things so old, so strange, that we wouldn't accept them as possibilities." He paused. "I used to date a Chinese girl."

"You did? When?"

"It was back in high school. She and her family had just come over from Shanghai. She was really sweet, really shy. And very old-fashioned."

"Maybe you should've married her instead of Alice."

"Well, you know what they say about hindsight. Wouldn't have worked anyway, because her family was dead-set against any white boy. But her great-grandmother, she was okay with me. I think she liked me because I was the only one who paid attention to her."

"Geez, Frost, is there an old lady alive who doesn't like you?"

"I liked listening to her stories. She'd talk and Jade would translate for me. The stuff she told me about China, man, if even a fraction of it was true . . ."

"Like what?"

He looked at her. "Do you believe in ghosts?"

"How many dead people have we been around? If ghosts are real, we're the ones who would've seen one by now."

"Jade's great-grandmother, she said that ghosts are everywhere in China. She said it's because China is so old, and millions and millions of souls have passed on there. They must end up somewhere. If they're not in heaven, then they've gotta be right here. All around us."

Jane braked at a stoplight. As she waited for the light to change, she thought of how many souls might still linger in this city. How many might be at this very spot, where the two roads intersected. Add up all the dead, century by century, and Boston was surely a haunted town.

"Old Mrs. Chang, she told me stuff

that sounded crazy, but *she* believed it. About holy men who walked on water. Fighting monks who could fly through the air and make themselves invisible."

"Sounds like she watched too many kung fu movies."

"But legends must be based on something, don't you think? Maybe our Western minds are too closed to accept what we can't understand, and there's so much more going on in this world than we're aware of. Don't you feel that in Chinatown? Whenever I'm there, I wonder what I'm not seeing, all the hidden clues that I'm too blind to notice. I go into those dusty herbalist shops and see all the weird dried things in jars. It's just hocus-pocus to us, but what if that stuff can actually cure cancer? Or make you live to a hundred? China's been a civilization for five thousand years. They must know things. Secrets they'll never tell us."

In the rearview mirror, Jane could see Tam's car right behind theirs. She wondered what he would think of this conversation, whether he'd be offended by this talk of the exotic and mysterious Chinese. The light changed to green.

As she drove through the intersection she said, "I wouldn't mention this to Tam."

Frost shook his head. "It'd probably piss him off. It's not like I'm racist, you know? I did date a Chinese girl."

"And that would definitely piss him off."

"I'm just trying to understand, to open my mind to what we're not seeing."

"What I'm not seeing is how this all fits together. A dead woman on the roof. An old murder-suicide. And now Ingersoll, muttering about a van watching his house. And something about girls."

"Why wouldn't he tell you over the phone? Who does he think is listening in?"

"He wouldn't say."

"Whenever someone starts talking about their phone being bugged, those psycho warning bells go off for me. Did he sound paranoid?"

"He sounded worried. And he mentioned *her.* He said he'd promised to keep *her* out of it."

"Iris Fang?"

"I don't know."

Frost looked ahead at the road. "Old cop like him, he's probably gonna be armed. We better take this nice and slow. Don't spook him."

Fifteen minutes later, Jane pulled up in front of Ingersoll's residence, and Tam parked right behind them. They all got out of their cars, doors thudding shut simultaneously. Inside the triple-decker town house, the lights were on, but when Frost rang the doorbell no one answered. He rang again and rapped on the window.

"I'll call him," said Jane, tapping in Ingersoll's number on her cell phone. They could hear his phone ringing somewhere inside the residence. Four rings, and then the answering machine picked up with the terse recording. *Not here now. Leave a message.*

"Can't see anything in there," said Tam, trying to peer through the curtained front windows.

Jane hung up and said to Frost, "You keep trying the bell. Tam, let's go around to the back. Maybe he can't hear us."

As she and Tam headed around the side of the building, she could hear Frost still banging on the front door. The narrow path between buildings was un- lit and overgrown with shrubbery. She smelled wet leaves, felt her shoes sink into sodden grass. Through a window, she glimpsed the blue glow of Inger- soll's TV set and she paused, looking into a living room where images flick- ered on the screen. On the coffee table was a cell phone and a half-eaten sand- wich.

"This window isn't latched," said Tam. "I can climb in. You want me to?"

They looked at each other in the shadows, both of them considering the consequences of entering a house with- out permission or a warrant.

"He did invite us," she said. "Maybe he's just sitting in the john where he can't hear us."

Tam slid open the window. In sec- onds he was up and over the sill, slith- ering into the house without a sound. How the hell did he do that? she won- dered, eyeing the chest-high sill. The

man really would make a superb cat
burglar.

"Detective Ingersoll?" Tam called out
as he walked into the next room. "It's
Boston PD. Are you here?"

Jane considered huffing and flailing
her way through the window as well,
then decided that by the time she could
finally scale that sill, Tam would have
the front door unlocked.

"Rizzoli, he's in here! He's down!"

Tam's shout swept away all indeci-
sion. She grasped the sill and was about
to launch herself through the window
headfirst when she heard bushes rustle
and footsteps thudded in the darkness.

Back of the house. Suspect in flight.

She took off in pursuit and reached
the rear of the building just in time to
see a dark figure scramble over the
fence and drop to the other side.

"Frost! I need backup!" she screamed,
sprinting to the fence. Sheer adrenaline
sent her up and over it, splinters lanc-
ing her palms. She landed on the other
side, and the impact of her shoes hit-
ting the pavement pounded straight up
her shins.

Her quarry was in view. *A man.*

She heard someone scrabble over the fence behind her but didn't glance back to see if it was Frost or Tam. She stayed focused on the figure ahead. She was gaining on him, close enough to see that he was all in black. Definitely dressed for crime. *But not fast enough to outrun this girl cop.*

Her backup's footsteps fell behind, but she didn't slow down, didn't give her quarry any chance to slip away. Already she was within a few dozen yards of him.

"Police!" she yelled. "Freeze!"

He darted right, slipping between buildings.

That pissed her off. Fueled by outrage, she sprinted around the corner and found herself in an alley. It was dark here, too dark. Her footsteps echoed back as she pounded ahead, half a dozen paces, then slowed. Stopped.

Where is he? Where did he go?

Weapon drawn, heart hammering, she scanned the shadows. Saw trash cans, heard broken glass clatter away.

The bullet slammed into her back,

right between her shoulder blades. The impact sent her flying and she sprawled on her belly, her palms scraping across pavement. Her weapon flew out of her hands. The Kevlar vest had saved her, but the force of the bullet stole the breath from her lungs and she lay stunned, her gun somewhere out of reach.

Footsteps slowly approached, and she struggled to her knees, fumbled around for her weapon.

The footsteps came to a halt right behind her.

She twisted around to see the man's silhouette towering above her. Shadows hid his face, but enough light spilled into the alley from a distant streetlamp that she saw him raise his arm. Saw the faint gleam of the gun he was pointing at her head. It would be a quick and efficient end, without killer and victim ever glimpsing each other's eyes. Gabriel, she thought. Regina. I never got the chance to tell you how much I love you both.

She heard Death whisper in the night, felt it hiss like the wind past her ear.

Something splashed her face and she blinked. When she opened her eyes again, the silhouette looming over her was already toppling forward. It landed across her legs like a felled tree. Trapped under the man's weight, she felt liquid warmth soaking into her clothes. Recognized all too well that coppery smell.

Something breathed in the darkness, something that now loomed where the gunman had stood only seconds before. She saw no face, just a black oval and a halo of silvery hair. It said not a word but as it turned away, something flashed in its hand, a bright arc of reflected light that was there and gone again. She heard what she thought was the wind as shadow swooped across shadow. Then she was alone, still pinned against the hard pavement by a man who spilled his last blood onto her clothes.

"Rizzoli? *Rizzoli!*"

She struggled to free herself from the deadweight trapping her legs. "I'm here! Frost!"

The beam of a flashlight flickered in

the distance. Moved closer, sweeping back and froth across the alley.

With a grunt of effort, Jane finally managed to shove the body away. Shuddering at the touch of dead flesh, she scrabbled backward. "Frost," she said.

The light landed squarely in her eyes, and she raised a hand against its glare.

"Jesus," Frost cried. "Are you—"

"I'm okay. I'm fine!" She took a deep breath and felt the lingering ache of the bullet's impact in her Kevlar vest. "At least, I think so."

"All this blood . . ."

"Not mine. It's his."

Frost aimed his flashlight at the body, and she sucked in a shocked breath that made her ribs hurt. The body was lying chest-down, and the decapitated head had rolled a few feet away. The eyes stared up at them, the mouth open as though in a last gasp of surprise. Jane gaped at the cleanly severed neck and was suddenly aware of her soaked trousers, the fabric clinging to her legs. The night began to spin and she stumbled away and sagged against a building where she dropped her head, desperately fighting the need to throw up.

"What happened?" said Frost.

"I saw it," she whispered. "The thing. Your creature on the roof." Her legs seemed to melt away beneath her and she slid all the way down to sit crumpled against the wall. "It just saved my life."

A long silence passed. Wind swept the alley, scattering grit that stung her eyes and pelted her face. I should be dead, she thought. I should be lying here with a bullet in my brain. Instead I'm going to go home tonight. I'm going to hug my husband and kiss my baby. And I owe this miracle to whatever it was that swooped out of the night.

She lifted her head and looked at Frost. "You must have seen it. Just now."

"I didn't see anything."

"It would have run right past you when you came into the alley."

He shook his head. "It's like what happened on the roof. I was the only one who saw it, and you didn't believe me."

She focused again on the body. On the gun that was still clutched in the headless corpse's hand. "I believe you now."

EIGHTEEN

From her parked car, Maura saw three police officers standing by the barrier of crime scene tape. They all glanced her way and almost certainly recognized her black Lexus, so they knew the medical examiner had just arrived. But as she climbed out of her car and walked toward them, they turned their backs and continued chatting among themselves. Only when she formally announced herself did they finally deign to meet her gaze.

"Is Detective Rizzoli in the residence?" she asked.

"I don't know, ma'am," one of the patrolmen answered. "Why don't you check inside?"

Was he being intentionally unhelpful? It was impossible to tell from his coolly neutral expression. As she ducked under the tape and walked toward the front door, she heard them laugh and wondered if that was directed at her. Wondered if this was what she'd face at every future death scene. The looks, the whispers, the thinly disguised hostility. She stopped at the front door to pull booties over her shoes, careful not to lose her balance and give them one more thing to snicker about. As she straightened, the front door opened and Detective Tam stood looking at her.

"Dr. Isles. Sorry to drag you out this time of night."

"Are both victims in the house?"

"One of them's in the kitchen. The second victim's a few blocks away, in an alley."

"How did number two end up so far away from number one?"

"He was trying to get away from Rizzoli. I guess she's a hard gal to shake."

Tam led her from the foyer and down the hall. Booties rustling over the floor, she followed him into the kitchen and was surprised to see the commander of Boston PD's homicide unit standing next to Barry Frost. It was rare to encounter Lieutenant Marquette at a crime scene, and his appearance here told her that something was very different about this homicide.

The victim lay on his side on the tiled floor, his face resting in a congealing pool of blood. He was a heavyset white man in his seventies, dressed in tan trousers, a knit shirt, and dark socks. One slipper was still on his foot. The bullet wound in his left temple left little doubt about the cause of death. Maura did not immediately move toward the body but remained where she stood for a moment, scanning the floor for a weapon. She saw no gun anywhere near the body. *Not a suicide.*

"He was a cop," said Jane quietly.

Maura had not heard her approach. She turned and stared at Jane's blood-splattered blouse. Instead of her usual dark trouser suit, Jane was wearing

baggy sweatpants, obviously an emergency change of clothes.

"My God, Jane."

"Things got a little rough out there."

"Are you all right?"

Jane nodded and looked down at the
dead man. "I can't say the same for
him."

"Who is he?"

Lieutenant Marquette answered. "Detective Lou Ingersoll. He retired from the
homicide unit sixteen years ago. He was
one of ours, Dr. Isles. He deserves our
very best effort."

Was he implying that she would give
this victim any less than her best? That
an ME who'd betray the thin blue line
would betray this cop as well? Cheeks
burning, she crouched down by the
body. It took her a few seconds to register the name. Lou Ingersoll.

She glanced up at Tam. "This was the
man who worked the Red Phoenix massacre."

"You already know about him?" asked
Jane.

"Detective Tam and I discussed it

when he brought me the autopsy reports."

Jane turned to Tam: "I didn't know you consulted her."

Tam shrugged. "I just wanted Dr. Isles's opinion. Whether something might have been missed nineteen years ago."

"Detective Rizzoli?" One of the criminalists stood in the kitchen doorway, a set of headphones looped around his neck. "We swept the room with a radio frequency scanner, and you're right. There's definitely a signal coming from his landline phone."

"A signal?" Marquette looked at Jane.

"Ingersoll thought someone was monitoring his phone calls," said Jane. "To be honest, I'm kind of surprised we actually found anything."

"Why would anyone bug his phone?"

"It wouldn't be for the usual reason. He's been widowed for eighteen years, so there's no divorce war. He's got one daughter, and she has no idea what's going on." Jane stared down at the dead man. "This just gets weirder and weirder. He complained about a van watching his house. He said someone broke in here while he was away. To me, it sounded like crazy talk."

"Not so crazy after all." Marquette looked at the criminalist. "You checked his cell phone yet?"

"We didn't detect any signal on that one. The battery's dead. Once we charge it up, we'll take a look at his call log."

"Let's get all his phone records, cell and landline. See who he's been talking to lately."

Maura rose to her feet. "I understand there's a second victim."

"The shooter," said Jane. "At least, the man we assume is the shooter. I chased him a few blocks away."

"You brought him down yourself?"

"No."

"Who did?"

Jane drew in a deep breath, as though steeling herself for what came next. "It's not easy to explain. I'll have to show you."

They walked outside, where a crowd was gathering, mesmerized by the invasion of law enforcement into their neighborhood. Jane forged a path through the gawkers and led Maura around the corner to a quiet side street. Although Jane walked at her usual brisk pace, the swagger was gone, and her shoulders were slumped as though the night had beaten her down and stolen her confidence.

"Are you really all right?" Maura asked.

"Aside from having my good pantsuit trashed? Yeah, I'm okay."

"You don't look okay. Jane, talk to me."

Jane's pace slowed, stopped. She stared down the street as if afraid to look at Maura, afraid to reveal how vulnerable she felt at that moment. "I shouldn't be standing here right now," she murmured. "I should be dead, like Ingersoll. Lying in the alley with a bullet in my head." She frowned at her hands, as if they belonged to someone else. "Look at this. I've got the goddamn shakes."

"You said you chased down the perp."

"Chased him, yeah. But I got cocky. Followed him into an alley. I'm the one who went down." She hugged herself, as though suddenly chilled. "Saved by my birthday present. Remember how Gabriel bought me a Kevlar vest? How you and I laughed about it? So romantic, what every gal wants. When I didn't wear it, he got royally pissed off at me, so just to keep the peace at home I put it on this morning. Now I'll never hear the end of it. That he was right."

"Does he know what happened to you?"

"I haven't called him yet." Jane swiped a sleeve across her face. "I haven't had the chance."

"You need to go home. Right now."

"In the middle of this?"

"Jane, you're barely holding it together. Your team can process the scene."

"Right, with Marquette here? Seeing that I can't handle a little thing like being shot in the back? Fuck that." Jane turned and walked away, as though in a hurry to get this business over with. To prove she was up to the task.

Oh Jane, thought Maura. You've proved yourself time and again, but it will never be enough for you. You'll always be that rookie fighting to be acknowledged. Afraid to show weakness.

They came to another barrier of crime scene tape, where a patrolman guarded the entrance to an alley. Once again, Maura was greeted with cold indifference. As she pulled on fresh shoe covers and ducked under the tape, she felt the patrolman watching her, and it was a relief to escape his stare and follow Jane into the gloom of the alley.

"And here's bachelor number two," announced Jane, aiming her flashlight at the pavement. The jarringly flippant remark left Maura unprepared for the horror lying at their feet.

The decapitation was complete. The head, wearing a dark knit cap, had come to rest a few feet away from the torso—a white male, perhaps forty. The body, garbed entirely in black, lay chest-down as though in mid-breaststroke through an ocean of its own spilled blood. Frozen in cadaveric spasm, the hand still clutched a gun. Swinging her flashlight, Maura saw stuttering arcs splashed across the walls, saw congealed pools, like puddles of black pudding on the pavement.

"Meet the asshole who ruined my favorite suit," said Jane.

Maura frowned at the headless torso. At the weapon in the man's hand. "This is the man you chased from the residence?"

"Yeah. Followed him from Ingersoll's backyard. He got off one round and hit me in the back. Still hurts like hell."

"Then how did he end up . . ."

"A third party stepped in. If you have any questions about the manner of death, just ask me, because I was here. I was here on the ground, and this guy was about to pump a bullet in my head. I thought I was dead. I thought . . ." She swallowed. "Then I heard a sound, this whoosh in the air. He just collapsed on top of me." Staring down, Jane said softly: "And I'm still alive."

"Did you see who did this?"

"Just a shadow. Silver hair."

"That's all?"

Jane hesitated. "A sword. I think he had a sword."

Maura looked down at the body and felt a puff of wind sweep down the alley. Wondered if the fatal blow had sounded like that same whisper of wind. She remembered the amputated wrist of Jane Doe, joints and tendons so cleanly divided. Her gaze sharpened on the gun in the dead man's grasp. "This gun has a suppressor."

"Yeah. He's dressed in black and carrying a hit man's special. Just like Jane Doe, the woman on the rooftop."

"This is not any run-of-the-mill burglar." Maura looked up. "Why was Ingersoll's phone bugged?"

"He never got the chance to tell me, but it was obvious he was worried and wanted to talk. Something about girls. *What happened to those girls,* he said."

"Which girls?"

"I think it's connected to the Red Phoenix. Did you know that two of the victims had their daughters go missing?"

Maura heard voices and the slam of vehicle doors. She looked up the alley and saw the approaching flashlights of

the CSU team. "Now I'm definitely going to read those files that Tam brought
me."

"Why did he? I was surprised to hear
he'd dropped that on you."

"He wanted an unbiased opinion. I
don't think he believes that the cook
was a suicide."

"What do you think?"

"I've been too busy to look at the
files. Rat's visiting this week, so I'm
spending time with him." Maura turned
to leave. "I'll do the autopsies first thing
in the morning. If you want to be there."

"You're going to do both of them?"

That struck Maura as an odd question and she looked back. "Why wouldn't
I?"

"Ingersoll was a cop. I'm just thinking
it's kind of a delicate time right now.
With you and the Graff trial."

Maura heard the discomfort in Jane's
voice and knew the reason for it. "Am I
no longer allowed to autopsy cops?"

"I'm not saying that."

"Trust me, you don't have to. I'm fully
aware of what's being said. I'm aware

of it every time a cop looks at me, or refuses to look at me. They consider me the enemy."

"It'll pass, Maura. It just takes time."

Until I testify against the next cop. "I wouldn't want to be politically incorrect," said Maura. "I'll ask Dr. Bristol to do the postmortem on Ingersoll." She ducked under the crime scene tape and walked away, past the CSU team. Felt the knot in her neck gradually ease only after she'd left the alley a block behind her. *It'll pass, Maura,* Jane had said, but would it? Cops had long memories. They recalled the details of cases that were decades old, and they held grudges, never forgetting who was with them or against them. I am always going to be placed in the second category, she thought. Twenty years from now, they're still going to remember that I helped send a cop to jail.

By the time she was back at Ingersoll's residence, more official vehicles had arrived. She paused, dazzled by the flashing lights and the carnival atmosphere of confusion. Suddenly a woman's sobs pierced the chatter of police radios.

"Let me see him! I need to see my father!"

"Ma'am, please. You can't go in there," a patrolman said, holding her back. "Someone will be out to talk to you as soon as they can."

"But he's my *dad.* I have a right to know what happened to him!"

"Father Brophy," the cop called out. "Can you help this lady, please?"

A tall man wearing a priest's collar quietly made his way through the crowd. As the clergyman for Boston PD, Daniel Brophy was frequently called to scenes of tragedy, so Maura was not surprised to see him here, but the sight of him stunned her nonetheless. She watched with hungry eyes as Daniel led Ingersoll's daughter away from the crime scene tape. Did he look thinner? Was his face haunted, his hair more gray? *Do you miss me the way I miss you?*

He guided the sobbing woman toward a patrol car, then suddenly he saw Maura and their gazes locked. For a moment the world dropped away and she saw only Daniel. Felt the drumming of her own heart, as frantic as the wings of a dying bird.

She was still staring as he walked away, cradling the sobbing woman against his shoulder.

NINETEEN

Jane stood before the morgue's light box, studying the dead man's X-rays. His bony structures appeared normal in every way, except for one glaring detail: His cranium had been separated from his body, severed cleanly between the third and fourth cervical vertebrae. Although Tam and Frost were already standing at the autopsy table, waiting for the postmortem to begin, Jane stayed rooted where she was, not yet ready to face what was lying beneath the drape. X-rays were abstract things, cartoon anatomy in black and white.

They did not look or smell like flesh; they did not have a face. And so she lingered longer than she needed to, focused on the shadow of lungs and heart, the same heart that had sent blood spurting across her clothes last night. If not for my nameless savior, my X-rays would be hanging here, she thought. My body would be lying on the table.

"Jane?" said Maura.

"It's hard to imagine a blade sharp enough to do this with one stroke," Jane said, her gaze still fixed on the X-ray.

"It's a matter of anatomy," said Maura. "The angle at which the blade hits the joint. In medieval times, a skilled executioner could behead a prisoner with one stroke. If he had to keep hacking away, that was a sure sign he was incompetent. Or drunk."

"Pleasant image to start off the morning," said Tam.

Maura whisked off the drape. "We haven't undressed him yet. I assumed you all wanted to be here when we did."

No, I don't want to be here, thought Jane. I don't want to see this. But she forced herself to turn to the table. Although what lay there was no surprise, she still sucked in a sharp breath at the sight of the severed head. She knew nothing yet about this man, neither his name nor his origins. The only clues they had so far came from the items removed from his pockets last night: an ammunition clip, a roll of cash, and keys to a stolen Ford van, which had been parked two blocks from Ingersoll's residence. He carried no ID of any kind.

Tam bent over the table, his expression unruffled as he took a closer look at the severed head. He didn't flinch when Maura peeled off the victim's stocking cap, revealing neatly clipped brown hair. The dead man's face was unremarkable, with an utterly average nose, average mouth, average chin. A man you'd forget a moment after you'd passed him on the street.

The hands had already been swabbed and his fingerprints collected last night upon arrival. Purple ink still stained the fingers. Maura and Yoshima worked together to remove the clothing, peeling off the sweatshirt and trousers, briefs and socks. The headless body was stocky and well muscled. A healed scar ran diagonally across the right knee—a souvenir of old surgery. Jane stared at the scar and thought: Now I know why I was able to run him down so easily last night.

Under the magnifier, Maura examined the incised soft tissues, searching for irregularities and bruising. "I don't see any serration marks," she said. "The wound is uniform, without secondary cuts. This was a single slice."

"That's what I told you," said Jane. "It was a sword. One slash."

Maura glanced up. "No matter how reliable I consider a witness, I always need to confirm." She refocused on the incision. "This cut was delivered at an odd angle. Which hand was holding the sword, right or left?"

Jane hesitated. "I didn't see the actual slash. But as he was walking away, it was . . . it was in his right hand."

"Are you sure?"

"Yes. Why?"

"Because this cut starts lower on the right, and angles upward as it exits the left side of the neck."

"So?"

"This victim is about five foot ten, five eleven. If the killer attacked from behind, slashing right to left, he was probably shorter." Maura looked at Jane. "Would you agree?"

"I was lying on my back. At that angle, everyone looks tall, especially someone with a big honking sword." She let out a breath, suddenly aware that Maura was looking at her with the analytical gaze that so irritated her. A look that invaded her privacy, made her feel like a specimen floating in formalin.

Abruptly Jane turned from the table. "I don't think I need to see any more of this. What's this autopsy going to tell us? Surprise, someone whacked off his head?" She tossed the gown in the contaminated linen bin. "You guys finish up here. I'm going to check with the crime lab, find out if Ingersoll's cell phone turned up anything."

The anteroom door suddenly swung open, and Jane was startled to see her husband walk in. "What are you doing here?"

Special Agent Gabriel Dean was no

stranger to autopsy rooms. It had been a serial murder case that introduced Jane to her husband, and over the course of that investigation they had spent more than a few malodorous hours together, bending over corpses that had been found in various stages of decomposition. Gabriel was already wearing a gown and shoe covers, and his face was focused and grim as he pulled on gloves and approached the table.

"This is the man from the alley?" he asked bluntly. "The one who almost killed you?"

"Hello to you, too, sweetheart," said Jane. She looked at Tam. "In case you're wondering who this crasher is, this is my husband, Gabriel. And I have no idea why he's here."

Gabriel's attention remained fixed on the cadaver. "What do we know about him so far?"

"We? Since when did you join the team?" asked Jane.

"Since this man took a shot at you."

"Gabriel." She sighed. "We can talk about it later."

"The time to talk about it is now."

She stared at her husband, trying to understand what was happening here. Trying to read his face, stony under the glare of morgue lights. "What is this all about?"

"It's about fingerprints."

"We've gotten nothing back on him from AFIS."

"I'm talking about Jane Doe's fingerprints. The woman on the rooftop."

"We didn't get any match on hers, either," said Maura. "She's not in the FBI database."

"I sent a black notice to Interpol," he said. "Because it's clear to me this is adding up to something bigger. A lot bigger. Think of how Jane Doe was dressed. The weapon she was carrying. The fact she had no ID and was driving a stolen vehicle." He looked at the corpse. "Like this man."

"You've heard back from Interpol?" said Jane.

He nodded. "An hour ago. She's in their database. Not her name, but her fingerprints. They turned up on components of a car bomb that exploded in

London two years ago. It killed the driver, an American businessman."

"Are we talking about *terrorism*?" asked Tam.

"Interpol believes the bomb was a hit by organized crime. A paid assassination. Your woman on the rooftop was clearly a professional, and I'm guessing this man was, as well." He looked at Jane. "A Kevlar vest isn't going to save you, Jane. Not against people like this."

Jane gave a startled laugh. "Man, we really hit the jackpot, didn't we?"

"You have a daughter," said Gabriel. "*We* have a daughter. Think about this."

"What's there to think about?"

"Whether Boston PD can handle this."

"Hold it right there. Can we take this into the next room, please?" She glanced at her colleagues. "Excuse me," she muttered and pushed through the swinging door. It wasn't until she and Gabriel were in the hallway and out of earshot that she blurted out: "What do you think you're doing here?"

"I'm trying to keep my wife alive."

"This is my turf, okay? I decide what happens here."

"Do you have any idea what you're dealing with?"

"I'm going to figure it out."

"In the meantime, you're taking bullets and collecting dead bodies."

"Yeah. It's turning into quite a collection."

"Including a cop. Ingersoll knew how to defend himself, and now he's in a body bag."

"So you want me to drop out? Run home and hide under the bed?" She snorted. "That is so *not* going to happen."

"Who brings in professional killers, Jane? Anyone who'd hire a hit on an ex-cop is not afraid of Boston PD. He's not afraid of you. This has got to be organized crime. The Russian mob. Or Chinese—"

"Kevin Donohue," she said.

Gabriel paused. "Irish mafia?"

"We're already digging for dirt on him. One of his men named Joey Gilmore died in the Chinatown massacre. Gilmore's mother believes it was really a paid hit on her son, ordered by Donohue. Ingersoll was the lead detective on that massacre."

"If it's Donohue, he has a very long reach. Maybe into Boston PD itself."

She stared at her husband. "Can the Bureau back up that charge?"

"There's not enough evidence to make it stick. But I'll tell you now, he's not someone you want to fuck with, Jane. If he has a channel into Boston PD, he already knows exactly what you're up to. He knows you're coming for him."

She thought about all the police officers who'd turned up at Ingersoll's residence last night, including Lieutenant Marquette himself. How many cops had been watching her, keeping tabs on what she said, what she planned? How much of that information had leaked to Donohue?

"Last night was a gift," said Gabriel. "You survived. Maybe you should take that gift home and savor it for a while."

"Drop out of this case? Is that what you're asking me to do?"

"Take a leave of absence. You need time to recover."

"Don't." She stepped so close she had to crane her neck to stare him in the eye. Gabriel didn't back down; he never did. "I don't need to hear this from you," she said. "Not now."

"Then when am I going to say it? At your funeral?"

Her ringing cell phone cut into the silence between them. Snatching it up, she answered with a curt "Rizzoli."

"Um, is this a bad time, Detective?"

"Who is this?"

"Erin. In the crime lab."

Jane huffed out a breath. "Sorry. What do you have for me?"

"Remember those weird hairs on Jane Doe's clothes? The ones I couldn't identify?"

"Yeah. The gray ones."

"I can't wait to tell you what they are."

The conversation with Gabriel was still weighing on Jane's mind as she and Frost drove together to Schroeder Plaza. He knew her moods well enough to stay silent for most of the drive, but as she turned into the parking garage, he said wistfully: "I miss that part about being married."

"Which part?" she said.

"The part about having someone worry about you. Hassle you about not taking any risks."

"That's supposed to be a good thing?"

"Well, isn't it? It means he loves you. It means he doesn't want to lose you."

"What it means is I have to fight battles on two fronts. Do my job while Gabriel tries to tie me into a straitjacket."

"What if he didn't? Do you ever think of that? What it'd be like to not have him care enough to say anything? What it'd be like to not be married at all?"

She pulled into a parking space and shut off the engine. "He doesn't want me working on this case."

"I'm not sure I want to be working on it, either. After what we've both been through."

She looked at him. "Scares you?"

"I'm not afraid to admit it."

They heard a door slam, and both turned to see Tam step out of his car a few spaces away. "Bet it doesn't scare him," she muttered. "I don't think anything rattles Bruce Lee over there."

"It's got to be an act. He'd be crazy not to be scared of Donohue and his boys."

Jane pushed open her door. "Come on, before someone thinks we're making out in here or something."

By the time they reached the crime lab, Tam was already sitting at Erin Volchko's microscope, peering at a slide.

"There you two are," said Erin. "Detective Tam and I were just looking at some sample primate hair strands."

"Any of them look like the hairs from our gal?" asked Jane.

"Yes, but microscopy can't pinpoint the precise species. For that, I went to a different technique." On the countertop, Erin spread out a page printed with columns in varying shades of gray. "These are keratin patterns. Hair has different protein components that you can separate by electrophoresis. What you do is wash and dry the sample, dissolve it in a soup of chemicals, and place the dissolved proteins on a thin layer of gel. Then you subject it to an electrical current. That makes the various proteins migrate across the gel at different rates."

"And you end up with these gray columns."

"Yes. That's after silver staining and rinsing, to deepen the contrast."

Frost shrugged. "Doesn't look all that exciting."

"But when I emailed this pattern to the Wildlife Forensics Lab in Oregon, they were able to match it against their database of keratin patterns."

"There's a database for that?" said Tam.

"Absolutely. Wildlife scientists around the world contribute to it. If US Customs seizes a shipment of animal skins, they need to know if those skins are from an endangered species. The database helps them identify which animal the fur comes from." Erin opened a file folder and pulled out another sheet of keratin patterns. "Here's what they compared our strands with. You'll notice the protein bands line up almost perfectly with one particular specimen."

Jane glanced back and forth between

the two pages. "Column number four," she said.

"Correct."

"So what is number four?"

"It's a nonhuman primate, as I guessed earlier. An Old World monkey, genus *Semnopithecus.* This particular species is known as the gray langur."

"Gray?" said Jane, glancing up.

Erin nodded. "The same color as those hair strands from your Jane Doe. These monkeys are quite large, with black faces and gray or blond hair. Their range is South Asia, from China into India, both terrestrial and arboreal." She paused. "Meaning, they live on the ground as well as in trees." She turned to her computer and requested a Google Images search. "Here's a photo. This is what the monkeys look like."

What Jane saw on the screen made her hands suddenly go cold. *Black face. Gray hair.* She felt the ache between her shoulder blades from the bullet slamming into her Kevlar vest. Remembered hot blood splashing her face, and the silhouette looming above her in the alley, its head crowned with silver hair.

"How large are these monkeys?" she asked softly.

"The males are about two and a half feet long."

"You're certain they don't grow taller?"

"They're not apes. They're just monkeys."

Jane looked at Frost. Saw his pale face, his stunned eyes. "It's what you saw, isn't it?" she asked. "On the roof."

Erin frowned. "What did you see?"

Frost shook his head. "It was way taller than two and a half feet."

Jane nodded. "I agree."

Erin looked back and forth between them. "You *both* saw this thing?"

"It had that face," said Frost. "And gray hair. But it couldn't have been a monkey. And what monkey carries a sword?"

"Now, *that* just sent a chill up my spine," said Erin softly. "Considering what kind of monkey this is. In India, these are also known as the Hanuman langur. Hanuman is the Hindu god known as the Monkey Warrior."

The same chill that Erin had just felt suddenly whispered like an icy breath up the back of Jane's neck. She thought of the creature in the alley. Remembered the gleam of its sword as it turned and slipped into the shadows.

"Is that the same character as the Monkey King?" said Tam. "Because I know that legend. There's a Chinese version of it, too. My grandmother used to tell me the stories."

"Who is the Monkey King?" asked Jane.

"In China, his name is Sun Wukong. He's born from a sacred rock and he starts off as just a stone monkey. Then he transforms to flesh and blood and gets crowned king of the monkeys. He becomes a warrior and travels to heaven to learn the wisdom of the gods. But up there, he gets into all sorts of trouble."

"So he's a bad character?" asked Frost.

"No, not evil. Just impulsive and mis-chievous, like a real monkey. There's a whole book of stories about him. How he eats all the peaches in the heavenly orchard. Drinks too much and steals a magic elixir. Gets into brawls with the

Immortals, who don't know how to deal with him. So they kick him out of heaven and temporarily lock him up inside a mountain prison."

Frost laughed. "He sounds like a few guys I went to high school with."

"So then what happens to him?" asked Jane.

"Sun Wukong has a whole series of adventures on earth. Sometimes he causes trouble. Sometimes, he performs good deeds. I can't remember all the stories, but I know there was a lot of magical fighting and river monsters and talking animals. Just your typical fairy tales."

"Fairy tales don't spring to life," said Jane. "They don't shed real hair on real victims."

"I'm just telling you what the legends say about him. He's a complex creature, sometimes helpful, sometimes destructive. But when faced with a choice between good and evil, the Monkey King almost always chooses to do the right thing."

Jane stared at the photo on Erin's computer screen. At a face that, only a moment ago, had so chilled her. "So he's not evil at all," she said.

"No," said Tam. "Despite his flaws, despite the chaos he sometimes causes, the Monkey King stands on the side of justice."

TWENTY

The savory scent of roasting chicken and rosemary drifted from Angela Rizzoli's kitchen, and in the dining room silver and chinaware clattered as retired detective Vince Korsak set the table. Outside in the yard, Jane's daughter, Regina, was laughing and squealing as Gabriel pushed her on a swing set. But Jane was oblivious to it all as she sat reading on her mother's sofa, half a dozen borrowed library books spread out before her on the coffee table. Books about Asian primates and gray langurs. And books about Sun Wukong, the

Monkey King. She discovered that Sun Wukong's adventures showed up not only in books, but also in movies and Chinese operas, dances, and even a children's television show.

In a collection of Chinese folktales, Jane found an introduction to the legend. Though the stories were written sometime during the 1500s by a Chinese author named Wu Cheng'en, the tales themselves were ancient and were said to date back to an era of ghosts and magic, a time when gods and monsters battled in both heaven and earth.

And one of the rocks of that earth, a rock that from the time of creation knew the sweet breath of the wind, the glow of moonlight, the favor of the divine, popped out a stone egg. That egg became a stone monkey. It could run and jump and climb, a monkey with eyes that flashed shafts of light so brilliant that even the Jade Emperor in heaven was startled.

The stone monkey, with neither

father nor mother, soon became king of all monkeys. They lived in perfect harmony, until one day the Monkey King came to understand that Death awaited them all. So he set out to learn the secret of immortality, a journey that took him to heaven and temptation, to mischief and imprisonment. While marching to his own execution, to be burned in a crucible with alchemic flames, the Monkey King sprang free, and his fight to survive turned heaven upside down until the gods were forced to seal him inside the Mountain of the Five Elements.

There he waits in stony darkness through the centuries, until the day when he is needed. A day when evil is in the world, and the Monkey King must emerge once again to wage battle.

Jane turned the page and confronted an image of Sun Wukong, clutching a long fighting staff. Though it was just an illustration, that glimpse of the Monkey

King made the hair on her arms stand straight up. She stared at sharp teeth jutting in a black mouth, at a crown of silver hair, and could not look away.

She remembered an afternoon at the zoo when she'd been six years old, and her father had held her up to see the spider monkeys. They took one look at her and the cage erupted in terrifying chaos, the monkeys shrieking and vaulting among the branches, as if they had just glimpsed the face of Satan himself. A zoo employee came running and ordered everyone, *Back away, back away! I don't know what's scaring them!* But as Jane's father carried her from that cage of screaming monkeys, Jane knew that she was the one who'd set them off. She was the one they were terrified of. What did they see but a six-year-old girl with dark curls? she wondered. Or was there something else that they'd recognized even then? Something about who and what she'd one day become?

"So how's it going with the monkey books?"

Korsak's voice made her glance up with a start. He was dressed in his Sunday best—at least, the best that he was capable of pulling together for dinner at Angela Rizzoli's. At least there were no ketchup stains on his white golf shirt and khaki Dockers. After a heart attack a few years earlier, he'd lost thirty pounds on a heart-healthy diet, but his weight was starting to creep back up again, and despite a newly punched hole in his belt it was straining against an ever-expanding belly.

"It's for a case," said Jane. She closed the book she'd been reading, relieved to blot out the image of Sun Wukong.

"Yeah, I heard all about it. Got yourself another weird one. Started off with that dead lady on the roof, didn't it? Makes me wish I was back in the saddle."

Jane looked at his belly and thought: God help any horse that you climb on.

Korsak flopped down in the armchair—the same armchair that her father used to sit in. It was weird to see him lounging in Frank Rizzoli's old perch, but her dad had forfeited all rights to that chair the day he walked out on Angela and moved in with the Bimbo. That's what they all called her now, though they knew her name well enough. Sandie Huffington, Sandie-with-an-e. Jane knew all about the Bimbo, including how many traffic tickets she'd racked up in the past ten years. Three. Because of the Bimbo, Vince Korsak was sitting in this armchair, fat and happy on Angela's cooking.

Jane didn't want to think about all the other ways that Angela made him happy.

"Chinatown," Korsak grunted. "Strange place. Good food."

He would, of course, mention food. "What do you remember about the Red Phoenix shooting?" she asked. "You must've heard the gossip back then."

"That one was a wicked shocker. Why would a guy with a cute little girl shoot four people and blow out his own brains? Never made sense to me." He shook his head. "Such a sweet kid, too. Real daddy's girl."

That surprised her. "You knew the cook's family?"

"Not really, but I used to eat there a lot. Those Chinese, they don't know how to take a day off, so the place was always open, all hours of the night. You could get off a late shift and still have dinner. I was there once at ten on a Sunday night, and that little girl brought out my fortune cookies. It's like child labor. But she looked like she was happy to be hanging out with Daddy."

"You sure it was the cook's daughter? She would've been pretty young."

"She looked pretty young. Maybe five? Cute as a button." He gave a sad sigh. "Can't believe a father would do that, leave a wife and kid behind. Not to mention all the other families he screwed up. A few weeks later, daughter of one of the victims got kidnapped."

"Charlotte Dion."

"Was that her name? I just remember it was like a Greek tragedy. Bad luck piled on top of bad luck."

"You know the really weird part?" said Jane. "Two years earlier, the daughter of one of the other victims was snatched as well. The waiter's kid. She disappeared on her way home from school."

"No shit? I didn't know that." Korsak thought about this for a moment. "That's freaky. Really makes you wonder if it's more than just a coincidence."

"One of the last things Detective Ingersoll said to me on the phone was something about girls. *What happened to those girls.* Those were his words."

"Those two girls? Or other girls?"

"I don't know."

He shook his head. "All these years later, and here we are still thinking about them. Weird to realize they're probably nothing but skeletons now." He paused. "But that's not what I want to be thinking about tonight. Let's pour some wine."

"I thought you were a beer man."

"Your ma's converted me. Wine's better for the old ticker anyway, you know." He heaved himself out of the armchair. "Time to talk about happy things, okay?"

Not about dead people, thought Jane. Not about mass shootings and kidnapped girls. But when Gabriel came into the house holding Regina by her tiny hand, Jane couldn't help thinking about Charlotte Dion and Laura Fang. She helped her mother carry platters to the table, a steady succession of ever-more-impressive dishes. Crisp roast potatoes. Green beans drizzled with olive oil. And finally two sumptuous roast chickens, fragrant with rosemary. But even as they sat down to eat, as she tied the bib around Regina and cut her meat into child-sized morsels, Jane was thinking about missing girls and devastated parents. How could a mother go on? She wondered if Iris Fang had ever considered ending her own misery. A leap off a rooftop, a handful of sleeping pills. How much easier than living with grief, day in and day out, pining for loved ones whom you'll never see again.

"Something wrong with your meal, Janie?" said Angela.

Jane looked up at her mother, who had the uncanny knack of knowing exactly what had gone into the mouths of every guest seated at her dining table. "It's great, Ma. You outdid yourself tonight."

"Then why aren't you eating?"

"I am."

"You took one bite of chicken, then you started moving things around on your plate. I hope you're not on a diet, because you don't need to lose any weight, sweetie."

"I'm not on a diet."

"All these girls, they're always on diets. Starving on salads, and for what?"

"Sure ain't doing it for men," mumbled Korsak around a mouthful of potatoes. "Guys like a little meat on a girl." He winked at Angela. "Take your ma. Built like a woman's supposed to be built."

Jane couldn't see what was happening under the table, but her mother suddenly bolted straight in her chair, laughing. "Vincent! Behave."

Please behave. Because I can't watch any more of this.

"You know," said Korsak, slicing into his chicken. "This is a good time to bring up you know what."

Never had three words sounded so ominous. Jane's chin snapped up, and she looked at her mother. "What's *you know what*?"

"It's something we've been talking about for a while," said Angela. "Vince and me."

Jane glanced at her husband, but as

usual Gabriel wore his FBI face, giving away nothing, even though he'd probably guessed where this conversation was going.

"Well, you know that Vince and I have been seeing each other for quite a while," said Angela.

"Quite a while? It's been only, what? A year and a half?"

"That's plenty of time to get to know someone, Janie. To see that he has a good heart." Angela beamed at Korsak, and they leaned in for a noisy, lip-smacking kiss.

"You dated Dad for three whole years," Jane pointed out. "Look where that ended up."

"I was fifteen when I met your father. He was only my second boyfriend."

"You were fifteen and you'd already had a boyfriend?"

"The point is, I was just a kid, and I didn't know what the world had to offer. I married too young, had kids too young. Only now do I know what I want."

Jane looked at Korsak and thought: You cannot seriously be talking about *him.*

"That's why we wanted you to come to dinner tonight, sweetie. You and Gabriel are going to be the first to know. I haven't told Frankie or Mike yet because, well, you know how they are. Still attached to their dad and all, despite the fact he's sleeping with the Bimbo." Angela paused to take a calming breath. Just mentioning the Bimbo made her voice rise half an octave. "Your brothers, they just won't understand. But you're my daughter, so you know what we women have to put up with in this world. You know how unfair things are."

"Ma, there's no need to rush into anything."

"Oh, we're not going to rush. We're going to have a nice long engagement and do it the old-fashioned way. Order real invitations from a printer. Rent a big reception hall and a caterer. And we can go shopping for dresses together, Janie! That'd be something, just you and me! I'm thinking peach or lavender, since I'm not—well, you know."

Jane glanced at Korsak to see how he was reacting to this feminine checklist, but he just grinned like a happy sailor.

"This time, I'm going to go slow and enjoy every minute of my wedding," said Angela. "And it'll give your brothers a chance to adjust to it all."

"What about Dad?"

"What about him?"

"How's he going to adjust?"

"That's his problem." Angela's gaze darkened. "He just better not try to rush up the aisle first. Ooh, I can see him doing that, you know. Marrying the Bimbo quick just to annoy me." She looked at Korsak. "Maybe, on second thought, we should move up our date."

"No! Ma, look, forget I even mentioned Dad."

"I wish I could forget him, but he's always gonna be there, like a splinter in my foot. Can't get it out and can't pretend it's not there. Just constantly poking at me. I hope you never have to know what that's like, Janie." She paused and glanced at Gabriel. "Of course you won't. You have such a good man here."

A good man who's still annoyed I'm a cop.

Gabriel wisely stayed out of the conversation and focused instead on coaxing tiny cubes of potato into Regina's mouth.

"So now you've heard our big news," said Korsak, and he lifted a glass of wine. "Here's to family!"

"Come on, Jane! Gabriel!" urged Angela. "Let's all toast!"

Stoically, Jane raised her glass and mumbled, "To family."

"Just think," said Korsak, laughing as he gave her a happy punch in the arm. "Now you can call me Dad."

"It's not as if you didn't see this coming," said Gabriel as he and Jane drove home with Regina asleep in the backseat. "They were two lonely people, and look how happy they are now. They're perfectly matched."

"Yeah. She cooks. He eats."

"They could do a lot worse."

"They're both on the rebound. It's too soon for them to get married."

"Life is short, Jane. You should know

that better than anyone. It can be gone in an instant. All it takes is an icy road, a drunk driver."

Or a bullet in a dark alley. Yes, she did know, because she saw life cut short far too often. Saw how every death cast ripples among the living. She remembered the ravaged face of Joey Gilmore's mother and the grief that clouded the eyes of Patrick Dion when he spoke of his daughter, Charlotte. Even nineteen years later, those ripples were still battering the survivors.

"I dread having to break this news to my brothers," she said.

"You don't think they'll take it well?"

"Frankie's going to throw a fit. He hates the idea of Mom and another man, you know . . ."

"Sleeping together?"

Jane winced. "I admit, that's what gives me the heebie-jeebies. I like Korsak. He's a decent man and he'll treat her right. But geez, she's my mother."

Gabriel laughed. "And your mother still has sex. Accept it. Just call Frankie and get it over with."

But when they got home, she put off

the assignment and avoided the phone entirely. Instead she set a kettle on the stove and sat down at the kitchen table to look at her library books again. The illustration of the Monkey King glared back at her, paws brandishing his staff, an image so threatening that only reluctantly did she touch the book to flip to the next page.

Chapter Nine. The Story of Chen O.
The great city of Ch'ang-an had long been the capital of all China. At this time, Tai Tsing of the dynasty of Tang was on the throne. The whole land was at peace.

It was a disarmingly pleasant beginning to a tale about a virtuous and scholarly young man named Chen O. After marrying a great beauty, he was appointed governor of a distant region. Together with his pregnant bride and their servants, he journeyed through the lush and flowering countryside toward his new post. But when they reached a river crossing, the charming fable suddenly transformed to a blood-splattered story of massacre when armed bandits attacked. This was not a sweet fable after all, but a tale of shrieks and terror, of butchered bodies thrown into the raging river. Only one person was not slaughtered that night: the pregnant wife, abducted for her beauty, imprisoned by the killers while she awaited the birth of her doomed child.

The scream of the teakettle wrenched Jane from the story. She looked up to see Gabriel shut off the flame and pour hot water into the teapot. She had not even heard him come into the kitchen.

"Fascinating reading?" he said.

"Jesus, this is a creepy book," she said with a shudder. "I sure wouldn't read these stories to my kid. Take this one, 'The Story of Chen O.' It's about a massacre at a ferry crossing, and the only survivor is a pregnant woman who's captured by the killers."

He brought the teapot to the table and sat down across from her. All night he had been subdued, and she noticed the telltale crease between his eyebrows. A hint of a frown that she noticed only now, in the bright light of their kitchen.

"I know I can't change your mind about this case," he said. "I just want to register my concern again."

She sighed. "Noted."

"Jane, I can't get it out of my head. The way you looked when you came home the other night. Shell-shocked. The blood all over your clothes. I haven't seen you look so shaken up since . . ."

He didn't say the name, but they both knew he was thinking of the monster who had brought them together. The man who had carved the scars on her hands, whose bloody footprints still tracked through her nightmares.

"You do remember what I do for a living?" she said.

He nodded. "And I knew there'd be days like this. I just didn't realize how hard it would be to live with."

"Do you ever regret it?" she asked softly.

"Marrying a cop?"

"Marrying me."

"Well, now." Rubbing his chin, he

gave an exaggerated *hmmmm.* "Let me think about that."

"Gabriel."

He turned as the phone rang. "Why do you have to ask that question?" he said, crossing the kitchen to answer the phone. "I'm not regretting a thing. I'm just telling you I don't like what's happening and what you're up against."

"I don't much like it, either," she said and looked at the book again. At the story of Chen O. Like the Red Phoenix, it was a tale of slaughter. And an abducted woman, she thought, remembering Charlotte Dion.

"Jane, it's for you." Gabriel stood with the phone in his hand and a look of concern in his eye. "He won't give me his name."

She took the phone. Felt her husband watching her as she answered, "Detective Rizzoli."

"I know you've been asking about me, so I figured I'd cut to the chase. Let's you and me talk, face-to-face. Four PM tomorrow, my house. Just you and no one else. You can tell your husband he has nothing to worry about."

"Who is this?" she demanded.

"Kevin Donohue."

She looked up sharply at Gabriel. Barely managed to keep her voice even as she said: "What is this about, Mr. Donohue?"

"The Red Phoenix. Your investigation's going way off the rails. I think it's time to set a few things straight."

TWENTY-ONE

Although both Frost and Tam sat watching her from their parked cars, Jane felt dangerously alone and exposed as she rang the bell at Kevin Donohue's front gate. A moment later two beefy men strode toward her down the driveway, both of them sporting the conspicuous bulges of sidearms under their jackets. They asked her no questions, merely admitted her through the gate and locked it again behind her. As she passed under the arch, she spotted a surveillance camera mounted overhead.

Every move she made was being monitored.

Following the men up the driveway, she noted the absence of trees and shrubbery. There was only a broad lawn and a concrete driveway lined with ugly lampposts, where yet more security cameras were mounted. Here was the stark evidence that being a prince of the Irish mob had its downside. You could never stop looking over your shoulder because you knew that somewhere, a bullet had your name on it.

As wealthy as he was, Donohue had depressingly pedestrian taste, something that was apparent as soon as Jane walked into the house and saw the bland pastel paintings hanging on the wall. They looked like the mass-produced landscapes for sale at every local shopping mall. Her escorts led her into the living room where an enormous man, bloated as a toad, sat in an extra-large armchair. He was in his sixties, clean-shaven and balding, with blue eyes that glared from beneath heavy lids. She didn't need to be introduced; she already knew that this Jabba the

Hutt character was Kevin Donohue, known for his impressive appetites and his equally impressive bad temper.

"Scan her, Sean," someone said. She hadn't noticed there was another man in the room, a skinny and nervous-looking fellow in a business suit.

One of her escorts moved toward her, holding a radio frequency scanner, and Jane snapped, "What the hell's this all about?"

"I'm Mr. Donohue's attorney," the skinny man said. "Before he talks to you, we need to make sure you're not bugged. And you'll have to hand us your cell phone."

"This wasn't part of the agreement."

"Detective Rizzoli," rumbled Donohue, "I'm granting you the privilege of keeping your weapon, on account of your voluntarily coming here. But I don't want any recording of this conversation. If you're worried about your safety, I'm sure your associates parked outside will come running to your rescue at the first sign of trouble."

For a moment Jane and Donohue traded stares. Then she handed her cell phone to the attorney and stood motionless while the bodyguard scanned her for radio signals. Only when Sean pronounced her clean did Donohue wave her toward the sofa, inviting her to sit. She chose an armchair instead, so that she would be at his eye level.

"Your reputation precedes you," said Donohue.

"So does yours."

He laughed. "I see the rumors are true."

"Rumors?"

He folded his hands on his bulging belly. "Detective Jane Rizzoli. Smart-ass tongue. Fucking bulldog."

"I'll take that as a compliment."

"Which is why I'm telling you to dig somewhere else for your bones. You're wasting your time on me."

"Am I?"

"You've been asking a lot of questions about me. So has your husband. Oh yeah, I know all about your husband, Mr. Special Agent Gabriel Dean. Quite the law enforcement couple. I'm not worried that you're gonna find anything useful, mind you. But with all these questions going around, it makes me look weak to my rivals. Like I'm about to topple. And if I look weak, that brings the vultures out." He leaned forward, his belly flopping over his belt. "There is nothing you're going to find, okay? *Nothing* that can link me to the Red Phoenix."

"What about Joey Gilmore?"

He sighed. "You've been talking to his old hag of a mother."

"She says you and Joey had a falling-out nineteen years ago."

"Small stuff. Not worth the price of a bullet."

"Can't be all that small if you're bringing in outside people to mop up now."

"What?"

Jane glanced at Donohue's two bodyguards. "I'm going to reach into my pocket for some pictures, okay? Don't freak out, boys." She pulled out two morgue photos and slid them across the coffee table toward Donohue. "Your hired help just can't keep their heads on straight."

Donohue stared. Of all the morgue photos Jane could have brought, she'd

chosen the two that were most graphi-
cally grotesque. Jane Doe with her
slashed throat gaping open. John Doe's
severed head lying beside his torso on
the autopsy table. The images had their
desired effect: Donohue's face had
turned as pasty as the corpses.

"Why the fuck are you showing me
this?" he demanded.

"Why did you hire these two killers?"

The lawyer cut in. "This conversation
has come to an end. Sean, Colin. Escort Detective Rizzoli out of the house."

"Shut up," said Donohue.

"Mr. Donohue, it's not in your best interests to—"

"I'm gonna answer her question,
okay?" Donohue looked at Jane. "I
didn't hire 'em. I don't even know who
that woman is." He eyed Jane Doe's
morgue photo with new interest and
grunted. "Nice-looking gal. What a
waste."

"And the man? Do you recognize
him?"

"Maybe. Looks a little familiar. What
do you think, Sean?"

His man Sean eyed the photo. "I think

I seen him around. Don't know his name, but he's local. Ukrainian or Russian."

Donohue shook his head. "Bad news, those boys. Completely lacking any moral conscience. I can tell you, this guy never worked for me." He looked up at Jane. "Now I guess he never will."

"Why don't I believe you?" she said.

"Because you've already decided I'm guilty. Even though I'll swear on my mother's Bible that I didn't hire these two." After the initial shock of seeing the morgue photos, his color and his cockiness had returned. "So you might wanna think of backing off."

"Are you threatening me, Mr. Dono-hue?"

"You're a smart girl. What do you think?"

"I think you're scared. I think you know you're cornered."

"By you?" He laughed. "*You* are the least of my worries."

"You called me a bulldog, remember? Well, I'm going to keep on digging in your backyard because that's where I'll find Joey Gilmore's bones."

"Come on. The cook killed those people and pulled a chuck. Everyone knows it was suicide, but Joey's old hag of a mother just can't let it go. That's why she sent me that fucking note."

Jane went very still. "You got one?"

"Few weeks ago, got a copy of Joey's obit. Plus some stupid message that she wrote on the back. *I know what really happened.* What the hell's that supposed to mean?"

"If Mrs. Gilmore is the reason you're investigating Mr. Donohue," said the attorney, "don't waste your time."

"How do you know Mary Gilmore's sending these notes?" Jane asked. "Did she sign yours? Was there a return address?"

The attorney frowned as he suddenly registered what Jane had said. "Notes, as in plural? Are you saying she's sent more than one?"

"There have been others. Mailings sent to all the family members of the Red Phoenix victims. The notes are similar to what Mr. Donohue received."

The attorney looked confused. "This doesn't make sense. Why would Mrs.

Gilmore harass other people with these mailings?"

"Maybe she's not the one sending them," said Jane.

The attorney and Donohue looked at each other. "We need to rethink this," said the attorney. "Obviously, something else is going on. If Mary Gilmore isn't doing this . . ."

Donohue's fingers rolled into two plump fists. "I want to know who the hell is."

TWENTY-TWO

Maura awakened just after dawn, and was happy to see that the sun was shining. She'd cook pancakes and sausages for the boy, and then they'd set off to tour Boston. First on the schedule was the Freedom Trail and the North End, then they'd go for a picnic and a run with the dog at Blue Hills Reservation. She'd planned a day packed with so many activities that there would be little time for awkward silences, for all the reminders that they were still very much strangers. Six months ago, in the Wyoming mountains, she had trusted Julian

"Rat" Perkins with her life. Now she had to acknowledge that this hulking teen-ager with the enormous feet was still a mystery to her. She wondered if he felt the same way about her. Did he worry that she would abandon him, the way everyone else in his life had?

She pulled on jeans and a T-shirt, ap-propriate attire for a romp with the dog. Thought about the chicken-and-avo-cado sandwiches she planned to make, and wondered if Rat liked avocados. Had he ever tasted an avocado or al-falfa sprouts or tarragon? I know so little about him, she thought. Yet here he is, a part of my life.

She walked down the hall and no-ticed that his bedroom door was open. "Rat?" she said. Peeking in, she did not see him.

In the kitchen, she found him sitting in front of the laptop computer that she'd left on the table the night before. The dog lay at his feet and his ears pricked up at the sight of Maura, as if here at last was someone who'd pay attention to him. Looking over the boy's shoulder, she was startled to see an autopsy image on the screen.

"Don't look at that," she said. "I should have put this all away last night." She punched the Exit key, and the morgue photo swooshed out of sight. Quickly she scooped up all the Red Phoenix files and set them on the counter. "Why don't you help me make breakfast?"

"Why did he do it?" the boy asked. "Why would he kill people he didn't even know?"

Maura looked into his troubled eyes. "Did you read the police report?"

"It was lying here on the table, and I couldn't help looking at it. But it doesn't make sense to me. Why someone would do that."

She pulled over a chair and sat down across from him. "Sometimes, Rat, there's no way to explain these things. I'm sorry to say that too often, I haven't a clue why people do things like this. Why they drown their babies or strangle their wives or shoot their co-workers. I see the results of their actions, but I can't tell you what sets them off. I just know that it happens. And people are capable of doing terrible things."

"I know," he murmured and looked down at the dog, who rested his enormous head in Rat's lap as though knowing that comfort was what the boy needed at that moment. "So this is what you do?"

"Yes, it is."

"Do you like your work?"

"I don't think *like* is the right word."

"What is the right word?"

"It's challenging. Interesting."

"And it doesn't bother you, seeing things like this?"

"Someone has to speak for the dead. I know how to do it. They tell me—their bodies tell me—how they died. If it was a natural death, or if it was violent. Yes, it can be upsetting. It can make you question what it means to be human when you see what people do to each other. But this is the job I feel I was always meant to do, to be their voice."

"Do you think I could do it?" He looked at the stack of files. "Your kind of work?"

"You mean, be a pathologist?"

"I want to learn the answers, too." He looked at her. "I want to be just like you."

"And that," she said with a smile, "is the most flattering thing anyone has ever said to me."

"At Evensong, my teachers say I'm really good at noticing things that other people miss. So I think I could do it."

"If you want to be a pathologist," she said, "you'll have to make very good grades in school."

"I know."

"You'll have to go to college, and then four years of medical school. After that, you'll have to do a residency, plus a fellowship in forensic pathology. That's a lot of years and a lot of commitment, Rat."

"Are you saying you don't think I can do it?"

"I'm just saying you really have to want it." She looked into the boy's dark eyes and thought she could glimpse the man that he would one day become. Intense and fiercely loyal. A man who would not only speak for the dead, but fight for them as well. "You'll have to learn science, because only science will prove your case on the witness stand. A hunch isn't good enough."

"What if your hunch is really strong?"

"It's never as convincing as what a drop of blood can tell you."

"But a hunch tells you when something's not right. Like in that picture."

"Which picture?"

"The Chinese man who killed himself. I'll show you." He got up and brought the laptop and file folders back to the table. With a few mouse clicks, he reopened the digital image of Wu Weimin's body, lying in the Red Phoenix kitchen. "The police said he shot himself once, in the head," said Rat.

"Yes."

"Look what's lying on the floor next to him."

Last night, she'd glanced at the photos only briefly. It had been late, she'd had a long day with the boy, and she'd been drowsy after two glasses of wine. Now she focused more intently on the dead cook, and on the weapon that was still clasped in his hand. Near his shoulder lay a spent bullet casing.

Rat pointed to what she'd missed, at the periphery of the photo. A second casing. "It says he had one bullet in his head," said Rat. "But if he fired twice, where did the other bullet go?"

"It could have ended up anywhere in the kitchen. Under the circumstances, the police probably saw no reason to go searching for it."

"And why did he shoot twice?"

"I've seen it before in suicides. The victim has to build up the courage to kill himself, and maybe he misses the first time. Or the gun misfires. I've even seen a suicide where the victim shot himself more than twice in the head. Another one who shot himself with his nondominant hand. And there was one man who . . ." She paused, suddenly appalled that she was having this conversation with a sixteen-year-old boy. But he was looking back at her as calmly as a fellow professional.

"It's certainly a valid concern to bring up," she said. "I'm sure the police considered it."

"But it didn't change their minds. They still say he killed those four people, even though they can't explain why."

"How could they? So few people really knew the cook."

"Like no one really knew me," he said quietly.

Now she understood what was really troubling the boy. He, too, had been called a murderer; he, too, had been judged by people who scarcely knew him. When Rat looked at Wu Weimin, what he saw was himself.

"All right," she conceded. "Let's assume for the moment that he didn't kill himself. Let's say it was staged to look like a suicide. Which means someone else must have shot those other four people, and then killed the cook."

Rat nodded.

"Think about it. Imagine you're the cook. You're standing in the kitchen and someone starts shooting in the other room. The gun had no silencer, so you'd hear those gunshots."

"Then how come no one else did? The report says there were people in the three apartments upstairs, but they heard only one bang. That's why no one called the police right away. Then the cook's wife went downstairs and found her husband's body."

"How much of this did you read?"

"Most of it."

"That's more than I have," she confessed. She opened the folder to the report filed by Staines and Ingersoll. When Detective Tam had dropped off the material, she had not welcomed the extra work, and had put it off until last night, when she'd given the photos only a cursory glance. Now she read the police report from beginning to end, and confirmed what Rat had just told her. Seven different witnesses stated that they'd heard only one bang, yet a total of nine bullet casings were found in the Red Phoenix restaurant.

Her sixth sense was starting to tingle. That uneasy feeling that something was not right, just as the boy had said.

She opened Wu Weimin's autopsy report. According to the pathologist, the cook was found lying on his side, his back wedged up against the closed cellar door. His right hand—the one still clutching the gun—was later swabbed and found positive for gunshot residue. Oblivious to the fact that Rat was watching, she clicked through the cook's autopsy photos. The fatal bullet had been fired into the right temple, and a close-up showed it to be a hard contact wound, the edges seared and blackened in a pressure abrasion ring caused by gases rushing out of the barrel. There was no exit wound. She clicked on the skull X-ray and saw metallic fragments scattered throughout the cranium. A hollow-point bullet, she thought, designed to mushroom and disintegrate, transferring its kinetic energy directly to tissues. Maximum damage with minimum penetration.

She moved on to the other files.

The second autopsy report was for James Fang, age thirty-seven, found slumped behind the cash register counter. He had been shot once in the head. The bullet had entered above his left eyebrow.

The third report was for Joey Gilmore, age twenty-five. His body fell in front of the cash register counter, take-out cartons scattered on the floor around him. He had been shot once, in the back of the head.

The last two victims were Arthur and Dina Mallory, both found near a corner table where they had been sitting. Arthur was shot twice, once in the back of the head, once in the spine. His wife was hit three times, the bullets punching into her cheek, her mid-back, and her skull. Scanning down to the pathologist's summary, she saw that he'd concluded the same thing she did: that Dina Mallory had been moving when she was shot the first two times, probably trying to flee her attacker. Maura was about to set the report aside when she noticed a sentence describing the dissection of the stomach and duodenum.

Based on volume of gastric contents, which appear to include spaghetti fragments with a tomato-based sauce, the postprandial period is estimated to be one to two hours.

Maura opened Arthur Mallory's autopsy report and scanned down to the examination of his stomach, which, as was routine in an autopsy, had been slit open and the contents collected.

Gastric contents appear to include cheese and meat, with partially digested fragments of lettuce. Postprandial interval estimated at one to two hours.

This did not make sense. Why would the Mallorys, their bellies full of what appeared to be an Italian meal, be sitting in a Chinese restaurant?

The description of gastric contents, of macerated lettuce and tomato sauce, had ruined her appetite. "This is not the way to start off breakfast," she said, closing the folder. "It's a beautiful day and I'm going to make pancakes, how about that? Let's not think about this anymore."

"What about the missing bullet?" said Rat.

"Even if we could find it now, it wouldn't change the conclusions. The

bodies have been long buried or cre-
mated, and the crime scene's been
cleaned up. To reopen a case, you need
new forensic evidence. After this many
years, there'd be nothing left."

"But there's something wrong about
all this, isn't there? You think so, too."

"Okay." She sighed. "Let's assume
the cook didn't kill himself. Let's assume someone else, a person unknown,
walked in and started shooting. Why
didn't the cook just run?"

"Maybe he couldn't get out."

"There's another exit from the kitchen.
The report said it opens into an alley."

"Maybe the door was locked from the
outside."

She pulled up the crime scene images on her laptop. This was completely
inappropriate viewing for the boy, but
he had raised good questions, and
nothing he'd seen or heard so far appeared to have rattled him. "Here," she
said, pointing to the kitchen exit. "It
looks like it's ajar. So there's no reason
he couldn't have fled. If he heard gunshots in the dining room, anyone with

common sense would have run out that kitchen door."

"What about that door?" He pointed to the cellar door, blocked by the cook's body. "Maybe he was going to hide down there."

"The cellar's a dead end. It makes no sense to head that way. Look at all the evidence, Rat. He's found holding the gun. There's gunshot residue on his hand, which means he was in contact with the weapon when it was fired." She paused, suddenly thinking about the extra bullet casing. The gun was fired twice in the kitchen, but only one blast was heard. And the Glock had a threaded barrel, so it could be fitted with a silencer. She tried to imagine an alternate sequence of events. An unknown killer executes Wu Weimin. Removes the silencer and places the weapon in the dead man's hand. Fires one last time to plant gunshot residue on the victim's skin. It would explain why only one blast was heard and why there were two bullet casings in the kitchen. But there was one detail she couldn't explain with that scenario: why Wu Weimin, given the chance to flee out the back exit, had chosen to remain in the kitchen.

She focused on the cellar door. On the cook's body, lying in front of it. Blocking it. Suddenly she thought: Maybe he couldn't flee.

Because he had a very good reason to stay.

TWENTY-THREE

"Luminol's probably going to make this whole place light up," said Jane. "According to the realtor, all they did after the event was wash down the walls and mop the floors. The linoleum was never replaced. So I'm not sure what this exercise is going to prove."

"We won't know until we look, will we?" said Maura.

They stood outside the old Red Phoenix restaurant, waiting for the crime scene unit to arrive. Total darkness was needed to properly examine the interior, and dusk was just now deepening toward night, bringing with it a damp chill that made Maura wish she had brought more than just her raincoat. At the far end of Knapp a lamp glowed, but this end of the street was deep in shadow, and the building, with its barred windows, its gated door, looked like a prison sealing in its ghosts.

Jane peered through the restaurant window and gave a visible shudder. "We've already been in there, you know. It's a creepy place, and it's probably crawling with roaches. Just bare walls and empty rooms. There's really nothing left to look at."

"The blood will still be there," said Maura. Soap and scrubbing erased only the visible evidence; the chemical ghost of blood remained on floors and walls. Luminol could reveal old smears and footprints that may have been missed during the original investigation.

The glare of headlights made her turn and squint as a vehicle rounded the corner and slowly rolled to a stop. Frost and Tam stepped out.

"You got the key?" Jane called out.

Frost pulled it from his pocket. "I had

to sign our lives away before Mr. Kwan would hand it over."

"What's the big deal? There's nothing to steal in there."

"He said if we damage anything, we'll hurt the resale value."

Jane snorted. "I could improve its resale value with a stick of dynamite."

Frost unlocked the door and felt around for the light switch. Nothing happened. "Bulb must've finally burned out," he said.

In the darkness beyond the threshold, something moved, startled by the sudden invasion. Maura turned on her flashlight and saw half a dozen roaches skitter away from the beam and vanish beneath the cash register counter.

"Ewww," said Frost. "I bet there's, like, a thousand of them swarming around under there."

"Thanks a lot," muttered Jane. "Now I'll never get that picture out of my head."

Their four flashlight beams sliced back and forth, crisscrossing in the darkness. As Jane had described, the room was bare walls and floor, but when

Maura looked around the room images from the crime scene photos superimposed themselves. She saw Joey Gilmore sprawled near the counter. Saw James Fang crumpled behind the counter. She crossed to the corner where the Mallorys had died and pictured the corpses as they had fallen. Arthur slumped facedown onto the table. Dina stretched out on the floor.

"Hello?" a voice called from the alley. "Detective Rizzoli?"

"We're in here," said Jane.

A new pair of dueling flashlight beams joined theirs as two men from the crime scene unit entered the room. "It's definitely dark enough in here," one of the men said. "And there's no furniture to move, so that'll make things quick." He squatted and examined the floor. "This is the same linoleum?"

"That's what we're told," said Tam.

"Looks it, too. Stamped linoleum, lots of dings and cracks. Should light up really well." He grunted as he stood up, his belly as big as an eight-month pregnancy.

His much thinner associate, who towered over him, said: "What are you hoping to find in here?"

"We're not sure," said Jane.

"Must have a reason you're looking again after nineteen years."

In the silence, Maura felt her face flush and wondered if the full responsibility for this outing was going to fall on her shoulders. Then Jane said, "We have reason to believe it wasn't a murder-suicide."

"So we're looking for unexplained footprints? Evidence of an intruder, what?"

"That would be a start."

His stouter colleague sighed. "Okay, we'll give you soup to nuts. You want it, you got it."

"I'll help you unload the van," said Tam.

The men carried in lighting equipment and video gear, electrical cords and chemicals. Although all the lightbulbs in the restaurant had burned out, the power outlets were still live, and when they plugged in the cord to illuminate the dining area, the glare of the lamps was as harsh as sunlight. While one of the criminalists videotaped the room, his partner unpacked boxes of chemicals from a cooler. Only now, in the light, did Maura recognize both men from the rooftop crime scene.

Slowly, the videographer panned the room with the camera and straightened. "Okay, Ed? You ready to start?"

"Soon as everyone gets on their gear," Ed answered. "Masks are in that box over there. We should have enough for everyone."

Tam handed Maura a pair of goggles and a respirator, which she pulled over her face to protect against the luminol fumes. Only after everyone was masked did Ed—at least she now knew the tall man's name—begin mixing chemicals. He swirled the solution in a jar, then decanted it into a spray bottle. "Someone want to be in charge of the lights?"

"I'll do it," said Frost.

"It's gonna be really dark in here, so stay by the lamp or you'll be fumbling for the switch." Ed glanced around the room. "Where do you folks want to start?"

"This section," said Jane, pointing to the area near the cash register.

Ed moved into position, then glanced at Frost. "Lights."

The room went black, and the darkness seemed to magnify the sound of Maura's breathing in the respirator. Only faintly did she hear the hiss of the spray bottle as Ed released a mist of luminol. A geometric pattern of blue-green suddenly glowed on the floor as the luminol reacted with traces of old hemoglobin. Wherever blood drips or splatters or flows, it leaves behind echoes of its presence. Nineteen years ago, blood had seeped into this linoleum, lodging so stubbornly in cracks and crevices that it could not be eradicated, even with the most thorough mopping.

"Light."

Frost flipped the switch and they all stood blinking in the glare. The blue-green glow had vanished; in its place was the same patch of floor they had seen earlier.

Tam looked up from his laptop, on which he'd loaded the Red Phoenix crime scene photos. "Corresponds with what I see here," he said. "No surprises. That's right where Joey Gilmore's body was found."

They moved the camera and tripod to the nook behind the counter, and everyone took their positions. Again the lights went out; again they heard the hiss of the spray bottle and more of the floor began to luminesce in checkerboard lines. Here was where James Fang died. The wall lit up as well, glowing spatters where traces of the waiter's blood had splashed, like the fading echoes of a scream.

In this building, there were still more screams to be heard.

They moved on to the corner where the Mallorys had perished. Two bodies meant twice as many splatters, and here were the loudest shrieks of all, a horror show of splashes and smears that flared in the darkness and slowly faded.

Frost turned on the lights and they all stood silent for a moment as they stared down at the tired patch of floor that had glowed so brightly only a moment earlier. Nothing had surprised them so far, but what they'd seen was nonetheless unsettling.

"Let's move on to the kitchen," said Jane.

They stepped through the doorway. It seemed colder in the next room, so cold that a chill rippled across Maura's skin. She looked around at a refrigerator, an ancient ventilation hood and stove. The floor was concrete in here, designed for easy swabbing in an area where grease and sauces would splatter. *And blood, too.* She stood shivering by the cellar door while the team transferred their equipment from the next room, bringing in their cameras and chemicals. With the room now brightly lit, Ed and his partner frowned at their surroundings.

"Got some rusty-looking kitchen equipment over there," said Ed. "That's going to react with the luminol and light up."

"It's the floor we need to focus on," said Maura. "Right here is where the cook was found."

"So we'll find more blood. Big surprise," said Ed, his note of sarcasm unmistakable.

"Look, if you think this is a waste of time, just give me the bottle and I'll do it," Maura snapped.

In the sudden silence, the two criminalists looked at each other. Ed said, "Do you want to tell us what you're looking for, Dr. Isles? So this might actually make sense?"

"I'll tell you when I see it. Let's start with that doorway leading into the dining room."

Ed nodded to Frost. "Lights off."

The sudden blackness was so complete in the kitchen that Maura felt herself sway, disoriented by the lack of any visual cues, any sense of who or what surrounded her. In this darkness, anyone could be standing beside her and she would not know he was there. The spray bottle hissed, and as glowing streaks of blue-green magically spread on the floor, she felt another chill whisper across her skin, as if a phantom had just brushed past her. Yes, there are indeed ghosts in this room, she thought, the ghosts of spilled blood that still cling to this floor. She heard another hiss of luminol, and more glowing patches materialized.

"I see footprints here," said Ed. "Maybe a woman's size five, six."

"Those are in the crime scene photos, too," Tam said. "The cook's wife was the first person to enter. She lived in the apartment right upstairs. When she heard the gunshot, she walked in through the alley door and found her husband. Tracked his blood into the dining room, where she found the other victims."

"Well, that's what it looks like here. Shoe impressions move in the direction of the dining room."

"The cook was right where I'm standing now," said Maura. "We should focus here."

"Cool your jets, Doc," the criminalist said, and Maura could hear his irritation. "We'll get to that spot."

"I've got this section recorded."

"Okay, moving on."

Maura heard more spray, and new footprints appeared, a luminous record of the wife's movements that night. They followed the prints backward, until suddenly a bright pool bloomed. Here was where Wu Weimin's blood had collected, spilling from the wound on his temple. Maura had read the autopsy report, had seen the close-up photo of what was just a small punch through skin and skull, belying the devastation to the brain. Yet for a few moments, his heart had continued pumping, and blood had poured out to form a congealing halo. Here was where his wife had crouched beside him, leaving her shoe print. *His body would still have been warm.*

"Lights."

Maura blinked at the floor where she now saw only bare concrete. But as Ed refilled the bottle with luminol, she could still see that pool, and the evidence of the wife's presence.

"We'll finish up over there," said Ed, pointing toward the kitchen exit leading to the alley. "Did the wife leave the same way she came in?"

"No," said Tam. "According to Ingersoll's report, she ran out the front exit, down Knapp Street. Headed toward Beach Street to call for help."

"So there shouldn't be any blood at this end."

Tam peered at his laptop. "I don't see any in this crime scene photo."

Maura saw Ed glance at his wristwatch, a reminder that it was growing late. What they had captured so far on video was exactly what they'd expected to find. She thought of what these two men would probably say to each other later, comments that would no doubt circulate among the rest of Boston PD. *Dr. Isles sent us on a wild goose chase.*

Was this a mistake? she wondered. Have I wasted everyone's evening, all because I listened to the doubts of a sixteen-year-old boy? But Maura, too, had shared Rat's doubts. After he'd returned to school, leaving her alone in a house that seemed sadly silent and empty, she had spent many hours combing through all the reports and photos from the Red Phoenix files. The baffling details that the boy had so quickly spotted became more and more troubling to her as well.

"Let's wrap this up and go home,"

said Jane, sounding both weary and a little disgusted.

The lights went out again, and Maura stood with hands clenched, glad that her face was hidden in the darkness. She heard the spray bottle once again deliver its mist of luminol.

Suddenly Ed blurted: "Hey, are you seeing this?"

"Lights!" Jane called out, and Frost turned on the lamp.

In the glare, they all stood silent for a moment, staring at bare concrete.

"That didn't show up in any of the crime scene photos," said Tam.

Ed was frowning. "Let me replay this video," he said. As they crowded around the camera, he rewound and hit Play. Glowing in the darkness were three blue-green patches that moved in a line toward the alley exit. Two were smeared and misshapen, but the third was un-mistakably a tiny footprint.

"Maybe they're not related to the shooting at all," said Jane. "These stains could be cumulative, over years."

"*Two* bloody incidents in the same kitchen?" said Tam.

"How do we explain the fact that these footprints aren't in any of the crime scene photos?"

"Because someone cleaned them up," said Maura softly. "Before the police arrived." Yet the traces remain here, she thought. Invisible to the human eye, but not to luminol.

The others looked stunned by what had just been revealed. A child had been in this kitchen, a child who had stepped into blood and had tracked it across the floor and out the door, into the alley.

"The cellar," said Jane. She crossed to the cellar door and swung it open. As Maura moved beside her, Jane shone her flashlight down the wooden steps. From the blackness below rose the smell of damp stone and mold. The beam of Jane's flashlight pierced shadows, and Maura glimpsed large barrels and giant tins of cooking oil, surely spoiled after two decades in storage.

"The cook died right here, blocking this door," said Jane. She turned to Ed. "Let's look at these top steps."

There were no impatient looks this

time, no sighs or glances at their watches. The criminalists moved swiftly to reposition the camera and tripod, aiming it down the cellar stairs. They all crowded in as the lights went out, and Ed unleashed a final hiss of luminol. Only then did they see that blood had trickled from the kitchen above and had dripped down onto the top step.

A step where they could see the treadmark of a small shoe.

TWENTY-FOUR

"Someone was in the kitchen cellar that night, Mrs. Fang. A child who may know what really happened," says Detective Rizzoli. "Do you know who that child was?"

The policewoman studies me, monitoring my reaction as I absorb what she has just told me. Through the closed door I can hear the sharp clacks of fighting sticks and the voices of my students chanting in unison as they practice their combat maneuvers. But here in my office it is silent as I weigh my possible responses. My silence alone is a reaction, and Detective Rizzoli is trying to read its meaning, but I allow no emotions to ripple the surface of my face. Between the two of us, this has become a chess game within a chess game, played with subtle moves that Detective Frost, who also stands watching, is probably not even aware of.

The woman is my true opponent. I look straight at her as I ask: "How do you know there was someone in the cellar?"

"There were footprints left behind in the kitchen, and on the cellar steps. A child's footprints."

"But it happened nineteen years ago."

"Even after many years, Mrs. Fang, blood leaves behind traces," explains Frost. His voice is gentler, a friend's, patiently explaining what he believes I do not understand. "With certain chemicals, we can see where blood has been tracked. And we know that a child came out of the cellar, stepped in Wu Weimin's blood, and walked out of the kitchen, into the alley."

"No one told me this before. Detective Ingersoll never said anything."

"Because he didn't see those footprints," says Detective Rizzoli. "By the time the police arrived that night, the prints were gone. Wiped away." She moves in closer, so close that I can see her pupils, two black bull's-eyes in chocolate-brown irises. "Who would do that, Mrs. Fang? Who would want to hide the fact a child was in the cellar?"

"Why do you ask me? I wasn't even in the country. I was in Taiwan visiting my family when it happened."

"But you knew Wu Weimin and his wife. Like them, you speak Mandarin. The child in the cellar was their little girl, wasn't it?" She pulls out a pocket notebook and reads from it. "Mei Mei, five years old." She looks at me. "Where did they go, the mother and daughter?"

"How would I know? I couldn't catch a flight home until three days later. By then, they were gone. They packed up their clothes, their belongings. I have no idea where they went."

"Why did they run? Was it because the wife was illegal?"

My jaw tightens, and I glare back at her. "Are you surprised that she *would* run? If I were illegal, Detective, and you thought my husband had just killed four people, how quickly would you put *me* in handcuffs and have *me* deported? The girl may have been born here, but Li Hua wasn't. She wanted her daughter to grow up in America, so can you blame her for avoiding the police? For staying in the shadows?"

"If she wiped away those footprints, then she destroyed important evidence."

"Maybe it was to protect her daughter."

"The girl was a witness. She could have changed the course of that investigation."

"And would you put a five-year-old girl in a courtroom and have her testify? Do you think a jury would believe a child of illegal immigrants, when the whole city has already called the father a monster?"

My answer takes her aback. She falls silent, thinking about the logic of what I've said. Realizing that Li Hua's actions were in fact reasonable. It was the logic of a mother desperate to protect herself and her child from authorities whom she did not trust.

Frost says, gently: "We're not the enemy, Mrs. Fang. We're just trying to learn the truth."

"I told the truth nineteen years ago," I point out. "I told the police that Wu Weimin would never hurt anyone, but that wasn't what they wanted to hear. It was so much easier for them to think he was a crazy Chinaman, and who cares what goes on in a Chinaman's head?" I hear the bitterness in my own voice, but don't try to suppress it. It spills forth, sharp and grating. "Searching for the *truth* is too much work. That's what the police thought."

"It's not what I think," says Frost quietly.

I stare back at him and see sincerity in his eyes. In the next room the class has ended, and I hear students departing, the door whooshing shut again and again.

"If Mei Mei was in that cellar," says Detective Rizzoli, "we need to find her. We need to know what she remembers."

"And you would believe her?"

"It depends on what kind of girl she is. What can you tell us about her?"

I think about this for a moment, looking back through the fog of nineteen years. "I remember she was afraid of nothing. She was never still, always running and jumping. *The little tiger,* her father called her. When my daughter, Laura, would babysit, she'd come home exhausted. She told me she never wanted to have children, if they were going to be as wild as Mei Mei."

"An intelligent girl?"

I give her a sad smile. "Do you have children, Detective?"

"I have a two-year-old daughter."

"And you probably think she's the cleverest child ever born."

Now it was Rizzoli's turn to smile. "I know she is."

"Because all children seem clever, don't they? Little Mei Mei was so quick, so curious . . ." My voice fades and I swallow hard. "When they left, it was like losing my own daughter all over again."

"Where did they go?"

I shake my head. "There was a cousin

in California, I think. Li Hua was only in her twenties, and so beautiful. She could have married again. She could have a different name."

"You have no idea where she is now?"

I pause just long enough to raise a doubt in her mind. To make her wonder if my answer is truthful. The chess game between us continues, move followed by countermove.

"No," I finally answer. "I don't even know if she's alive."

There is a knock on the door, and Bella steps into the office. She is flushed from the exertions of teaching class, and her short black hair stands up, stiff with sweat. She dips her head in a bow.

"*Sifu,* the last class of the day has left. Will you need me?"

"Wait a moment. We are just finishing here."

It is clear to the two detectives that I have nothing more to offer them, and they turn to leave. As they walk to the door, Rizzoli pauses and regards Bella. It is a long, speculative look, and I can almost see the thoughts whirring in her head. *Mei Mei was five years old when she vanished. How old is this young woman? Could it be possible?* But Rizzoli says nothing, merely nods goodbye and walks out of the studio.

After the door shuts, I say to Bella: "We are running out of time."

"Do they know?"

"They're closer to the truth." I draw in a deep breath, and it worries me that I cannot cast off the new fatigue that now drags me down. I am fighting two battles at once, one of them against the enemy that smolders in my own bone marrow. I know that one of these enemies is certain to take my life.

The only question is, which one will kill me first?

TWENTY-FIVE

Now there were three missing girls.

Jane sipped lukewarm coffee and ate a chicken salad sandwich as she reviewed her growing stack of folders. On her desk were files on Jane Doe, the Red Phoenix massacre, and the disappearances of Laura Fang and Charlotte Dion. She'd started a new file on yet another missing girl: Mei Mei, the cook's daughter who had vanished along with her mother nineteen years ago. Mei Mei would be twenty-four years old now, perhaps married and living under a different name. They had no photos of her, no fingerprints, no idea what she looked like. She might not even reside in the country. Or she could be right under their noses, teaching martial arts in a Chinatown studio, Jane thought, and she pictured Iris's stony-faced assistant, Bella Li, whose background they were already looking into.

Of the three girls, Mei Mei was the only one likely to be alive. The other two were almost certainly dead.

Jane turned her attention back to Laura Fang and Charlotte Dion. To the startling connection between them, despite the gulf that separated their lives. Charlotte was wealthy and white. Laura was the daughter of struggling Chinese immigrants. Charlotte grew up in a Brookline mansion, Laura in a cramped Chinatown apartment. Two such different girls, yet both had lost parents in the restaurant shooting, and now their files shared equal space on Jane's desk in the homicide unit—not a place where anyone wanted to end up. Paging through their files, she heard the echo of Ingersoll's last words to her:

It's all about what happened to those girls.

Were these the girls he'd meant?

Patrick Dion's estate looked no less impressive the second time she saw it.

Jane drove between the twin stone pillars onto the private road that took her past birch trees and lilacs and up the rolling lawn to the massive Colonial. As she pulled up under the porte cochere, Patrick emerged from the house to greet her.

"Thank you for seeing me again," she said as they shook hands.

"Is there news about Charlotte?" he asked, and it was painful to see the hope in his eyes, to hear the tremor in his voice.

"I'm sorry if I wasn't clear about the reason for my visit," she said. "I'm afraid I don't have anything new to report."

"But you said on the phone that you wanted to talk about Charlotte."

"This is in connection to our current investigation. The murder in Chinatown."

"What does that have to do with my daughter?"

"I'm not sure, Mr. Dion. But there've been developments that make me think Charlotte's disappearance is connected with another missing girl."

"That was already explored years ago, by Detective Buckholz."

"I'd like to look at it again. Even though it's been nineteen years, I won't let your daughter be forgotten. Charlotte deserves better than that."

She saw him blink away tears, and she knew that for him the loss was still raw, the pain still alive. Parents never forget.

With a weary nod, he said: "Come inside. I've brought her things down from the attic, as you requested. Please take as long as you need to look through them."

She followed him into the foyer and was once again impressed by gleaming hardwood floors, by oil portraits that appeared to be at least two centuries old. She could not help comparing this house with Kevin Donohue's residence, with its pedestrian furniture and shopping mall art. Old money versus new money. Patrick led her into the formal dining room, where Palladian windows looked out over a lily pond. On the rosewood dining table, large enough to seat a dozen guests, was a collection of cardboard boxes.

"This is what I saved," he said sadly. "Most of her clothes, I finally gave away to charity. Charlotte would have approved, I think. She cared about that sort of thing, feeding the poor, housing the needy." He looked around at the room and gave an ironic laugh. "You probably think it sounds hypocritical, don't you? Saying that while I live in this house, on this property. But my daughter really *did* have a good heart. A generous heart." He reached into one of the boxes and lifted out a pair of frayed blue jeans. Stared at it, as if he could still see them clinging to his daughter's slim hips. "Funny, how I never could bring myself to give these away. Blue jeans never go out of style. If she ever comes back, I know she'll want them." Gently he set them back in the box and breathed out a long sigh.

"I'm so sorry, Mr. Dion. About bringing all this pain back to you. Would it be easier for you if I looked through these boxes on my own?"

"No, I'll need to explain things. You won't know what some of it means." He reached into a different box and pulled out a photo album. Clutched it for a moment, as if reluctant to release it. When he held it out to Jane it was with both hands, a precious offering that she took with equal reverence. "This is what you probably want to see."

She opened the cover. On the first page was a photo of a young blond woman holding a red-faced newborn, the baby swaddled like a tiny mummy in a white blanket. OUR CHARLOTTE, EIGHT HOURS OLD was written beneath it with the extravagant loops and flourishes of a woman's hand. So this was Dina when she was still Patrick's fresh-faced bride. Before Arthur Mallory stepped into their lives and fractured their marriage.

"Charlotte was your only child?" Jane asked.

"Dina insisted that we have only one.

At the time, I was fine with it. But now . . ."

Now he regrets it, she thought. Regrets pouring all his love and hopes into a child he would one day lose. She turned the pages and studied other photos of Charlotte as a blue-eyed, golden-haired toddler. Occasionally Dina appeared, but Patrick was in none of the photos, except as an elusive shadow cast at the edge of the frame while he held the camera. Jane turned to the final page in the album, the year Charlotte turned four years old.

Patrick handed her the next volume.

The years seemed to accelerate in this second album, the girl growing, changing every few pages. After the flurry of attention devoted to a child's first years, after the novelty of new parenthood wears off, taking photos becomes an afterthought, the camera brought out only when the special occasion calls for it. A fifth-birthday party. A first ballet recital. A visit to New York City. Suddenly that cherubic toddler transformed into a glum-faced adolescent, posing in her school uniform at the front gate of the Bolton Academy.

"She was twelve years old in this photo," said Patrick. "I remember she hated that uniform. Said that plaid makes a girl look fat, and that was why the school made them wear it. To make the girls look so ugly, they wouldn't get into trouble with any of the boys."

"Did she not want to go to Bolton?"

"Oh, she certainly did want to go. But I admit, I wasn't happy about seeing her leave. I had such a hard time losing my little girl to boarding school. Dina insisted because it was the school that she graduated from, a place where a girl could *meet all the right people.* That was how Dina put it." He paused. "God, that probably sounds so superficial, but Dina was completely focused on things like that. On Charlotte making the right friends and marrying the right man." He paused and added, ironically, "As it turned out, it was Dina who met a husband at Bolton."

"That must have been hard for you when Dina left."

Patrick gave a resigned shrug. "I accepted it. What else could I do? And oddly enough, I rather liked Arthur Mallory. Liked the whole Mallory family, in fact—Barbara, their son. Mark. All of them were decent people. But hormones are an irresistible force. I think I lost my wife to Arthur the very first time they laid eyes on each other. All I could do was stand by and watch my marriage fall apart."

Jane turned to the last page and studied the final image in the album. It was a wedding photo, and standing at the center were the new bride and groom, Dina and Arthur Mallory, both dressed in formal attire. Flanking them were their respective children, Mark standing at his father's side, Charlotte at her mother's. While bride and groom were beaming, Charlotte looked dazed, as if she did not know how she'd come to be standing with these people.

"How old is Charlotte in this photo?" Jane asked.

"She would have been thirteen there."

"She looks a little lost."

"It happened so fast, I think we were all stunned. We'd met the Mallorys only a year before, when Charlotte and Mark both performed at the Bolton Academy Christmas pageant. A year later, all of us once again attended the Bolton Christmas pageant, but by then Dina had left me for Arthur. And I was just another single father, raising a daughter on my own."

"Charlotte stayed with you after the divorce?"

"Dina and I discussed it, and we both felt it was best if I had custody so that Charlotte could stay in the house where she'd grown up. Every few months, Charlotte was supposed to spend a weekend with Dina and Arthur, but they traveled so much they were seldom home."

"And there was no legal battle, no tug-of-war over your daughter?"

"Just because two people get divorced doesn't mean they don't care about each other. We did care. And we were now all part of an extended family. Arthur's ex-wife, Barbara, had some difficulty accepting the divorce, I'm afraid, and she remained bitter to the end. But

I saw no point in hanging on to resentments. It's called being civilized."

That was what Ingersoll had written in his report, that Patrick Dion and his ex-wife had stayed cordial even after the divorce. Now, hearing it from Patrick himself, she could believe it.

"They even spent their last Christmas here, with me," he said. "Arthur and Dina and Mark. We had dinner together, in this room. Opened gifts." He looked around the table, as if seeing their ghosts still seated there. "I remember Charlotte was there, at that end of the table, asking Mark about Harvard and whether he liked it there. Dina gave her a pearl necklace. We had pumpkin pie for dessert. And afterward, I took Mark downstairs to my woodshop, because he loves working with his hands. The Harvard kid who'd rather be building fine furniture." Patrick blinked and looked at her, as if suddenly remembering she was there. "Now they're gone. And there's only Mark and me left."

"You two seem close."

"Oh, he's a fine young man." Patrick paused and suddenly smiled. "Mark's already thirty-nine, but at my age, any-one under forty still seems like a young man."

Jane pulled another book out of the box—not a family album this time, but a Bolton Academy yearbook with the school's seal embossed in gold on the maroon leather.

"She was a sophomore that year," said Patrick, looking at the cover. "That was the year before she . . ." He paused, his face darkening. "I thought about su-ing the school for negligence. They took my daughter on a field trip without ad-equate supervision. There they were, in a public place. Faneuil Hall! They should have known some of the kids might wander off, or some stranger might ap-proach them. But the teachers, they didn't pay attention, and suddenly my girl was gone. I was an ocean away, where I couldn't do a damn thing to save her."

"I understand you were in London."

He nodded. "Meeting with some po-tential investors, adding to my goddamn fortune. I'd throw this all away, if only I could . . ." Suddenly he stood up. "I think I could use a stiff drink right now. Can I pour you one?"

"Thank you, but no. I'm driving."

"Ah. The responsible policewoman. If you'll excuse me," he said, and walked out.

Jane opened the Bolton yearbook to the sophomore section and spotted Charlotte in the bottom row of photos. Her blond hair hung loose to her shoulders, and her lips were barely curved in a wistful smile. She was a beautiful girl, but tragedy already seemed stamped into her features, as if she knew that the future held only heartbreak for her. Printed beneath her photo was a list of her interests and activities. DRAMA CLUB. ART. ORCHESTRA. TENNIS TEAM.

Orchestra. She remembered that Charlotte had played the viola. She also remembered that Laura Fang had played the violin. The girls might have grown up in different universes, but they had music in common.

She paged through the book until she found the activities section, where she once again spotted Charlotte, posing with two dozen other music students.

The girl was seated in the second row of string players, her instrument propped in her lap. The caption read: CANDACE FORSYTH, MUSICAL DIRECTOR, AND THE BOLTON ACADEMY ORCHESTRA.

She heard Patrick return to the dining room, carrying a drink that tinkled with ice cubes. "Did your daughter know a girl named Laura Fang?" Jane asked him.

"Detective Buckholz asked me that same question, after Charlotte disappeared. I told him I hadn't heard the name before. I only found out later that Laura Fang was a girl who vanished two years before Charlotte. That's when I understood why he asked me about her."

"You can't think of any link between the girls? Charlotte never mentioned Laura's name?"

He looked at the photo of the Bolton orchestra. "Your child comes home from school and talks about this girl or that boy. How can any parent possibly remember all the names?"

He was right; it was an impossible thing to expect of a parent.

Jane flipped to the back of the book, to the section of senior students, and scanned the photos of clean-cut boys dressed in their Bolton uniforms of blue blazers and red neckties. There was Mark Mallory, his face a bit thinner, his hair longer and curlier. Already he was a handsome young man, bound for Harvard. Beneath his photo, his interests were listed: LACROSSE, ORCHESTRA, CHESS, FENCING, DRAMA.

Orchestra again. That was, after all, how the Dions and Mallorys had met—through their musical children at the Christmas pageant.

"I'm not quite sure how any of this is going to help you," said Patrick. "Detective Buckholz asked me all these questions nineteen years ago."

She looked up at him. "Maybe the answers have changed."

As Jane left Brookline and drove west on the Massachusetts Turnpike, the afternoon sun was in her eyes. She made good time to Worcester, but the drive north from that point was slow, on secondary roads where traffic funneled into a single lane because of repaving work. By the time she reached the Bolton Academy, it was nearly five PM. She drove through the front gate, onto a curving drive shaded by ancient oak trees. At the main hall, three girls sat chatting on the stone steps. They did not even bother to look up as Jane parked and climbed out of her car. They appeared to be fifteen or sixteen, all of them slim and pretty, perfectly designed by Mother Nature to fulfill their biological purpose on earth and attract young men.

"Excuse me. I'm looking for Mrs. Forsyth, the music director," said Jane.

The three goddesses responded with passive stares. Even in their plaid skirts and white cotton blouses, they managed to make Jane feel hopelessly unfashionable.

"She's in Bennett Hall," one of the girls finally said.

"Where's that?"

The girl extended a graceful arm to point at the stately building across the lawn. "There."

"Thanks." As Jane walked across the

lawn, she felt their eyes following her, the alien specimen from the world of merely ordinary people. So this was what boarding school was like, not a fun place like Hogwarts at all. More like sorority hell. She came to the steps of Bennett Hall and gazed up at the white columns, the elaborately carved pediment. It's like scaling Mount Olympus, she thought as she climbed the stairs into the central hall.

The sound of a scratchy violin drifted from the corridor to her left. She followed it to a classroom where a teenage girl sat bowing with fierce concentration while a silver-haired woman frowned at her.

"For heaven's sake, Amanda, your vibrato sounds like a high-tension wire! It makes me nervous just listening to it. And you're practically strangling the neck. Relax your wrist." The woman tugged at the girl's left hand and gave it a hard shake. "Come on, loosen up!"

The student suddenly noticed Jane and froze. The woman turned and said: "Yes?"

"Mrs. Forsyth? I called earlier. I'm Detective Rizzoli."

"We're just finishing up here." The teacher turned to her student and sighed. "You're all tensed up today, so there's no point continuing the lesson. Go back to the dorm and practice shaking your wrists. Both hands. Above all, a violinist must have flexible wrists."

Resignedly the girl packed up her instrument. She was about to walk out of the room when she abruptly stopped and said to Jane: "You said you're a detective. Are you, like, with the police?"

Jane nodded. "Boston PD."

"That is *so* cool! I want to be an FBI agent someday."

"Then you should go for it. The Bureau could use more women."

"Yeah, tell that to my parents. They say police work is for *other* people," she muttered and slouched out of the room.

"I'm afraid that girl is never going to be much of a musician," said Mrs. Forsyth.

"The last I heard," said Jane, "playing

the violin isn't a requirement for the FBI."

That sarcastic remark did not win Jane any points with this woman. Mrs. Forsyth eyed her coolly. "You said you had questions, Detective?"

"About one of your students from nineteen years ago. She was in the school orchestra. Played the viola."

"You're here about Charlotte Dion, aren't you?" Seeing Jane's nod, the woman sighed. "Of course it *would* be about Charlotte. The one student no one ever lets us forget. Even all these years later, Mr. Dion still blames us, doesn't he? For losing his daughter."

"It would be hard for any parent to accept. You can understand that."

"Boston PD thoroughly investigated her disappearance, and they never considered our school negligent. We had more than enough chaperones on that excursion, a ratio of one to six. And these weren't toddlers on the outing, these were teenagers. We shouldn't have to babysit them." She added under her breath, "But with Charlotte, maybe we should have."

"Why?"

Mrs. Forsyth paused. "I'm sorry, I shouldn't have said that."

"Was Charlotte difficult?"

"I don't like to speak ill of the dead."

"I think the dead would want justice served."

After a moment the woman nodded. "I'll just say this about her: She was not one of our academic stars. Oh, she was bright enough. That showed up in her entrance exam scores. And the first year she was here, she did fine. But after her parents divorced, everything went downhill for her and she barely passed most of her classes. Of course we felt sorry for her, but half our students come from divorced families. They're able to adjust and move on. Charlotte never did. She just remained a morose girl. It's as if, just by her poor-me attitude, she *attracted* bad luck."

For a woman who didn't like to speak ill of the dead, Mrs. Forsyth certainly had no trouble letting loose.

"She can hardly be blamed for losing her mother," Jane pointed out.

"No, of course not. That was awful, that shooting in Chinatown. But have you ever noticed the way misfortune seems to target certain people? They'll lose their spouse, their job, and get cancer all in the same year. That was Charlotte, always gloomy, always attracting bad luck. Which may be why she didn't seem to have a lot of friends."

This was certainly not the impression of Charlotte that Jane had picked up from talking with Patrick. It surprised her to hear about this side of the girl.

"In the school yearbook, she seemed to have a healthy list of activities," Jane said. "Music, for instance."

Mrs. Forsyth nodded. "She was a decent violist, but her heart never seemed to be in it. Only in her junior year did she finally manage to pass the auditions for the Boston summer orchestra workshop. But it helped that she played the viola. They're always in demand."

"How many of your students attend that workshop?"

"At least a few every year. It's the best in New England, taught by members of the Boston Symphony Orchestra. Very selective." Mrs. Forsyth paused. "I know who you're going to ask about next. That Chinese girl who disappeared, right?"

Jane nodded. "You read my mind. Her name was Laura Fang."

"I understand she was a talented girl. That's what I heard after she vanished. A number of my students attended the workshop with her."

"But not Charlotte?"

"No. Charlotte didn't pass the audition until the year after Laura disappeared, so they wouldn't have met each other. Another question you were about to ask, I'm sure."

"You remember all these details, even after nineteen years?"

"Because I just went over it again with that detective."

"Which detective?"

"I can't remember his name. It was a few weeks ago. I'd have to check my appointment book."

"I'd appreciate it if you looked up his name right now, ma'am."

A look of irritation flickered in the woman's eyes, as if this was more effort than she cared to make. But she crossed to her desk and rummaged through a drawer until she came up with a daily planner. Flipping back through the pages, she gave a nod. "Here. He called me April second to schedule an appointment. I thought he looked a bit old to be a detective, but I guess experience counts for something."

A bit old. And asking about missing girls. "Was his name Detective Ingersoll?" Jane asked.

Mrs. Forsyth glanced up. "So you do know him."

"Haven't you heard the news? Detective Ingersoll is dead. He was shot to death last week."

The appointment book tumbled from Mrs. Forsyth's hands and slapped onto her desk. "My God. No, I didn't know."

"Why was he here, Mrs. Forsyth? Why was he asking about Charlotte?"

"I assumed it was her father pushing for it, still hoping for answers. I mentioned it to Mark Mallory at the alumni dinner a few weeks ago, but he didn't know anything about it."

"Did you ask Mr. Dion?"

She flushed. "The Bolton Academy avoids any contact whatsoever with Mr. Dion. To avoid dredging up . . . bad feelings."

"Tell me exactly what Detective Ingersoll said to you."

The woman sank into the chair behind her desk. Suddenly she looked smaller and less formidable, stunned by this intrusion of the brutal outside world into her sheltered universe of books and orchestral scores. "I'm sorry, give me a moment to think about it . . ." She swallowed. "He didn't actually ask very much about Charlotte. It was more about the other girl."

"Laura Fang."

"And others."

"Others?"

"He had a list. A long list with maybe two dozen names. He asked if I recognized any of them. If any had attended Bolton. I told him no."

"Do you remember any of the names on that list?"

"No. As I said, I didn't know any of them. He told me they were all girls who'd gone missing like Laura." Mrs. Forsyth straightened and looked up at Jane. "Girls who've never been found."

TWENTY-SIX

"These are Detective Ingersoll's cell and landline phone records for the past thirty days," said Tam, spreading out the pages on the conference table so Jane and Frost could see them. "It's a list of every call he made and received over the past month. At first glance, nothing jumps out at you. It's mostly mundane stuff. Calls to his daughter, his dentist, his cable company, his credit card company. A call to the fishing camp where he stayed in Maine. And multiple calls to the pizza parlor down his street."

"Geez. He sure ate a lot of pizza," observed Frost.

"You'll also notice that he called family members of the Red Phoenix victims. Those particular calls were made on March thirtieth and April first. Right around the anniversary of the massacre."

"I spoke to both Mrs. Gilmore and Mark Mallory," said Frost. "They confirmed that Ingersoll called them, to find out if they received the usual anonymous mailing that he did. The one they've all been getting every year."

"But then there are a few calls on the list that don't make sense to me," said Tam. "The ones that seem completely random." He tapped his finger on one of the phone numbers. "This one, for instance. April sixth, Lowell. My Best Friend Dog Groomers." Tam looked up at his colleagues. "As far as we know, Ingersoll never owned a dog."

"Maybe he was dating the groomer," said Jane.

"I called the number," Tam said. "They'd never heard of him, and he wasn't on their doggy client list. I thought

maybe he'd called a wrong number."
He pointed to another entry. "Then
there's this call, April eighth, to Worcester. It's the number for the Shady Lady
Lingerie store."

Jane grimaced. "I'm not sure I want
to know the details on that one."

"When I spoke to the store," said
Tam, "no one recognized the name Ingersoll. So I assumed it was just another wrong number."

"A reasonable assumption."

"But incorrect. He *did* mean to call
that number."

"Please tell me he was buying sexy
underwear for a girlfriend and not for
himself," said Jane.

"Sexy underwear was not involved.
His phone call wasn't meant for the
Shady Lady at all, but for the party who
used to have that number."

Jane frowned. "How did you figure
that out?"

"After your visit to the Bolton Academy, I pulled up the state database of
missing girls, just as you asked. I put
together a list of every girl who's van-

ished in Massachusetts over the past twenty-five years."

"You went that far back?" said Frost.

"Charlotte vanished nineteen years ago. Laura Fang twenty-one years ago. I arbitrarily chose twenty-five as the cut-off, to give myself a good margin, and I'm glad I did." Tam pulled a page from a bulging folder and slid it across the table to Jane. Midway down the page was a phone number circled in red ink. "This is the number Ingersoll called, the one now assigned to Shady Lady. Twenty-two years ago, that same number was listed under the name Mr. Gregory Boles in Worcester. Twelve years ago, the number was reassigned to another party. And then four years ago, it became the number for Shady Lady Lingerie. Phone numbers turn over all the time, and with more and more people giving up landlines, the turnover's even more frequent. I think that's the party Detective Ingersoll was actually trying to reach. Gregory Boles. But Boles moved out of state twelve years ago."

"Who is Gregory Boles?" asked Frost.

Scanning down the page of phone numbers, Jane suddenly felt a thrill of comprehension. "These are the contact numbers from the missing children's database." She looked up.

Tam nodded. "Gregory Boles is the father of a missing girl. I was planning to review all the cases that are currently open in the state. Every female under eighteen who's vanished during the past twenty five-years." He pointed to the bulging folder he'd brought in. "But I realized it was a monumental task, sifting through them all, trying to find any links with Charlotte or Laura. And to be honest, I was kind of pissed off about getting assigned the task, because I thought it was just busywork."

"But you ended up finding something," Jane said.

"Yes I did. I got the idea of cross-referencing all the phone numbers from Ingersoll's phone log. Every number he called from either his landline or his cell phone. Judging by the numbers on his call log, he started tracking down certain families in early April. Then he abruptly stopped making any phone calls at all. From either his cell phone or his landline."

"Because he thought he was being monitored," said Jane. A suspicion that had proven true; the crime lab had indeed found an electronic bug in Ingersoll's landline phone.

"Based on the calls he made before he stopped using those phones, these are the missing girls he was homing in on." Tam slid a single page in front of her.

Jane saw only three names. "What do we know about these girls?"

"They were different ages. Thirteen, fifteen, and sixteen. They all vanished within a hundred and fifty miles of Boston. Two were white, one was Asian."

"Like Laura Fang," said Frost.

"Also like Laura," said Tam, "these were what you'd call good girls. A or B students. No delinquency, no reason to think they'd be runaways. Maybe that's why Ingersoll grouped them together on his list. He thought that was the common denominator."

"How old are these cases?" asked Frost.

"These girls all vanished more than twenty years ago."

"So he was just looking at old cases? Why not more recent ones?"

"I don't know. Maybe he was just getting started. If he hadn't been killed, maybe he would have come up with more names. The thing that puzzles me is why he got himself involved in this in the first place. He didn't work these disappearances when he was with Boston PD, so what drew him to this now? Was retirement so boring?"

"Maybe someone hired him to do PI work. Could have been one of the families."

"That was my first thought," said Tam. "I've been able to reach all three families, but no one hired Ingersoll. And we know Patrick Dion didn't, either."

"So maybe he was doing this for himself," said Frost. "Some cops just can't handle retirement."

"None of these three girls would have been Boston PD cases," said Jane. "They're all from different jurisdictions."

"But Charlotte Dion vanished in Boston. So did Laura Fang. They could have been Ingersoll's starting points, the reason he got involved."

Jane looked at the names of the three new girls. "And now he's dead," she said softly. "What the hell did he get himself into?"

"Kevin Donohue's territory," said Tam.

Jane and Frost looked up at him. Although Tam had been working with them for barely two weeks, he had already acquired a hint of cockiness. In his suit and tie, with his neatly clipped hair and icy stare, he could pass for Secret Service or one of those comic book Men in Black. Not someone you could easily get to know, and certainly not a guy Jane could imagine ever knocking back beers with.

"Word on the street," said Tam, "is that Donohue's been running girls for years. Prostitution's just one of his sidelines."

Jane nodded. "Yeah. Another meaning of *Donohue Wholesale Meats.*"

"What if this is how he obtains those girls?"

"By kidnapping A students?" Jane shook her head. "Somehow, it seems like a risky method of picking up under-aged prostitutes. There are easier ways."

"But it would tie everything together. Joey Gilmore, missing girls, and the Red Phoenix. Maybe Ingersoll discovered the link to Donohue, and that's when he got spooked. Why he stopped using his phones. Because if Donohue got wind of it, Ingersoll knew he'd be a dead man."

"Ingersoll *is* a dead man," said Jane. "What we don't know is *why* he started asking questions. After all these years in retirement, why did he suddenly get interested in missing girls?"

Tam said, "Maybe what we really need to ask is: Who was he working for?"

Now there were six.

Jane sat at her desk, reviewing what she knew about the three new names on the list. The first to vanish was Deborah Schiffer, age thirteen, of Lowell, Massachusetts. Daughter of a doctor and a schoolteacher, she'd been five foot two, one hundred pounds, with brown hair and brown eyes. Twenty-five years ago, she vanished somewhere between her middle school and her piano teacher's house. A straight-A student, she was described as shy and bookish, with no known boyfriends. Had that been the age of the Internet, they would probably know a great deal more about her, but Facebook and MySpace and online chat groups had yet to be invented.

A year and a half later, the next girl on the list disappeared. Patricia Boles, fifteen, was last seen at a shopping mall, where she'd been dropped off by her mother. Three hours later, Patricia did not show up at the appointed meeting place. She was five foot three, 105 pounds, with blond hair and blue eyes. Like Deborah Schiffer, she was an above-average student who had never been in trouble. Her disappearance no doubt contributed to the subsequent breakup of her parents' marriage. Her mother died seven years later; her father, whom Jane was finally able to reach at his current residence in Florida, scarcely wanted to talk about his long-lost daughter. "I'm remarried and I have three kids now. It hurts too much to even hear Patty's name," he told Jane over the phone. Yes, he'd received calls from the police over the years about the case. Yes, he'd spoken to Detective Ingersoll recently. But nothing had ever come of those calls.

After Patty Boles's disappearance, more than a year passed before the next girl went missing. Sherry Tanaka was sixteen, petite, and a high school junior in Attleboro. She vanished from her own home one afternoon, leaving the front door ajar, her homework still spread across the dining room table. Her mother, who was now living in Connecticut, had recently received a letter from Detective Ingersoll asking to speak with her about Sherry. It was dated April 4, and had been forwarded through a series of old addresses. She had tried calling his phone number just yesterday, but it rang unanswered.

Because Ingersoll was now dead.

Mrs. Tanaka did not know any of the girls on the list, nor had she heard of Charlotte Dion. But the name Laura Fang was familiar, because she was an

Asian girl like Sherry, and that detail had stuck in Mrs. Tanaka's mind. It had made her wonder if there was a link. Years ago, she had called the Attleboro police about it, but had heard nothing back since.

Having three Massachusetts girls go missing over a period of six years was not in itself surprising. Each year across the country, thousands of children between the ages of twelve and seventeen went missing, many no doubt abducted by non–family members. Dozens of girls in Massachusetts had vanished during that same time period, girls in the same age group, who had not made it onto Ingersoll's list. Why had he focused on these particular victims? Was it because they were of similar ages and statures? Because they were all taken from locations within an easy drive of Highway 495, which encircled the Boston metropolitan area?

And then there was seventeen-year-old Charlotte Dion. Unlike the other girls, she'd been older and a disinterested C-minus student. How did she fit into the pattern?

Maybe there was no pattern. Maybe Ingersoll had been searching for links that did not exist.

Jane set aside the notes on the three girls and turned her attention to the folder on Charlotte, which had been compiled by Detective Buckholz. It was a great deal thicker than Laura Fang's file, and she had to assume it was because of the Dion name. Wealth did count, even in matters of justice. Especially, perhaps, in matters of justice. A child's disappearance would forever haunt any parent, would make him wonder as the decades passed if that young woman he glimpsed on the street might be a long-lost daughter, grown up. Or was she just another random stranger like all the others, whose smile or curve of a lip seemed, for an instant, heart-breakingly familiar?

Jane opened the envelope containing what were probably the last images ever recorded of Charlotte, which they'd obtained from the *Boston Globe* photo files. There were a dozen photos taken at the double burial service of Arthur and Dina Mallory. The horrific nature of their deaths, and the extensive publicity surrounding the Red Phoenix massacre, had drawn nearly two hundred people to the cemetery that day, according to the *Globe* article, and the photographer had taken several long shots of the somberly dressed gathering standing beside two open graves.

But the most arresting images were the close-ups of the family. Charlotte stood dead center, the dramatic focus of the composition, and no wonder: With her pale features, her long blond hair, she was the fragile embodiment of grief. Her hand was lifted to her mouth, as though to stifle a sob, and her face was contorted in a look of physical pain. Standing on her right was her father, Patrick, looking at her with concern. But her body was turned away from him, as though she did not want him to see her distress.

At the periphery of the photo stood Mark Mallory, his dark hair longer and more unruly. At twenty, he already had a man's well-muscled build and broad shoulders. He towered over the gaunt and middle-aged woman seated in a wheelchair beside him, his hand resting on her shoulder. Jane assumed the woman was Mark's mother, Barbara, Arthur's ex-wife. Barbara sat staring at the coffins, unaware that the click of a camera shutter would forever capture her expression, not of grief but an unsettling gaze of cold detachment. As if the man in that coffin meant nothing to her. Or perhaps less than nothing; after all, Arthur had left her for Dina, and although Mark claimed there were no bitter feelings between his parents, that view of Barbara's face told a different story. Here was the discarded wife, standing at the graves of her ex-husband and the woman who had stolen him. Did she feel some trace of satisfaction at that moment? A twinge of triumph that she had survived them both?

Jane flipped to the next photo. It was taken from the same vantage point, but Charlotte's face was blurred as she turned even further from her father, her whole body bent forward in motion. In the next photo, Patrick was frowning at her as she continued to move, her hand still pressed to her mouth, her face grimacing. By the next shot, she was half-way off the frame, only her back still in view, her skirt a black blur. One more click of the shutter, and Charlotte was no longer visible at all; neither was Mark. Patrick Dion and Barbara Mallory remained in place, both their faces registering puzzlement that their children had slipped away from the gathering.

What was going on between Mark and Charlotte? Had he followed her to offer his support?

In the next shot, Patrick was leaning over to awkwardly embrace Barbara, the two discarded spouses comforting each other. It was an artfully composed image, with the embrace reflected in a casket's gleaming surface.

The final shot was of the crowd as it dispersed, their backs turned from the twin grave sites. A metaphor, perhaps, of how the living always move on with their lives. In that final photo, Charlotte was once again visible, walking beside her father, Patrick's arm firmly wrapped around her waist. But Charlotte's head was turned in a backward glance toward her mother's grave, and on her face was a desperate look of yearning, as if she longed to throw herself atop her mother's coffin. That same mother who had walked out of her life five years earlier.

Jane set down the photo, overwhelmed with sadness for Charlotte. She thought of her own mother, thought of all the ways Angela annoyed her. But never once did Jane doubt that her mother loved her and would give her own life for her, just as Jane would give her own life for Regina without a second thought. When Dina divorced Patrick and left the family, Charlotte had been only twelve, that tender age at childhood's end. Even with a devoted father, there were secrets that a girl could learn only from her mother, the secrets of womanhood. *Who was there to teach you, Charlotte?*

At lunchtime, Jane went downstairs to the cafeteria for coffee and a ham sandwich. She brought both up to eat at her desk, fueling up not with pleasure but out of sheer necessity. She wiped mayonnaise from her fingers and turned to her computer to review the digital file of crime scene photos from the Ingersoll residence. As she cycled through the images of his home and re-membered the smell of the shrubbery along the walkway, the glow of his TV screen through the window, she felt her heart begin to thump hard. *That was the night I should have died.* She took a deep breath and forced herself to focus on the photos and critically view the scene with a calmer perspective. She studied the kitchen, where Ingersoll lay with blood pooled around his head. Clicked to the photo of his home office with the ransacked drawers, the bare desktop where a computer must have been. During their last phone conversa-tion, Ingersoll told Jane that someone had broken into his house. This was the chaos that he'd found when he got home from his fishing trip: the evidence of a burglary. Finally she clicked on a photo of the bedroom, where Ingersoll's closed suitcase still sat on the floor. He'd never had the chance to unpack.

She advanced to the photos of his Ford Taurus, which was parked on the street in front of the residence. The car was still littered with the detritus of a long road trip: empty coffee cups, a wadded Burger King sack, a *Bangor Daily* newspaper. That night she'd been covered in blood and shaken by what had happened in the alley, so she had not personally searched the car but had left that task to Frost and Tam. Frost reported finding a week-old receipt in the glove compartment from a Greenville, Maine, gas station. It corroborated the daughter's statement that Ingersoll had left for a fishing trip up north.

She went back through all the photos again, clicking through image after image. Living room, dining room, kitchen, bedroom. When she did not find what she was searching for, she picked up the phone and called Frost.

"Did you find a tackle box anywhere in the house?" she asked.

"Um, no. I don't remember seeing one."

"Who goes fishing without a tackle box?"

"Maybe he rented everything up at the camp where he was staying."

"You talked to the manager up there?"

"Yeah. But I didn't ask him about fishing gear."

"I'll give him a call."

"Why?"

"Just strikes me as odd, that's all." She hung up and pulled out the page with Ingersoll's call log. Scanning down it, she spotted a 207 area code. Ingersoll had made the call from his landline on April 14.

She dialed the number. It rang five times, and a male voice answered with a no-nonsense: "Loon Point."

"This is Detective Jane Rizzoli, Boston PD. May I ask who I'm speaking to?"

"Joe. Did you folks have another question?"

"Excuse me?"

"Someone else called from Boston PD yesterday. Spoke to my son Will."

"That would have been Detective Frost. Where is Loon Point located, exactly?"

"We're on Moosehead Lake. Got a dozen nice little cabins up here."

"You had a guest up there recently, name of Ingersoll."

"Yeah, Will said you folks were asking about him. It was my wife who checked him into the cabin, but she's not here today. All I can tell you is he stayed five days, pretty much kept to himself." He paused and yelled to his son: "Will, you wanna help those folks unload the gear from their boat? They're already tied up at the dock!" Then, back to Jane: "Sorry, ma'am. Starting to get busy around here. Really want to help you and all, but there's not much more to say. We were sorry to hear the man died."

"Was that the first time Mr. Ingersoll stayed at Loon Point?"

"Don't remember seeing him before."

"How long have you worked there?"

"Since it opened. I own the place. Look, I gotta get off and help some guests."

"One last question. Did Mr. Ingersoll rent any fishing gear while he was there?"

"Yeah, he did. Will helped him choose a rod and reel. Don't think he caught much, though."

She glanced at her ringing cell phone. "Thank you, Mr. . . ."

"Patten. You have any more questions, just call back."

She hung up the desk phone, picked up her cell phone, and saw the call was from the crime lab. "Rizzoli."

Criminalist Erin Volchko answered: "I've seen some pretty surprising things over the years, but this just might take the cake."

"What are we talking about?"

"That metallic fragment that came over from the ME's office. It was embedded in the cervical spine of Jane Doe."

"Yeah. A fragment from the blade."

"It's unlike any metal I've ever come across."

TWENTY-SEVEN

Frost and Tam were waiting for her in the crime lab when Jane walked in. So was a man she'd never met before, a soft-spoken African American gentleman whom Erin introduced as Dr. Calvin Napoleon Cherry from Harvard's Arthur Sackler Museum.

"When I realized what this metal might be, I asked Dr. Cherry to take a look at it," said Erin. "If anyone has an answer, it'll be him."

Dr. Cherry responded with an embarrassed laugh. "You make me sound far too impressive."

"Well, your name shows up on half the published articles on this subject. I can't imagine there's any better expert to consult."

"What is your role at the Sackler Museum, Dr. Cherry?" asked Jane.

He gave a modest shrug. "I'm curator of their weapons collection. I wrote my doctoral thesis on the metallurgic analysis of blades. Specifically, the blades of China and Japan. They're closely related, even though the methods of craftsmanship diverged centuries ago."

"So you think this blade was made in Asia?"

"I'm almost certain it was."

"You can tell that with just a fragment?"

"Here," said Erin, settling down in front of her computer. "Let me show you the images I sent to Dr. Cherry earlier this week. These are micrographs of the fragment." She tapped the keyboard, and on the monitor they saw an image of gray swirls and waves.

"What you're looking at," said Dr. Cherry, "is called lamellar or Damascus steel. It forms this wavy pattern when different layers of metal are folded and hammered again and again, sandwiching together both soft and hardened steel. The more layers you see beaten together, the finer the workmanship, and the stronger the sword. In China, the best steel is called *bailian jinggang,* or 'hundred-times-forged steel.' And that produces these patterns you see here, which we call the blade's veins."

"If this is a Chinese weapon," said Frost, "why is it called Damascus steel?"

"To explain that, I have to tell you a little about the history of Chinese weaponry. That is, if you want to hear it." He paused, glancing at the three detectives to gauge their interest.

"Go on," said Jane.

Dr. Cherry's eyes lit up, as if there was no subject he enjoyed more. "Let's go back to the beginning of swordcraft. Thousands of years ago, the Chinese started off making blades out of stone. Then they progressed to bronze, a soft and heavy metal that has its limitations as weapons material. The next advance was iron, but we don't find many examples of those swords because iron

corrodes, leaving very little behind. Ironically enough, you're more likely to come
across a bronze sword than an iron
sword, even though bronze is centuries
older."

"But we're talking about steel here,"
said Tam. "Not iron."

"And do you know the difference between steel and iron?"

Tam hesitated. "If I remember right, it
has something to do with the addition
of carbon."

"Very good!" Dr. Cherry beamed. "Not
everyone knows that, not even some of
my freshman students at Harvard. So
now we're into the middle Han dynasty,
about two thousand years ago, when
swordmakers learned to forge and fold
steel, to hammer it into bands and
sheets. The technique probably origi-
nated in India and later spread to China
and the Middle East. And that's how it
got the name Damascus steel."

"But it's not from Damascus at all,"
said Frost.

"No, it's originally from India. But
good ideas are bound to spread, and
once the technique reached China,

swordmaking truly advanced to an art. As the centuries passed, their technical quality varied, depending on the state of warfare. With every new conflict, weapons always evolve. When the Mongols invaded during the Song dynasty, they introduced sabers. The Chinese adapted that saber into their own curved sword. It's known as the *dao,* and it was used by cavalry to cut and slash while on horseback. We're talking about blades that were razor-sharp, so you can imagine the carnage on the battlefield. There would have been mass dismemberment and decapitation."

It was a gruesome image that Jane could picture only too vividly. She remembered the alley. The whoosh of the blade, the spray of hot blood on her face. The gentleness of Dr. Cherry's voice grotesquely underplayed the horror of what he was describing.

"Who the hell would sign up to be a soldier? Not me," said Frost.

"You might not have a choice," said Dr. Cherry. "For much of ancient history, armed conflict was part of life in China.

Warlord pitted against warlord. Invasions by Mongols and pirates."

"Pirates? In China?"

Dr. Cherry nodded. "During the Ming dynasty, Japanese pirates terrorized the Chinese coast. Then a hero named General Qi marched in and defeated them."

"I remember hearing about him," said Tam. "My grandmother told me that General Qi cut off the heads of five thousand pirates. His adventures made great bedtime stories."

"Geez," muttered Jane. "To think all I got was Snow White and the Seven Dwarfs."

"General Qi's elite soldiers were renowned for their ingenious tactics," said Dr. Cherry. "And their weapon of choice was the *dao*. The Chinese saber." He pointed to the magnified image on Erin's computer screen and said, with a note of awe: "It's amazing to think that's what this fragment probably came from."

"A Chinese saber?" said Jane.

"Yes."

"How can you tell, from that little

piece? Couldn't it be from a Japanese samurai sword?"

"That's possible, I suppose, since the Japanese learned their swordmaking techniques from the Chinese."

"And samurai swords are easy to find," said Tam. "You see them for sale in specialty knife stores."

"Ah, but those stores don't sell swords like this one."

"What's so special about it?" asked Jane.

"Its age. Based on carbon-fourteen dating."

Jane frowned. "I thought carbon-fourteen dating was only used for organic material. This is steel."

"Let's go back to how ancient swords were made," said Dr. Cherry. "The traditional technique was to melt iron sand in a forge. That iron was then combined with carbon to form steel. But where do you get the carbon? They used wood ash."

"And wood is organic," said Tam.

"Exactly. We extracted the carbon component of this specimen using sealed-tube combustion," said Erin. "And that carbon was then analyzed."

"The fragment had to be destroyed?"

"Unfortunately, yes. To date the carbon, the specimen had to be sacrificed. It was the only way we could get an accurate age."

"And that's where the big surprise came in," said Dr. Cherry, a lilt of excitement in his voice.

"I take it this weapon wasn't bought in some local knife store," Jane said.

"Not unless that store deals in very old antiques."

"How old are we talking about?"

Dr. Cherry pointed to the micrograph. "That steel you see there was crafted during the Ming dynasty. Carbon-fourteen dating narrows it down to sometime between the years 1540 and 1590." He looked at Jane, his eyes aglow. "That just happens to be the era of General Qi's legendary army. A saber with this degree of craftsmanship could have been wielded by one of his elite soldiers. Maybe it even cut off the heads of a few pirates."

Jane stared at the image on the computer. "This weapon is over five hundred years old? And it's still usable?"

"It's possible to preserve such a sword for a long, long time, but it takes special care, especially if this weapon actually saw use on the battlefield. Blood corrodes steel, even if it's assiduously wiped away. Exposure to air causes rust and pitting. The blade would need repeated cleaning and polishing over the centuries, and that alone abrades the metal, making the cutting edge brittle. That may be why this particular blade chipped off in the victim's neck. It's simply reached the end of its useful life as a killing tool." He gave a wistful sigh. "What I'd give to examine it! A *dao* from General Qi's era would be priceless, if you could just find it." He paused and frowned at Frost, who had suddenly paled. "Is something wrong, Detective?"

Frost said, softly: "I know where to find that sword."

TWENTY-EIGHT

Once again, Detectives Rizzoli and Frost have invaded my studio, and this time they've brought along a well-dressed black gentleman whose soft-spoken diffidence indicates that he is not a policeman like them. The sudden interruption startles my class, and the dozen students stand frozen, their sparring exercises abruptly halted. Only Bella strides into action, slipping past the students to plant herself beside me. She acts as my fierce guardian, all five foot, four inches of her, including her spiky black hair. I am not surprised to see the visitors, and I cast a glance at Bella that says: *Stand down. Allow me to deal with this.*

She gives the subtlest of nods but stubbornly remains at my side.

Detective Rizzoli assumes command of the conversation. Of course she would; she wears her authority like a coat of armor. "We understand you're in possession of an antique sword, Mrs. Fang," she says. "We ask you to surrender it to us now."

I look at Detective Frost. It is a cold stare of accusation, and shame darkens his eyes. On the night we shared dinner, the night that a friendship warmed between us, I allowed him to hold Zheng Yi and I shared the sword's history with him. That night, I saw kindness in his face. Now that face tightens into a mask that closes off any hint of our earlier connection. It is clear that he is a policeman above all, which poisons any possibility of friendship between us.

"If you choose not to hand over the weapon," says Detective Rizzoli, "we have a search warrant."

"And if I give you my sword, what will you do with it?" I ask.

"Examine it."

"Why?"

"To determine if it was used in the commission of a crime."

"Will it be returned to me undamaged?"

"Mrs. Fang, we're not here to negotiate. Where is the sword?"

Bella steps forward, fury radiating off her like the hum of a high-voltage wire. "You can't just confiscate it!"

"The law says I can."

"Zheng Yi has been in my family for generations," I say. "It has never left my possession."

Detective Rizzoli frowns at me. "What is Zheng Yi?"

"The name it was given when it was forged. It means 'justice.' "

"The sword has a name?"

"Why are you surprised? Don't you have a legend in Western culture, about a sword named Excalibur?"

"Madam Fang," says the black man, his voice quietly respectful. "Believe me, I don't want the sword damaged in any way. I understand its value, and I promise I'll treat it with care."

"And why should I believe you?" I ask.

"Because it's my job to protect and preserve such weapons. I'm Dr. Calvin Cherry from the Arthur Sackler Museum, and I've examined many ancient swords. I know their history. I know the battles they've fought." He dips his head, a gesture of regard that impresses me. "I would be honored if you'd allow me to see Zheng Yi," he says quietly.

I look into his soft brown eyes and see a sincerity that I did not expect. This man pronounces the name with a perfect accent, so I know he speaks Mandarin. Even more important, he understands that a fine weapon is to be revered for the skill of its craftsman, and for the centuries it has survived.

"Come with me," I say. "Bella, please take charge of the class."

I lead the visitors into the back room and shut the door. From my pocket I take out a key and unlock the closet to reveal the silk-wrapped bundle that lies on the shelf. With both hands, I present it to Dr. Cherry.

He receives it with a bow and carefully sets it on my desk. Detectives Rizzoli and Frost watch as he peels back the layers of red silk, exposing the sheathed weapon. He pauses for a moment to examine the scabbard, which is made of lacquered wood with bronze fittings. The handle, too, is lacquered wood, but covered with stingray skin that has been stained green. When he pulls out the sword, the blade makes a musical whine that sends a thrill across my skin.

"Liuye dao," he says softly.

I nod. "A willow leaf saber."

"And you say this comes from your family?"

"It was my mother's. And before that, her mother's."

"How many generations does it go back?"

"All the way to General Washi."

He looks up, clearly startled. "Truly?"

"It is our family bloodline."

Detective Rizzoli asks, "Who was he, this general?"

"You'd appreciate this bit of history, Detective," says Dr. Cherry. "General Washi was a woman, and the most famous of the double *dao* masters. A warrior who fought with two swords, one in each hand. She commanded thousands of soldiers during the Ming dynasty, leading them in charges against those Japanese pirates I told you about." He looks at me in wonder. "And you're her descendant."

Smiling back at him, I nod. "I'm pleased you know of her."

"But this is astonishing! To think—"

"Dr. Cherry," cuts in Detective Rizzoli. "What about the sword?"

"Oh yes. Of course." He pulls out his glasses and slips them on his nose. Behind the lenses, his brown eyes squint in concentration. "This has the typical curve of a willow leaf *dao.* It's a very old design," he explains to the two detectives. "This one is somewhat shorter than usual, but I guess you'd expect it if this weapon was designed specifically for a woman's hand. These blood grooves here are also typical, meant to make the blade a little lighter. Look at these etchings in the steel! I'm amazed how deep they still are! And this grip, you'd almost think it was original, if you didn't know it has to be at least five hundred . . ." He pauses. Above his spectacles, I can see his frown deepen. For the next few moments he says nothing at all. He brings the *dao* close to his glasses, minutely studying the cutting edge of the blade. He tests the flexibility. Finally, he reaches into his pocket for a magnifier, through which he examines the etched panels.

At last he straightens, and when he looks at me, I see a strange sadness in his eyes. A look that is almost regretful. Quietly, he slides the *dao* back into the scabbard and holds it out to me. "Madam Fang," he says. "Thank you for allowing me to see Zheng Yi."

"Then you are finished with her?" I ask.

"There's no need for us to take it after all."

Detective Rizzoli protests, "Dr. Cherry, the crime lab needs to examine it."

"Trust me, this is not the weapon you're looking for."

Rizzoli turns to Detective Frost. "Is it the same sword you saw?"

Frost looks confused. His gaze flicks up and down, between my face and the sheathed sword that I am holding. His face deepens to scarlet as he realizes he may have made a mistake.

"Well, is it?" she asks again.

Frost shakes his head. "I'm not sure. I mean, I only saw the sword for a moment."

"Detective Frost," I say coldly, "the next time you visit, I hope you'll be courteous enough to tell me what it is you really want from me."

My barb finds its mark, and he flinches as though stung.

Detective Rizzoli sighs. "Mrs. Fang, regardless of what Dr. Cherry says, we still need to take the sword for further study." She holds out her hands, waiting for me to surrender the prize.

After a pause, I place it in her hands. "I expect it returned to me undamaged."

As the visitors leave, I see Detective Frost cast a regretful look back, but I wear my disdain like a shield, deflecting any apology. His shoulders are drooping as he walks out the door.

"Sifu?" Bella says softly, stepping into my office.

In the next room, the students continue sparring and kicking, grunting and sweating. She closes the door so they cannot see the look of satisfaction that passes between us.

Move, countermove. The chess game continues, and the police are still one step behind us.

TWENTY-NINE

Jane waited until they were halfway down the block, where their cars were parked, before she confronted Dr. Cherry. "How can you be so sure this isn't the weapon?"

"Take it to the crime lab. Let them examine it if you don't believe me," he said.

"We're looking for an ancient Chinese sword, and she just *happens* to have one."

"That sword you took from her isn't the one you're looking for. Yes, the blade's edge has nicks and scars from use, but the etchings and blood grooves are too distinct. Also, the handle appears to be original to that weapon. A wooden handle crafted in the Ming dynasty wouldn't have survived all these centuries in such good condition."

"So this sword isn't old?"

"It's certainly well made, and it has the proper heft and balance of a Ming dynasty saber. But that sword is just a very good reproduction. At most, it's maybe fifty, seventy-five years old."

"Why didn't you say any of this while we were there?"

"Because it's clear that *she* believes it's real. *She* believes it was passed down from her ancestors. I didn't have the heart to disillusion her, not when it means so much to her." He looked toward the *paifang* gate. It was now late afternoon, and dinnertime visitors were descending on Chinatown, roaming its narrow streets, staring at menus in windows. Dr. Cherry surveyed the crowd with a look of sadness. "At the museum where I work," he said, "I'm often asked to evaluate family heirlooms. People bring in all sorts of junk from their attics. Vases and paintings and musical instruments. Things that come with all sorts of mythology attached to them. Almost always, my verdict is disappointing for them because what they bring aren't treasures, but worthless reproductions. It forces people to question everything they were ever told as children. It destroys their personal mythologies, and I hate having to do it. People want to believe they're exceptional. They want to believe their family has a unique story to tell, and for proof they point to Grandma's antique ring, or Grandpa's old fiddle. Why force them to hear the brutal truth, which is that most of us are utterly ordinary? And the hand-me-down relics we cherish are almost always fakes."

"Mrs. Fang believes she's descended from warrior women," said Frost. "Do you think that's just another family fantasy?"

"I think it's something that her parents told her. And they gave her that sword to prove it."

"So it's not true. About General Washi."

"Anything's possible, Detective Frost. You could be descended from King Arthur or William the Conqueror. If that's important to you, if it helps you get through your day-to-day life, then go on believing that. Because family mythology has far more meaning to us than the truth. It helps us cope with the sheer insignificance of our own lives."

Jane snorted. "My family mythology was all about how much beer Uncle Lou could chug at one sitting."

"I doubt that's the only lore you heard," said Dr. Cherry.

"I also heard that my great-grandma gave a whole wedding party food poisoning."

Dr. Cherry smiled. "I'm talking about heroes. There must be at least one of those in your family. Think about it, Detective. Think about how important those heroes are to the way you view yourself."

Jane did think about it as she drove home, but the first personalities that came to mind were the roguish and the ridiculous. The Rizzoli cousin who tried to prove Santa Claus really could make a traditional entrance, resulting in the emergency dismantling of his mother's chimney. Or the uncle who livened up a New Year's party with homemade fireworks and left the hospital minus three fingers.

But there were also stories of quiet dignity, told about a great-aunt who was a nun in Africa. Another great-aunt who struggled to feed eight children in Italy during the war. They could be called heroes, too, but of a quieter kind. Real women who endured, nothing like Iris Fang's legendary ancestor who fought with two sabers and led soldiers into battle. A fable was what that sounded like, no more real than Sun Wukong the Monkey King, who protected the innocent and battled demons and river monsters. Iris was living in just such a fairy-tale world, where a lonely widow could believe herself a swordmaster with the blood of ancient warriors in her veins. And who could blame her for retreating into such a fantasy? Iris was dying of leukemia. Her husband and daughter were gone. Alone in her sad home, with

that sad furniture, did she dream of bat-
tlefields and glory? *Wouldn't I?*

As she braked at a stoplight, her cell
phone rang. Without looking at the caller's number she answered it, and was
treated to an angry voice blasting in her
ear.

"What the hell, Jane? Why didn't you
tell me?" said her brother Frankie. "We
can't let her do it."

She sighed. "I take it this is about
Mom's engagement?"

"I had to hear the news from Mike."

"I was going to call you, but I've been
kind of busy."

"She can't marry that guy. You gotta
stop her."

"You wanna tell me how I should go
about that?"

"She's still married, for Chrissakes!"

"Yeah. To a man who left her for a
bimbo."

"Don't talk about Dad like that."

"Well, he did."

"That's not gonna last. Dad'll come
home, you'll see. He just needs to get
out his ya-yas first."

"Tell that to Mom. See what she says about it."

"Fuck's sake, Jane, I can't believe you're letting this happen. This is the Rizzoli *family. Families* oughta stick together. And what do we really know about this Korsak guy, anyway?"

"Come on. We both know he's okay."

"What does that mean, he's *okay*?"

"He's a decent human being. And he's a good cop." She paused, struck by the fact that she was defending the same man whom she had not particularly relished as a stepfather. But everything she'd said about Korsak was true. He *was* a decent human being. He *was* a man you could count on. A woman could do much worse.

"And it's fine with you that he's boinking Ma?" said Frankie.

"You have no problem with Dad boinking the Bimbo."

"That's different. He's a guy."

Now, that pissed her off. "And Mom's not allowed to boink?" Jane shot back.

"She's our *mother.*"

The light turned green. As she drove through the intersection, she said,

"Mom's not dead yet, Frankie. She's good-looking and fun and she deserves another chance at love. Instead of harassing her about this, you go talk to Dad. He's the reason she went out with Korsak in the first place."

"Yeah, I will talk to him. Maybe it's time he took control of this situation." Frankie hung up.

Control? It was Dad's lack of control that got us here.

She tossed the phone on the seat, fretting over how her dad was going to react to the news. Angry that this was yet one more thing to worry about, one more ball to juggle when she already had a dozen whirling in midair.

The phone rang again.

Abruptly she pulled over to the curb to answer it. "I don't have time for this, Frankie," she snapped.

"Who the fuck's Frankie?" came an equally irritated retort. "Listen, Rizzoli, I've had enough of this Red Phoenix crap and I want you to make it stop." There was no mistaking Kevin Donohue's gravelly voice. Or his delightful vocabulary.

"I don't know what you're talking about, Mr. Donohue," she said.

"I got another one this afternoon. This time they shoved it under my windshield wiper. Can you believe they had the nerve to touch my *fucking car*?"

"You got another what?"

"Another copy of Joey's obituary. *Enjoyed basketball and target shooting, survived by his loving mother and sister,* blah blah blah. And there's a message on the back."

"What does it say?"

"It's coming for you."

"And you think it's worth taking seriously?"

"Two people have been chopped up by some freak monkey creature, and you think I shouldn't take this seriously?"

She said, evenly: "What monkey creature are you talking about?"

"What, I'm not supposed to know about that?"

"That information isn't public."

"I ain't *the public,* okay? I'm a tax-paying citizen whose life is being threatened."

He has a channel into our investigation, she thought. He's found a way into Boston PD. It shouldn't surprise her. A man as powerful as Donohue could buy eyes and ears everywhere, including City Hall and Schroeder Plaza.

"Do your job, Detective," said Donohue. "You're supposed to serve and protect, remember?"

Too bad that includes protecting garbage like you. She took a breath and managed to sound civil. "I'll need to examine the latest note. Where are you right now?"

"I'm at my warehouse on Jeffries Point. I'm not gonna wait around long, so get here soon."

THIRTY

Darkness had fallen when Jane drove through the open gate of Donohue Wholesale Meats and parked between a BMW and a silver Mercedes. Mobsters did seem to like their flashy imports. As she climbed out, she heard the roar of a jet taking off from nearby Logan Airport; she looked up to watch as it banked and headed south. She thought of Florida beaches and rum punches and palm trees. How nice it would be to take a sunny vacation from murder.

"Detective Rizzoli."

Turning, she recognized one of the burly bodyguards she'd met at Donohue's residence a few days ago. Sean was his name.

"He's waiting inside," Sean said, and eyed her holstered weapon. "First, you're gonna have to hand that over."

"Mr. Donohue didn't mind me carrying the other day."

"Yeah, well, he's a lot more nervous now. On account of that message on his windshield." He held out his hand.

"I don't surrender my weapon to anyone. So you tell Mr. Donohue he can come see me at police headquarters. I'll be happy to talk to him there." She turned toward her car.

"Okay, okay," the man relented. "But just so you know, I'll be watching you like a hawk."

"Yeah. Whatever."

She followed him into the warehouse, and as the insulated door thudded shut behind her, she suddenly wished she'd brought a heavier jacket. It was freezing inside, a windowless cavern that was so cold she could see her own breath swirl. Sean led her through a curtain of slitted plastic, into the refrigerated area beyond. From ceiling hooks hung enormous sides of beef, row upon row of them, a forest of suspended corpses. The chill mist stank of blood and slaughtered flesh, a smell she feared would cling to her hair and clothes long after she left this place. They walked through that forest of hanging meat to an office at the rear of the building, and her escort knocked on the door.

It swung open and she recognized the second bodyguard, who waved her in. Jane walked into the windowless room, and the door gave a solid thud as it closed behind her. She was trapped in a fortress within a meat locker, guarded by armed thugs, yet she felt less nervous about the situation than her host appeared to be. This was what it meant to be a prince of the Irish mob, permanently afflicted by paranoia and fear. Wielding power meant always dreading the moment when you'd lose it.

Kevin Donohue looked more bloated than before, sitting behind his desk, his sausage-like fingers resting on the zip-lock bag containing the latest message. He held up the bag. "Unfortunately," he said, "my brilliant associates here got their fingerprints all over it before they showed it to me."

"These notes never have any fingerprints," she said, taking the bag. "Whoever sends them is far too careful." She looked at the photocopied side. It was the identical *Boston Globe* obituary of Joey Gilmore, published nineteen years ago. Flipping it over, she read the message, written in block letters: IT'S COMING FOR YOU.

She looked at Donohue. "What do you think the *it* refers to?"

"Are you a retard? Obviously, it's that thing running around town, playing vigilante with a sword."

"Why would this vigilante come after you? Are you guilty of something?"

"I don't have to be guilty of a damn thing to recognize a threat when I see one. I get enough of them."

"I had no idea that shipping fancy cuts of meats was such a dangerous business."

He stared at her with pale eyes.

"You're too smart a girl to be playing dumb."

"But not smart enough to figure out what it is you want from me, Mr. Donohue."

"I told you over the phone. I want this crap to stop, before any more blood gets spilled."

"You mean your blood, specifically." She glanced at the two men flanking her. "Looks to me like you've already got plenty of protection."

"Not against that—that *thing*. Whatever it is."

"Thing?"

Donohue rocked forward, his face florid with impatience. "Word around town is, it sliced up those two professionals like lunch meat. And then it vanished without a trace."

"Were they your professionals?"

"I told you the last time. No, I didn't hire them."

"Any idea who they were working for?"

"I'd tell you if I knew. I've put out feelers, and I hear the contract went out on that cop weeks ago."

"A contract on Detective Ingersoll?"

Donohue nodded, his three chins jiggling. "Soon as that offer hit the street, he was a walking dead man. Must've made someone really nervous."

"Ingersoll was retired."

"But he was asking a lot of questions."

"About girls, Mr. Donohue. Girls who've gone missing." Jane stared straight into his eyes. "Now, that's a subject that should make *you* nervous."

"Me?" He leaned back, his massive weight setting off a loud creak in the chair. "No idea what you're talking about."

"Prostitution? Trafficking underaged girls?"

"Prove it."

She shrugged. "Gee, now that I think about it, maybe I should just let the monkey creature do its thing."

"It's coming after the wrong guy! I had nothing to do with the Red Phoenix! Sure, Joey was a weasel. I didn't shed any tears when he got whacked, but I didn't order it."

She looked down at Joey's obituary. "Someone thinks you did."

"It's that crazy lady in Chinatown. Gotta be her behind it."

"You mean Mrs. Fang?"

"I'm thinking she hired Ingersoll to ask those questions, to find out who killed her husband. He got too close to the truth and that's how this war got started. If you think the Irish play rough, you haven't seen what the Chinese can do. They have people who can get past anything. People who can practically walk through walls."

"Are these people or fairy tales we're talking about?"

"Didn't you see that movie *Ninja Assassin*? They're trained to kill since childhood."

"Ninjas are Japanese."

"Don't split hairs with me! It's the same skills, the same training. You know who she is, don't you? Where Iris Fang comes from? I've been looking into her background. She grew up in some secret monastery up in the mountains, where they train kids for that sort of thing. Probably could snap a man's neck by the time she was ten. And now she has all those students working for her."

"She's a fifty-five-year-old widow." An ailing woman with sad delusions of grandeur, thought Jane. A woman who believes she's descended from a mythical general and has a fake sword to prove it.

"There are widows, and then there's *her.*"

"Do you know for a fact that Iris Fang is threatening you?"

"That's *your* job to prove it. I'm just telling you what it smells like to me. She lost her husband that night, and she figures that I ordered the hit. I'm being blamed for the Red Phoenix and for once, goddamn it, I *didn't do it.*"

A loud bang suddenly rocked the building. Jane caught a glimpse of Donohue's face, frozen in surprise, just before the room went pitch-black.

"What the fuck?" yelled Donohue.

"I think the power's out," one of his men said.

"I can see the power's out! Get the generator going!"

"If I can find a flashlight . . ."

A noise overhead made them all fall silent. Jane looked up as a rapid *thump-thump-thump* pattered on the roof. Staring up at the darkness, she felt her own heart thumping, felt her palms slicken with sweat as she reached down to unsnap her holster. "Where's the generator switch?" she asked.

"It—it's in the warehouse," one of the men responded, his voice close to her and thick with fear. "Electrical box is against the back wall. But I ain't gonna be able to find it in the dark. Not with that thing—" He stopped as they heard the sound again, light as raindrops skittering across the roof.

Jane dug in her purse and pulled out her SureFire flashlight. She clicked it on and the beam landed on Donohue, his face gleaming with sweat and fear. "Call nine one one," she ordered.

He grabbed the portable phone on his desk. Slammed it down again. "It's dead!"

She pulled her cell phone from her belt. No signal. "Is this place lined with lead, or what?"

"These walls are bulletproof and blast-proof," said Donohue. "It's a safety feature."

"Great. The ultimate dead zone."

"You'll need to go outside to get a signal."

But I don't want to go outside. And neither does anyone else.

It was getting warm in the room, the walls trapping both their body heat and their fear. We can't stay in here forever, she thought; someone has to step out and make the call, and it doesn't look like it's going to be anyone but me.

She drew her weapon and went to the door. "I'll lead," she said. "Stay close."

"Wait!" Donohue cut in. "No way are my boys going with you."

"I need backup."

"They're paid to guard *me.* They stay here."

She turned, aiming the light straight into his eyes. "Okay then. *You* go out there, and take your boys with you. I'll just hang out here and wait till you get back." She grabbed a chair, sat down, and turned off the flashlight.

A moment passed in darkness, the building silent. The only sound was Donohue's panicked wheezing.

"All right," he finally said. "Take Colin with you. But Sean stays."

She had no idea whether she could trust Colin; she only hoped he had enough functioning gray cells not to accidentally shoot her in the back. At the door she paused, listening for sounds beyond it, but the barrier was too thick. *Bulletproof and blast-proof,* Donohue had said.

She slid open the dead bolt and pulled the door open a crack. The darkness wasn't as deep outside the office; through a high warehouse window shone the dim glow of the city, just enough light for Jane to make out dark rows of hanging meat, like shadowy warriors in formation. Anything could be lurking in that gloom, posing as one more silhouette among those sides of beef.

Jane turned on her flashlight and quickly scanned the perimeter. In one sweep she registered hanging carcasses, the concrete floor, the fog of her own breath. She heard Colin standing right behind her, his breathing shaky with fear. An armed and terrified man was not the sort of backup she'd had in mind. I could wind up with a bullet in my spine, she thought. If the creature doesn't slice off my head first.

"Where's the closest exit?" she whispered.

"Straight ahead. Far end of the building."

Swallowing hard, she started down the row of carcasses. She swept the light back and forth, scanning for movement, for a glimpse of a face, the flash of steel. All she saw were the products of the slaughterhouse, living creatures reduced to hanging muscle and bone. The flashlight felt slippery in her trembling hand. Whoever, whatever you are, she thought, you spared me once before. But that didn't mean it would repeat the favor, not when it saw the company she was keeping.

More carcasses loomed ahead. Aiming her light straight ahead, she could not see the end of the row. Abruptly she halted, trying to hear through the thunder of her own heartbeat.

"What?" whispered Colin.

"Listen."

It was just a faint creak, the sound that a tree makes when a rising wind causes it to sway. But the creak rose to a rhythmic groan, as if that tree were swaying with ever-building violence. *It's coming from above us.* Jane lifted her light toward the ceiling and saw a suspended carcass swinging back and forth, as if shoved by an invisible hand.

They heard another creak, this time to their left. "There!" said Colin, and Jane swung her light toward the sound. Found herself staring at a second swaying carcass, moving like a giant pendulum back and forth across the narrow beam of her flashlight.

"Behind us!" said Colin, voice rising to shrill panic now. "No, over there!"

Jane spun, her light catching movement everywhere as the darkness came alive with a noisy chorus of clanks and groans and squealing metal.

"Where the fuck *is it*?" yelled Colin, whirling beside her, wildly swinging his weapon as carcasses swayed all around them. He fired, and somewhere in the darkness metal clanged. He fired again, and the bullet thunked into cold meat.

"Will you *stop it,* before you kill us both!" Jane yelled.

He ceased fire but was still jerking one way and then the other, in search of a target. No doubt he imagined the creature everywhere, just as she did. Over there, was that the flash of a face, the gleam of an eye? How could anything move so swiftly, so soundlessly? Suddenly she remembered the illustration in the book of Chinese folktales. The Monkey King, clutching his staff, his long tail curling like a serpent. She thought of a sword whispering through the night, the blade slicing through her throat. Her gaze shot upward and for an instant she thought she saw it perched above, its feral eyes shining from the darkness. But there was no creature there, just an empty steel hook awaiting a fresh side of meat.

Slowly the groans and creaks faded to silence. Yet she and Colin stood in place, backs pressed against each other, both of them frantically scanning the shadows. In every direction that Jane aimed her flashlight, she spotted no intruder, yet the darkness seemed to be watching them. And with this light in my hand, she thought, whatever is here knows exactly where we are.

"Keep moving," she whispered. "To the door."

"What is this thing? What are we dealing with?"

"Let's not wait around to find out."

He was not about to be left behind. As she moved toward the door, she could almost feel his breath on her neck. For a man like Colin, a gun was fake courage, enough to transform a coward into a bully and a killer. But put that man in the dark where he can't see the enemy, where blindness is the equalizer, and the coward is stripped bare again. Only after they'd reached the exit and stepped outside did she hear him give a relieved sigh. The air smelled of the sea, and in the sky, circling jets glittered like moving stars. She pulled out her cell phone, but hesitated before making the call. What would she say? *The power failed and we all freaked out. Heard things in the dark and imagined monsters.*

"You gonna call or what?" said Colin. The coward was gone, and the bully was back.

She lifted her phone to dial and went instantly still, her gaze riveted on the warehouse rooftop. On the figure squatting there, silhouetted like a gargoyle against the night sky. It was watching her, just as she was watching it. *Does it see me as friend or enemy?*

"There it is!" yelled Colin.

Just as he raised his gun to fire, Jane grabbed his arm. The bullet went wild, flying harmlessly into the sky.

"What the fuck?" Colin yelled. "It's right there, kill it!"

On the rooftop, the figure didn't move; it simply sat staring at them.

"If you don't take it down, I will," said Colin. Once again he lifted his gun and suddenly froze, scanning the rooftop. "Where is it? Where'd it go?"

"It's gone," said Jane, staring up at the empty rooftop. *You saved my life once; now I've saved yours.*

THIRTY-ONE

"Donohue's a dirtbag," said Tam. "I say we just let the thing take him out. Let it take them all out."

The thing. They had no other name for whatever it was that had perched on the warehouse last night. No one had seen its face or heard its voice. They'd caught only glimpses of it, and always in darkness, where it was little more than shadow moving across shadow. In the battle between good and evil, *the thing* had clearly staked its position. Already it had cut down two hired killers. Now its gaze was fixed on Donohue.

But it spared me, thought Jane. *How does it know I'm one of the good guys?*

"Whatever it is," said Frost, "it's pretty damn clever at avoiding surveillance cameras."

The three detectives had spent all morning in the second-floor conference room, reviewing video footage from cameras mounted throughout the Jeffries Point neighborhood where Donohue's warehouse was located. The feed from one of Donohue's cameras was now playing on the monitor, and it showed an evening view of his parking lot. Jane watched her own car pull in through the gate and park in the stall next to Donohue's Mercedes.

"Smile. You're on candid camera," said Frost.

On the video, Jane stepped out of her car and paused to look at the sky, as though sniffing the wind. Is my hair really that messy? she thought, wincing at her own image. Do I really slouch that badly? Gotta learn to stand straight and hold in my stomach.

Now Donohue's man Sean appeared, and they had their conversation about

Jane's weapon, Sean insisting, Jane squaring her shoulders in resistance.

"Why didn't you ask us to go there with you?" said Tam.

"I was just there to pick up the note. It was nothing."

"Turned into a lot more than nothing. You could have used us."

On the screen, Jane and the bodyguard disappeared into the warehouse and the view went static. There was no movement, no change in the parking lot except for the transitory glow of a car's headlights as it passed by on the street. Frost fast-forwarded the video five minutes. Ten minutes. The image suddenly flickered and went blank.

"And that's it," said Frost. "The same thing happens in all four of his surveillance cameras. The power cuts out, and the picture goes blank."

"So we don't have a single shot of the thing," said Tam.

"Not on Donohue's cameras."

"Is this thing invisible?"

"Maybe it just knows what it's doing." Frost brought up thumbnail photos of the warehouse exterior. "I brought my camera out there this morning and took these pictures. You can see where all the cameras are mounted. As you might expect, they're focused on entrance points. The doors and the truck bays. But the back side of the building is just uninterrupted wall, so it wasn't under surveillance. Nor was the rooftop." He looked at Jane. "So it is physically possible to evade the cameras. Which means this doesn't have to be some supernatural creature."

"Last night, it was easy to believe it was," said Jane softly, remembering the eerie creaks and squeals of the meat hooks swaying around her in the warehouse. "He has a security system and bodyguards. He's armed to the teeth. But against this thing, Donohue has no idea how to protect himself and he's scared shitless."

"Why should we care, exactly?" said Tam. "The thing's doing our job for us. When it comes to cleaning up the bad guys, I say let it rip."

Jane stared at the photos of Donohue's warehouse. "You know, I have a hard time disagreeing with you. I owe that thing my life. But I want to know how it penetrated the building. I was right there, yet I didn't see it until the very end. When it *allowed* me to see it. When it sat up on the roof long enough for Donohue's man to see it, too."

"Why would it do that?" said Frost.

"Maybe to prove to us it actually exists? Maybe to scare Donohue, show him it can take him down anytime it wants to?"

"Then why didn't it? Donohue's still alive and kicking."

"And scared to death," said Jane. "Funny thing is, I'm not afraid of it anymore. I think it's here for a reason. I just want to know how it does what it does." She looked at Tam. "What do you know about wushu?"

He sighed. "Of course you'd turn to the Asian guy."

"Come on Tam, you're the logical man to ask. Seems like you know a lot about Chinese folktales."

"Yeah," he conceded. "Courtesy of my grandmother."

"Donohue thinks that ninja warriors are after him. I looked it up last night and I found out ninja techniques actually come from China. Donohue says these guys are raised from childhood to kill, and they can penetrate any defenses."

"We both know half of that is fantasy."

"Yeah, but which half?"

"The half that made it into *Crouching Tiger, Hidden Dragon.*"

"I liked that movie," said Frost.

"But did you ever once believe that warriors can fly through the air and fight in treetops? Of course not, because it's a fairy tale. Just like all the other tales my grandma told me about monks who could walk on water. Immortals who came down from heaven to mingle with men."

"But legends sometimes have an element of truth to them," said Jane. "And there really were fighting monks in China."

"Okay," admitted Tam. "Maybe that part is real. There actually were fighting Shaolin monks from a mountain temple. They got famous for their combat skills after they defended the emperor against an uprising. But the art of wushu goes back long before those monks. It's thousands of years old, so old that no one really knows its true history. And with every century that goes by, the tales get more and more outlandish. That's how you end up with people thinking that wushu warriors are like ghosts. Impossible to kill."

"After last night, I'd almost believe it's true," said Jane.

"Come on."

"You weren't there. You didn't see it."

"I'd almost believe it's a ghost, too," Frost said as he studied another video on the screen. "I pulled footage from cameras all over that neighborhood, and so far I haven't caught a glimpse. It managed to slip through blind spots everywhere." He pointed to the monitor. "This camera is mounted right across the street from Donohue's warehouse. It was recording the whole time, yet nothing shows up."

"If it's flesh and blood, it's going to turn up somewhere," said Jane.

Frost switched to a different video. "Okay, now this camera's about a block away, almost to Summer Street." He hit

Play, and a view of an alley appeared, a chain-link fence blocking the far end. Minutes passed and nothing moved, nothing changed. "Again, nothing."

Jane gave Frost a sympathetic pat on the back and finally stood up. "Happy viewing. Call me if you spot anything."

"Yeah, yeah."

She was almost out the door when she heard Frost suck in a sharp breath. She turned. "What?"

"It went by so fast!"

"I didn't see a thing," said Tam.

Jane moved back to the monitor and watched as Frost rewound and hit Play again. The same static image reappeared. The same dimly lit alley with the chain-link fence at the far end.

"There," said Frost.

The figure seemed to materialize out of darkness, its back to the camera as it moved in a blur down the alley. In one swift leap it launched itself up and over the fence and landed in a crouch on the other side. There it paused and straightened to its full height.

Frost froze the image.

It was garbed head-to-toe in black.

They could not see a face, but the figure clearly stood out in silhouette, revealing a slender waist and the unmistakable curve of hips.

"It's a woman," said Frost.

Bella Li strode into Boston PD's Schroeder Plaza wearing low-slung blue jeans, tall boots, and a black leather jacket. Before stepping through the metal detector, she made a grand show of peeling off that jacket, a strip tease for all the cops who were watching, and revealed a skintight T-shirt that hugged every curve of her braless breasts. She returned their stares with a lethal smile and swaggered through security to meet Jane, who was waiting for her on the other side.

"Didn't know I'd have to pass inspection," Bella said.

"Everyone does. Even the mayor." Jane waved her toward the elevator. "We're going upstairs."

As they rode up to the second floor, Bella stood with hip cocked, leather jacket slung over her shoulder. Her short hair stood up even spikier than usual, like the fur of a cat that's been riled and is ready to fight. And this is one gal who could probably take me down, Jane thought. Bella might not be big, but she was all muscle and as lithe as a panther. Staring at her, Jane wondered: Are you the creature I saw perched on the rooftop? Are you the one who saved my life in that alley?

On the second floor, Jane escorted Bella to the interview room. "Make yourself comfortable. I'll let Detective Frost know you're here," she said, and left the young woman alone.

In the adjoining room, Jane joined Frost, who was watching Bella through the one-way mirror. Their guest appeared not in the least nervous, and was leaning back in her chair, boots propped up on the table. Head tipped back, Bella stared at the ceiling, looking bored.

"Did she say anything interesting on the way up?" asked Frost.

Jane shook her head. "Never even asked why we called her in."

"That's interesting. You think she knows that we know?"

"I think she's trying to show us that she doesn't give a damn."

In the next room, Bella looked straight at the mirror and arched one eyebrow, her expression unmistakable: *Can we get this over with?*

"Okay." Jane sighed. "Let's go rattle her cage."

As Jane and Frost walked into the interview room, Bella dropped her feet from the table but remained slouched in her chair, arms crossed, as she answered Jane's questions in a monotone. The deceptively easy queries came first: Name? Bella Li. Date of birth? May 18. Occupation? Martial arts instructor. Bella sighed loudly, the picture of disinterest. But the next question made the muscles in her forearm twitch.

"Where were you last night, between the hours of six PM and nine PM?" Jane asked.

Bella shrugged. "I was home."

"Alone?"

"Why do you want to know?"

"We want to verify your whereabouts."

"I consider my love life private. I don't

see why I should have to share names with anyone."

"So someone was with you that night?" asked Frost. "Could you tell us his name?"

"Why do you assume I'm interested in men? Do you really think a woman can't do better?" She shot a provocative smile at Jane.

"Okay," Jane said with a sigh. "What was *her* name, then?"

Bella looked down at her own hands, studying her close-clipped fingernails. "There was no one. I was home alone."

"You could've said that earlier."

"You could have told me why you asked me here."

"So you were home by yourself. Did you leave your residence at any time?"

"I don't remember."

"Maybe if we showed you a photo, you *would* remember."

"What photo?"

Frost said, "From a security camera on Jeffries Point. You're very good at eluding surveillance cameras, Ms. Li. But you didn't spot all of them."

For the first time, Bella didn't have a

ready response, though her expression did not change and her eyes remained as unperturbed as forest ponds.

"We know it's you in the video," Jane lied. Leaning in closer, she saw the girl's pupils twitch, a reaction that was both involuntary and telling. Bella might appear calm, but her internal fight-or-flight instincts were on full alert. "We know you were there at the warehouse. The question is, why?"

The girl laughed, an impressive rally of nerves in someone so clearly at a disadvantage. "You tell me. Since you seem to know everything."

"You went there to scare Kevin Donohue."

"Why would I?"

"First you placed a threatening note on his windshield. Then you broke into his warehouse. Disabled his security system and his phone line."

"I did that all by myself?"

"You have extensive martial arts training. You were taught at one of the best academies in the world, in Taiwan." Jane slapped a folder on the table. "The file on your travel records for the past five years."

Bella cocked her head. "I have a file?"

"You do now."

Bella opened the folder and flipped through the pages with feigned disinterest. "So I've been in and out of the country. Aren't we Americans free to travel where we want?"

"Not many Americans spend five years in a Taiwan monastery, studying an ancient art like wushu."

"Different strokes for different folks."

"And here's the interesting part. You were sponsored by Mrs. Fang. She's not wealthy, yet she paid for those years of training. Paid for your plane flights, your tuition. Why?"

"She saw that I had talent."

"When did she recognize that?"

"I was seventeen and living on the streets when she found me. She dusted me off and took me on, maybe because I reminded her of her daughter."

"Is that what you're doing in Boston? Playing her surrogate daughter?"

"I teach at her studio. We practice the

same style of martial arts. And we share the same philosophy."

"What philosophy would that be?"

Bella looked her in the eye. "That justice is a responsibility shared by all."

"Justice? Or vengeance?"

"Some would say that *vengeance* is simply another word for justice."

Jane stared at Bella, trying to read her. Trying to decide if this was the same creature who'd saved her life in the alley, who'd perched on the warehouse roof. Bella was flesh and blood, like any other twenty-four-year-old, but she was definitely not ordinary. Looking into those eyes, Jane glimpsed a strangeness, a wildness. An animal spirit that made her suddenly draw back, a chill raising the hairs on her arms. As if she'd glimpsed something in those eyes that was not quite human.

Frost broke the silence. "Ms. Li, it's time to tell us the truth."

Bella gave him a dismissive look. "Which part isn't the truth?"

"The part about why Iris Fang chose you in particular."

"She could have chosen anyone."

"But she didn't. She flew all the way to San Francisco to find one particular seventeen-year-old girl whose mother had just died. A girl who ran away from her foster home and was living on the streets. What was so special about you in particular?"

When Bella didn't answer, Jane said: "We have your school records from California. They don't mention your mother's immigration status."

"My mother's dead. What does it matter now?"

"She was an illegal immigrant."

"Prove it."

"What about you, Bella?"

"I have a US passport."

"Which says that you were born in the state of Massachusetts. Six years later, you're registered in a public school in San Francisco. Your mother is working as a hotel maid with a fake Social Security number. Why did you move there? Why did you two suddenly pull up stakes and run to California?" Jane leaned in close enough to see her own reflection in those bottomless eyes. "I have a pretty good idea who you really are. I just can't prove it yet. But trust me, I will." She glanced at Frost. "Show her the search warrant."

Bella frowned. "Search warrant?"

"It authorizes us to enter your residence," said Frost. "Detective Tam is at your address now, with the search team."

"What do you think you're going to find?"

"Evidence that will link you to the deaths of an unidentified female Jane Doe on the night of April fifteenth, and an unidentified male, John Doe, on the night of April twenty-first."

Bella shook her head. "Sorry to disappoint you, but I have a rock-solid alibi for April fifteenth. I was onstage at a wushu demonstration in Chinatown. There were at least two hundred witnesses."

"We'll verify that. In the meantime, if you want an attorney, now is the time to call one."

"You're *arresting* me?" Bella snapped forward, a move so sudden that Jane flinched, fully aware of how quickly and lethally this girl could move. "This," she said quietly, "is a *very bad mistake.*" Something deep in Bella's eyes seemed to stir, like a creature awakening in the inky depths.

"Tell us why it's a mistake, and maybe we'll reconsider," said Jane.

Bella took a breath, and someone else seemed to take possession of her. Someone who stared back with eyes as cold as polished stone. "I have nothing more to say."

Bella's apartment was clean. Far too clean. Jane stood in the living room, staring down at a carpet that still bore the parallel tracks of recent vacuuming.

"This is the way we found it," said Tam. "Kitchen and bathroom are scrubbed spotless. Not even a stray scrap of paper in the trash cans. It's like no one lives here. Either she's obsessive-compulsive about housecleaning, or she was scouring away any trace evidence."

"How did she know we'd be coming here?"

"Anyone who gets a call to visit Boston PD is going to figure out they're a suspect. She must have realized we'd be coming."

Jane went to the window and peered through spotless glass at the street below, where two elderly women hobbled along the sidewalk, their arms linked. It was quiet on this corner of Tai Tung Village, at the south end of Chinatown. Iris Fang's residence was right up the street, a minute's walk away. The neighborhood was very much its own universe, and Jane felt like the alien here. It was a feeling reinforced by every stare, every nervous murmur among the neighbors. With her badge and her authority, Jane was the alien wherever she went, the outsider who could be either your best friend or your worst enemy.

She turned from the window and went into the bathroom, where Frost was down on his knees scanning the cabinet beneath the sink. "Nothing," he said and rose to his feet, face flushed from bending. "Not a single hair in the shower or sink. All I found in the medicine cabinet was aspirin and a roll of Ace wrap. It's like no one lives here."

"Are we sure she does?"

"Tam spoke to the neighbor next door. Old guy in his eighties. Says he hardly ever sees her, but he does hear voices in here every so often." Frost rapped the wall. "They're pretty thin."

"Voices, as in plural?"

"Could be the TV. She lives alone."

Jane looked around at the pristine bathroom. "If she lives here at all."

"Someone's paying the rent."

"Looks like someone's also been through here with the bleach and a vacuum cleaner."

"Funny thing about the vacuum cleaner. We can't find one, so we have no bag to look at, no trace evidence."

Jane headed into the bedroom, where she found Tam talking on his cell phone. He gave a nod as Jane stepped into the room. The floor was wood, swept clean. The sheets and bedcovers had been pulled back, the mattress exposed. Dropping to her knees, Jane peered beneath the bed and saw that the floor under the box spring was just as dust-free. A pair of shoes walked into view and Jane popped up to see a Boston

PD criminalist looking at her across the mattress.

"We didn't find any weapon," he reported. "Unless you count the cooking knives in the kitchen."

"You didn't see anything like a sword?"

"No, ma'am. We went through the closets and drawers. Pulled out all the furniture and looked behind it." He paused, glancing around at the bare walls. "I'm guessing she hasn't been here very long. Not long enough to settle in."

"If she planned to stay at all."

"Didn't bring much in the way of clothes, either."

Jane opened the closet and saw no more than a dozen items hanging there, all size two. Three pairs of black pants, a few dark sweaters and blouses, and one sleeveless summer dress of soft peach silk. It was the wardrobe of a temporary visitor who clearly planned to move on. A girl who remained a mystery to them. Jane stared at the dress, trying to picture Bella Li wearing something so feminine, so flirty, but could not see it. Instead she saw the girl's fierce eyes, her spiky black hair.

"Sorry to tell you this," said Tam, holding up his cell phone. "But her alibi for April fifteenth is solid. I just spoke to the program director at the cultural center. That night they hosted a martial arts demonstration. Bella Li performed with eight students from the Dragon and Stars Academy."

"What time was it?"

"The group arrived at six PM, ate dinner, and went onstage about nine PM. They were there for the whole evening." He shook his head. "This isn't going to stick, Rizzoli."

"She has no alibi for April twenty-first."

"That's not a reason to hold her."

"Then let's find a reason, goddamn it."

"Why?" Tam's gaze was so probing, it made her uncomfortable.

She turned back to the closet, to avoid his eyes. "Something about her trips my sensors. I *know* she's involved, but I don't know how."

"All we have is a surveillance video

with a female figure. It might be her, but it might be someone else. We don't have any weapon. We don't have any trace evidence."

"Because she blitzed this place with bleach before we got here."

"So what do we have, besides your gut feeling?"

"It's served me well before." She reached into the closet and poked a gloved hand into pockets, searching. Not knowing what she was looking for. She found only stray change, a button, a folded tissue.

"You know, Tam's right," said Frost, standing in the doorway. "We have to release her."

"Not till I know more about her. Who she really is," said Jane.

"We're just guessing."

"Then let's find what we need to prove it. There's a trail somewhere, there has to be." She crossed to the bedroom window and looked down at an alley. The sash was unlocked, the window open just enough to let in fresh air. A fire escape landing was right outside, and there was no screen on the window. Any other female tenant would feel nervous about this lack of security, but Bella Li was fearless, striding through life ready for battle. At night, in her bed, did she ever startle awake at the odd noise outside her window, the creak in the floor? Or did she sleep like a warrior as well, unafraid even in her dreams?

Jane turned from the window and suddenly stopped, her gaze on the curtain. The fabric was a polyester blend that never wrinkles, a print of beige bamboo stalks against a forest of green. On that multicolored background, the silvery streak was almost invisible. Only at that angle, with the room light glancing across the fabric's surface, did Jane see the strand clinging to the fabric.

She pulled an evidence bag out of her pocket. Afraid to even breathe, she delicately plucked the strand from the curtain and slipped it into the bag. Holding the bag up to the light, she stared through plastic at the single hair. Then she looked at the window, and at the fire escape just beyond it.

It was here. The creature was in this room.

THIRTY-TWO

The hunter seldom realizes when he is the one being hunted. He walks in the woods, rifle in hand, eyes alert for his quarry's prints on snow-dusted ground. He searches for spoor or sits perched in his tree blind, waiting for the bear to lumber into view. It never occurs to him that his prey might be watching *him,* biding its time until he makes a mistake.

The hunter who stalks me now would see little to fear. I appear to be merely a middle-aged woman, my hair streaked with gray, my gait slowed by weariness and the weight of the bags I carry, bulging with my weekly supply of groceries. I walk the same route I always walk on Tuesday evening. After shopping at the Chinese market on Beach Street, I turn right onto Tyler and head south, toward my quiet neighborhood of Tai Tung Village. I keep my head down, my shoulders drooped, so that anyone who sees me will think: *Here is a victim.* Not a woman who will fight back. Not a woman you need to fear.

But by now my opponent knows he should be wary, just as I am wary of him. So far we have sparred only in the shadows but have never actually connected, except through his surrogates. We are two hunters still circling each other, and he must make the next move. Only then, when he emerges into the light, will I know his face.

So I walk down Tyler Street as I have so many times before, wondering if this is the night. I have never felt so vulnerable, and I know the next act is about to begin. The bright lights of Beach and Kneeland streets fade behind me. I move through shadows now, past dark doorways and unlit alleys, the plastic grocery sacks rustling as I walk. Just a tired widow minding her own business. But I am aware of everything around me, from the mist on my face to the scent of cilantro and onions wafting from my bags. No one escorts me. No guardian stands watch. Tonight I am alone, a target waiting for the first arrow to come flying.

As I draw near my home, I see the light over the porch is dark. Deliberate sabotage or merely a burned-out bulb? My nerves hum with alarm and my heart accelerates, rushing blood to muscles that are already tensing for battle. Then I spot the parked car and see the man who steps out to greet me, and my breath rushes out in a sigh of both relief and exasperation.

"Mrs. Fang?" says Detective Frost. "I need to speak with you."

I pause beside my front stoop, arms weighed down by groceries, and stare at him without smiling. "I'm tired tonight. And I have nothing more to say."

"At least let me help you with those," he offers and before I can protest, he snatches the grocery sacks from my hands and carries them up the steps to my porch. There he waits for me to open the door. He looks so earnest that I don't have the heart to reject his offer.

I unlock the door and let him in.

As I turn on lights, he carries the sacks into the kitchen and sets them on the counter. He stands with his hands in his pockets and he watches as I put pungent herbs and crisp vegetables in the refrigerator, as I stock pantry cabinets with cooking oil and paper towels and cans of chicken broth.

"I wanted to apologize," he says. "And to explain."

"Explain?" I ask, sounding as if I really don't care what he has to say.

"The sword, and why we took it. In a murder investigation, we have to explore all avenues. Follow every line of inquiry. The weapon we've been looking for is a very old sword, and I knew you owned one."

I shut the pantry cabinet and turn to him. "By now you must have realized the mistake you made."

He nodded. "The sword will be returned to you."

"And when will Bella be released?"

"That's more complicated. We're still looking into her background. Something I was hoping you could help us with, since you know her."

I shake my head. "The last time we spoke, Detective, I ended up being considered a suspect, and my family heirloom was confiscated."

"I didn't want that to happen."

"But you're a policeman, first and foremost."

"What else would you expect me to be?"

"I don't know. A friend?"

That makes him pause. He stands beneath the harsh kitchen lights, which make him look older than he is. Even so, he is a young man, young enough to be my son. I don't want to think about how those unflattering fluorescent lights must age my face.

"I *would* be your friend, Iris," he says. "If only . . ."

"If only I weren't a suspect."

"I don't consider you one."

"Then you aren't doing your job. I could be that killer you're searching for.

Can't you picture it, Detective? This middle-aged woman swinging a sword, leaping around on rooftops and cutting down enemies?" I laugh in his face and he flushes, as if I've slapped him. "Maybe you should search my house. There could be another sword hidden here somewhere, a weapon you don't even know I have."

"Iris, please."

"Maybe you'll report back to your colleagues that the suspect has turned hostile. That she's not going to be charmed into giving away any more information."

"That's not why I'm here! The night we had dinner, I wasn't trying to interrogate you."

"What were you trying to do?"

"Understand you, that's all. Who you are, what you think."

"Why?"

"Because you and I—because . . ." He gives a heavy sigh. "I felt like we both needed a friend, that's all. I know I do."

I regard him for a moment. He is not looking at me; his gaze is focused somewhere beyond me, as if he can't bring himself to look me in the eye. Not because he's untruthful, but because he's vulnerable. He may be a policeman, but he's afraid of my opinion of him. There's nothing I can offer him now, not comfort or friendship or even a touch on the arm.

"You need a friend your own age, Detective Frost," I say quietly. "Not someone like me."

"I don't even see your age."

"I do. I feel it, too," I add, massaging an imaginary kink in my neck. "And my illness."

"I see a woman who'll never get old."

"Tell me that in twenty years."

He smiles. "Maybe I will."

The moment trembles with unsaid words, with feelings that make us both uncomfortable. He is a good man; I see that in his eyes. But it's absurd to think we could ever be more than mere acquaintances. Not because I am nearly two decades older than he is, although that alone is a barrier. No, it's because of the secrets that I can never share

with him, secrets that place us on opposite sides of a chasm.

As I walk him to the door, he says:
"Tomorrow I'll bring the sword back to
you."

"And Bella?"

"There's a chance she'll be released
in the morning. We can't hold her in-
definitely, not without evidence."

"She's done nothing wrong."

In the doorway he stops and looks
straight at me. "It's not always clear
what's right and what's wrong. Is it?"

I stare back at him, thinking: Could
he know? Is he giving me permission
for what I'm about to do? But he merely
smiles and walks away.

I lock the door behind him. The conversation has left me off balance, unable to focus. What to make of such a
man, I wonder as I head up the stairs to
change my clothes. Yet again, he makes
me think of my husband. His kindness,
his patience. His open mind, so ready
to welcome possibilities. Am I a vain
fool to entertain such an unlikely friendship? I am distracted, mulling over the
conversation, and I miss the clues that

should have warned me. The tremor in the air. The faint scent of unfamiliar flesh. Only when I flip my bedroom light switch and nothing happens do I suddenly realize I am not alone.

The bedroom door slams shut behind me. In the darkness, I cannot see the blow hurtling toward my head, but my instincts spring to life. Something whooshes just above me as I duck and spin toward the bed, where my sword is concealed. Not the decoy reproduction that I surrendered to the police, but the real Zheng Yi. For five centuries she has been passed down from mothers to daughters, a legacy meant to protect us, defend us.

Now, more than ever, I need her.

My attacker lunges, but I slip away like water and roll to the floor. Reach under the box spring for the niche where Zheng Yi is hidden. She fits into my hand like an old friend and makes a musical sigh as she slides from her scabbard.

In one fluid motion I rise and whirl to face the enemy. The creak of the floor announces his location, to my right.

Just as I shift weight to attack, I hear the footfall, but this one is behind me.

Two of them.

It's the last thought I have before I fall.

THIRTY-THREE

Jane crouched down beside Iris's bed, reading the evidence and not liking what it said to her. There were red splatters on the floor and on the edge of the sheets where a body had fallen. The blood loss was minimal, certainly not enough to be fatal. Rising to her feet, she stared down at smeared drops, across which a body had been dragged. She had already spotted more blood on the stairs, and on the front porch where the door had been left wide open, alerting Iris's neighbors that something was very wrong.

Jane turned to Frost. "You're sure about the time? It was nine PM when you left last night?"

He nodded, a dazed look in his eyes. "I didn't see anyone else around when I came out of the house. And I was parked right outside."

"Why were you here?"

"To talk to her. I felt bad about what happened. About taking the sword."

"You came to apologize for doing your job?"

"Sometimes, Rizzoli, the job makes me feel like an asshole, okay?" he shot back. "Here's a woman who was already a victim. She lost her husband and her daughter. And we turn her into a suspect. We interrogate her. We made her a victim all over again."

"I don't know what Iris Fang is. I do know that she's been at the center of this from the beginning. Everything that's happened seems to revolve around *her*." Jane's cell phone rang. "Rizzoli," she answered.

It was Tam on the line. "Kevin Donohue says he has an alibi for last night."

"And his men?"

"That's the problem. They're each other's alibis. All three swear they spent the evening together in Donohue's residence, watching TV. Which means we can't believe a word from any of them."

"So we can't rule them out."

"We can't prove it in court, either."

Jane hung up and turned in frustration to the window. On the street below, a trio of elderly Chinese women stood staring up at her, chattering among themselves. *What do they know that they're not telling us?* Nothing about Chinatown was ever straightforward, nothing was as it seemed. It was like peering through a silk screen, never getting a clear image, a complete picture.

She turned to Frost. "Maybe Bella will finally talk to us. It's time to put all our cards on the table."

Bella looked even more hostile today, her hands closed in fists, gaze hard as diamonds. "It's *your* fault this happened," she said. "I should have been there. I would have stopped it."

Jane looked into those glittering eyes

and suddenly imagined the young woman springing up like a wildcat, attacking with teeth and claws. But she kept her voice calm as she said: "So you knew this would happen? You knew they would take her?"

"We're wasting time! She needs me."

"How will you help her when you don't even know where she is?"

Bella opened her mouth to speak, then glanced at the one-way mirror, as if aware that others were watching.

"Why don't we start at the beginning, Bella," said Jane. "With who you really are. Not the name you called yourself in California, but the name you were born with." Jane placed a photocopy of a birth certificate on the table. "It's signed by a Chinatown doctor. You were born right here in Boston. A home birth, at a Knapp Street address. Your father's name was Wu Weimin."

Bella didn't answer, but Jane read the acknowledgment in her eyes. Not that she needed it; the document was only exhibit number one. Jane brought out other photocopied documents. Her records from the San Francisco public schools where the girl was registered under the name Bella Li. The death certificate of her mother, who went by the name of Annie Li, dead at age forty-three of stomach cancer. It was all there in black and white, the paper trail that Jane's team had doggedly pursued over the last forty-eight hours, a trail obscured in that pre-9/11 era by different jurisdictions, and by the hidden world in which undocumented aliens moved. A world in which a lone mother and child could so easily vanish and reappear under new names.

"Why did you come back to Boston?" asked Jane.

Bella looked her in the eye. "*Sifu* Fang asked me to come. She's not well, and she needed another instructor at her school."

"Yes, that's the story you keep telling us."

"Is there a different story?"

"It has nothing to do with what happened in the Red Phoenix? Nothing to do with your father killing four people?"

Bella's face snapped taut. "My father was innocent."

"Not according to the official report."

"And official reports are *never* wrong."

"If it's wrong, then what's the truth?"

Bella glared back. "He was murdered."

"Is that what your mother told you?"

"My mother wasn't there!"

Jane paused, suddenly registering the unspoken meaning of those last words, *my mother wasn't there.* She remembered the glow of luminol on the cellar step, the bloody imprint of a child's shoe. "But someone *was* there," Jane said quietly. "Someone who was hiding in the cellar when it happened."

Bella went absolutely still. "How did you . . ."

"The blood told us. Even if you try to wash it away, its traces remain. Decades later, with a chemical spray, we can still see it. We found your footprint on the cellar steps, and on the kitchen floor, leading toward the exit. Footprints that someone had wiped away by the time the police arrived that night." Jane leaned in closer. "Why did your mother do it, Bella? Why did she try to erase the evidence?"

Bella didn't answer, but Jane saw the inner debate play out on her face, a struggle between telling the truth and keeping it secret.

"She did it to protect you, didn't she?" said Jane. "Because you saw what happened, and she was afraid for you. Afraid that someone would come after you."

Bella shook her head. "I didn't see it."

"You were there."

"But I didn't *see* it!" Bella cried. For a moment her outburst seemed to hang in the air between them. Her head drooped and she whispered: "But I heard it."

Jane didn't ask any questions, didn't interrupt. She simply waited for the story she knew would now be told.

Bella took another breath. "My mother was asleep in bed. She was always so tired after working all day at the grocery store. And that night she was sick with the flu." Bella stared at the table, as though she could still picture her mother huddled in bed under blankets. "But I wasn't tired. So I climbed out of bed. I went downstairs to see Daddy."

"In the restaurant."

"He was annoyed with me, of course." A sad smile tugged at her mouth. "There he was, juggling pots and pans. And I was whining for attention and ice cream. He told me to go back upstairs to bed. He was busy, and he didn't have time for me. Uncle Fang didn't have time for me, either."

"Iris's husband?"

Bella nodded. "He was in the dining room. I looked through the door and saw him sitting at a table with a man and woman. They were drinking tea."

Jane frowned, wondering why the waiter would be sitting with two patrons. It added to the other puzzle about the Mallorys: Why were they in a Chinese restaurant when their autopsies showed they had just dined on Italian food?

"What were they talking about?" asked Jane. "Mr. Fang and the two customers?"

Bella shook her head. "It was too noisy in the kitchen to hear anything in the dining room. My father banging his pots. The fan blowing."

"Did you see Joey Gilmore come in to pick up his take-out order?"

"No. All I remember is my father, working at the stove. Sweating. And his old T-shirt. He always worked in his T-shirt . . ." Her voice faltered and she wiped a hand across her eyes. "My poor father. Working, always working. His hands scarred from all the burns and cuts from the kitchen."

"What happened then?"

Bella's mouth twisted in a rueful smile. "I wanted ice cream. I was whining, demanding attention, while he was trying to fill the take-out cartons. Finally he gave in. Told me to go downstairs and choose an ice cream from the freezer."

"In the cellar?"

She nodded. "Oh, I knew that cellar very well. I'd been down there so many times. There was a big chest freezer, tucked in the corner. I had to climb onto a chair to lift the lid. I remember looking inside for just the flavor I wanted. They were in these little cardboard cups, just big enough to hold one scoop. I wanted the one with stripes of chocolate and vanilla and strawberry. But I couldn't find any. I kept digging and digging through those little cups, but they were all vanilla. Nothing but vanilla." She took a deep breath. "And then I heard my father shouting."

"At whom?"

"At me." Bella looked up and blinked away tears. "He was screaming at me to hide."

"Everyone in the restaurant must have heard him."

"He said it in Chinese. The killer couldn't understand, or he would have come looking for me. He would have known I was in the cellar."

Jane glanced toward the one-way mirror. She couldn't see Frost and Tam, but she imagined their astonished faces. Here was the tale's missing chapter. The clues had been there all along on the cellar step and on the kitchen floor, but footprints are silent. Only Bella gave them a voice.

"And you hid?" asked Jane.

"I didn't understand what was hap-pening. I climbed off the chair and started to go up the steps, but then I stopped. I heard him pleading. Begging for his life, in his broken English. That's when I understood this wasn't a game, wasn't some trick he was playing on me. My father didn't play games." Bella swallowed and her voice dropped even lower. "So I did what he told me to do. I didn't make a sound. I ducked underneath the stairs. I heard something fall. And then a loud bang."

"How many gunshots in all?"

"Just the one. That single bang."

Jane thought of the weapon found in Wu Weimin's hand, a Glock with a threaded barrel. The killer had used a suppressor to muffle the sound of those first eight gunshots. Only after dispatching his victims did he remove the suppressor, place the grip in Wu Weimin's lifeless hand, and fire the final bullet, ensuring that gunshot residue would be found on the victim's skin.

A perfect crime, thought Jane. Except for the fact there was a witness. A silent girl, huddled under the cellar steps.

"He died for me," whispered Bella.

"He should have run, but he wouldn't leave me. So he stayed. He died right in front of the cellar door. Blocking it with his body. I had to step in his blood to get past him. If I hadn't been there that night, begging for my goddamn ice cream, my father would still be alive."

Jane understood it all, now. Why Wu Weimin did not flee when he had the chance. Why there were two bullet casings on the kitchen floor. Had the staged suicide been a last-minute idea, something that occurred to the killer as he stood over the cook's body? It was such a simple thing, to wrap a dead man's fingers around the grip and fire the last round. Leave the gun behind and walk out the door.

"You should have told the police," said Jane. "It would have changed everything."

"No, it wouldn't. Who would believe a five-year-old girl? A girl who never saw the killer's face. And my mother wouldn't let me say a word. She was afraid of the police. *Terrified* is a better word."

"Why?"

Bella's jaw tightened. "Can't you

guess? My mother was here illegally. What do you think would have happened if the police focused on us? She had my future to think of, and hers as well. My father was dead. Nothing we could do would change that."

"What about justice? That had no part in the equation?"

"Not then. Not that night, when all she could think about was keeping us both safe. If the killer knew there was a witness, he might come looking for me. That's why she wiped up my footprints. That's why we packed our suitcases and left two days later."

"Did Iris Fang know?"

"Not then. Not until years later, when my mother was dying of stomach cancer. A month before she died, she wrote *Sifu* Fang and told her the truth. Apologized for being a coward. But after so many years, there was nothing we could prove, nothing we could change."

"Yet you've been trying, haven't you?" said Jane. "For the past seven years, either you or Iris has been mailing obituaries to the families. Keeping their memories and their pain alive. Telling them that the truth hasn't been told."

"It *hasn't* been. They need to know that. That's why the letters were sent, so they would keep asking questions. It's the only way we'll find out who the killer is."

"So you and Iris have been trying to draw him out into the open. Sending notes to the families, to Kevin Donohue, hinting that the truth's about to be revealed. Taking out that ad in *The Boston Globe,* hoping the killer will get worried and finally attack. And what was the plan then? Turn him over to us? Or take justice into your own hands?"

Bella laughed. "How could we possibly do that? We're *only* women."

Now it was Jane's turn to laugh. "As if I'd ever underestimate *you.*" Jane reached into her briefcase and pulled out the Arthur Waley translation of *Monkey,* the ancient Chinese folk novel. "I'm sure you've heard of the Monkey King."

Bella glanced at the book. "Chinese fairy tales. What do they have to do with anything?"

"One particular chapter in this book

caught my attention. It's called 'The Story of Chen O.' It's about a scholar who travels with his pregnant wife. At a ferry crossing, they're attacked by bandits and the husband is killed. His wife is abducted. Do you know this one?"

Bella shrugged. "I've heard it."

"Then you know how it turns out. The wife gives birth to a son while in captivity and secretly places him on a wooden plank, with a letter explaining her plight. Just like baby Moses, the child's set adrift on the river. He floats to the Temple of the Golden Mountain, where he's raised by holy men. He grows to manhood and learns the truth about his parents. About his butchered father and his imprisoned mother."

"Is there a point to this?"

"The point is right here, in the words spoken by the young man." Jane looked down at the page and read the quote. *"He who fails to avenge the wrongs done to a parent is unworthy of the name of man."* She looked at Bella. "That's what this is all about, isn't it? You're like the son in this story. Haunted by the murder of your father. Honor-bound to avenge him." Jane slid the book in front of Bella. "It's exactly what the Monkey King would do, fight for justice. Protect the innocent. Avenge a father. Oh, Monkey may wreak a bit of havoc in the process. He may break all the chinaware and set fire to the furniture. But in the end, justice is done. He always does the *right thing.*"

Bella said nothing as she stared at the illustration of the warrior monkey brandishing his staff.

"I understand completely, Bella," said Jane. "You're not the villain in this. You're the daughter of a victim, a daughter who wants what the police can't deliver. Justice." She lowered her voice to a sympathetic murmur. "That's what you and Iris were trying to do. Draw out the killer. Tempt him to strike."

Was that the hint of a nod she saw? Bella's inadvertent acknowledgment of the truth?

"But the plan didn't work out so well," said Jane. "When he did strike, he hired professionals to do the killing for him. So you still don't know his identity. And now he's taken Iris."

Bella looked up, fury burning in her eyes. "It went wrong because of *you.* I should have been there to watch over her."

"She was the bait."

"She was willing to take the risk."

"And you two were going to deliver justice all by yourselves?"

"Who else is going to do it? The police?" Bella's laugh was bitter. "All these years later, they don't care."

"You're wrong, Bella. I sure as hell do care."

"Then let me go, so I can find her."

"You have no idea where to start."

"Do you?" Bella spat back.

"We're looking at several suspects."

"While you keep me locked up for no reason."

"I'm investigating two homicides. That's my reason."

"They were hired killers. That's what you said."

"Their deaths are still homicides."

"And I have an alibi for the first one. You *know* I didn't kill that woman on the roof."

"Then who did?"

Bella looked at the book and her mouth twitched. "Maybe it was the Monkey King."

"I'm talking about real people."

"You say I'm a suspect, but you know I couldn't have killed the woman. You might as well blame some mythical creature, because you have just as much of a chance of proving it." Bella looked at Jane. "You do know how the folktale starts, don't you? How Sun Wukong emerges from stone and transforms into a warrior? The night my father was killed, I emerged from that stone cellar just like Monkey. I was transformed, too. I became what I am now."

Jane stared into eyes as hard as any she had ever looked into. She tried to imagine Bella as a frightened five-year-old, but she could see no trace of that child in this fierce creature. *If I'd witnessed the murder of someone I loved, would I be any different?*

Jane stood up. "You're right, Bella. I don't have enough to hold you. Not yet."

"You mean—you're letting me go?"

"Yes, you can leave."

"And I won't be followed? I'm free to do what I have to?"

"What does that mean?"

Bella rose from her chair, like a lioness uncoiling herself for the hunt, and the two women stared at each other across the table. "Whatever it takes," she said.

THIRTY-FOUR

I can hear him breathing in the darkness, beyond the blinding glare that shines in my eyes. He has not allowed me to see his face; all I know about him is that his voice is as smooth as cream. But I have not cooperated, and he is starting to grow angry because he realizes I am not easily broken.

Now he is worried as well, because of the personal tracking device he found strapped to my ankle. A device that he has disabled by removing the battery.

"Who are you working with?" he asks.

He shoves the device in my face. "Who was tracking you?"

Despite my bruised jaw, my swollen lips, I manage to answer in a hoarse whisper: "Someone you never want to meet. But you soon will."

"Not if they can't find you." He tosses down the tracking device, and when it hits the floor it is like the sound of shattering hope. I was still unconscious when he took it from me, so I don't know when the device ceased its transmissions. It might have been long before I arrived in this place, which means that no one will be able to find me. And this is where I will die.

I don't even know where I am.

My wrists are trapped by manacles bolted to the wall. The floor beneath my bare feet is concrete. There is no light except what he shines in my eyes, no hint of sunlight through window cracks. Perhaps it is night. Or perhaps this is a place where light never penetrates, where screams never escape. I squint against the glare, trying to make out my surroundings, but there is only that bright light and beyond it, darkness. My hands twitch, aching to close around a weapon, to complete what I have waited so many years to finish.

"You're looking for your sword, aren't you?" he says, and waves the blade in the light, so that I can see it. "A beautiful weapon. Sharp enough to slice off a finger without an ounce of effort. Is this what you used to kill them?" He swings it, and the blade hisses past my face. "I hear her hand was sliced off clean. And his head came off with a single stroke. Two professional killers, yet they were both taken by surprise." He brings the blade to my neck, pressing it so tightly that my bounding pulse makes the metal throb. "Shall we see what this can do to *your* throat?"

I hold still, my gaze fixed on the black oval that is his face. I have already resigned myself to death, so I am prepared for it. In truth, I've been ready to die these past nineteen years, and with a slash of the blade, he'll free me at last to join my husband, a reunion that I have put off only because of this unfinished business. What I feel now isn't fear but regret that I have failed. That this man will never feel my sword's bite against his own throat.

"That night, in the Red Phoenix, there was a witness," he says. "Who was it?"

"Do you really think I would tell you?"

"So someone *was* there."

"And will never forget."

The sword digs deeper into my neck. "Tell me the name."

"You're going to kill me anyway. Why should I?"

A long pause, then he lifts the blade from my skin. "Let's make a deal," he says calmly. "You tell me who this witness is. And I'll tell you what happened to your daughter."

I try to process what he's just said, but the darkness suddenly spins around me and the floor seems to be dissolving beneath my feet. He sees my confusion and he laughs.

"You had no idea, did you, that this was always about her. Laura, wasn't that her name? She was about fourteen years old. I remember her, because she was the first one I got to choose. Pretty little thing. Long black hair, skinny hips.

And so trusting. It wasn't hard to talk her into the car. She was carrying all those heavy books and her violin, and was grateful for the ride home. It was all so easy, because I was a friend."

"I don't believe you."

"Why would I lie?"

"Then tell me where she is."

"First tell me who the witness is. Tell me who was in the Red Phoenix. Then I'll tell you what happened to Laura."

I am still struggling with this revelation, trying to understand why this man knows my daughter's fate. She disappeared two years before my husband died in the shooting. I never imagined any connection between the events. I had believed that fate simply delivered a double blow, a karmic punishment for some cruelty I'd committed in a past lifetime.

"She was such a talented girl," the smooth voice says. "That first day we rehearsed, I knew she was the one I wanted. Vivaldi's Concerto for Two Violins. Do you remember her practicing that piece?"

His words are like a blast that hurls shrapnel through my heart because I know now that he's telling the truth. He heard my daughter play. He knows what happened to her.

"Tell me the name of the witness," he says.

"This is all I'll tell you," I say quietly. "You are a dead man."

The blow comes without warning, so violent that it whips my head backward and my skull slams against the wall. Through the roaring in my ears I hear him speaking to me, words that I don't want to hear.

"She lasted seven, maybe eight weeks. Longer than the others. She looked delicate, but oh, she was strong. Think of it, Mrs. Fang. For two whole months, while the police were searching for her, she was still alive. Begging to go home to her mommy."

My control shatters. I cannot stop the tears, cannot suppress the sobs that rack my body. They sound like an animal's howls of pain, wild and alien.

"I can give you *closure,* Mrs. Fang,"

he says. "I can answer the question that's been tormenting you all these years. Where is Laura?" He leans in closer. Though I can't see his face, I smell his scent, ripe with aggression. "Tell me what I want to know, and I'll put your mind at rest."

It happens before I even think about it, a feral reaction that surprises us both. He flinches away, gasping in disgust as he wipes my spit from his face. I fully expect that another blow will follow and I brace myself for the pain.

It does not come. Instead he bends down and picks up my tracking device, which he had earlier tossed to the floor. He waves it in my face. "Really, I don't need you at all," he says. "All I need to do is replace this battery and turn it on again. And I'll just wait to see who shows up."

He leaves the room. I hear the door swing shut, and footsteps thud up the stairs.

Grief is my only companion, gnawing with teeth so sharp that I cry and flail against the manacles, scraping skin from my wrists. He had my daughter. He kept her. I remember the nights after Laura vanished, when my husband and I clung to each other, neither daring to say what we were both thinking. *What if she is dead?* Now I realize there was a far worse possibility, something that we had not imagined: that she was still alive. That during those two months, as James and I felt hope die and acceptance take its place, our Laura was still breathing. Still suffering.

I slump back exhausted, and my screams fade to whimpers. The frenzy has left me numb. Leaning against the concrete wall, I try to reconcile what he has just told me with what I already know, which is this: Two years after my daughter's abduction, my husband and four other people were massacred in the Red Phoenix restaurant. How could these events be related and what ties them together? This he never explained.

I struggle to remember everything he said, searching through the fog of grief for clues. One sentence suddenly comes back to me, words that instantly freeze the blood in my veins.

She lasted seven, maybe eight weeks. Longer than the others.

My head lifts at the revelation. *The others.*

My daughter was not the only one.

THIRTY-FIVE

What did Detective Ingersoll know, and why was he killed for it?

That was the question that consumed Jane as she sat late into the afternoon, sifting through her notes about Ingersoll's murder. Spread across her desk were the crime scene photos of his residence, ballistic and trace-evidence reports, his cell phone and landline logs, and his bank card charges. According to Donohue, a death contract had gone out on Ingersoll weeks ago, right about the time when he began asking questions about missing girls. All the cases were old ones that had since dropped off the radar of departments across Massachusetts. She stared at a photo of Ingersoll's body and thought: What monster did you awaken?

And what do missing girls have to do with the Red Phoenix?

She reached for the files on those missing girls. She was thoroughly familiar with the details of Laura's and Charlotte's disappearances, so she focused on the other three cases. All the victims were pretty and petite. All were good-to-excellent students. All were multitalented.

Patty Boles and Sherry Tanaka played in tennis tournaments. Deborah Schiffer and Patty Boles participated in art fairs. Deborah Schiffer played the piano in her school orchestra. But none of the three knew one another, at least according to their parents. And they were different ages at the times of their disappearances. Sherry Tanaka was sixteen. Deborah Schiffer was thirteen. Patty Boles was fifteen. One in middle school, two in high school.

Jane thought about this for a moment. Remembered that Laura Fang was fourteen years old when she vanished.

She jotted down the order in which the girls disappeared.

Deborah Schiffer, age thirteen.

Laura Fang, age fourteen.

Patty Boles, age fifteen.

Sherry Tanaka, age sixteen.

Charlotte Dion, age seventeen.

It was like staring at a royal flush. Every year, a different girl, a different age. As if the kidnapper's taste had matured as the years passed.

She reached for the folder with the last photos of Charlotte, taken at the double funeral of her mother and stepfather. Again she flipped through the sequence of images taken by the *Boston Globe* photographer. Charlotte looking pale and thin in her black dress, surrounded by mourners. Charlotte stumbling away toward the edge of the crowd as Mark Mallory, her stepbrother, stares in her direction. The photo where Charlotte and Mark are absent, and her father, Patrick, looks confused by the sudden abandonment. Finally she came to the last image, where both were back in the frame, Mark walking behind Charlotte. Tall and broad-shouldered, he could easily have overpowered his step-sister.

Every year, an older girl.

The year that thirteen-year-old Deborah Schiffer vanished was a year after Dina and Arthur Mallory married, forming a new and reconstituted family, with all the joint activities that this would have entailed. School assemblies. Orchestra performances. State tennis tournaments.

Is this how the victims were chosen? Through Charlotte?

Jane picked up the phone and called Patrick Dion.

"I'm sorry to bother you at dinner-time," she said. "But would it be possible for me to take another look at Charlotte's school yearbooks?"

"You're welcome to come anytime. Has something new turned up?"

"I'm not sure."

"What are you looking for, exactly? Perhaps I could help you."

"I've been thinking a lot about Charlotte. About whether she's the key to everything that's happened."

Over the phone, she heard Patrick give a mournful sigh. "My daughter has always been the key, Detective. To my life, to everything that's ever mattered. There's nothing I want more than to know what happened to her."

"I understand, sir," Jane said gently. "I know you want the answer, and I think I might be able to provide it."

He answered the door wearing a baggy pullover sweater, chino slacks, and bedroom slippers. Patrick's face, like his sweater, was sagging and careworn, every crease etched deeply with old grief. And here was Jane to bring back the awful memories. For that she felt guilty, and when they shook hands, she held on longer than necessary, a grasp meant to tell him that she was sorry. That she understood.

He gave her a sad nod and led the way into the dining room, his slippers shuffling across the wood floor. "I have the yearbooks waiting for you," he said, pointing to the volumes on the dining table.

"I'll just bring these out to my car and be on my way. Thank you."

"Oh dear." He frowned. "If it's all right, I'd rather you didn't take them out of the house."

"I promise I'll look after them very carefully."

"I'm sure you will, but . . ." He placed his hand on the stack of books, as though blessing a child. "This is what I have left of my daughter. And it's hard, you know, to let any of it out of my sight. I worry that they'll get lost or damaged. That maybe someone will steal them from your car. Or you'll have an accident and . . ." He paused and gave a rueful shake of his head. "That's terrible of me, isn't it? To value a stack of books so much that I I focus only on what happens to *them.* When they're just cardboard and paper."

"They're worth more than that to you. I understand."

"So if you could humor me? You're perfectly welcome to sit here as long as you need and look through them. Can I get you something? A glass of wine?"

"Thanks, but I'm on duty. And I have to drive home."

"Coffee, then."

Jane smiled. "That would be wonderful."

As Patrick went to the kitchen to make coffee, she sat down at the dining table and spread out the books. He had brought them all out, including the volumes from Charlotte's elementary school years. She set those aside and opened the volume from Charlotte's first year at the Bolton Academy, when she was a seventh grader. Her photo showed a fragile-looking blonde with braces on her teeth. The caption read: CHARLOTTE DION. ORCHESTRA, TENNIS, ART. Jane flipped through the book to the older students and found Mark Mallory's photo in the sophomore high school class. He would have been fifteen then, and his interests were listed as orchestra, lacrosse, chess, fencing, drama. It was music that had brought them together, music that had changed the course of their lives and their families. The Dions and the Mallorys had met because of their children's performances at school. They became friends. Then Dina left Patrick for Arthur, and nothing would ever be the same for them again.

"Here you are," said Patrick, carrying in a tray with the coffeepot. He poured her a cup and set the sugar and cream on the table. "You must be hungry, too. I can make you a sandwich."

"No, this is perfect," she said, sipping hot coffee. "I had a late lunch, and I'll eat supper when I get home."

"You must have an understanding family."

She smiled. "I have a husband who knew what he was getting when he married me. Which reminds me." She pulled out her cell phone and tapped out a quick text message to Gabriel: HOME LATE. START DINNER WITHOUT ME.

"Are you finding what you need here?" Patrick asked, nodding at the yearbooks.

She set down her phone. "I don't know yet."

"If you tell me what you're looking for, I might be able to help."

"I'm looking for connections," she said.

"Between what?"

"Between your daughter. And these girls." Jane opened the file she'd brought with her and pointed to the list of four names.

Patrick frowned. "I know about Laura Fang, of course. After Charlotte went missing, the police explored whether there was any connection. But these other girls, I'm afraid I'm not familiar with their names."

"They didn't go to Bolton, but like your daughter, they disappeared without a trace. From different towns, in different years. I'm wondering if Charlotte knew any of them. Maybe through music or sports."

Patrick thought about this for a moment. "Detective Buckholz told me that children vanish all the time. Why are you looking at these girls in particular?"

Because a dead man named Ingersoll pointed the way, thought Jane. What she said was: "These names have come up in the course of the investigation. There could turn out to be no connection at all. But if a link with Charlotte does exist, I might be able to find it right here."

"In her yearbooks?"

She flipped through the student activity pages. "Look," she said. "I noticed this the last time. The Bolton Academy's very good about chronicling everything their students do, from school concerts to tennis meets. Maybe because it's such a small student body." She pointed to a page with photos of smiling students standing beside their science projects. The caption read: NEW ENGLAND SCIENCE FAIR, BURLINGTON, VERMONT, MAY 17. "With this documentation," she said, "I'm hoping to reconstruct Charlotte's school years. Where she was, what activities she participated in." Jane looked at Patrick. "She played the viola. That's how you got to know the Mallorys. At the kids' musical performances."

"How does that help you?"

Jane turned to the section for the music department. "Here. This was the year she first played in the orchestra." She pointed to a group photo of the musicians, which included Charlotte and Mark. Below it was the caption: THE ORCHESTRA'S JANUARY CONCERT BRINGS A STANDING OVATION!

Just the sight of the photo made Patrick wince with what seemed like physical pain. He said softly, "It's hard, you know. Looking at these photos. Remembering how . . ."

"You don't need to do this, Mr. Dion." Jane touched his hand. "I'll go through these books on my own. If I have any questions, I'll ask."

He nodded, suddenly looking far older than his sixty-seven years. "I'll leave you alone, then," he said. Quietly he retreated from the dining room, sliding the pocket doors shut behind him.

Jane poured another cup of coffee. Opened another yearbook.

It was for Charlotte's eighth-grade year, when she would have been thirteen and Mark sixteen. His growth spurt was already under way, his photo now showing a square jaw and broad shoulders. Charlotte still had a child's face, pale and delicate. Jane flipped through the school activities section, searching for photos of either one. She found both of them in a group portrait, taken at the statewide "Battle of the Orchestras," March 20, in Lowell, Massachusetts.

Deborah Schiffer lived in Lowell, and she played the piano.

Jane stared at the image of Charlotte and her fellow musicians. Two months after that photo was taken, Deborah vanished.

Jane's hand was humming with excitement and caffeine. She drained her coffee cup, poured another. Searched the volumes for Charlotte's ninth-grade yearbook. She already knew what she would find when she flipped to the music section. To the photo of eight music students, posing with their instruments with the caption: BOLTON'S BEST QUALIFY FOR BOSTON SUMMER ORCHESTRA WORKSHOP. She did not see Charlotte in the photo, but there was Mark Mallory. By this time he was seventeen years old, darkly handsome, a boy who could turn the head of any teen girl. That year, Laura Fang had been fourteen. She, too, had attended the orchestra workshop in Boston. Had Laura been dazzled by one particular boy's good looks and wealth, a boy for whom a girl of Laura's humble upbringing would be invisible?

Or was Laura very much on his radar?

Jane's throat felt parched, the buzzing in her head louder. She took another sip of coffee and reached for the next volume, Charlotte's tenth-grade yearbook. When she opened it, the words seemed smudged, the faces indistinct. She rubbed her eyes, turned to the activities section. There, once again, was Charlotte in the orchestra with her viola. But Mark had graduated, and another boy stood behind the tympanies.

Jane turned to the athletics pages. Again she rubbed her eyes, trying to clear away the fog that seemed to hang over her vision. The photo moved in and out of focus, but she could still pick out Charlotte's face in the lineup of tennis players. BOLTON TEAM TAKES SECOND PLACE AT OCTOBER'S REGIONALS.

Patty Boles was a tennis player, too, thought Jane. Like Charlotte, she was in her sophomore year. Had she competed at those regionals? Had she caught someone's eye, someone who could easily learn who she was, and which school she attended?

Six weeks after that regional tournament, Patty Boles vanished.

Jane gave her head a shake, but the fog seemed to thicken before her eyes. *Something is very wrong.*

The distant jangle of a ringing phone penetrated the buzz in her ears. She heard Patrick talking. She tried to call for help, but no sound came out.

Struggling to her feet, she heard the chair topple over and crash to the floor. All feeling was gone from her legs; they were like wooden stilts, senseless and clumsy. She staggered toward the pocket doors, afraid that she'd collapse before she got there, that Patrick would find her on the floor in a humiliating heap. As she reached out toward the doors they seemed to recede, taunting her efforts, always just beyond her fingertips.

Just as she lurched toward them, they suddenly slid open, and Patrick appeared.

"Help me," she whispered.

But he didn't move. He simply stood

watching her, his expression coldly dispassionate. Only then did she realize what a mistake she'd made. It was her last thought before she slumped unconscious at his feet.

THIRTY-SIX

She was thirsty, so thirsty. Jane tried to swallow, but her throat was parched, her tongue as dry as old leather against the roof of her mouth. Slowly she registered other sensations: the tingling in her left arm from lying too long in one position. The cold and gritty surface beneath her cheek. And the voice calling out to her, urgent and persistent. A woman's voice that would not let her sleep but kept nagging, wheedling her back to consciousness.

"Wake up. You must wake up!"

Jane opened her eyes—or thought

she did. The darkness she saw was so impenetrable that she wondered if she was trapped in the shadowy borderland between sleep and wakefulness, paralyzed but aware. Or was there another reason she could not move? She tried to roll onto her back and realized that her hands and feet were immobilized. She strained to free her wrists and met the unyielding resistance of duct tape. The floor beneath her cheek was concrete that bruised her hips and chilled straight through her clothes. She did not know how she'd come to be in this cold, black place. The last she remembered was sitting in Patrick's dining room, paging through Charlotte's yearbooks. Sipping coffee. *Coffee that he served me.*

"Detective Rizzoli! *Please* wake up!"

Jane recognized Iris Fang's voice, and she turned her head toward the sound. "How . . .where . . ."

"I cannot help you. I'm here, against the wall. Chained to the wall. We are in a cellar, I think. Maybe in his house. I don't know because I can't remember how I got here."

"Neither can I," groaned Jane.

"He brought you here hours ago. We don't have much time. He's just waiting for the other one to return."

The other one. Jane struggled to think through the lifting fog in her head. Of course Patrick was not working alone. At sixty-seven, he would need someone to help him with the strenuous tasks. That's why he'd hired professionals to kill Ingersoll, to attack Iris.

"We have to prepare," said Iris. "Before they come back."

"Prepare?" Jane couldn't help a desperate laugh. "I can't move my arms or legs. I can't even feel my hands!"

"But you can roll toward the wall. There's a set of keys hanging near the door. I saw it when he turned on the light and brought you down here. They might unlock my handcuffs. You free me, then I'll free you."

"Which way is the door?"

"It's to my right. Follow my voice. The keys are hanging on a hook. If you can get to your feet, grab the keys with your teeth—"

"That's a lot of ifs."

"Do it." The command pierced the darkness, sharp as a blade. But the next words were soft. "He took my daughter," she whispered, sobs suddenly stuttering through. "He's the one."

Jane listened to Iris crying in the darkness, and she thought of the other girls who'd vanished. Deborah Schiffer. Patty Boles. Sherry Tanaka. How many others had there been, girls whose names they did not yet know? *Even his own daughter, Charlotte.*

She fought against her bonds, but duct tape was indestructible, the favorite tool of MacGyver and serial killers alike. No amount of straining and twisting would tear those straps from her wrists.

"Don't let him win," said Iris. Her voice had steadied; the steel was back in it.

"I want him, too," said Jane.

"The keys. You have to reach them."

Already Jane was twisting, rolling across the floor. Her bruised hip banged against the concrete and she gasped, breathing deeply for a moment as the pain faded. Then it was another twist, another tumble across the floor. This time her face landed on the concrete, scraping her nose, banging her teeth. She rolled onto her unbruised side, knees drawn up in a fetal position, fighting tears of pain and frustration. How was she going to do this? She couldn't even make it across the floor, much less rise to her feet and reach the keys.

"You have a daughter," said Iris softly.

"Yes."

"Think of her. Think of what you'd do to hold her again. To smell her hair, touch her face. Think. *Imagine.*"

That quiet command seemed to come from somewhere inside her own head, as if it were her own voice demanding action. She thought of Regina in the bathtub, slippery and sweet-smelling with soap, dark curls clinging to pink skin. Regina, who would grow into a young woman, never knowing her own mother except as a ghost reflected in her own face, her own features. And she thought of Gabriel, growing old and gray. *A lifetime we'll never have together if I don't survive this night.*

"Think of her." Iris's voice drifted

through the darkness. "She'll give you the strength you need to *fight*."

"Is that how you did it all these years?"

"It was all I had. It's what kept me alive, the hope that my daughter might come home to me. I lived for that, Detective. I lived for the day I'd see her again. Or if it never happened, for the day I would see justice done. At least I'll know that I died trying."

Jane rolled again and her battered hip thumped against the floor, her face scraping across rough concrete. Suddenly her back collided with a wall and she lay on her side, panting, resting for what would be the next, and most difficult challenge. "I've reached the wall," she said.

"Get to your feet. The door's at the far end."

With the wall as a support, Jane tried to squirm up to a kneeling position, but lost her balance and collapsed facedown, her mouth slamming against the floor. Pain shot straight from her teeth into her skull.

"Your daughter," said Iris. "What is her name?"

Jane licked her lip and tasted blood. Felt the soft tissues already puffing up, swelling. "Regina," she said.

"How old is she?"

"Two and a half."

"And you love her very much."

"Of course I do." With a grunt, Jane struggled to her knees. She knew what Iris was doing; she could feel new strength in her muscles, new steel in her spine. No, she would not be kept away from her daughter. She would survive this night, the way Iris had survived these past two decades, because nothing mattered more to a mother than seeing her child again. She fought gravity, straining her back and neck to rise to a kneeling position.

"Regina," said Iris. "She is the blood in your veins. The breath in your lungs." Her voice was hypnotic, her words a whispered chant that sent heat rushing through Jane's limbs. Words spoken in the universal language that every mother understands.

She is the blood in your veins. The breath in your lungs.

Get to your feet, Jane thought. Get those keys.

She rocked forward on her knees, coiling her muscles, and sprang up. Landed on her feet, but only for a few tottering seconds before she lost her balance and fell forward, her kneecaps slamming onto concrete.

"Again," ordered Iris. No hint of sympathy in her voice. Was she as ruthless with her students? Was this the way real warriors were honed, without mercy, pushed beyond their limits?

"The keys," said Iris.

Jane took a deep breath, tensed, and sprang up. Again she landed on her feet and wobbled, but the wall was right beside her. She propped her shoulder against it as she waited for the cramp in her calf to ease. "I'm up," she said.

"Get to the far corner. That's where the door is."

Another hop, another wobble. She could do this. "Once we get free, we still have to get past him," said Jane. "He has my gun."

"I don't need a weapon."

"Oh, right. Ninjas just fly through the air."

"You don't know anything about me. Or what I can do."

Jane hopped again, landing like a kangaroo. "Then tell me. Since we're probably going to die, anyway. Are you the Monkey King?"

"The Monkey King is a fable."

"It leaves behind real hair. It kills with a real sword. So who is it?"

"Someone you want on your side, Detective."

"First I want to know who it is."

"He's inside you and me. He's inside everyone who believes in justice."

"That's not an answer."

"It's as much as I can tell you."

"I'm not talking mystical mumo jumbo," Jane panted and hopped again. "I'm talking about something real, something I've actually seen. Something that saved my life." She paused to catch her breath. And said quietly: "I just want to thank him—or her—for that. So if you know who it is, could you pass that message along?"

Iris answered, just as softly: "It already knows."

Jane made one last hop and her forehead banged against a door. "I'm here."

"It's hanging about the level of your head. Can you feel it?"

Brushing her cheek against the wall, Jane felt metal suddenly bite into her skin. Heard the soft clink of the hanging keys. "Found it!"

"Please don't drop them."

Jane gripped the keys in her mouth and lifted the ring off the wall hook. *We're going to do this. We're going to beat them* . . .

The squeal of the opening door made her freeze. Lights blazed on, so bright that she shrank back, blinded, against the wall.

"Well, this is a complication," said a voice she recognized. Slowly she opened her eyes against the glare and saw Mark Mallory standing beside Patrick. It has always been the two of them, she thought. Hunting together. Killing together. And the bond that linked these men was Charlotte. Poor Charlotte, whose every interest, every activity, had introduced predators to their prey, turning something as innocent as a tennis meet or an orchestra performance into an opportunity for killers to glimpse and choose fresh faces.

Mark grabbed the key ring and wrenched it from Jane's mouth. Gave her a shove and sent her toppling to the floor. "Does anyone know she came here?"

"We have to assume so," said Patrick. "That's why we need to get rid of her car. We should have done it hours ago, if only you'd gotten back sooner."

"I wanted to see if anyone would show up."

"No one came for her?"

"Maybe the tracker's broken." He looked at Iris. "Or maybe no one cares about her. I waited for four hours, and not a soul turned up."

"Well, someone's going to be coming for *this* one," said Patrick, looking down at Jane.

"Where's her cell phone?"

Patrick handed it to Mark. "What are you going to do?"

"It looks like her last text message

was to her husband." He began to tap out a new message on Jane's phone. "Let's tell him she's headed to Dorchester and won't be home for a while."

"Then what?"

"It has to look like an accident. Or a suicide." He looked at Patrick. "You made it work before."

Patrick nodded. "Her gun's up in the dining room."

"My husband will know," said Jane. "He knows I'd *never* kill myself."

"The spouse always says that. And the police never believe them. Do they, Detective?" said Mark, and he smiled.

If her limbs had not been trussed, she would have been on her feet and pummeling him, fists slamming into those perfect teeth. But even with rage fueling her muscles she could not tear free, could do nothing but watch as he finished the text message and sent it into the ether. She thought of how it would probably happen: a bullet to her head to kill her, followed by a second gunshot to plant residue on her hand, the way Wu Weimin's suicide had been staged. What Mark said was true: It was too easy to ignore the denials of a victim's family. She'd been guilty of it herself. She remembered standing over the body of a young man who was missing half his head from a shotgun blast. Remembered the mother sobbing, *He'd never kill himself! He'd just turned his life around!* And she remembered her own remark to Frost afterward, about clueless families who never saw it coming.

"You've made so many mistakes," said Iris. "You have no idea what's about to happen."

Mark turned to her and laughed. "Look who's talking. The lady chained to the wall."

Iris regarded him with an eerily calm gaze. "Before it all ends for you, tell me. Why did you choose my daughter?"

Mark crossed toward Iris until they were face-to-face. Though he was far taller, though he held every advantage, Iris revealed not a flicker of fear. "Pretty little Laura. You do remember her, Patrick?" He glanced at the older man. "The girl we picked up as she walked out of school. The one we offered a ride to."

"*Why?*" said Iris.

Mark smiled. "Because she was special. They all were."

"We're wasting time," said Patrick, stepping toward Jane. "Let's get her out of here."

But Mark was still looking at Iris. "Sometimes I chose the girl. Sometimes Patrick chose. You never know what will catch your eye. A ponytail. A cute little ass. Something that makes her stand out. Makes her worthy."

"Charlotte must have known," said Jane, looking up at Patrick in disgust. "She must have realized what you were. Jesus, her own *father.* How could you kill her?"

"Charlotte was never part of this."

"Never part of it? She was at the *center* of it!"

Jane's cell phone rang. Mark glanced at the caller's number and said, "Hubby seems to be checking on his wife."

"Don't answer it," said Patrick.

"I wasn't planning to. I'll just shut this off, and let's get her in the car."

Iris said, "You think it will be that simple?"

The men ignored her and bent down to grab Jane. Patrick picked up her feet and Mark hauled her up under her arms. Though Jane squirmed, she could not resist them, and they easily lifted her and carried her toward the door.

"You've already lost," said Iris. "You just don't know it yet."

Mark snorted. "I know who's chained to the wall."

"And I know who followed you back here."

"No one followed me—" His voice suddenly cut off as the lights went out.

In the pitch black, both men released their grips on Jane and she fell to the floor, skull slamming against concrete. She lay stunned, trying to make sense of what was happening in a room where she could see nothing, where the darkness was chaotic with curses and panicked breathing.

"What the fuck?" said Mark.

Iris's voice whispered through the gloom: "Now it begins."

"Shut up! Just *shut up*!" Mark yelled.

"It's probably nothing," said Patrick, but he sounded unnerved. "Look, maybe we just blew a fuse. Let's go upstairs and check."

The door banged shut and their footsteps faded up the stairs. Jane heard only the thumping of her own heart.

"You must lie very still and stay calm," said Iris.

"What's happening?"

"What was always meant to happen."

"You knew? You expected this?"

"Listen carefully to me, Detective. This is not your battle. It was planned a long time ago, and it will be fought without you."

"Fought by whom? What's out there?"

Iris did not answer. In the silence, Jane felt, rather than heard, the brush of air against her cheek, as though the wind had whispered into the room and was stirring the darkness. *Something else is here with us.*

She heard the soft clatter of handcuffs falling free. And a whisper: "Apologies, *Sifu.* I would have come sooner."

"My sword?"

"Here is Zheng Yi. I found it upstairs."

Jane knew that voice. "Bella?"

A hand was pressed across her lips and Iris murmured: "Stay."

"You can't leave me like this!"

"You're safer here."

"At least cut me free!"

"No," said Bella. "She'll just cause trouble."

"And if you fail?" said Jane. "I'll be trapped down here, and I won't be able to defend myself. At least give me a fighting chance!"

She felt a tug on her hands, heard the hiss of the blade slicing through her duct tape bindings. Another slice freed her ankles. "Remember," Iris whispered into her ear. "This is not your battle."

It is now. But Jane stayed silent and still as the two women melted into the darkness. She could neither see nor hear their departure; all she sensed was the kiss of air again, as if they had dissolved into wind and had whispered through the door and up the stairs.

Jane tried to rise to her feet, but dizziness sent her staggering blindly in the dark. She sat back down again, her skull aching from being dropped on concrete. That and the lingering effects of the drug left her weak. She reached out, felt the wall nearby, and once again tried to stand, this time propping herself, as unsteady as a newborn foal.

A gunshot made her chin snap up.

I can't be trapped down here, she thought. I have to get out of this house.

She felt her way to the door. It was unlocked and softly creaked open. Somewhere upstairs, she heard heavy footsteps running. Two more gunshots.

Get out now. Before the men come back for you.

She started up steps, moving slowly, afraid to make a sound. Afraid to alert anyone to her presence. Without a weapon, without any way to defend herself, she could not join this fight. She was the noncombatant trying to slip through a war zone to safety, wherever that might be. Find the exit, get out of the house. She didn't have her car keys, so she'd have to run to the neighbors. She tried to picture the property. Remembered the long driveway, the woods and lawns and the tall hedge that surrounded it all. By daylight, it had looked like a private garden of Eden, enclosed to keep the world out. Now she knew that the gate, with its spiked posts, was not meant just to keep people out, but also to keep them in. This was no garden of Eden; it was a death camp.

She reached the top of the stairs and felt another closed door. Pressing her ear against it, she heard nothing. The silence was unnerving. How many gunshots had there been? At least three, she thought, enough to have taken down both Iris and Bella. Were the women lying dead, beyond that door? Were Patrick and Mark now on their way back to the cellar to find her?

Her hand was slick with sweat as she grasped the knob. The door swung open soundlessly, to darkness that was every bit as thick as in the cellar. She could not make out any shapes or shadows. This floor, too, was concrete, and as she slowly inched her way across it, arms outstretched for unseen obstacles, she heard something small and metallic skitter away from her shoe. She collided with an edge that hit her hip and she halted, trying to discern what it was. It felt like a table, coated with dust. Jagged metal suddenly bit her fingers and she pulled back, startled. It was a table saw. She shifted a few feet farther into the darkness and hit another obstacle. This time, a drill press. This was Patrick's woodworking shop. She stood among the power tools, thinking of saw blades and drills, wondering if mahogany and maple were the only things this equipment had sliced into.

Renewed panic sent her fumbling in the darkness for a way out. She touched a wall and followed it to a corner.

More gunshots. Four in a row. *Get out, get out!*

At last she located the door and wasted no time slipping through it, to find yet another set of steps to climb. How far belowground had she been?

Deep enough so that no one would have heard my screams.

At the top of the stairs, she exited through a door and found herself in a carpeted hallway. Here she could barely make out shapes in the darkness, and a balustrade to her right. Hand brushing across a wall, she inched ahead. She had no idea if she was moving toward the front or the rear of the house; all she wanted to find was a way out.

On the second-floor landing above, footsteps creaked and started down the stairs.

Frantically she ducked through the first open doorway to her left, into a room where moonlight glowed through the windows, reflecting off a desk and bookshelves. An office.

The footsteps had reached the first floor.

She scrambled forward, seeking a hiding place in the shadows, and her shoes crunched across broken shards of glass. Suddenly her foot snagged an obstacle and as she went sprawling, she put out a hand to catch herself. Her palm slid through something warm and sticky. By the glow of moonlight, she stared at the dark form lying on the floor right beside her. A body.

Patrick Dion.

Gasping, she scrabbled away, sliding backward across the floor. Felt something heavy spin away from her hand. A gun. She reached for it, and the instant her fingers closed around the grip, she knew it was her own weapon. The gun that Patrick had taken from her. *My old friend.*

Footsteps creaked behind her and came to a halt.

Trapped in the light of the window, Jane was framed by moonglow that seemed as bright and inescapable as a searchlight. She looked up to see Mark's silhouette standing above her.

"I was never here," he said. "When the police come to talk to me, I'll tell them I was home in bed the whole time. It was Patrick who killed all those girls and buried them in his yard. Patrick who killed you. And then he shot himself."

Behind her, hand concealed in shadow, she clutched her weapon. But Mark already had his gun pointed at her. He would have the first shot, the best shot. There'd be no time for her to aim, no time to do anything but squeeze off the last bullet she would probably ever fire. Even as she lifted her weapon, she knew she was too slow, too late.

But at that instant Mark gasped in a startled breath and turned away from her, his attention shifting, his gun swinging toward someone—something—else.

Jane brought up her gun and fired. Three shots, four. Her reflexes on automatic. The bullets slammed into his torso and Mark staggered backward, collapsing against an end table. It gave way in a crash of splintering wood.

Pulse whooshing in her ears, Jane rose to her feet and stood over his body, her weapon aimed and ready should he miraculously spring back to life. He did not move.

But the shadows did.

It was just a whisper of air, utterly soundless. A flutter of black against black at the periphery of her vision. Slowly she turned toward the figure that stood cloaked in darkness. Though she was clutching a gun, though she could have fired, she did not. She simply stared at a face crowned with silvery fur. At jagged teeth that gleamed in the moonlight.

"Who are you?" she whispered. "What are you?"

A breath of wind brushed her face, and she blinked. When she opened her eyes again, the face was gone. Frantically she glanced around the room, searching for whatever had been standing there, but she saw only moonlight and shadow. *Was it really here, or did I imagine it? Did I create a creature out of darkness and my own fear?*

Through the window, a movement caught her eye. She looked out at the moonlit garden and saw it, then, darting across the lawn and vanishing into the cover of trees.

"Detective Rizzoli?"

With a start, Jane whirled around to see the two women in the doorway, Iris sagging heavily against Bella.

"She needs an ambulance!" said Bella.

"I am not as young as I once was," groaned Iris. "Or as swift."

Gently, Bella lowered her teacher to the floor. Cradling Iris in her lap she began to murmur in Chinese, words that she repeated again and again, as though chanting a magical spell. Words of healing.

Words of hope.

THIRTY-SEVEN

Jane stood among the jumble of Brookline PD and Boston PD vehicles parked in Patrick Dion's driveway and watched the sun come up. She had not slept in twenty-four hours, had not eaten since lunch the day before, and her first glimpse of dawn was so dazzling that she closed her eyes, suddenly dizzy, and swayed backward against a police cruiser. When she opened her eyes again, Maura and Frost had emerged from the house and were now walking toward her.

"You should go home," said Maura.

"That's what everyone tells me." She looked toward the residence. "You finished in there?"

"They're bringing out the bodies now."

Frost frowned as Jane bent down to pull on shoe covers. "You know, you probably shouldn't go in the house," he said.

"Like I haven't already been in there?"

"That's the point."

He didn't need to explain; she already understood. She'd been the one to take down Mark Mallory, and it was almost certainly her gun that had fired the bullet into Patrick Dion's brain. Her weapon was now in the custody of ballistics, and she missed its weight on her belt.

The front door opened and the first stretcher came out, bearing one of the bodies. In silence they watched it roll toward the waiting morgue van.

"The older man had one bullet wound. Right temple, close range," said Maura.

"Patrick Dion," said Jane.

"I have a feeling we're going to find gunshot residue on his right hand. Does that remind you of another crime scene?"

"The Red Phoenix," said Jane softly. "Wu Weimin."

"His death was called a suicide."

"What are you going to call this one, Maura?"

Maura sighed. "We have no witnesses, do we?"

Jane shook her head. "Bella said that she and Iris were upstairs when it happened. They didn't see it."

"But there was another intruder in the house," Frost pointed out. "You said you saw him."

"I don't know what I saw." Jane looked toward the garden. There, last night by moonlight, she had caught a glimpse of something slipping into the woods. "I don't think I'll ever know."

Maura turned as the second body was wheeled out of the house. "I could call Patrick Dion's death a suicide, but it's too similar to the Red Phoenix, Jane. It feels staged."

"I think it's meant to be similar. It's meant to be an echo from the past. Justice completing its circle."

"*Justice* doesn't qualify as a manner of death."

Jane looked at her. "Maybe it should."

"Hey, Frost! Rizzoli!" Detective Tam waved to them from a grove of trees, where he stood with a team of criminalists.

"What is it?" said Jane.

"Cadaver dog's just scented on something!"

The missing girls. Surely there were more names that had not made it onto Ingersoll's list, other girls who'd vanished in the years since Charlotte Dion disappeared. And what more convenient place to hide the bodies than in this private sanctuary, closed off from prying eyes? As they approached the CSU team, she saw the dog watching her with alert eyes, tail happily wagging. The dog was the only cheerful one among them. The men and women gathered in the shadow of those trees stood silent and grim-faced because they understood what most likely lay beneath their feet.

"The soil's been disturbed here," Tam said, pointing to a patch of bare earth under the trees. "It was covered with loose brush to conceal it."

A recent burial. Jane looked around at the tree-shaded grounds and the dense shrubbery, at all the secret spots hidden by shade and brush. This was evil on a scale she could scarcely comprehend. How many bodies are lying here, she wondered. How many silent girls who will finally be able to speak? Suddenly she felt overwhelmed by the task ahead of them. She was bruised, hungry, and weary of death.

"Frost, I think I'll leave this to you. I'm going home," she said and walked away, back across the lawn. Back into the sunshine.

"Rizzoli," said Tam. He followed her toward the driveway. "Just wanted to let you know, I spoke to the hospital a little while ago. Iris Fang is out of surgery and awake."

"Is she going to be okay?"

"She took a bullet to the thigh and lost a lot of blood, but she'll recover. She seems to be a pretty tough bird."

"We should all be so tough."

It was bright on that driveway with the morning sun in their faces. Tam pulled sunglasses from his pocket and slipped them on. "Maybe I should head over to the hospital? Get a statement from her?" he suggested.

"Later. Right now, I need you here. Brookline asked us to assist, so we're going to be spending a lot of time on this property."

"So I'm staying with the team?"

She squinted at him, the sun's glare piercing her tired eyes. "Yeah, until we wrap this up, I'll ask your District A-1 supervisor to let us keep you. That is, if you want to stay with homicide."

"Thanks. I'd like that a lot," he said simply. As he turned to leave, she suddenly noticed a bright streak reflecting off the back of his head. Clinging to his jet-black hair, the lone strand stood out like glitter. *A silver hair.*

"Tam?" she said.

He turned. "Yeah?"

For a moment she just looked at him, wanting to read his eyes, but he was wearing sunglasses, and in those mirrored lenses all she saw was her own reflection. She remembered how he'd slipped so quickly and silently through Ingersoll's window. Remembered how the Knapp Street surveillance camera had captured both her and Frost clumsily tumbling onto the fire escape, but not Tam. *Maybe I'm a ghost,* he had joked. Not a ghost, she thought, but someone just as elusive. Someone who'd been present at every step of the investigation, who knew what was being said and what was being planned. She could not see his expression, could not probe for secrets, but she knew they were there, waiting to be discovered. Secrets that she decided she would let him keep.

For now.

"Did you have a question, Rizzoli?" he asked.

"Never mind," she said. And she turned and walked away.

It was happy hour at J. P. Doyle's, and the bar was packed with so many off-duty cops that Jane had trouble spotting Korsak. Only after the waitress pointed her toward the dining room did she finally find him, sitting alone in a booth keeping company with a fried seafood platter and a pint of ale.

"Sorry I'm late," she said. "What's doin'?"

"Hope you don't mind that I already ordered."

She eyed his mound of deep-fried shrimp. "Guess you're off the diet, huh?"

"Don't get on my case, okay? Day's been lousy like a bastard and I need my comfort food, I really do." He stabbed four shrimp and stuffed them into his mouth. "You gonna order something or what?"

She waved over the waitress, ordered a small salad, and watched Korsak polish off another half dozen shrimp.

"That all you're eating?" he asked when her order arrived.

"I'm going home for supper. Haven't spent much time there the past few days."

"Yeah, I hear it's been a real circus over there in Brookline. How many bodies they dig up so far?"

"Six, all look to be females. It'll be months before we're done searching the property, and they may have other burial spots we don't know about. So we're looking at Mark Mallory's residence as well."

Korsak lifted his ale in a toast. "What is it you ladies like to say? *You go, girl!*"

She looked at his grease-splattered shirt and thought: He has the man breasts to actually pull off that phrase. She raised her glass of water and they made an impressive clunk, splashing beer on his ever-shrinking mound of shrimp.

"Just one fly in the ointment," she said as she picked up her fork. "There's no way I'll ever close the files on either John Doe or Jane Doe. And it was her death that set off the whole thing."

"Never found the sword that killed her?"

"Vanished. Probably walked off that night with whatever I saw disappear into the trees. We're never going to get anyone to confess. But I have a pretty good idea who did it."

"Enough to convict?"

"Honestly? I don't want to convict. Sometimes, Korsak, just doing my job means I'd have to do the wrong thing."

Korsak laughed. "Don't ever let Dr. Isles hear you say that."

"No, she wouldn't understand," Jane agreed. What Maura understood was facts, and those facts had led to the conviction of Officer Wayne Graff a few days ago. Yes or no, black or white, for Maura the line was always perfectly clear. But the longer that Jane was a cop, the less certain she was of where that line between right and wrong was drawn.

She dug into her salad and took a bite. "So what's doing with you? What'd you want to talk to me about?"

He sighed and put down his fork. Very few things, other than an empty plate, could make Vince Korsak surrender his fork. "You know I love your mom," he said.

"Yeah, I think I got that part figured out."

"I mean, I *really* love her. She's fun and smart and sexy."

"You can stop right there." She set down her own fork. "Just tell me where this is going."

"All's I want is to marry her."

"And she's already said yes. So?"

"The problem is your brother. He calls her three times a day, trying to talk her out of it. It's pretty clear he despises me."

"Frankie doesn't like any kind of change, period."

"He's got her all upset and now she's thinking of calling off the wedding, just to keep him happy." His deep sigh ended on what sounded close to a whimper, and he turned to stare at the booth across the aisle. At a toddler in a high chair who took one look at him and wailed. The mother shot Korsak a dirty look and pulled the baby into her arms. Poor Korsak, homely enough to scare small children who couldn't see past his coarse exterior to the kind heart inside. *But Mom sees it. And she deserves a good man like him.*

"It's okay," she said. "I'll talk to Frankie." If that didn't work, she'd also give her brother a good whack upside the head.

His head lifted. "You'd do that for me? Really?"

"Why wouldn't I?"

"I don't know. I got the idea you weren't wicked crazy about me and your ma, you know. Getting it on."

"I just don't want to hear the sweaty details, okay?" She reached across the table and gave him an affectionate punch on the arm. "You're cool, Korsak. And you make her happy. That's all I care about." She stood up. "I gotta get home. You okay now?"

"I love her. You know that."

"I know, I know."

"I love you, too." He scowled and added: "But *not* your brother."

"That I totally understand."

She left him to his seafood platter and exited through the crowded bar. Just as she reached the door, she heard someone call out: "Rizzoli!"

It was retired Detective Buckholz, who had investigated Charlotte Dion's disappearance nineteen years ago. He was sitting at his usual place at the counter, a glass of scotch in front of him. "I gotta talk to you," he said.

"I'm on my way home."

"Then I'll walk out with you."

"Could we talk tomorrow, Hank?"

"No. I got something to say, and it's really bugging me." He drained his glass and slapped it down on the bar. "Let's step outside. Too damn noisy in here."

They walked out of Doyle's and stood in the parking lot. It was a cool spring evening, the smell of damp earth in the air. Jane zipped up her jacket and glanced at her parked car, wondering how long this would take and whether she had time to pick up milk on the way home.

"You know your case against Patrick Dion and Mark Mallory? You got it wrong," he said.

"What do you mean?"

"It's been plastered all over the news. Two rich guys hunting girls together for twenty-five years. The whole country's talking about it, wondering why we didn't notice it. Why we didn't stop them."

"They were smart about it, Hank. They didn't escalate and they didn't get sloppy. They managed to stay in control."

"Patrick Dion had alibis for some of those disappearances."

"Because they took turns snatching the girls. Mallory abducted some of them, Dion took the others. We've already found six bodies on Dion's property, and I'm sure we'll find others."

"But not Charlotte's. I guarantee you won't find her there."

"How do you know?"

"When I worked that case, I didn't do a half-assed job, okay? It may have been nineteen years ago, but I remember the details. Last night, I pulled out my old notes, just to be sure of my facts. I *know* Patrick Dion was in London the day Charlotte went missing. He flew home that evening, right after he got the news."

"Okay, so you're right about that detail. It's easy to confirm."

"I'm also right about Mark Mallory. He couldn't have snatched Charlotte, either, because he had an alibi, too. He was visiting his mother. She'd had a stroke a year earlier, and she was in a rehab hospital."

She eyed him in the fading daylight. Buckholz was defending his own record, so he couldn't possibly be objective. Judging by his wasted face, his frayed shirt, retirement had not been kind to him. He practically lived at Doyle's, as if only there, surrounded by cops, did he feel alive again. Useful again.

Humor the old guy. She gave him a sympathetic nod. "I'll review the case file and get back to you."

"You think you can just brush me off? I was a *good* cop, Rizzoli. I checked out that boy. When you're talking about abduction, you always look at the family first, so I took a good long look at her stepbrother. Every move he made that day. There was no way Mark Mallory could have snatched Charlotte."

"Because he said he was visiting his mother? Come on, Hank. You can't take his word, or his mother's. She would have lied to protect her own kid."

"But you can trust the medical record."

"What?"

He reached into his jacket and pulled out a folded paper, which he thrust at her. "I got that from Barbara Mallory's hospital chart. It's a photocopy of the nurses' notes. Look at the entry for April twentieth, one PM."

Jane scanned down to what the nurse had written at that time. *BP 115/80, Pulse 84. Patient resting comfortably. Son here visiting and requests that his mother be moved to a quieter room, away from nurses' station.*

"At one PM," said Buckholz, "Charlotte Dion was with her school group in Faneuil Hall. The teachers first noticed her missing around one fifteen. So tell me how Mark Mallory, who's sitting in his mom's hospital room twenty-five miles away, manages to snatch his stepsister off a street in Boston only fifteen minutes later?"

Jane read and reread the nurse's entry. There was no mistaking the date and time. This is all wrong, she thought.

Except it wasn't. It was there in black and white.

"Stop making it look like I screwed up," said Buckholz. "It's obvious that your two perps didn't take Charlotte."

"Then who did?" Jane murmured.

"We'll probably never find out. I'm

betting it was just some guy who saw her and made an opportunistic grab."

Some guy. A perp they had yet to identify.

She drove home with the photocopied page on the seat beside her and thought about the odds. Two killers in her family, and Charlotte gets snatched by an unrelated stranger? She pulled into her apartment parking space and sat brooding, not yet ready to walk into the noise and the chaos of motherhood. She thought about what they knew for certain: that Dion and Mallory had been stalking and killing girls together. That they'd buried at least six bodies on Dion's property. Had Charlotte discovered her father's secret? Was that the real reason they had to dispose of her? Had it been arranged through a third party, so that both Patrick and Mark had solid alibis?

Jane massaged her scalp, overwhelmed by the questions. Once again, the mystery revolved around Charlotte. What she knew and when she learned about it. And with whom she shared it. She thought of the last photos ever taken of Charlotte, at the funeral of her mother and stepfather. She remembered how Charlotte had been flanked by her father and Mark. Surrounded by enemies and unable to escape.

Jane sat up straight, suddenly struck by the answer that should have been obvious from the beginning.

Maybe she did.

THIRTY-EIGHT

At noon, Jane crossed the New Hampshire border and drove north, into Maine. It was a soft May day, the trees leafed out in their spring flush, a golden haze hanging over fields and forest. But by the time she reached Moosehead Lake in the late afternoon, the air had turned chilly. She parked her car, wrapped a wool scarf around her neck, and walked to the landing, where a motorboat was moored.

A boy of about fifteen, his blond hair tousled in the wind, waved at her. "You Mrs. Rizzoli? I'm Will, from the Loon

Point Lodge." He took her overnight bag. "Is this all the luggage you brought?"

"I'm only staying for one night." She glanced around the dock. "Where's the skipper?"

Grinning, he waved his hand. "Right here. Been driving this boat since I was eight. In case you're nervous, I've made this crossing, oh, a few thousand times."

Still dubious about the kid's skills as a skipper, she climbed aboard and buckled on the offered life jacket. As she settled onto the bench she noticed the boxes filled with groceries, and the bundle of newspapers with *The Boston Globe* on top. Obviously this boat trip had also been a shopping run for the boy.

As he started up the engine, she asked: "How long have you worked at the lodge?"

"All my life. My mom and dad own it."

She took a closer look at the boy. Saw a strong jaw and sun-bleached hair. He was built like a lifeguard, slim but muscular, the kind of kid who'd look right at home on a California beach. He seemed utterly at ease as he guided the boat away from the pier. Before she could ask him any more questions, they were skimming across choppy water, the motor too noisy for conversation. She held on to the gunwale and stared at dense forest, at a lake so vast that it stretched ahead of them like a sea.

"It's beautiful here," she said, but he didn't hear her; his attention was focused on their destination across the water.

By the time they reached the opposite shore, the sun was dropping toward the horizon, leafing the water with flame and gold. She saw rustic cabins ahead, and a cluster of canoes pulled up on the bank. On the pier, a towheaded girl stood waiting to catch the mooring line. As soon as Jane caught a closer look at the girl's face, she knew that these two were brother and sister.

"This troublemaker here is Samantha," Will said with a laugh and he affectionately mussed the girl's hair. "She's our general gofer around here. You need a toothbrush, extra towels, whatever, just give her a shout."

As the girl went scampering up the pier with the guest's bag, Jane said: "She looks like she's about eight, nine? Don't you both go to school?"

"We're homeschooled. Too hard getting to town in the winter. My dad always tells us that we're the luckiest kids in the world, to be living out here in paradise." He led her up the path to one of the cabins. "Mom put you in this one. It's got the most privacy."

They climbed the steps to the screened porch, and the door squealed shut behind them. Samantha had brought Jane's bag into the cabin and it sat on a rustic luggage rack at the foot of the bed. Jane looked up at open beams, at walls of knotty pine. A fire was already crackling in the stone hearth.

"Everything look okay?" asked Will.

"I wish I'd brought my husband here. He'd love this place."

"Bring him back next time." Will gave her a salute and turned to leave. "Once you get settled in, come over to the lodge for dinner. I think we're having beef stew."

After he left, she sank into a rocking chair on the screened porch and sat watching the sunset burn a fire in the lake. Insects hummed, and the sound of lapping water made her drowsy. She closed her eyes and did not see the visitor approach her cabin. Only when she heard the knock did she look out to see the blond woman standing outside the screen door.

"Detective Rizzoli?" the woman said.

"Come in."

The woman stepped inside, careful to keep the door quiet as it swung shut. Even in the shadowy porch, Jane could see the woman's resemblance to Will and Samantha, and she knew that this was their mother. She also knew, without a doubt, what her name was. It was Ingersoll's oddly timed fishing trip that had made Jane focus on Loon Point, a trip on which he'd brought no tackle box. This was the real reason Ingersoll had come to Maine: to visit the woman who now stood on Jane's cabin porch.

"Hello, Charlotte," said Jane.

The woman glanced through the screen, scanning the area for anyone within earshot. Then she looked at Jane. "Please don't ever use that name again. My name is Susan now."

"Your family doesn't know?"

"My husband does, but not the children. It's just too hard to make them understand. And I never want them to know what kind of man their grandfather . . ." Her voice trailed off. With a sigh she sank into one of the rocking chairs. For a moment the only sound was the creak of her chair on the porch.

Jane stared at the woman's profile. Charlotte—no, Susan—was only thirty-six, yet she looked much older. Years in the outdoors had freckled her skin, and her hair already had silvery streaks. But it was the pain in her eyes that aged her the most, pain that had left deep creases and a haunted gaze.

Leaning her head back against the rocker, Susan stared off at the darkening lake. "It started when I was nine years old," she said. "One night, he came into my room while my mother was sleeping. He told me I was old enough. That it was time for me to learn what all daughters were supposed to do. We're supposed to please our daddies." She swallowed. "So I did."

"Didn't you tell your mother?"

"My mother?" Susan's laugh was bitter. "My mother's concerns never extended beyond her own selfish interests. After she started her affair with Arthur Mallory, it took her only two months to fly the coop. She never looked back. I'm not sure she even remembered that she *had* a daughter. So I was left behind with my father, who was only too happy to retain custody. Uncontested, of course. Oh, a few times a year, I was scheduled to spend weekends with Mom and Arthur, but she pretty much ignored me. Arthur was the only one who showed me any real kindness. I didn't know him well, but he seemed like a decent man."

"What about his son, Mark?"

There was a long silence. "I didn't realize what Mark was," she said softly. "He seemed perfectly harmless when our families first got together. Soon we were all seeing way too much of each other. Dinners at our house, then at Mark's. We got along so swimmingly. The trouble was, my mom and Arthur were getting along better than I realized at the time."

"It seems that your father and Mark were getting along rather well, too."

Susan nodded. "Like best friends. It was as if my dad finally found the son he'd always wanted. Even after my parents divorced, Mark would come over to visit Dad. They'd go downstairs to Dad's workshop and build birdhouses or picture frames. I had no idea what was really going on down there."

A lot more than woodworking, thought Jane. "You didn't think it was strange, the two of them spending so much time together?"

"I was mostly relieved to be left alone. It was around then, when I was thirteen, that my dad stopped coming to my room at night. At the time I didn't know why. Now I realize that was when the first girl disappeared. When I was thirteen, and my dad found someone else to amuse him. With Mark's help." Susan ceased rocking and sat very still, her gaze fixed on the lake. "If I'd known, if I'd realized what Mark really was, my mother and Arthur would still be alive."

Jane frowned. "Why do you say that?"

"I'm the reason they went to the Red Phoenix restaurant that night. They were there because of something I told them."

"You?"

Susan took a deep breath, as if collecting the strength to continue. "It was the scheduled weekend for my visit with Mom and Arthur. I'd just gotten my license, and I drove myself to their house for the very first time. I took my father's car. That's when I found the pendant. It had fallen between the seat and the console, where nobody noticed it for two years. It was gold, in the shape of a dragon, and it had a name engraved on the back. Laura Fang."

"Did you recognize the name?"

"Yes. The story was in the newspapers when she disappeared. I remembered the name because she was my age, and she played the violin. At Bolton, some of the students talked about her because they knew her from the summer orchestra workshop."

"Mark attended that workshop."

Susan nodded. "He knew her. But I couldn't understand the connection with my father. How did Laura's pendant end up in my *father's* car? Then I started thinking about all the nights that he'd come into my bedroom, and what he'd done to me. If he'd abused me, maybe he'd done it to other girls. Maybe that's what happened to Laura. Why she disappeared."

"And then you told your mother?"

"That weekend, when I visited her, it all came out. I told her and Arthur everything. What my dad had done to me years earlier. What I'd found in his car. At first, Mom couldn't believe it. Then, in her usual self-centered way, she started worrying about the bad publicity and how her name would get dragged into the newspapers. That she'd be known as the clueless wife who had no idea what was going on in her own house. But Arthur—Arthur took it seriously. *He* believed me. And I'll always respect him for that."

"Why didn't they go straight to the police?"

"My mom wanted to be certain of the facts first. She didn't want to attract any attention until they knew this wasn't some weird coincidence. Maybe there was another Laura Fang, she said. So they were going to show the pendant to Laura's family. Confirm that it belonged to the same Laura who'd disappeared two years earlier." Susan's head drooped, and her next words were almost inaudible. "That's the last time I saw them alive. When they left to meet with Laura's father, at the restaurant."

This was the final piece of the puzzle: the reason why Arthur and Dina had gone to Chinatown that night. Not to eat a meal, but to speak with James Fang about his missing daughter. Gunfire ended the conversation, a bloody massacre that was blamed on a hapless immigrant.

"The police insisted it was a murder-suicide," said Susan. "They said my mom and Arthur were just in the wrong place at the wrong time. The pendant was never found, so I had no evidence. I had no one else to turn to. I kept wondering if it was connected. Laura and the shooting. And then there was Mark. He was home with us that weekend, so he knew what was going on."

"He called Patrick. Told him your mother and Arthur were going to Chinatown."

"I'm sure he did. But it was only at the funeral that I finally put it all together. My father and Mark, working together. Without the pendant, I couldn't prove anything. My dad held all the power, and I knew how easy it would be for him to make me disappear."

"So you made yourself disappear."

"I didn't plan it ahead of time. But there I was with my class, walking Boston's Freedom Trail." She gave a sad laugh. "And suddenly I thought, *I* want to be free, too! And now is the time to do it. So I slipped away from the teachers. A few blocks later, I started thinking about how to throw everyone off track. I dropped my backpack and ID in an alley. I had enough cash to buy a bus ticket north. I wasn't sure where I was going, I just knew I had to get away from my father. When I got to Maine, and I stepped off the bus, I suddenly felt like . . ." She sighed. "Like I'd arrived home."

"And you stayed."

"I got a job cleaning cabins for tourists. I met my husband, Joe. And that was the biggest gift of my life, finding a man who loves me. Who stands by me, no matter what." She breathed in deeply and lifted her head. Sat up straight. "Here, I remade my life. Had my children. Together, Joe and I built these cabins. Built the business. I thought I'd be happy, just hiding away here forever."

The sound of laughter drifted from the lake where Will and his sister, now dressed in bathing suits, were racing down the pier. They leaped off and their laughter turned to squeals as they plunged into the cold water. Susan rose from her chair and stared at her children, happily splashing in the lake.

"Samantha's nine years old. The same age I was when it started. When my father first came into my bedroom." Susan kept her back turned to Jane, as if she could not bear to let her see her face. "You think you can put the abuse behind you, but you never can. The past is always there, waiting to meet you in your nightmares. It pops up when you least expect it. When you smell gin and cigars. Or hear your bedroom door creak open at night. Even after all these years, he's still tormenting me. And when Samantha turned nine, the nightmares got worse, because I saw myself at her age. So innocent, still untouched. I thought of what he did to me, and what he might have done to Laura. And I wondered if there were other girls, other victims I didn't even know about. But I didn't know how to bring him down, not all by myself. I didn't have the courage."

Outside, Will and Samantha climbed back onto the pier and stood drying off, laughing. Susan pressed her hand to the screen, as if drawing courage from her children.

"Then on March thirtieth," said Susan, "I opened *The Boston Globe*."

"You saw Iris Fang's ad. About the Red Phoenix massacre."

"The truth has never been told," Susan whispered. "That's what the ad said. And suddenly I knew I wasn't alone.

That someone else was searching for answers. For justice." She turned to face Jane. "That's when I finally got the nerve to call Detective Ingersoll. I knew him because he'd investigated the Red Phoenix massacre. I told him about Laura's pendant. About my dad and Mark. I told him there might be other missing girls."

"So that's why he started asking questions about the girls," said Jane. Questions that had put him in danger, because word got back to Patrick that Ingersoll was gathering evidence, linking him not only to vanished girls but also to the Red Phoenix. He would have assumed that Iris Fang was behind it, because she'd placed the ad in the *Globe.* She'd lost both a daughter and a husband. Killing Iris and Ingersoll would eradicate the problem, so Patrick had hired professionals. But the killers had underestimated what they were up against.

"I was terrified that my father might find me," said Susan. "I told Detective Ingersoll not to say *anything* that could be traced back to me. He promised that even his own daughter wouldn't know what he was working on."

"He kept his word. We had no inkling that you were the one who hired him. We assumed it was Mrs. Fang."

"A few weeks later, he called me. He said we had to meet, and he drove up here. Told me he'd found a pattern. He'd come up with the names of three girls who might have met me before they vanished. Girls who'd attended the same tennis meet or the same music camp. It turned out *I* was the link. *I* was the reason they were chosen." Her voice broke and she sank into the chair again. "Here I've been living with my little girl, safe and secure in Maine. I never knew there were other victims. If only I'd been braver, I could have stopped this a long time ago."

"It *has* been stopped, Susan. And you *did* have a role in it."

She looked at Jane, her eyes glistening. "Only a minor role. Detective Ingersoll died for it. And you're the one who finished it."

But not alone, thought Jane. I had help.

"Mom?" The girl's voice drifted in from the shadows outside. Samantha stood beyond the screen, her slim figure silhouetted against the reflected light from the lake behind her. "Dad said to come get you. He's not sure if it's time to take the pie out of the oven."

"I'm coming, sweetheart." Susan rose to her feet. As she swung open the screen door, she glanced back and smiled at Jane. "Dinner's ready. Come when you get hungry," she said, and she stepped out, letting the door squeal shut behind her.

From the porch, Jane watched Susan take Samantha's hand. Together, mother and daughter walked away along the water's edge and faded into the twilight. They held hands the whole way.

THIRTY-NINE

**THREE MONTHS LATER
FUJIAN PROVINCE, CHINA**

The sweet scent of incense wafts across the courtyard where Bella and I stand before the tomb of her father's ancestors. It is an ancient cemetery. For at least a thousand years, generations of the Wu family have been interred here, and now Wu Weimin's ashes lie joined with his forefathers. No longer does his tormented soul wander the spirit world, crying out for justice. Here he will finally lie, for an eternity, in peace.

As the shadows deepen to night, Bella and I light candles and bow to her father's memory. Suddenly I sense the presence of someone else, and I turn to see a figure step through the courtyard gate. Although I cannot see his face in the gloom, I know by his silent approach, by the easy grace with which he moves, that it is Wu Weimin's son by his first wife, the son who has never forgotten him and has continued to honor him. As the man moves into the glow of candlelight, Bella nods to her half brother and he returns the greeting with a sad smile. They are so alike, these two, both as unyielding as the stone that entombs their father's ashes. Now that their duty has been fulfilled, I wonder what will become of them. When you have devoted half your young life to a single goal, and you finally reach it, what is left to be accomplished?

He gives me a respectful bow. "*Sifu,* I am sorry to be late. My flight from Shanghai was delayed because of weather."

I study his face in the candlelight and I see more than fatigue in the worry lines around his eyes. "Are there problems in Boston?"

"I believe she knows. I feel her watching and probing. I sense her suspicion every time she looks at me."

"What will happen now?"

He gives a long sigh and stares at the burning candles. "I think—I hope—that she understands. She wrote me a glowing commendation. And she wants me to work with her on another Chinatown investigation."

I smile at Johnny Tam. "Detective Rizzoli is not so different from us. She may not agree with the way we accomplished our objective, but I believe she understands why we did it. And she approves."

I touch a match to the courtyard fire pit, lighting the tinder. Flames leap up like ravenous teeth, and we feed them joss papers of spirit money. The fire consumes them, and as the smoke lifts, it carries comfort and fortune to the ghosts of those we love.

There is one final item we must burn.

As I pull the mask from its sack, the silvery hair reflects firelight and suddenly seems alive, as if the spirit of Sun Wukong himself has sprung from the shadows. But the mask hangs limp in my grasp, merely a dead object made of leather and monkey fur, a moldering prop that I bought years ago from a Chinese opera company. All three of us have worn the mask. All three of us have shared the role. I, while defending myself on the rooftop against a woman assassin. Bella, while saving a policewoman's life. And Johnny last of all, when he fired the bullet into Patrick Dion's head, completing the circle of death.

I drop the mask into the flames. Instantly the hairs catch fire and I smell sizzling fur and charred leather. In one bright flare, the mask is consumed, returning Sun Wukong to the spirit world, where the Monkey King belongs. But he is never truly far away; when we need him most, each one of us will find him within ourselves.

The flames die down and the three of us stare into the fire pit, seeking in those glowing ashes what we each want to see. For Bella and Johnny, it is their father's smile of approval. They have done their filial duty; now their lives are their own.

And what do I see in those ashes? I behold the face of my daughter, Laura, whose remains were recovered ten weeks ago from a vine-choked corner of Patrick Dion's property. I see the face of my beloved husband, still young, his hair as black as the day we married. Though they do not age, here I linger on this earth, my health faltering, my hair turning silver, the years etching their lines ever more deeply in my face. But with every year that I grow older, I also draw closer to James and Laura, to the day when we will once again be together. So I march through the deepening shadows, serene and unafraid.

Because I know that, at the end of my journey, they will be waiting for me.

ACKNOWLEDGMENTS

No novel I've written has been quite as personal as this one. The story was inspired by my mother's tales of growing up in China, tales of ghosts and mysterious martial arts masters and, yes, the heroic Monkey King. So thank you, Mom, for introducing me to the wondrous world of Chinese fables.

Thanks also to Tony Yee and Boston PD officer Tommy Yung for their insights into Boston's Chinatown; to Halford Jones for long encouraging me to write a story about martial arts; to my son Adam Gerritsen for his help with Mandarin words and obscure firearms; to Dr. Reena Roy, associate professor at the Penn State University Forensic Science Program, for her invaluable help on primate hair analysis; to John R. Michaud, assistant professor of legal studies, and his Criminal Justice Club students at Husson University for their advice on the metal analysis of ancient swords; and to Detective Russell Grant, Boston PD, for always being willing to field my questions. Any errors I've made in this novel are mine, and mine alone.

Then there's the stalwart team that has been behind me every step of the way with advice, encouragement, and sometimes a much-needed martini: my peerless literary agent, Meg Ruley, of the Jane Rotrosen Agency; my Ballantine editor, Linda Marrow; my Transworld champion, Selina Walker; and the man who keeps me safe and sane while I'm on the road, Brian McLendon.

Most of all, thanks to my husband, Jacob, who so cheerfully endures the trials of being married to a writer. After spending all day with people who exist only in my head, I'm so grateful to have a real flesh-and-blood hero to return to.

ABOUT THE AUTHOR

TESS GERRITSEN is a physician and an internationally bestselling author. She gained nationwide acclaim for her first novel of suspense, the *New York Times* bestseller *Harvest*. She is also the author of the bestsellers *Ice Cold, The Keepsake, The Bone Garden, The Mephisto Club, Vanish, Body Double, The Sinner, The Apprentice, The Surgeon, Life Support, Bloodstream,* and *Gravity.* Tess Gerritsen lives in Maine.
www.tessgerritsen.com